Six helicopters came over the top of Paolos Verdes and descended through the night mist like vultures from hell. The men who flew in them were under orders to kill everyone in sight. Not a living soul was to leave the estate alive. The swimming pool area became the first killing field. As bullets traced through the night, naked people ran in every direction. Screams of terror mixed with screams of death as the soft sounds spitting from the automatic rifles were nearly drowned by the *thumpa-thumpa* of the aircraft.

David watched speechlessly as the first wave of gunfire erupted. Then he heard the shattering of glass and the ricocheting of bullets as gunfire ripped through the second floor of the computer center.

Get out! Run! Run!

His instincts told him he had to get to the shadows of the perimeter of the compound to even stand a chance. He went to a window on the far wall and jerked it open.

He thought: I hope this isn't the one over the loading dock.

Then as shots popped in the background, seemingly from all directions, he kicked out the screen and jumped into the darkness.

THE FINEST IN SUSPENSE!

THE URSA ULTIMATUM   (2310, $3.95)
by Terry Baxter
In the dead of night, twelve nuclear warheads are smuggled north
across the Mexican border to be detonated simultaneously in major cities throughout the U.S. And only a small-town desert law-
man stands between a face-less Russian superspy and World War
Three!

THE LAST ASSASSIN   (1989, $3.95)
by Daniel Easterman
From New York City to the Middle East, the devastating flames
of revolution and terrorism sweep across a world gone mad . . .
as the most terrifying conspiracy in the history of mankind is
born!

FLOWERS FROM BERLIN   (2060, $4.50)
by Noel Hynd
With the Earth on the brink of World War Two, the Third Reich's
deadliest professional killer is dispatched on the most heinous assignment of his murderous career: the assassination of Franklin
Delano Roosevelt!

THE BIG NEEDLE   (2776, $3.50)
by Ken Follett
All across Europe, innocent people are being terrorized, homes
are destroyed, and dead bodies have become an unnervingly common sight. And the horrors will continue until the most powerful
organization on Earth finds Chadwell Carstairs — and kills him!

John D Randall (signature)

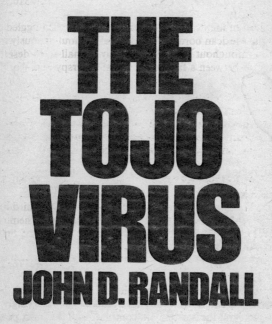

THE TOJO VIRUS

JOHN D. RANDALL

ZEBRA BOOKS
KENSINGTON PUBLISHING CORP.

ZEBRA BOOKS

are published by

Kensington Publishing Corp.
475 Park Avenue South
New York, NY 10016

First printing: April, 1991

Printed in the United States of America

To the members of the 18W "pit"
and to a special friend, Marcia Davies

Table Of Contents

Preface

Personal Computer Security Considerations
National Computer Security Center
Document #NCSC-WA-002-85

Despite a growing interest in securing computer systems — especially against mischievous "hackers" — most (if not all) computer systems (both PCs and mainframe computers) are susceptible to software attacks.

One attack, known as a trapdoor attack, involves the insertion of a mechanism that provides the attacker the means to later gain unauthorized access to the system. Such a mechanism inserted in a mainframe computer could, for example, grant the attacker access to a privileged system account after he presents a control sequence or password.

Another attack, called the Trojan horse attack, involves the insertion of unauthorized algorithms into the system. Many times, a trapdoor is used to activate a Trojan horse. A Trojan horse is a body of code that is designed to subvert the person or process that uses it. A sample Trojan horse might be a text editor that copies every file it creates into the attacker's directory. Beware of programs on bulletin boards and in the public domain. These programs purport to be useful utilities, but, in reality, may be designed to sack your system.

A "virus" is a software attack that infects computer

systems much the same way as a biological virus infects humans. A computer virus is a small program that searches the computer for a program that is uninfected, or "germ-free." When it finds one, it makes a copy of itself and inserts the "germ" in the beginning of the healthy program. This insertion could take place in a fraction of a second—a delay that is impossible to detect. The infected program will subsequently execute the virus code prior to beginning its normal processing. A sample PC virus might copy itself onto any diskette inserted into the disk drive, and after a certain number of operations on that disk, erase it.

The knowledge needed to create a Trojan horse or virus is basic, and no foolproof system exists to detect it. PCs are especially susceptible to these attacks because of the volume of software exchanged between users.

Remote connections to other systems make PCs susceptible to remote attacks. A PC connected to a network, for example, may be subjected to attack by other network users. The attacker could transmit control characters that affect the interrupt logic of the PC in such a way as to permit him to obtain full access to the PC and its peripherals, even if he is incapable of passing the system's log-in challenge. No foolproof system exists to detect it.

Vin McLellan
the *New York Times*
"Deadly 'viruses' spread among computers"

It could be a science-fiction nightmare come to life. In the last nine months, computer viruses—which could subvert, alter or destroy the computer programs

10

of banks, corporations, the military and the government — have infected personal computer programs at several corporations and universities in the United States, as well as in Israel, West Germany, Switzerland, Britain and Italy.

Like its biological counterpart, a computer virus can be highly contagious. It has the capability of instantaneously cloning a copy of itself and then burying those copies inside other programs. All infected programs then become contagious, and the virus passes to other computers that the software comes into contact with.

The most virulent outbreaks so far have occurred in personal computers. But security experts say the greatest risk would come from infected large computers, such as those governing the air traffic controller's system or the Internal Revenue Service.

"The solution is to put a wall with a good solid gate around the jungle — most computers still have the equivalent of a sleepy guard at the door," Weiss said (Kenneth Weiss, technical director at Security Dynamics Technologies, Inc). "But the larger problem is how to secure the system against people who have legitimate work inside."

Seattle Post-Intelligencer
November 4, 1988
Page 1 Headline

Computer Virus Sweeps the Country

A virus invaded computers at major universities and research institutions — ranging from a nationwide Department of Defense system to the University of Washington — before apparently being brought under control yesterday afternoon.

The infection, apparently caused by a computer science student's experiment, raged for about 24 hours before it was identified and removed, clogging systems linking thousands of military, corporate, and university computers around the country, but not destroying any data.

Viruses, the communicable diseases of computers, are tiny programs created in computers either as a joke or vandalism. They can attach themselves to other programs and spread through shared software.

In their mildest form, a message flashes on a user's screen; as malignancies, they can destroy data and cripple a computer.

Penetrating a security hole in the electronic mail systems that connect UNIX-language computers, yesterday's virus moved into two networks linking 2,000 computers worldwide.

"The big issue is that a relatively benign software program can virtually bring our computing community to its knees and keep it there for some time," said Chuck Cole, deputy computer security manager at Lawrence Livermore Laboratory in Livermore, Calif., one of the sites affected by the intrusion. "The cost is going to be staggering."

Clifford Stoll, a computer security expert at Harvard University, added: "There is not one system manager who is not tearing his hair out. It's causing enormous headaches."

University of Washington systems programmer Ken Lowe said the virus causes him more concern about the vulnerability of computers.

The infection appears to have come in through a security hole in the affected computers' electronic mail systems.

12

"It looks like it infected most of the computers through the National Science Foundation network, which links a number of supercomputers," Lowe said.

The virus worked by invading some computers through the mail system, making copies of itself in each machine it reached, then directing that machine to send the copies to other computers. It also apparently was transmitted from system to system in other ways as well, Lowe said.

The *New York Times* reported that the virus program was apparently the result of an experiment by a computer science graduate student trying to sneak what he thought was a harmless virus into the Arpanet computer network, which is used by universities, military contractors and the Pentagon, where the software program would remain undetected.

Chapter One
Zack's Been A Bad Boy

The black limo turned off the San Diego Freeway onto Hawthorne Boulevard and headed due south through the city of Torrance, smoothly crossed the intersection with the Pacific Coast Highway, then gently gained altitude as the four-lane road rose through Rolling Hills Estates before ending its journey in Rancho Palos Verdes, one of the richest bedroom communities of Los Angeles. Consisting of a large hill approximately ten miles long by five miles wide, the Palos Verdes peninsula is a nub of land that separates Santa Monica Bay to the west and north from San Pedro Bay and Long Beach to the east and south. Unlike Beverly Hills and Bel Air, home of movie moguls and old LA money, the red-tiled million-dollar homes dotting the peninsula house the captains of industry, the technocrats who rule modern society—executives of TRW, Hughes, Rockwell, Northrop and a hundred other service and specialty companies supporting the aerospace giants.

At the top of the peninsula the limo turned left onto Crest Road and proceeded slowly past secluded and well-manicured properties. The view on either side of the road was spectacular. It was dusk and the air was unusually clear. To the left was the huge expanse of

Los Angeles, its lights twinkling in the smog-free evening. Rumpling against the pale blue-black horizon were the gray outlines of the Santa Monica and San Gabriel mountains and the complete downtown skyline of Los Angeles, which stretched twenty-five miles east to west in a glittering line along Wilshire Boulevard, from Civic Center to downtown Santa Monica. On the opposite side the view was just as spectacular, with the vast expanse of the Pacific Ocean melting into a pink sky in the distance. The twenty-six miles between Point Vicente and Catalina Island seemed an optical illusion. The night was so clear that tiny dots of light from the village of Avalon could be seen.

The limo slowed to a crawl, then turned left into a bricked driveway, stopping at a drawn set of wrought iron gates. Through a television monitor a uniformed security guard verified the chauffeur's identification and that of the single passenger seated behind the glassed partition. Under electronic control the gates noiselessly swung inward, allowing the limo to quietly approach the front of the mansion, which faced south and was a seven thousand-square foot, two-story Spanish contemporary constructed with old brick and topped with a red tiled roof. The driveway was illuminated by the soft light from a series of subdued light posts that looked like tiny straight-backed soldiers standing at attention. The entire six-acre mansion grounds were ringed by a ten-foot-tall stone-and-brick fence with built-in sensors that provided a multilayered defense against intruders.

Connected to the home via vine-covered stone walkways were two symmetrical but smaller buildings to the northwest and northeast, each two stories in height. Between these smaller buildings, and directly to the rear of the main home, was a large grassy expanse that surrounded an adult playground consisting of a fenced tennis court, two swimming pools, a shuffleboard court, a horseshoe pit, and a single story recreation center that housed vending machines, three table tennis tables, a full-sized billiard table, and four comfortable card tables.

The home belonged to Makato Shinogara, who patiently stood at the bottom of two exquisitely sculpted white marble steps and waited for the limo to arrive. Shinogara, a distinguished Japanese gentleman of fifty-six, was dressed in a carefully pressed navy blue business suit worn over a crisp white long-sleeved shirt fastened by half-inch black cuff links in an emerald cut. His tie was gray, which matched his neatly trimmed hair.

The stretch Cadillac stopped so that the right passenger door was precisely in front of Shinogara, who personally opened the heavy door and offered his hand to his guest. His offer was accepted by a pristine white-gloved hand, which was followed by a silk dress in a deep blue-and-black design that carefully swung out to the right. The dress that clung closely to slender young hips was slit on either side, and carefully exposed stockinged legs up to midthigh.

Up from the comfortable seat stood Marcia Lee, her long black hair pulled to the left and worn back. She was five feet, eight inches tall and a beautiful young woman, with just a trace of Oriental heritage in her facial features, around the eyes.

"Welcome to my home, Miss Lee. Thank you for coming. Was your trip comfortable?" Shinogara asked politely.

"Limousine to and from the airports, a private ride in a private jet — first class door to door, thank you," replied Marcia, brushing her hair off her forehead

17

with the back of her right hand in a gesture that was both stylish and drew subtle attention to her face. She preferred the habit to changing her hairstyle.

"The others are waiting. They may ask you to say a few words," said the older man as he led her to the front door, which was already opened by a waiting houseboy.

"Speaking to a group is a lot like acting—and I'm a good actress," she replied, stepping through the entrance as the front door was opened by one of Shinogara's servants precisely as they reached it.

Marcia's first impression wasn't what she expected. Although a Spanish contemporary on the outside, she expected the interior to reflect the tastes and decor of a traditional Japanese home. Instead the interior was as American and as Western as apple pie and John Wayne. Finely stained polished oak hardwood floors were mixed with soft beige carpeting in blended islands through the house, which had the feeling of being entirely open. Rooms melded together, separated not by walls but by furniture and artwork. The furniture was large and comfortable and contemporary.

"Very nice," she complimented sincerely.

"Thank you—we've enjoyed our stay here," Shinogara replied. "But the men are anxious to return home—and so am I."

Marcia didn't press for an explanation. She did pick up on the past tense of "enjoyed," which implied that the future might not be as pleasant nor as permanent. Her high-heeled shoes clicked on the hardwood as Shinogara led her through the house and out the back. Four men were playing tennis on a lighted court. There was activity in the pool and she could hear the *pick-pock* of table tennis being played well in the clubhouse. She thought, I'm the only woman on the property.

"The building we're headed toward is the computer facility," Shinogara pointed as they walked down the pathway to the left of the main house. "The building to your right is our dormitory, which has been divided into work group sleeping areas. I have three supervisors, each of whom has his own private quarters. Each supervisor has a project leader and three or four assistants, all of whom share common sleeping facilities."

"Sounds very efficient," said Marcia with just a note of sarcasm in her voice, sarcasm that was taken as a compliment by her host.

"Thank you, we believe it's the best way to run our project."

"What do the groups do?" Marcia asked, curious.

"Your part of this project doesn't require an in-depth knowledge of the operation, Miss Lee," Shinogara said, clearly reminding Marcia that she was an outsider, a hired hand—someone who was to perform a task and be paid for it.

With no more words to exchange, the two walked toward the computer building eighty feet away. Marcia's high heels click-clacked on the brick walkway.

"This way, please. The elevator is to your left."

"I'm perfectly capable of taking the stairs, Mr. Shinogara," said Marcia. "I do get my exercise, you know."

"Yes, I'm sure you do," Shinogara laughed, his eyes crinkled around the edges.

On the second floor, Shinogara led her through a set of double doors that swung freely in both directions. Marcia found herself in a miniature classroom with perhaps thirty-five seats in a sloped auditorium configuration that curved around a center presentation area. All seats were good seats. In the middle of the room

19

was a raised podium with a personal computer on a work table. Unseen and cabled beneath the floor, the computer was connected to a controller that allowed the PC's screen to be displayed on the large projection screen that hung from the ceiling behind the workstation. The screen was hung high enough to be comfortably seen from any seat. The floor was covered with a durable carpet which gave Marcia the feeling that the room was well used. She was correct.

Walking in front of her, Shinogara's body language wordlessly cautioned her to watch the steps as they descended to first level. Seated in the first row were three men, who on cue turned as one to watch them descend. Two were Shinogara's age and indistinguishable; the third was a husky man in his twenties, a foot taller than the others, and wore his hair in a near crew cut chop. Perched on his nose was a pair of heavy-duty rose-tinted glasses, which out of habit he constantly pushed back up onto his bridge.

Techno-nerd, she noted. Tech weenie. Technoid. They're easy to spot.

All three rose in unison as Shinogara escorted Marcia to the front of the room and introduced her. One old man was a Yamamoto and the other a Sukawa. The tech weenie was named David Kimura and unlike the others spoke English as a native language.

The others are not of this country, she smiled to herself.

"Nice to meet you, Miss Lee," said David, who along with his elders gave Marcia an approving top-to-bottom eyeball. "Please be seated."

Marcia sat down next to one of the older gentlemen and casually crossed her legs, left over right, and exposed a good deal of attractive leg, a move that caused Sukawa's eyes to flutter.

20

"This past Tuesday I met with Miss Lee in her San Francisco home—which, by the way, is so beautiful," Shinogara complimented. Marcia thanked him with a nod of her head. "I briefly outlined our need for the special . . . *services* of her organization, and that our project was at a critical point where we needed some-one with her . . . *unique* skills. We briefly discussed contractual arrangements and came to a mutually-agreeable fee."

Again Marcia nodded in thanks.

"She said that she was interested, but wanted to know more about our project and what would be ex-pected—so that she could better assess the risks and resources that would be required. Since this was a rea-sonable request, I invited her down here this evening, with a full understanding that anything disclosed to her in this meeting would be considered the highest or-der of corporate confidentiality, and that she would as-sume the risks that accompany such disclosure. Isn't that correct, Miss Lee?"

"Yes. Without knowing any details, I'm very cogni-zant of your need for privacy. *All* of my clients have had the same need. I don't discuss any client's business with any other client, or potential client. Believe me, I've gained a lot by keeping my mouth shut."

"I'd like to know more about Miss Lee and her orga-nization," said Yamamoto.

Shinogara nodded to Marcia, who stood up.

"I'm thirty-two years old and live in San Francisco. You would refer to me as a high-class call girl. I prefer to think of it in different terms, but a rose is a rose in any case," Marcia said, smiling. "I've been on my own since I was thirteen—since the day my mother found my stepfather in my room on one of his four-times-a-week visits. It was easier for her to kick me out than

21

him — she needed him more."

Marcia was no longer smiling; neither were the men.

"Since then I've educated myself, stayed off drugs, and kept my . . . *assets* in good shape. It may not be much, but I've found something that I'm good at and I plan to take advantage of as best I can — as long as I can.

"The first job I did was for free — and it was the last. I was in a bar when a friend of mine told me about her obnoxious boss who was about to fire her because she wouldn't put out. I decided to see if I could help. I knew two men who were camera freaks and talked them into helping me. My objective was to set him up so there could be no connection, no suspicion that my friend was in any way involved. She didn't know anything about it until we were done and her boss had been disgraced and fired. She never saw him again. After that, jobs just *came* to me. Somehow word got around in the right places and all of a sudden I was doing jobs in Los Angeles, Sacramento, Tahoe, Vegas — all over the West. What I do is a perfect example of supply and demand in a free economy. I've raised my rates tenfold over the years and I still have more requests than I can satisfy. I even did a job for the CIA in Mexico. They didn't know who I was then, and they still don't know.

"Now I have five full-time employees and fixed expenses of one hundred thousand dollars a month. I use the latest in technology and don't take jobs where the client is trying to reduce expenses. I don't run an on-the-cheap operation. None of my employees are in any police or FBI computer, and neither am I — and we intend to stay that way."

Marcia stopped and looked at each of the men in

22

turn.

"Do you have any questions?"

There weren't any.

"This is David Kimura, our chief programmer. David will be working with you on this project." Shinogara nodded to David, who stood up and went to the computer on the work table. His fingers floated over the PC's keyboard, tapping at a rapid pace. A map of the United States appeared on the large screen. Every major city was identified by a dot, as were many smaller ones.

"Are you familiar with IGC Corporation, Miss Lee?"

"World's largest manufacturer of computers—most widely held stock next to AT&T—every year has the largest net income after taxes—pays lousy dividends. Regular, but lousy. I'm heavily invested in them," replied Marcia.

All but Marcia laughed.

"You may want to reorganize your investment portfolio at some future date. It's only a suggestion."

Whoa. The hairs on the back of Marcia's neck prickled.

"The dots on this map indicate IGC locations across the country. In larger cities . . ."

Using a pointing device called a "mouse," David zeroed in on the Los Angeles dot, pressed a button, and instantly the screen was changed to a map of the greater Los Angeles area. There were many dots on this map.

". . . you can see that IGC has multiple locations. In the Los Angeles area alone there are twenty-five separate offices, representing more than seven thousand employees."

"Yes, they're big," added Marcia rhetorically.

23

For the first time Marcia turned her head to look at the others. Their eyes were already fixed on her. It was an eerie sensation. She couldn't tell if they were undressing or appraising her. What she could see was that they were serious.

Marcia turned her attention back to David.

"Yes, they're large. Over three hundred and fifty thousand employees worldwide. As you can imagine, the problems of internal communications and managing the logistics of such a huge operation are staggering in proportions. Yet they do it very well. Their internal technical support systems are absolutely the best of any company in the business. They're careful to pay their people salaries that are slightly above average for the industry—not too much. Nobody ever breaks the bank while at IGC. But nobody goes hungry, either. There hasn't been a single layoff in the company's seventy-year history. Not one! Job security is there, and a high degree of company loyalty. Not as much as it used to be—but that's natural with the change in American values in the last decade."

David pressed another button and a grid appeared across the country. Lines zigged and zagged between cities. The map was labeled IGC Internal Communications, and showed the physical and logical connections of IGC's internal computer networks, where the gateways existed, and where the most used internal application programs were housed—none of which made sense to Marcia in the brief time the map flashed on the screen.

"Your objective, Miss Lee, is to find one IGC employee. Only one. The *right* one. Someone in a marketing position, either a salesman or systems engineer."

Marcia's face wrinkled into a frown.

"So you don't have anybody particular in mind?"

24

Marcia looked down the line to Shinogara.

"No," replied Shinogara. "That will be your job. We'll show you the way, prepare you—but we're depending on you to find the right person."

"That's not the way I normally operate. I like to think the people I . . . compromise . . . have deserved what they've gotten."

"*We* like to think of companies not as a collection of individuals, but as an entity—and this one deserves the back of your hand and the spike of your heel, Miss Lee," replied Shinogara, and nodded toward David to continue.

"The only criterion," David explained, "is that the employee must have remote personal computer access to his or her office from home. I worked for IGC for three years before joining Mr. Shinogara's organization. We have the means to teach you the things you'll need to know. In less than a week you'll be able to pass yourself off as a true-blue IGCer, a 'lifer.' "

"Why Dallas?"

"Initially, we had two locations to choose from—Atlanta or Dallas. Both are major internal education centers for the corporation. However, most of the entry-level marketing training has been shifted to Atlanta. These people are more likely to be newer employees and will be less likely to have offices at home. For that reason we've selected Dallas. We have much to teach you, Miss Lee—Marcia," David corrected himself, as he tried to be more personal. "You must appear to be one of them. You must be able to mingle among them without distraction. I'll teach you what technical things you need to know—but you're a very beautiful woman. We have no doubt you'll be able to present yourself to attract any man you want."

The stone-faced Sukawa raised his hand in question.

"Now I have a question for Miss Lee."

"Yes?"

"What if the . . . victim . . . is a woman?"

"Do you mean, can I sexually blackmail a woman as well as a man?"

"Yes," replied Sukawa.

"I've found that my business requires me to learn something new every day. Learning to make love to another woman was an early requirement."

"I see," said Sukawa.

I bet you do, Marcia thought, and stood up to face the four men.

"Now I have a question for all of you. Blackmail is a risky business. As you know, it's illegal. So are some of the things done to blackmail people — drugs may be involved, laws broken. What degree — what level of risk are you willing to take?"

"Risk and reward go hand in hand," Shinogara replied. "The more risk you must take, the higher should be the reward — so is the effort required to achieve it. My associates and I are not gangsters. We are not murderers or criminals. We are businessmen. But the stakes are high. Where the stakes are high, only the bold can succeed. We are willing to do *anything* to accomplish this mission. And we expect you to be prepared to do the same. If this breaks an American law, then so be it." Shinogara leaned back in his chair. "I know you have done work outside the United States. You know that laws are not universal, that what is commonplace in one country may be illegal in another. We are businessmen. Risk is part of existence. Just so there is no discussion at a later point" — Shinogara raised his finger in emphasis — "we expect this client to be so thoroughly disgraced, that he — or she — will gladly offer what we want. Use your imagi-

26

nation, Miss Lee. I've heard it's quite good," Shinogara smiled.

For two million dollars, she smiled to herself, I can even go to Dallas.

Marcia and Shinogara shook hands and sealed the deal.

"This calls for a celebration, don't you think?" smiled Shinogara. "You will stay over, of course?"

"I know you'll want to get me started quickly. I've got to get my own organization back in gear. My crew will have to drive to Dallas. If your pilot is available, I'd like to fly back this evening. I can be back tomorrow afternoon, if that's OK?"

"I understand."

Marcia shook hands with each of the others, receiving two cold fish, and a warm vice grip from David.

As he did when he entered the room, Shinogara led the way up the steps and to the elevator. Once outside, the night air had noticeably changed. It was more chilly, even damp.

"Just like home. The fog must be coming in. You must get socked in pretty well up here," remarked Marcia.

"Yes, quite often. But some nights we seem to be just above the fog. It can be quite a strange sensation—the compound looks like it has a halo around it."

"Not from good deeds, I assume," Marcia joked. "I'll be back tomorrow afternoon," she said as Shinogara closed the limo's door.

A gray-and-blue 1988 Chevy Camaro was parked at the corner of Crest and Hawthorne, its hood up. The name of the man in the driver's seat was Juan Carlos "Buddy" Gault. He was the epitome of what police call the BHS, the Bushy-Haired Stranger, a man who had a rubber face and lips that remained permanently chapped from neglect, so neglected that they would bleed on occasion, as they were now. Gault made the problem worse by constantly ticking the sores with his tongue. He had a head of sandy hair that struggled to stay under a Dodgers cap and a cut across his forehead from a recent close encounter with two black men over on Crenshaw near Western. The pair had sincerely regretted their inability to reimburse Buddy and had paid the price as a result.

"Buddy!" came the urgent, nonprocedure call on the walkie-talkie. "How long do I have to walk this fucking dog?"

Buddy Gault had to laugh. Tough guys don't walk dogs, not unless there's a woman involved. And there was Bennie, out schlepping up and down the street with a mutt on a leash in the pitch dark while at the same time watching the front of the Jap's house. The dog was a perfect way to walk through an expensive neighborhood without getting the residents up in a heat, even places with those nosy neighbors signs posted everywhere. Besides, the fog was coming in and pretty soon nobody was going to see nothing.

Jimmy C. had called him three hours ago from San Francisco and told him to get his butt down to the Santa Monica airport and wait for a private jet to come in at six, maybe six-thirty or so. If a woman got off, then follow her. If not, then watch who gets on. And for Christ's sake, take some pictures. Photos, Jimmy C. always wanted photos. OK, photos he'll get. The woman was beautiful, all blue and all legs, long black hair and a knockout figure.

"Hey, Buddy — the limo's coming out. She's in back!"

Buddy Gault jumped out of the car and slammed

28

down the hood, then got back inside and had the Camaro ready to roll by the time the limo got to the corner of Crest and Hawthorne.

"Buddy! You ain't gonna leave me up here?"

"Catch a cab, Bennie, I gotta roll," replied Buddy, flicking the walkie-talkie off before Bennie had a chance to complain.

The black limo moved along the street like it was an electric train on fixed tracks, smooth and straight. The limo turned right at the intersection and headed down the hill on Hawthorne, away from the insulation of the peninsula and back into Ordinary People's Land.

Buddy drove the Camaro with the tips of his fingers. He was so in tune with the automobile that oftentimes he felt like he could just think and the car would obey. It was the perfect machine for his personality, capable of hitting 140 on the freeway, which he did only once on the Santa Monica early one Saturday morning last December. The son of a bitch had a two-mile lead on him and was headed for the beach, but from downtown Buddy caught up to him by the time they both crossed over the San Diego Freeway. The guy had been so surprised that he died with his mouth open. Buddy wished he could have seen himself in the guy's rear-view mirror. Slowing to seventy, Bennie had blown him off the road at the West LA exit. The guy's car left the road, flew off the embankment, and headed for New Mex Land—the area between Westwood and Santa Monica which had been a white neighborhood in the sixties but was now a barrio.

Buddy wasn't afraid of losing the limo. After all, the driver hadn't gone over forty-five from the airport down to the peninsula. In fact, he let the limo get on the San Diego, then caught up with it a few minutes later—anything to make a game out of it. This was real boring work. Buddy followed the black beast all the way back to the Santa Monica airport and made sure that it was the woman who got back aboard.

Some chick! he thought, and his libido departed for Fantasyland as he imagined what it must be like to be able to fly a beautiful whore in from San Francisco, screw her, then pat her on the butt and send her home like a good little girl.

"It must be nice," he said, shaking his head in envy as he reached for the phone and pressed an autodial combination. "Your package is back in the mail. Two hours thirty-eight minutes door-to-door."

Buddy hung up and watched the jet warm up, then taxi out to the end of the runway and take off. His fantasy about the woman in blue stayed with him as long as the jet's lights were visible, then just as suddenly vanished as he went back to work.

One by one, Marcia's crew arrived. The names and faces were familiar to Benson, the uniformed lobby guard. While Benson looked official, Marcia doubted he'd ever used his revolver except to get certified. A private express elevator zipped to the twentieth floor, which was the penthouse and all Marcia's — paid in full, thank you very much.

As usual, Joe came first, jumping like a puppy to her every word. He was in love with her, and she knew it. It was an unattainable and inexpressible love, a match that Joe knew would never take place outside of his own mind. He was the perfect bodyguard, someone who at times knew her better than she did herself, and who was constantly anticipating what could or would happen next. As a result of constant thinking, Joe's face looked like a worried basset hound most of the time. He was a lot more intelligent than he looked, although he was oftentimes slow tongued around her, which made him appear dim witted. He wasn't. He was, however, a big man—tipping in at six-five and 260 pounds. Marcia could never take more luggage than Joe could carry.

Tony and Bill were best friends and were constantly in each other's face, laughing and jabbing like two kids, although Tony was in his late forties and Bill a decade younger. They were a matching pair of electronic geniuses.

Then there were Marcia's ladies.

Heather was a tall blond of twenty-six who physically matched Marcia nearly leg for leg. She was a hungry animal who could take a man on a trip to the far edge of reality, to the point where fantasies no longer existed. Unlike Marcia, who was sleekly and elegantly desirable, Heather exuded *want-it want-it* twenty-four hours a day, a black hole of sexual desire. Her metabolism was set on high warble. As a result, she ate like a lumberjack but never gained an ounce. She always had to have something in her mouth, and she didn't care what it was.

The last of the crew was a nymphette named Jo Jo Joslin, but the crew just called her Baby. She was a small pouty blond of twenty-one, who, when dressed for action, looked no older than an innocent girl of fourteen.

"It's about time you showed up," Heather sparred as the elevator opened and Baby popped out. Her white leather boots softly padded across the black marble foyer to the huge open living area, which was sunk two plushly carpeted steps down. To the left was a well-stocked open bar with stools in front, a semiformal dining room with a contemporary glassed table, a

31

small but gleaming kitchen with microwave, and a utility room with stacked washer and dryer. To the right was a short hallway to the master bedroom, which passed two bathrooms and an inboard small bedroom along the way. The master bedroom, living room, and dining room all had an unobstructed view of San Francisco through floor-to-ceiling glass windows.

"I thought we'd have a little more time off, but it looks like we've got a big one. It's enough for double bonuses," she opened. "Maybe even triple!"

Double bonuses got everyone's attention. While a triple had been joked about here and there, Marcia had never paid one out. Not that anybody had any complaints about money. They were all paid very well—a base salary plus a completion bonus based on a percentage of the net take on the job. Whatever number was agreed upon, the client paid half up front and the other half when the job was done. When the pot reached a certain number—which would vary from job to job depending upon expenses, duration, difficulty, or any combination—Marcia would kick in the double bonus schedule, which could mean anywhere from twenty-five to fifty thousand dollars extra per person.

On Monday Shinogara had deposited one million dollars in her Swiss bank account as up-front money.

"A triple bonus?" asked Heather, amazed. "You're not kidding us, are you?"

"No, I'm not. Right now I can guarantee a double, with a good chance for a triple."

There were "Oh, yeahs!" and happy smiles around.

"We're going to earn it. Our client is"—Marcia paused—"our clients are a group of Japanese businessmen. As far as I can tell they aren't a company and they aren't individuals, except for the leader, a man named Shinogara. What makes this case different is that I have to find the mark."

Marcia could see the puzzled looks on their faces.

"And we have to do this in Dallas."

Groans and catcalls.

"And I don't know how long it will take."

"Have you ever thought about quadruple bonuses?" asked Bill.

"Way to go!" laughed Tony.

Marcia joined in their laughter.

"We're going to be away from our home base, so I want all of our equipment with us. If you think we might need it, take it. My guess is we'll be in a house or apartment . . ."

"A house is better, Marcia," interrupted Tony.

"Tony says a house is better, so it's a house," Marcia laughed. "I want the panel truck and the Caravan and all of you there when we start. This is going to be a team effort. Pack for . . . six weeks, I don't know — we may be longer, maybe not. I hope not. Joe and I are going back to Los Angeles tomorrow. Shinogara's going to make me into a computer whiz in less than a week."

"You never cease to amaze me, Marcia," said Heather, shaking her head.

"Plan on meeting me at the Omni Hotel in downtown Dallas next Tuesday."

"We'll be there," said Tony.

Three men sat around a four hundred-year-old teak table, its once yellowish brown wood now stained the color of a rich coffee. Like a bank where everything depends on the placement of the vault, all the furni-

33

ture in the living room rotated in relationship to the antique table. If the table had been moved six inches the room would have been in complete disarray. But all was harmony. Vases and prints and tie-dyed Malaysian batiks stood and hung in just the right places. Across the floor was a two-centuries-old Chinese rug, fifteen by twenty feet wide, in rich blues and reds, with a delicate hand-sewn fringe. A pair of golden lions danced in the middle.

Seated at one end of the rectangular table in an uncomfortable looking straight-backed chair was financier Xiang Wu. Since his Chinatown apartment offered the easiest guarantee of privacy, Wu had offered it to host the meeting. Located in the 800 block of Grant Street, the apartment was accessed by climbing an unassuming but steep flight of wooden stairs which were wedged between a busy restaurant and a laundry. Once inside, the apartment expanded to cross the top of several first floor businesses and with vaulted ceilings managed to reach the top of the three-story building, which opened up to a view east, toward the Embarcadero section of San Francisco, the financial heart of the West Coast and Xiang Wu's home turf.

Wu, sixty-eight years old, smiled as his beautiful twelve-year-old consort softly padded around the room refilling drinks which had been offered to the guests. "A lovely girl. She keeps an old man warm at night. She was a gift from the Huang brothers."

Seated on the sofa was forty-one year old E. Dexter Albright, B.S. Yale University, MBA Wharton School of Business. Albright represented Eastern Establishment. A proper man, Dexter was dressed in a business suit, vest, polished black wingtips, with a two-day-old haircut that made every hair seem just in place. Albright was a senior partner of White, Tifton and Reynolds, or WTR as it was known on Wall Street. The agency was called other names by other brokers, but it had managed an unbroken string of successes without once being caught with its fingers in the cookie jar.

Across the table from Albright sat Jimmy Chimichanga, or Jimmy C. as he was known on the street. Chimichanga, forty-nine, was a first generation Irish-American-Mexican mongrel thug with thick hands, dark eyebrows, and a misshapen nose that looked like a large blob of putty. Even when dressed to the teeth he was still an ugly man. But good looks had never been a requirement to succeed in the thug business. Jimmy C. controlled over forty percent of the South American drug traffic to the West Coast, and because of his business relationship with Xiang Wu, one hundred percent of the Far East heroin traffic entering the port of San Francisco. It was enough to keep a man busy. Chimichanga, besides being ugly as a pit bull, was blunt as a spent bullet. He had not one ounce of finesse in his psyche. When something had to get done, it got done.

"Don't ever tell me you want something done if you don't mean it. When I do something, it can't get fixed—if it gets broke, you ain't going to put it back."

It was a simple philosophy, but one that was easy to understand. It made the relationship among the New York-based stockbroker, the San Francisco financier, and the LA mobster one that seemed to work. Each was legitimate in his own way, yet crooked to the bone. The alliance among the three men had been on-again, off-again for the last five years. Each man brought strengths that made their union an example of how the whole is more than the sum of its parts. Wu got heroin for Chimichanga and accounts for Dexter. Dexter laundered money for Jimmy C. and beat SEC and

NYSE rules for Wu. Chimichanga provided muscle and logistical support for them both.

"I'm going to ask you both a simple question. What would you do if you knew — I mean really *knew* — that a stock would lose twenty-five points next Monday?" asked Albright.

"I did the same thing on a horse at Bay Meadows on Tuesday. Came in fifth," replied Jimmy C.

"No, I mean it. What would you do?" repeated Albright, turning to Xiang Wu. "Wu? I think I know what you'd do." Albright nodded to his mentor.

"I would want my investors to make as much as possible without seeming greedy," nodded Wu.

"Without calling attention to yourself."

"Correct," replied Wu.

"James?" asked Albright, turning to the squat, balding man across the table from him.

Chimichanga's face turned from amusement to a hard stare into the stockbroker's eyes.

"Guaranteed? A dead cinch lock?" he asked.

"Mortal," replied Albright.

"I'd bet the fucking farm," replied Jimmy Chimichanga.

"Yes, I thought you would," smiled Albright.

"And what would you do, Dex?" asked Jimmy.

E. Dexter Albright hated to be called Dex, not even by his mother and father, but it was such a natural nickname that he'd found himself with only two choices — reverse the initials and go by Eaton D. Albright, or get a new name. Instead, he lived with the irritation.

"If I knew a particular stock was going to nose-dive, I'd invest in the ancillary industries — "

"English, stockbroker — English," gruffed Chimichanga.

36

"The side issues, James," explained Wu, gently.

"Yes, the side issues. What companies service or supply critical parts to the target? What companies are in the same industry? Is the industry weak? Do the stocks in the industry move together on the stock market? Will it affect the market as a whole? What about futures? What I *wouldn't* do is put all my money in a short buy of the stock. That would guarantee a visit from an SEC team," briefly analyzed Albright.

"Well, that's what I would have done too," added Jimmy C. "So big deal? Is that what you think this is going to come to?"

"Yes," replied Dexter. "I do. I think very shortly we will have, as the former president was fond of saying, a window of opportunity for a financial windfall unparalleled in the history of money."

In the four years Jimmy C. had been doing business with E. Dexter Albright, he'd known the man to be an enthusiastic, often pedantic pain in the ass, but not naive or careless. For Dex to make such an obvious overstatement meant that there was a real good chance they'd all make some dough.

"And the girl is the key," stated Jimmy.

"Yes, the girl is definitely the key," replied Dexter. "And Xiang Wu's itchy-fingered investors."

Xiang Wu had become the most important investment banker on the West Coast by developing contacts in the Republic of China, to the point that all major Taiwanese investors came to him for advice, and to handle transactions. The fact that Wu had been born in Taipei gave him a natural advantage. Wu had been with them before the ROC had amassed its nearly one hundred billion-dollar cash reserves, achieved mainly through low-cost manufacturing processes in the electronics and garment industries. With pockets bulging with cash, rich Taiwanese merchants flocked to Xiang Wu, eager to break into the American markets by financing new U.S. upstart companies. The upstart companies were just as eager to receive the offshore cash. By the late eighties, Taiwanese venture capital seed money had been potted in every pocket of silicon high technology along the West Coast.

"She's been very successful," said Dexter.

"How is it I don't know her?" asked Jimmy Chimichanga, a bit put out that his two "legitimate" partners had a good make on a broad that was nothing more than a call girl.

"She deals in subtlety, Jimmy," laughed Dexter. "Definitely not your style. Twenty years ago she'd be in your pocket."

Jimmy C. leaned forward and took half of his glass of Coors in a single swallow.

"I first heard of Miss Lee from an acquaintance in the investment department at Bank of America who told me secondhand that a particular state senator had decided to change his vote on a bill that potentially could cost certain investors large sums of money. He assured me that the bank had nothing to do with it, that he had heard through a friend that the senator had been caught in an indiscreet situation with an underage girl. That was about three years ago. My offices are in the financial nerve center on this coast, and the grapevine is a fairly reliable source for the truth. There were several business executives and more than a handful of politicians who either made startling career decisions or changed their opinions on views that were thought to be ironclad. Finally, last year I was even offered her name and phone number by an associate who thought I might use her services one day," Wu added.

"Shinogara may be ready to make his move," added Albright.

Chimichanga's face was grooved with deep furrows of doubt. In turn he looked at the two men.

"You two talk like you've been onto this Shinogara for a long time. Why is this the first time I've heard about it?"

Chimichanga's voice had raised a half octave, indicating his displeasure at what he perceived as being a slight.

"We weren't aware that you were terribly interested in the fluctuations of the worldwide computer industry," replied Albright dryly.

Jimmy C.'s face remained furrowed. Xiang Wu raised his hand in placation.

"Let me explain, my friend. Makato Shinogara is a representative of the Japanese government. When I say government, in this case I mean industry — business — corporate Japan. In many circles the words business and government are synonymous. In this case it's true. Shinogara doesn't come from their embassy, but his function is governmental nevertheless."

Wu's hand motioned for Jimmy Chimichanga to have patience.

"As best we can determine, Shinogara was sent to the United States in the fall of 1987."

"By who?" asked Chimichanga.

Wu sighed, then continued.

"By a consortium of Japanese electronics corporations, mainly in the computer industry. Shinogara was selected because of his organizational skills and willingness to sacrifice everything to achieve the corporate goals of the combined companies."

"Which is?" asked Chimichanga.

"Do you know which computer company has the

largest sales in Japan?"

"Don't you *ever* answer a fucking question straight?"

Wu laughed at his rough compatriot's impatience.

"IGC Corporation," said Wu simply. "IGC sells more computers inside Japan than do the rest of the Japanese national companies themselves. It's true."

"So? Good for them," replied the mobster.

"In 1982 the FBI was ready to award a large computer contract to Hitachi. The award was canceled when it was learned that the company authorized the theft of trade secrets from IGC's San Jose laboratory. The result — damages, loss of esteem, loss of business. And replacement of the Hitachi equipment by IGC.

"In 1986 Toshiba Corporation was banned from doing business with the American government because of its sales to Iron Curtain countries. It was a minor breach of American rules, but major penalties were exacted against the company. In private, some Japanese officials believe IGC was involved in the background of the disclosure. In 1987, American microchip manufacturers complained bitterly about the Japanese practice of 'dumping,' a term used when a company comes into a market and offers a product at below cost, drives out its competitors, then raises its prices to monopolistic levels."

Wu had Chimichanga's attention.

"While all American semiconductor companies had a lot to lose, IGC had the largest stake. In 1987 the American government put a severe limit on the number of computer chips that Japan could export to the U.S.

"There are other instances, but the trail always seems to lead back to IGC. The Japanese fear and loathe the American computer giant. They resent the holier-than-thou approach to business, the veneer of cleanliness that coats their employees, and the constant preaching of the fair play code of ethics. To the Japanese, IGC sounds like an American evangelical preacher."

"And they don't like getting slapped around in public," Jimmy C. added.

"That's right. That's why Makato Shinogara was sent over to the United States. He's on a mission that will in some way undermine or wreak a measure of revenge on IGC. Shinogara's not on any payroll, nor does he receive a government subsidy. His seed money is all in cash, all untraceable. That includes the mansion he's bought and the men he's brought to it—*smart* men, *dedicated* men. All with a mission."

"Which is?"

"We don't know. We are trying to find out. If we know what he is doing, and we know that it will work . . ."

"And we know when," added Dexter Albright.

"Yes, when—timing is always important. If we know all of that, then the three of us can make certain . . . investments . . . that can take advantage of the situation."

"And you think the girl has something to do with this plan?" asked Jimmy C.

"Yes, and that's why we need you to follow her," replied Dexter.

"Why not just have her picked up?" Jimmy C. interrupted. "I could take care of it tonight. I could have taken care of it last night, easy as could be. She came home, met with these people . . ."

Chimichanga handed a stack of photos to Wu, who recognized them and handed them to Dexter Albright.

". . . then left this morning with five suitcases of luggage and a dopey-looking bodyguard. Right now she's

41

back in LA at Shinogara's estate."

"Those are her associates." Wu spoke to Albright, who quickly sifted through the pictures of Tony, Bill, Heather, and Baby.

"Very nice," mused Albright, pausing over Baby's picture.

"Yes, they are. This Lee woman runs a clean operation. To my knowledge, nothing's ever blown up in her face," complimented Wu.

"Until now," said Jimmy C.

"Yes, until now. Right now, all we need is to have her followed. Mr. Wu and I believe that Shinogara is starting something and"—Dexter leaned over the table toward Jimmy C.—"it's vital that we know what it is. We're talking big bucks, Jimmy. We don't want him spooked. We need to know what he's planning," Dexter instructed his mobster partner.

"She'll never know we're there," Chimichanga smiled.

Marcia was crawling the walls by the end of the week. She was the only woman in a luxurious compound filled with thirty Japanese tech nerds, all about thirty years old, all wearing glasses thick as Coke bottles. She'd walk through the computer building and people would be hunched over terminals. Everyone spoke Japanese and everyone was excruciatingly nice to her.

David gave her several books to read and tried to give her a short course in computers and current terminology, but the alphabet soup that passed for language was simply too much.

"David, I'm not going to talk business with these people. If I get somebody out one-on-one, they're dead meat. No man is going to talk about work when he can get laid. I need enough surface knowledge to get along, to ask the right questions, and to recognize the right answer. That can't be too tough. I'm perfectly capable of nodding my head and looking smart even when I don't have the foggiest idea what the hell is going on. And, all guys are the same," Marcia laughed. "Give 'em a whiff and they don't care if you don't know the difference between a computer and a toaster. And they won't remember afterward, either."

"I've got a realtor lined up for us this afternoon," said David.

"What's the nicest suburb?" asked Marcia.

"Highland Park—far and away the best," David answered.

"That's where I want to go," Marcia said firmly.

David could see that Marcia didn't want to talk. For most of the week she'd patiently listened to his advice—something she wasn't used to doing, he was sure. Besides that, other than the task ahead, the two of them had very little in common to begin with—and the interior of a 767 wasn't the place to talk about blackmail and computer viruses.

While both of them were lost in their thoughts, neither David or Marcia paid attention to the details of the other passengers, who for the most part were just bodies who filled seats. Seated three rows behind them was Buddy Gault, who along with two other men would follow their every move for as long as it would take—whatever *it* turned out to be.

An hour later, David started Marcia on her tour of the architectural misery along Highway 114 north of Irving—past the IGC training center at Williams

Square, the apartment complex and concrete minicity called Las Colinas, a place where there were moats and boats to get about, but no sidewalks—a common suburban trait. People drove, they didn't walk.

The IGC facility at Williams Square consisted of three thirty-story reddish brick buildings, each topped with a distinctive tapered roof, so distinctive that the buildings were nicknamed the Coneheads. Separating the buildings was a massive concrete plaza that gradually stair-stepped down to an impressive, larger-than-life-size series of sculpted mustang ponies, bronzed beauties frozen in poses while crossing an artificial stream that ran through the plaza. The sensation of movement was highlighted by well-placed fountains that splashed water at the point where the horse's hooves met the stream.

"It's good to see that things haven't changed much since I was here," smiled the congenial Kimura. "It is so boring to be here for more than a couple of days. There's nothing to do except drink, which they do very well. To pay for their drinking everybody crowds into the pubs and tries to make up their meal money in free hors d'oeuvres."

David was a graduate of UC Berkeley in computer sciences and had joined IGC directly out of college. He'd been quickly accepted and trained in the IGC Way, a process that Kimura found to be both illuminating and degrading. The instruction was rote and patterned, a highly structured approach to learning—a process that would easily turn off a young professional, and did. The principles of selling were intertwined with a constant barrage of intensive product training, on subjects that weren't easy to understand. IGC didn't ask new marketing people to come to the company already pretrained. In fact, it was better to come

44

with a clean mental slate — just be prepared for the fire hose method of training. Throw enough information at a student and some is bound to stick. Do it often enough and apply some pressure to learn, and the company could easily weed the good from the average.

The entire year of training, which was sliced into periods of classroom study with breaks of real life back home in the branch office, was based around the development and perfection of the elements involved in the Planned Sales Call: State the objectives, ask open-ended questions, develop interest, two-way communications, transitions to the Business Portion, set proper goals, How much-by when, verify customer understanding, verify interest, paraphrase and overcome objections, find a relevant IGC solution, relate the advantages, trial close, plan of action, realistic commitment, gain agreement, close the sale . . . Calls plus Demos equal Sales.

"Why'd you quit?" Marcia asked.

"It wasn't for me. Too structured, too many rules. Mr. Shinogara has treated me very well," David replied, not answering her question.

Marcia scrutinized her new companion.

"What's going on here, David?" she asked point blank.

He looked her in the eyes and returned a small shake of his head.

"Sorry," he replied seriously. "I can only say that the future has much to offer — much more than I could possibly dream of anyplace else."

Highland Park was more than Marcia had expected — quiet, old, and moneyed. People tended to their own business. The agent had taken them to four

45

homes before driving by a two-story Spanish-style traditional with stucco finish and a red-tiled roof. The lawn of zoysia grass, white-tipped and dormant because of the warm Texas autumn, was carefully manicured in the owner's absence.

"I like it," said Marcia, after inspecting the upstairs. "Is there a basement?" she asked the agent.

"Completely finished."

"It's perfect," she said, smiling to David. "We'll take it."

Later, the papers signed, deposit and six months' rental paid in full—in cash—David turned the keys over to Marcia.

"We're going to need a lot of furniture. I want lived in stuff—no new carpet smell. You know what I mean."

"Consider it done—tasteful, somewhat modern, but comfortable—make the house look used—no new carpeting—no new carpet smell," David read from his notepad, then smiled at Marcia. "You'll need an automobile. I'll arrange it. What kind do you prefer?"

"I want something tasteful, but with borderline flash. Get me either a Camaro or a Mustang. Make it red, and make it a convertible."

Tony looked approvingly at the high ceilings and the ornate light fixtures. He ran his hand along the side of a large mirror that hung over the living room fireplace.

"I can get a camera in that one, but we'll need mirrors on all three walls to get the other angles. I assume we can get through to downstairs," he said to Bill, who tapped on the walls.

"Real plaster. It'll take some digging. Where do you

46

want us to set up?" Bill asked Marcia.

"There's a finished basement. I'd hoped that you could make it your control room. It's out of the way, and can give us all a bit of breathing room when the show's on. Upstairs are four bedrooms and two baths. I thought we'd do the living room, kitchen, master bedroom, and the master bath. That's all the furniture I've ordered."

"Where are we going to sleep?" asked Heather.

"Sorry—I've got two of the upstairs bedrooms set as crash rooms," Marcia replied. "Let me show you the rest of the house. You'll figure out what to do. You always do," she added, smiling to her crew.

Marcia led the troop upstairs to the master bedroom.

"Nice size," said Heather.

"Look at this bathroom," added Baby.

"There's going to be a lot of action in these two rooms, Tony—probably with low lighting," said Marcia.

"The film's no problem. Bathrooms are tough—the damn fog from the steam causes problems."

"Maybe we can adjust the air-conditioning," suggested Marcia.

The group nodded their heads in approval. The house was big enough so they wouldn't get on one another's nerves. More importantly, they had time to set up and prepare the electronics so that things had a chance to run smoothly.

"Today's Friday. Monday night I'm going to start trolling, so I want to be ready. If I don't get somebody Monday or Tuesday night, then we'll have to wait until the next week. We need at least three nights—"

"For the drugs, right?" interrupted Heather.

"Right. It takes at least seventy-two hours to get

47

enough drugs into his system to alter his personality. Most of these IGC classes don't go from week to week, so we need to catch our guy early," Marcia explained. "At worst, you'll have weekends off."

Cheers from the group.

"I thought you'd like that. All right, we've got a lot of work to do. Let's get this house ready for some action!"

Tony and Bill were very pleased to find out that the walls were thick enough to handle the minicameras without having to alter the outside of the home. Platforms were constructed inside the walls for the cameras and coax cables dropped through to the basement. One-way mirrors were installed in the living room, bedroom, and bathroom. Downstairs, Tony had a monitor for each camera and could control the zoom or pan at will. Joe and Bill set up interroom communications via wireless headsets. While someone could obviously talk to the control room from any of the four rooms, there had to be a way for two-way communications. It was critical if something went drastically wrong and somebody needed help in a hurry.

Cheryl Coldsmith Colby, a pretty blond of twenty-eight, sat cross-legged on her newly purchased king-size bed and watched as her husband Zack quickly and efficiently finished packing the second of two suitcases for his upcoming week in Dallas.

"Mom said that she talked with Scotty yesterday," said Cheryl, feeling the need to attach as much family to Zack as she could before he left the house.

And with Mom and Dad Coldsmith living only forty-nine miles away in Laramie, it was nearly impossible for Zack to escape the ominipresent family anytime, which was another reason he was looking forward to the week in Dallas. And as much as he tried to hide it, Zack somehow generated high-frequency thought patterns that broadcast his relief at being away from home for a few days. Zack simply oozed anxiety.

"Scotty? How is he?" replied Zack, his conversation politely keeping up with Cheryl even though his mind was on his suitcase and the upcoming trip.

Cheryl switched positions and lay on her right side, stretching her five-foot ten-inch frame across the bed. Even at that height Cheryl was the runt of the Coldsmith family. Her parents were both over six feet tall and her younger brother Scotty was a lanky six foot four.

"He's doing OK. He doesn't like New York much, though," she said wistfully.

"Why doesn't he transfer?" asked Zack, nearly finished. "The FBI office in Denver has to have room for him—especially since he's a hero and all."

"Mom says they won't let him. They won't consider it until that spy trial is finished, which Scotty says has been going on *forever*. Apparently, he's become kind of a media star. Just think—our Scotty, a star!" Cheryl spoke lovingly of her younger brother.

"Well, I still think you got the good looks in the family," Zack said with a smile.

With a single motion Zack zipped his garment bag closed and wordlessly announced that he was ready to leave.

"Ready?" asked Cheryl, an anxious tone in her voice.

Will he come back? she thought. It was a silly fear, she knew. He was a good-looking man and she was a good-looking young woman. They'd had a happy four years of marriage and two wonderful children. Still, there was part of Zack's background that he'd never let her get close to, and Cheryl always had a nagging feeling that Zack might have had a fling or two, even though she had not one bit of evidence to back up her suspicions. There was a wildness that lay barely masked in his eyes, which hinted of things done but never discussed. Zack would be the first to admit that he had a constant high-level appreciation for the female form.

"Don't forget to bring something home for the kids," Cheryl whispered in Zack's ear as she softly kissed his cheek.

"I won't," Zack smiled as he returned her embrace, then bent down to say good-bye, first to little Brian, then to his sister Anne.

The entire Colby family stood cooing and kissing out on the front porch. It was a beautiful afternoon. Perched on a small bluff near the northern limit of town, the young Colbys had an unsurpassed view of Cheyenne below them. With the air always crisp and clean, the Rocky Mountains seemed much closer than forty miles away. To their right and down the hill was the small Cheyenne airport, then the cluster of downtown office and government buildings, including the state capital, the four lanes of I-25, and finally Warren AFB.

With Zack's good job with IGC, he and Cheryl had managed to get a larger loan than they could afford, and more house than they needed—a five-bedroom, three-bath, two-level home that had been converted to a doctor's office on the first floor. But with the arrival of Brian and then Anne, they'd grown into it, and his income with IGC had risen to the point where the once-burdensome mortgage was no longer a problem. In fact, the two of them had seriously discussed how they could go about paying it down at a faster rate.

The main floor and residence was on the level with the top of the bluff, with the front of the home facing north, offering a 360-degree panorama of Cheyenne and four hundred miles of empty prairie to the north and east. The back of the home was all glass and had a spacious deck and patio off of the living room, kitchen, and master bedrooms.

The doctor's office was one level down and had its own separate driveway and parking area, with excellent views to the south and sunshine for most of the day. Zack had combined several of the doctor's patient rooms and made replicas of two business offices, each with the latest in IGC equipment. The office worked very well from Zack's point of view, but more importantly, the arrangement satisfied picky IGC management. It was hard for management to say no to a good idea that brought in sales. With Cheryl and the kids upstairs, the downstairs was isolated and insulated, connected by a spiral staircase and an intercom system. From the IRS standpoint, the downstairs of the Colby home was a good example of separation of business and personal space.

In addition to the two demonstration rooms, he had two bathrooms, a nice kitchen, and a large area for presentations. Zack could put on the best of multimedia dog-and-pony shows.

"Have a good class," Cheryl said, her hands dropping from his shoulders.

"I hope so," Zack replied, now anxious to leave. "Daddy's got to go now," he said to the children as he turned for his car, which was in the driveway with Zack's two suitcases already in the backseat. "I'll be back Friday night for dinner."

"I love you," Cheryl said simply. "Take care. Call me," she gushed.

"You, too. I will," he replied, getting into his car.

Cheryl stood and watched until Zack's car turned left onto College Drive and drove down the bluff, finally losing him in the traffic near Lincolnway. She couldn't tell if he'd returned her wave, but thought so.

Jeez, is this bad.

Scotty had long since lost interest in what the lawyers were saying—on both sides. It had taken a year just to get the case to court, what with the internal squabbles over jurisdiction, location, and endless blah-blah-blah from Justice. Once they'd agreed to hold the trial in Los Angeles, Scotty thought things would pick up—but no. The trial itself was in its fourth month and had threatened to become a millstone on the careers of several government lawyers.

Oh—you were on the Soviet spy case.

From Scotty's perspective, the Justice Department had very nearly botched a wired open-and-shut lead-pipe cinch mortal fucking lock case. At certain points in the proceedings, Scotty wanted to jump up and take over for the Justice team—to use his three years at Columbia Law School and his intimate personal knowledge of the case. The criminals, Soviet spies Katrina Tambov and Alexander Rostov, had been caught red-handed, and a confession from the Soviet government had been heard all over the world.

But was it admissible in court?

Gimme a break.

Scott Coldsmith, twenty-seven years old and forever a Scotty, was now two years out of the FBI's rookie school and light years away from his home in Laramie. While still a rookie he'd been assigned to track a Soviet courier named Rostov. Together with a senior agent

52

from North Carolina—J. J. Carteret—he'd tracked Rostov and broken a spy ring and an attempt to bring the country to its knees.

Damn you, J. J.

Scotty always suspected J. J. had used a two-tailed coin when they'd flipped to see which of them would give deposition and which would stay with the case to the bitter end. Now J. J. had gotten his reward and a temporary assignment as FBI liaison to Sequoia National Park.

My reward is to sit in this courtroom and listen to these damn bozos, he thought.

The Special-Agent-in-Charge at the Los Angeles office, the second largest regional office in the FBI's network, had made life bearable at least, for which he was appreciative. He'd even given Scott some real work to do when there were recesses. There was no sense in flying back and forth to New York every time there was a delay—a fact that his boss, Manhattan SAC Murphy Monahan, simply hated.

"I can't help it, Murphy! It's not my fault! Justice is letting the defense clobber us with the god-damned Constitution. *Our* constitution."

While he was in Los Angeles, Scotty had been assigned to the organized crime unit and had been fortunate enough to participate in the Big Fucking Bust, as the 20 billion-dollar Colombian seizure was internally referred to. While the bust hadn't been formally connected to James "Jimmy C." Chimichanga, the unit thought they were getting close.

Scotty's six-foot-four frame was nearly paralyzed by the small and uncomfortable courtroom seats. By midafternoon the lawyers all started to sound alike—like the annoying drone of the Goodyear blimp hovering overhead.

Being an FBI agent is less fun than meets the eye.

The hour-and-a-half drive to Stapleton gave Zack more time to think than he wanted. He should have been happy but he wasn't. Work was great, home was great, the kids were great, Cheryl was great. So why didn't he *feel* great? Why did he look forward to the week in Dallas? If ever something should be a pain in the ass, a week-long workstation update in Dallas would be it.

A full week of boring shit.

Why was he glad to be away from his family? It didn't make any sense at all. It was unsettling to Zack, who at age thirty appeared to have the world by the tail—a great job with IGC, a beautiful blond wife, two healthy children, and the respect of all who knew him.

The feeling of anxiety, of something being wrong, was very unsettling, and it didn't get any better until he was on the plane and had two gin and tonics on his service tray.

Every couple needs time off from each other every once in a while, he thought.

Filled with warm rationalizations and a soft buzz, Zack waited for the dinner service to be completed before going back to chat up one of the flight attendants, a pretty young woman about his age named Leslie.

"Long day?" he started.

"Really," said the weary attendant, trying to cram in a quick meal before preparing for landing.

"Going home?"

"No—I'm out of Houston. But not tonight. We've got a thirty-six-hour layover, then Wednesday morning back to Denver, San Francisco, Dallas again, LA, and back to Houston."

"In *one day?*"

The attendant smiled and nodded yes, hoping Zack would let her get back to her meal.

"How about dinner tonight?"

With tired eyes she scanned him from head to toe. Zack might as well have worn a neon sign.

Young Married Bullshitter on the Make.

"What would your wife say?"

"I'm not asking you to marry me — just have dinner," Zack responded seriously.

It was a better reply than most men gave. Some lied, most badly. Some stammered and turned red, some walked away — which was exactly what Leslie wanted Zack to do.

"No, I'm busy," she turned him off, and went back to her meal.

Walking back to his seat, Zack's body was pumped with adrenaline as his imagination leaped over reality, nearly convincing his mind that he'd almost scored.

Dallas.

The thought was enough to make his stomach turn.

Even after four years, the experience of going through IGC's entry-level marketing training had left such a bad taste in his mouth for the city that he hated to go back. And he wasn't the only one. A lot officers hated Dallas.

At least this class had the promise of real education. Most classes had two days of information stuffed into five days of time, classes that quickly degenerated into Brain Drain — a race to see whether the brain cells created during the day could keep up with the brain cells damaged at night. After the second no-content lecture, Zack's head would begin to feel like someone shot it

55

with novocaine.

Is it still there? he thought. Am I brain dead?

Landing was a blur. As was deplaning. Zack knew the routine. "Take the SURTRANS bus marked "Downtown" to the IGC . . ." He had the instructions memorized. He could take a cab if he wanted, but the twenty-dollar fare wouldn't be reimbursable. Only the $6.25 SURTRANS bus tickets were reimbursable. One rental car was provided for every four students, and designated drivers appointed. It wasn't a bad system. Rental cars were a tremendous expense, yet without some form of transportation the students were prisoners.

Check-in at the Sheraton went smoothly enough, although Zack hated sharing a room with someone he didn't know. But the Sheraton was infinitely better than the IGC Ghetto in Las Colinas, apartments that smelled of entry-level training, of trainees, of late nights and pressure studies for pretend sales calls.

Zack shook his head at the powerful memories.

It wouldn't have been so bad if they'd somehow managed to treat you as adults, he thought.

It was the biggest gripe of all, the worst memory of Dallas training. Yes, it was programmed. Yes, it was unreal. But there were elements he'd learned that he used in his sales calls every day of his career. But it was being treated like a child that bothered him the most. The instructors taught their courses the Dallas Way, which meant that there was no deviation from the program and certainly no original thinking. The experience would be enough to cause the loss of many good people to competing companies.

By seven Zack had had supper and called home. On the last normal day of his life, Zack Colby had four shooters of gin, a Denny's cheeseburger combo, and went to bed early with a headache and a mildly upset stomach.

It is one of the truths of corporate education that bad classes always end early in the day. Even the instructors get tired of presenting fluff and concept. Today was no exception. The last foil went up at 4:28 and the overhead turned off at 4:30.

"A mercy kill," said Zack.

"Free the hostages," replied the rep who sat next to him, a fellow called Meyers.

A group of eight or nine classmates gathered for the next major decision. Where are we going to drink? The choice quickly narrowed to TGI Friday's or Houlihan's. Houlihan's won by a six-to-three vote, but not without discussion. The waitresses were much better looking at Friday's, but the drinks at Houlihan's were larger and less watered. The finger food was determined to be equal. So Houlihan's it was. They got there early enough to get the large corner booth in the rear, the one with the good view of the large-screen TV. In another couple of hours Monday Night Football would be on, and by then they'd be well into a three-digit bar tab and dinner would have been long forgotten.

By six-thirty the group had grown to fifteen or so, with additions from other classes. Conversations were laced with industry jargon, acronyms mixing with numbers and abbreviations, turning their pseudo-language into a nearly indecipherable foreign tongue.

IGC tables were easy to spot.

The content of the conversation was nearly always business, and depending on how straitlaced the women were, could go off on good-natured sexual tangents, as could the vocabulary used. The group was always loud, the laughter boisterous. By seven o'clock the group was sixty percent to forty percent men, a higher-than-normal mixture of women. After three rounds of drinks at least two unannounced products had been disclosed along with the marketing problems, equipment backlog, and future plans of eight to ten major IGC installations. It was all so innocent and trusting—and so easy. Even with constant management reminders about loose lips and security, the average IGCer was impervious to the realities of the way business was conducted.

The talk quickly bounced through unannounced products, types of managers, airports, hobbies, goals, a small bit of politics, the class they were attending, their accounts, their office—topics that would be totally boring to anybody outside IGC. Topics that were never discussed were religion and home. Wives, husbands, and children were left behind, to mentally reappear in more quiet times, but not in the middle of a good joke.

"Does everybody have a PC at home?" asked the woman sitting across from Zack. She was tall and slender, raven-haired—nearly too pretty for IGC. Elegant was the word. She seemed to make eye contact with everybody in the room at the same time—a difficult thing to do.

She is very attractive, Zack thought.

She wore a soft blue dress tied at her narrow waist with a dark blue sash. Her shoes matched the sash. Her long legs were casually crossed and exposed the area slightly above her knee.

The conversation went around the group with yeas and nays, the opinion about equally divided between the benefits of doing work at home, and not wanting to turn life into the Endless Workday. At one point during the tail end of the conversation, Zack jumped in.

"I've got a PC *and* a 9350 at home. I've set up my own demonstration areas—my own private office in the downstairs of my house," Zack bragged.

Hoots and guffaws.

"A 9350? Perfect for home use!" came a friendly but sarcastic response to the thought of having a down-sized mainframe computer in a home.

"Don't laugh. It works out pretty well. I'm a remote rep. I've got most of Wyoming and part of Nebraska to cover. I've got a home that used to be a doctor's office. Now when I go to work, I just go downstairs. And I've got a view of the Rocky Mountains from my desk. Life is great." Zack leaned back in his chair.

More laughter, but this time mixed with admiration.

"I can demo all the IBM software we use internally—PROFS, AS, GDDM—you name it—right from home. Hell, I can even passthrough to the Yorktown disk," Zack boasted. "And, I've even got an eight hundred number to call."

"This turkey's got the best of all worlds—remote territory, no competition, *no manager*," said one of the guys. The group rolled their collective eyes in envy, groaning—including the pretty woman in the blue dress.

As the clock approached seven-thirty, the bar was full and noisy. People came and left at the IGC wing, as some decided to go out and get something to eat, some went back to study, and some went to their rooms because they were tired. With the ebb and flow, Zack found himself sitting next to the blue dress. A slight trace of a wonderful female fragrance reached his nostrils at the same time his eyes fell on her legs. Engaged in a laughing conversation with someone else, she sat in such a position so that her skirt exposed a generous length of right thigh, nearly up to *there*. And the view was only available to him!

Oooh.

He mentally sucked his breath. In that same instant she broke off her conversation, turned to him, and introduced herself.

"Hi, I'm Marcia Lee, and you are . . . ?"

Zack was caught off guard. His eyes were on her legs, and it was obvious. He looked up, ready to be embarrassed, but her smile said it's OK, so he wasn't. She made no effort to adjust her dress.

"Zack Colby, from Cheyenne."

"And I'm Marcia Lee, from right here in Dallas," she laughed prettily. "Do you want to go to dinner, Zack Colby from Wyoming?" Marcia asked with a smile.

"Yes," he replied a nanosecond later, with enthusiasm. "I sure would. Let's go," he said, standing to go. Marcia shifted her body and the skirt covered what it was intended to. Zack politely held his hand out as she rose, and the offer was accepted with grace.

Zack threw a twenty on the table to cover their tab and left to a chorus of good-natured hoots, this time of a sexual theme.

"Happy hunting," Meyers whispered in his ear. "She's beautiful," he added, shaking his head in envy.

Marcia had gone ahead. From Houlihan's lobby he could see her tucking in the boot of her red convertible. The hot Texas wind fluffed her skirt with invisible fingers as she bent and stretched to finish the task. The back of her legs were firm and tight. Flipping on his sunglasses, suit coat casually thrown over his shoulder,

Zack Colby walked out into an evening that offered promise. Not even a tiny ounce of guilt crossed his mind.

"OK, it's your city, where do you want to go?" Zack asked, expansively.

"How about my place? I think I can come up with something to keep us satisfied," she smiled, her eyes twinkling. "Or we could go out someplace, if you'd like."

"Home is good," Zack replied, laughing.

This was OK, he thought.

With a firm hand, Marcia scooted for the entrance to the inbound Stemmons. The outbound traffic was backed up for miles as the downtown glass towers slowly disgorged their tired worker bees to suburban havens even at the late hour. Still a bit high from Houlihan's, Zack felt exhilarated as they sped along. The two chatted animatedly over the noise of the wind and the radio. Seemingly uncaring, Marcia let the wind billow and ruffle her dress, which revealed a long expanse of tanned legs up to her thighs.

Marcia reached for her car phone and quickly punched out a fast dial code.

"Maria? My plans have changed. You can have the evening off after all, if you'd like. I'd appreciate it if you could fix something for us before you go. We'll be there in twenty minutes or so. Thanks." She turned to Zack. "My housekeeper. I think we'll eat in tonight," she smiled and winked.

Zack couldn't keep his eyes off of her as Marcia skillfully navigated through the freeway traffic before turning off onto Mockingbird Lane, which she followed across town to Highland Park.

Zack's hormones abated long enough for him to notice and appreciate the well-to-do older neighborhood, homes that had a maid and a gardener as standard equipment.

"Well, this is it—humble home!" she said.

"They must be buying a lot of computers down here in Dallas," Zack said, with a touch of awe. "You must be on a different sales plan."

Marcia laughed. "I got my inheritance early."

The home combined Spanish style with simple elegance. The staircase leading upstairs was wide, its molding polished and finely detailed. The walls were all twelve feet tall and each room was equipped with a large, slowly turning ceiling fan. A cool porch was located in back and the kitchen was well stocked with oversize pots and pans, and gave the appearance of being used by someone who knew what she was doing. Zack walked to the glass doors that led to a stone patio and a completely protected backyard.

"You could get an all-over tan out there," Zack said.

"I do . . . quite often," she replied, laughing, from the kitchen.

Although nearly on the other side of the house, he could see her profile through two sets of doors.

"Don't look," she shouted.

She put both hands under her dress and slowly wiggled her panty hose down over her slender hips to the floor.

"God, I hate panty hose! I can't wait to get home and get them off."

Zack walked back into the kitchen.

"I'm afraid I looked. You have . . . nice legs," Zack said unapologetically. "But, if you don't like them, why wear them?"

A subtle change had come into Marcia's eyes. They were more knowing, sensual.

"Oh? What should I wear?" she asked, somewhat

coy. "Oh, I know—stockings and a garter belt," Marcia laughed. "That's all you men want. You just like to think of women wearing nothing but stockings and a garter belt, of having sex while she still has them on—right?" She said sex like it was dirty. Marcia smoothly closed the distance between the two of them. "It's so—*virile*, so—*nasty*." She bit the words off, and softly poked him in the chest with her right index finger.

Zack's mouth went dry.

"It's on my list," he managed to reply, gently taking her finger, then her hand. She made no effort to disjoin. Wordlessly, they joined eyes. Marcia's said yes.

"What other fantasies do you have?" she said, her voice dropping an octave. "You tell me yours, and I'll tell you mine."

She moved ever so slightly closer to him. Zack's heart jumped.

"I want to know," Marcia said, her voice very soft, her body close.

Marcia's hand softly squeezed his, her fingers played with his fingertips. Zack's eyes were locked on hers. He felt his other hand touched, then held. She softly kissed his cheek, then their lips met and seemed to melt together. She let him release his passion, her tongue found his, his hands slipped to cup her firm bottom. They wriggled and rubbed against each other before breaking.

"I could use a drink. Let's go into the living room, where we can be more . . . comfortable. Come with me," she said, her voice filled with throaty lust. "I have fantasies as well," she said, her voice now near a growl.

She closed his hand in hers and led him into the living room.

"Over here," she said, pointing to the couch.

Zack did as he was told. Marcia went over to the wet

63

bar, opened a cabinet, and pulled down a tumbler. She turned back to Zack.

"Scotch OK?"

"OK." Zack's voice was a near croak.

In the bottom of the glass was a pale liquid. Marcia dropped ice into the glass, then the golden liquor, and gave it a quick finger stir. She walked back to the couch, stood in front of him, and handed Zack the drink, which he took. His eyes never left hers.

"Drink up, big guy."

In agonizingly slow motion, Marcia undid the sash around her waist and pulled her dress over her head, then dropped it in a pile at her feet. She stood no more than two feet in front of him, so close that he could smell her fragrance. Zack took the liquor down in a single gulp. She wore nothing but a lacy half-cup brassiere and a soft V-shaped bikini that rose up her hips in front and tapered off to a thong in back. The white undergarments were highlighted against the darkness of a well-tanned body.

With the tips of her fingers she began to slowly caress her breasts, rubbing the soft lacy material against her barely concealed nipples.

"Oooh, this feels good, Zack," her eyes spoke to him. Soon her right nipple came out from its restraint. She wet the fingers of her left hand with saliva and began to rub the nipple in earnest, alternating between direct finger contact and kneading it with the stiffer material of the brassiere. She leaned forward and unclasped the bra, popping it from the front.

Oh, God—she has perfect breasts!

They were equal in proportion, not excessive, firmly shaped, with nipples that begged to be touched and stroked. She leaned forward even farther and let them nearly touch his face, while communicating "not yet."

They shimmered in front of his mouth. Zack watched in erotic amazement as she then let the fingers of her right hand slowly slip under the thin bikini, first one, then several. They darted and rubbed, then began to stroke.

Marcia lost eye contact and began to groan. At the same time Zack's body began to feel the effect of the drug. He felt displaced—tingly all over. Marcia's legs seemed to turn to rubber. She came down to him on the couch and straddled him, then locked him in a passionate kiss.

Zack was a goner.

"Screen two is better," said Bill.

"Is she awesome, or what?" Tony said, as he adjusted the picture on the screen labeled Living Room #2.

With deft fingers Tony zoomed in on the action.

"Yes . . . yes . . . oh, yes, Zack," Marcia cried as she rocked to his touch. Then he slapped her on the right buttock.

"Yes! Yes, hit me! Hit me!"

"How many times has she been to the drugstore?" asked Heather, sifting through a copy of *People*.

"Three, I think—maybe four," replied Baby.

"By Friday morning that boy won't know up from down," said the tall blond, fingering a vial of pale liquid. "Yes, sir—a friendly pecker-upper."

Baby laughed. Tony and Bill paid no attention to the girl talk and kept on filming.

"Awesome—absolutely awesome," Tony repeated.

"Time to get up, Zack," Marcia said sweetly.

Zack groaned, then rolled over. His eyes were baggy and red, and his body ached from the unusually long bout of sex and the aftereffect of the cocaine. Marcia was nearly dressed and looked impossibly bright and cheery. Zack groaned again and ducked his head under the covers, which smelled of her body and their coupling.

"No, no . . . it's time to get up! You're a busy boy. We've got to get you to class. But first we've got to go to the hotel and get checked out," she said.

"What?" he said from under the covers.

"You heard me," she replied. "You're checking out. You're staying with me this week. Unless you don't *want* to," she said seductively. "You *do* want to stay with me, don't you Zack?"

More than anything in the world, he thought.

As the day slowly dragged on, Zack began to feel the affect of Newton's Law—what goes up, must come down. Ten minutes of feel-too-good had to be paid off in ten minutes feel-too-bad, as did seven hours of feel-too-good. Nature had to balance things out, and did so with ruthless ignorance. By midmorning Zack had a headache and felt like he had a mild case of the flu. Gradually during the afternoon he started to rally as the instructors droned on and on.

During one of the afternoon breaks the Lie started—Zack's official recognition that he wanted to hold, fondle, and have sex with a woman not his wife. Cheryl was glad he called and immediately went on about what Brian and Anne had been doing for the last two days.

"Listen, honey, the phones at the hotel aren't working very well. I'll call you during the day, if that's OK?

66

Besides, I know quite a few of the guys here, so I think we'll be drinking dinner," Zack said with a hearty laugh.

Cheryl understood, and was happy enough that he called.

All I can think about are her legs and her tongue and her perfect breasts, Zack thought.

He managed to complete the call without hearing a word she said. At appropriate intervals he inserted verbal flotsam, unseen nods of the head, reassurance that he was listening.

"I've got to run—it looks like class is starting up again," Zack said, closing the conversation.

"I love you, Zack," Cheryl said earnestly.

"I love you, too, honey," Zack replied. It was the first time in nearly eight years that he lied when he said it. There was no love in his body, only lust.

The last half hour of the class seemed six days long, as if some evil entity had somehow inserted a weight on the wall clock's big hand. But even bad things must eventually end, as did Zack's wait at five o'clock.

Zack found himself on the first elevator down, packed with students. All of a sudden his brain elected to go into Altered States. The sensation lasted for no more than ten seconds, enough time for the elevator to go from the third to the first floor. While he could hear the other students talking, their words seemed to be in a foreign language. Zack seemed . . . apart from them, as if the elevator were much bigger than it was. Then just as quickly the sensation vanished and the elevator doors opened.

Whoa! What the hell was that?

Jack didn't associate the brief side trip to Altered States as a reaction to Marcia's chemistry—a cross between liquid cocaine and crystal meth. Then in an instant Zack found himself outside and his head clear. There she was! She wore a red dress with a white sash around her waist and a white-and-red scarf around her neck, hiding only a bit of her décolletage. Word had quickly gotten around class that Zack had made a local connection. A few of the salesmen stood near the door, watching and gossiping as Zack walked across the plaza toward O'Donnell Street.

"Wow," was all one man could say.

"You've *got* to be kidding," was another envious comment.

"You look wonderful!" Zack exclaimed, feeling better already.

Indeed, she did look wonderful. She met him with a full embrace and a passionate kiss, which was instantly returned. He could feel the push of her breasts against his shirt and the probing of her tongue as it urgently sucked his.

God, is she good! Zack thought. I don't care if she's done this with nineteen guys before me. I don't care. Jesus, how can a kiss make you want to jump out of your shorts?

"How was your class?" she asked, breaking off.

"Just awful, all I could think of was you," Zack said seriously.

"Here—I bet you could use a drink!" she said, reaching for a thermos.

As she sped off, Zack quickly downed two cups of cold spiked scotch. He was soon in buzzland. Their conversation bantered back and forth about each other's day, the weather, and other random topics that she seemed to initiate. She drove with her left hand; the long, well-manicured fingers of her right hand absentmindedly stroked and massaged the outside of her right leg, which pulled her dress about halfway up her thigh.

"Have you ever masturbated in a car?" she asked, playfully, catching him off guard. "I love it!" she exclaimed, laughing. "Sometimes I'll just come out on the highway, dressed like this, and pull up alongside a truck. I'll wear this scarf, no bra—and open the dress up a little up top, just enough so the wind will give him a peek down my dress. Then, I'll slowly pull up my dress and start—oh, it's great! They love it!"

Zack had no words for her, just amazement.

She's on the edge, he warned himself. Trouble. Back off, Zack.

But he couldn't.

"By the way, I've got a friend coming over for dinner tonight. Her name is Heather. I think you'll like her," she said as they pulled into the driveway.

Fifteen minutes later the doorbell rang, just as the first round of drinks had been made. From the living room came the high-pitched greetings of old friends. Heather had arrived.

"Zack, I'd like you to meet one of my best all-time friends," Marcia said as she guided her good friend through the doorway into the kitchen.

Wow.

Heather was a knockout. Actually, he'd never met any Heather that wasn't. This Heather had short blond hair, fair skin, small features, blue eyes, and wore lipstick that was just the right shade of blush. She wore a peach-colored short summer skirt, narrow white belt, matching shoes, and a white blouse with no brassiere. Her small nipples pressed against the soft material, as did a clear outline of the top of her breasts. She nearly looked transparent.

Good enough to eat, Zack thought.

The chitchat continued as they carried their drinks

from the kitchen to the living room. Zack sat on the couch, his arm casually around Marcia's shoulders. Heather sat on the floor in front of them, curled up, with her legs casually offering Zack a view up her dress. It was all very relaxed and social. Soft music played in the background. Heather leaned forward and gently kissed the inside of Marcia's left knee. Zack could feel Marcia shudder with the touch. Her weight shifted toward her friend, her legs opened slightly to allow easier access. Marcia reached out and lovingly touched her younger friend's cheek, then moved up, gently twisting Heather's hair in her fingers while caressing the lobe of her left ear.

"It's been a long time, Marcia," Heather said softly, looking up at her lover.

"Help me take her dress off," Heather said softly but firmly to Zack, who did what he was told. The dress seemed to know what to do, and presented no obstacle. Her stockings were attached to a very thin red garter belt. Underneath was a thong bikini in matching red.

"Take off your clothes," Marcia spoke for the first time, her voice husky with lust. Zack's heart pounded as he watched Heather stand up and slowly pull the zipper on her short skirt down far enough so she could wriggle it over her slender hips, letting it fall to the floor in a peachy pile.

Zack soon found himself in a PleasureDome. Every possible combination of human connection was tried. It was a bizarre sexual cornucopia, a decadent debauchery. And it was all on tape.

Wearing only a thin housecoat, a weary Heather quietly left the bedroom and walked downstairs, then went down to the basement.

"I'm getting fantastic pictures. You look great!" Tony laughed.

"I feel like shit," Heather replied. "I don't know how that guy's pecker can still be attached to his body. That stuff we're giving him must paralyze his dick—"

"In the on position," laughed Tony. "That boy does have staying power."

"That stuff we're giving him is *po-tent*. Stay away from it. I don't even like to be in the same room with it! He's lost touch with everything. In two days he's turned from a nice everyday kind of guy into a demented slime. He can't stop. He's hooked. He'll never know what hit him," said Heather.

"God! You look like shit!" said Tom Meyers, hardly believing his eyes.

Indeed, Zack looked and felt like shit wrapped in a blue suit. He'd thrown up twice already, once on the way over—just barely managing to give Marcia enough time to stop the car—and again inside the building in the men's room. His body hurt everywhere. Ached. His temples throbbed. For two nights in a row the trio had ended up in Marcia's king-size bed in a ring of pleasure and had fallen into a comalike sleep at midnight. The kitchen had been ravaged at nine and again at eleven, and the living room nearly destroyed. But by five-thirty, when Marcia shook Zack awake, it was clean as a whistle. He woke up to a snoring Heather, whose blond tousled head rested near his feet, her beautiful bottom near his chest. She'd slept all night in the position of her last orgasm. While the shower had felt great, stepping into the bright sunshine of morning didn't, not even with several good

71

cups of coffee.

"Don't let me snore," he said to the smiling Meyers.

In IGC there was no requirement for a student to be awake during the class, only that he or she be there during the day. Daily rosters were kept, checked, and followed up with—you didn't skip class. Noiselessly, Zack managed to regain nearly three lost hours of sleep, although he received tremendous grief from the other reps during coffee breaks.

Not once did Zack think of not getting into Marcia's car that afternoon, of ending the sexual marathon, or of what the possible consequences might be. Although an intelligent young man, not once did he analyze the character of Marcia Lee and compare it to that of the typical IGCer. She was pretty, bright, and dressed well—that was enough.

Zack's mind had been turned to mush. He was unable to drift off into new areas of fantasy. He'd just *lived* everything that was possible, and more. There was no guilt, no remorse. His mind slipped into neutral and went on an eight-hour coast.

If I close my eyes, he mused, I can even feel the breeze.

"OK, this is it," Marcia started.

All of them were in the living room, including David Kimura, who stood off to the side.

"He's disoriented, tired, and half-crazy. He can't control himself. Is the room set?" Marcia asked Joe.

"Just like we've done before. I got it right into a stud in the ceiling. There'll be no problems with the weight," replied Joe.

"Are you implying that I'm *fat?*" pouted Baby, which drew hoots from the rest of them.

Hardly.

"The timing tonight is critical. Baby—Joe and Heather will be in the next room if something goes wrong. But it shouldn't. We've done this before. You've just got to make it last for seven minutes, give or take thirty seconds or so. The mix is different to-night. Seven minutes and he'll be out cold."

Zack's eyes were dull as he walked out of class on Thursday night. He hadn't shaved that morning. Dark puffy bags cushioned his red-rivered eyes. Methodically and without enthusiasm he fell into the passenger seat of Marcia's convertible. He didn't notice that she wasn't her normal effervescent self. She was more— businesslike. With hardly a greeting, he reached for the thermos and gulped a cupful of cold laced scotch, spilling some on his shirt.

"Tastes different—"

"Oh?"

"Better—want some?"

"No thanks—I've got to drive, remember?"

The drive to Highland Park took a half hour, which was nearly wordless. Zack just stared out the window, lost in his thoughts. But by the time they reached the living room at least part of Zack had risen to the occasion. As Marcia's hands softly massaged his back, Zack felt like a displaced person. His heart was pounding, his fingers and legs tingled, and he had an erection that wouldn't quit. The alcohol and drugs were sending conflicting messages to his inexperienced brain. He'd had virtually no sleep in thirty-six hours.

"Zack, I've got something special for you tonight," Marcia whispered softly in his right ear with a throaty earthiness. "Up in our bedroom is a very, very bad

73

girl," Marcia instructed him like he was a little boy. "She needs to be spanked, Zack. She likes it *rough. Rough, Zack—rough.* She's a liar, Zack—a dirty little liar. She'll say anything. She *must* be punished. You've got to punish her."

"Punish—"

In a trance, Zack moved for the steps.

"Here, you'll want these." Marcia handed him four lengths of nylon cord, a gag, and a riding crop. "You look terrible. Drink this—it'll pep you up."

Zack drained the drink and took the bizarre sexual accessories absentmindedly, then slowly climbed the stairway to the second floor. Upstairs, he found Marcia's door locked from the outside. He turned the key and stepped inside.

His eyes were drawn to the ceiling. Hanging down directly above the bed was a short but heavy chain, secured solidly by a four-inch bolt into the ceiling. The round eye of the last link hung approximately six feet above the very firm bed.

Sitting on the edge of the well-used bed was Baby— the bad girl—a nymph who looked no older than fourteen. She had a scared look in her eyes. Her eyes radiated a practiced look of terrified innocence. She was a slender, nearly fragile young thing, with smooth white skin, long blond hair, full hips, and voluptuous breasts. She wore a schoolgirl's uniform: a simple plaid wraparound skirt held together with a large pin at the hem just above the knee, and a crisp white short-sleeved blouse. She was barefoot and wore no hose. A small gold cross dangled on a chain around her neck. To Zack, she appeared terrified.

It's all an act, he thought to himself. It's only a game. Isn't it?

Baby stayed where she was, but made anxious eye

74

contact with Zack. Zack closed and latched the door behind him, walked over to the bed, and stood in front of her. She began to tremble. Zack's adrenaline rushed.

"You've been a bad girl," Zack said, following Marcia's instructions. "I'm going to have to spank you."

It is just a game.

The drugs and lack of sleep had turned his disposition mean.

"Mister, please help me," Baby began to cry, both hands up to her face. "I haven't done anything. Please! They kidnapped me. Help me, please!"

Zack's mind had long since turned reality off. Zack dropped the bondage toys on the bed beside her, then put his left hand on top of her head and roughly grabbed a handful of blond hair, twisted her head backward, and forced her to look up at him. Tears ran down both her cheeks.

"Please, mister . . . I haven't done anything . . . please!" she sobbed.

"Stop that crying!" Zack shouted while he slapped her face with his opened right hand.

That felt good.

The blow left red impressions of his fingers on Baby's pale cheek. He began to become aroused with the violence, the domination of the girl.

Remember, she likes it rough.

The physical abuse Zack had given his body was reflected in his face. His eyes reflected a brain that had already shut down contact with common sense and decency. Subconsciously, he was starting to face up to all that he'd done during the week. He was ashamed and angry. His hair was disheveled, his face drawn and haggard from the sexual excess and lack of food. In four days he'd had only one real meal and had lost

75

eight pounds.

"Don't!" she screamed, her high-pitched voice nearly breaking. "Let me go," she squealed, squirming to get out of his grasp.

Still holding on to her hair, Zack started to lower himself on her, to pin the girl down on the bed.

"You've got to get your spanking, you little whore," Zack said, a low meanness in his voice.

At the instant Zack shifted his weight to pin her backward on the bed, Baby shrieked and made a dash for the door.

Get her!

She was quick, but fumbled with the handle. Zack lunged for her just as she turned the lock and started to open the door, managing to dive far enough to catch her skirt as he fell to the floor, twisted onto his right side. She screamed as his weight knocked her against the door, which slammed shut. With a fury she kicked at his half-prone body and tried to knee him in the face, while Zack tried to get a grip on more than just her skirt.

Her skirt could no longer stand the pressure of his grasp and slipped over her hips and down her legs. This gave Zack a free shot at her body, but more importantly, it tangled her feet up and stopped the foot assault. It also prevented her from running. Using the tangled skirt, Zack grabbed both legs at her ankles, regained his balance, and yanked her feet out from under her. Baby slammed to the carpet face first in a very painful fall. She was stunned. She grunted in pain as Zack lumbered on top of her and put his full weight on her back. She could barely breathe.

"Bitch!" He slapped the back of her head.

Zack's brain turned dark in midthought as the lights went out. His head bounced on the hardwood floor

76

with a thud.

Untangling, Baby pulled herself out from under Zack's body.

"Creep," she muttered.

With some effort she stood up and opened the door. "OK, everybody—he's out!"

Zack's right eye opened. His head was in an odd position and his vision fuzzy.

Please focus, he thought.

A clock tocked loudly on a nearby end table, but the damn thing was tilted ninety degrees. It was either quarter of three or eleven-thirty. Zack's left eye opened. Together they saw a floor strewn with clothes—a shirt, panties, bra, skirt, shoes. His eyes went back to the clock, which now was in focus.

Eleven-thirty? Shit!

Then Zack felt something in his right hand. His body was so sore that even the thought of moving was painful. His eyes went to his right hand.

Jesus—what the fuck?

He was holding a whip in his hand; its knotted nine tails hung over the edge of the bed. He felt a breeze on his back from the air-conditioning, which just clicked on.

I'm naked.

He was naked and sprawled atop Marcia's bed, his head over the side. His mind cried—begged—for mercy. He felt like he wanted to retch, but he hurt too bad.

What's that?

Something wet fell on his cheek. Although his shoulders hurt like hell, he reached up with his right hand, which seemed like it was part of somebody else's body, and touched his cheek.

Blood! Shit — it's fucking blood!

"Wha — ?"

In a lurching spasm, Zack flipped over onto his back — just as several more drops fell, this time onto his face.

Oh my God. Oh my God!

Above him the young girl hung from the chain which was secured into the ceiling; her feet dangled off the bed only by inches. Her hands were tied above her, then attached to the chain. She was naked but for the remains of the blouse on her shoulders. She slowly spun to the air currents of the room. Her head hung limply in front and her straggled hair covered part of her face, which was desecrated by an ugly black rubber ball that bulged through her lips, which bled. Tiny streamlets of blood oozed down the back of her legs from nasty sores on her bottom and legs, where she had been whipped. She had been completely violated.

Did I do this?

Zack knew the answer. He lay on the bed, his emotions careening down a bottomless canyon. His chest heaved with the exertion, his head felt like exploding. Marcia had given him one fantasy after another, each one dipping into a darker and more forbidden part of his head.

It had felt good.

Everything had felt good.

But this didn't feel good.

"Oh God oh God oh God what I have done?"

Zack's naked and spent body curled back into a fetus position and he began to sob uncontrollably. He never heard the bedroom door open, nor Marcia sit quietly down beside him. For a brief second she smiled at the totality of Zack's disintegration.

You poor schmuck, she thought.

The feeling wasn't as good as she thought it would be.

Poor Zack—

She cradled him in her arms.

"There, there, Zack. It's all right. You'll be all right," she said soothingly as she patted his head and wiped his forehead.

"Oh no . . . oh no . . . oh no," he sobbed. "Why did you do this to me? Why did you do this to me? You took my fantasies," he cried, as he accepted the gentleness of her touch.

"What do you mean, Zack?" Marcia replied quietly. "These were *your* fantasies. I was fulfilling *your* fantasies. *You* did this, Zack."

"That . . . that poor little—" he broke down again with tears. "I didn't know, I thought it was part of the game, I didn't know," Zack blubbered.

"You knew, Zack," Marcia corrected, softly. "You knew all along. You could have stopped. But you didn't."

"Bu . . . but I didn't know." Zack turned to her with a plea in his eyes.

"Didn't know what, Zack?" Marcia replied.

"I . . . I . . . I didn't know . . . I didn't know that I would f . . . feel so bad—that I really didn't want those things. I . . . I . . . can't go back—God, I hate myself!" Zack cried.

"There, there. Everything will be all right. The girl's all right. Nobody will know. I'll take care of her—she's just a girl we picked up for you. I'll dispose of her for you. Come on, Zack—you need to get some rest. Up you go," Marcia mothered.

She held him and led him to the door, then down a dark hallway to a very small bedroom, where a bed had been prepared for him.

"Here, take this." She offered a lukewarm cup of tea laced with a powerful sleeping tablet.

"Night-night, Zack," Marcia said.

Zack waved a hand, then closed his eyes and let his body follow his brain down into the darkness of hell.

Marcia let Zack sleep an extra hour in the morning, but had to go in and wake him from the sleep of the dead. It wasn't until they were almost to IGC, with his bags neatly packed and sitting in the backseat, that Zack came out of his stupor.

"You don't work for IGC, do you?" he asked, now realizing that he'd been played the fool by an eccentric nymphomaniac, used by Marcia for her own perverse gratification.

"No, Zack, I don't," Marcia answered honestly.

Her smooth features were just as desirable after a week of hedonistic indulgence. Strands of her long black hair blew across her face as she turned to him with her answer. His eyes involuntarily went to her breasts, to her legs, and back.

Jesus Christ, will you stop?

"You were very bad last night, Zack. Very bad. But I'll clean up after you."

Zack turned away, oblivious of the inbound traffic on the Stemmons, to her legs, to the rising sun shining in his face. They'd each gotten what they wanted. They'd each gotten their fantasies exercised. She'd used him, but he'd used her, too.

"Why me?" Zack asked, as she turned onto O'Donnell.

"You were there and I was there. We were both willing—both grown adults. Why you? I don't know, maybe you were just lucky, that's all," Marcia replied, smiling but serious.

"Will I see you again?" Zack answered.

He was willing to throw everything aside for her—the love of his family, his job, everything.

"No, I don't think so, Zack," she lied. "I don't know, maybe I'll get up to Wyoming sometime—but I doubt it. Here you are," Marcia said as she whisked up in front of IGC.

Without a wave Marcia drove off, leaving Zack at the curbside in front of Williams Square, surrounded by luggage and with a lost and forlorn look on his face. Behind him, the bronze mustangs still proudly danced through a concrete stream.

I still don't know—why me? he wondered. Luck?

The vote had been six to three to go to Houlihan's Monday night. Zack had been one of the three to vote for Friday's.

If we'd gone to Friday's . . .

If I'd gone back to the room . . .

If I . . .

"All right crew, let's get humping!" Marcia ordered, totally in control. "Bill—how much longer?" she shouted downstairs.

"Twenty minutes!" came the return shout.

It was time for Marcia to back off and let her people do their jobs. They were pros and knew what needed to be done.

"Well done, Marcia," said a pleased David Kimura.

"It was too easy, David. I don't like doing that to somebody like Zack Colby. It's not my style, you know?"

Marcia was troubled, but not troubled enough to

81

forget the two million dollars, nor the attention to detail that had kept her out of police computers for the last five years.

"It's done, Marcia," said Bill, gently shaking her from a deep sleep. "It's time to go."

In the three hours she'd slept on the cot the house had been stripped of equipment, wires, microphones, cameras, fingerprints, bloodstained sheets, drug-laced glasses—everything. The chain had been removed from the ceiling, the holes in the walls plugged as well as possible. There was no intention to leave the house the way it was—just to remove anything that could be incriminating.

"Is everything wiped down?" Marcia asked, getting up.

Her body ached with a weariness that would take a week to repair.

"I think so, but in a house this size, you just don't know. We'll do our best. Meanwhile, Tony and I have finished. Do you want to see it?"

As the group convened for the last time in Dallas, Tony inserted the tape into the living room VCR and let it go.

"Devastating . . . can you imagine? How long is it, Tony?" Marcia asked after fast-forwarding through sections.

"Eighty-eight minutes—full-length porno."

"Time to go. Well done. I'll meet you all back home and we'll talk about triple bonuses," Marcia smiled.

"Gentlemen—Zack Colby, IGC marketing representative from Cheyenne, Wyoming," Marcia said as she punched the Play button on the VCR.

Skillfully edited, the tape began with a voice-over of Zack's admission of his sexual fantasies as the film showed his first snort of cocaine and the acrobatic high saddle offered by Marcia. The voice-over ended and was followed by three minutes of flesh-slapping sex, complete with all orgasms.

Sukawa and Yamamoto sat down next to Makato Shinogara. David preferred to stand. As Marcia watched she had to smile. The film was obviously provoking a reaction in the men. Sukawa shifted in his chair and the corner of Yamamoto's mouth twitched in a near smile.

"Oh . . . look at that," Sukawa said involuntarily.

The film made it clear that Zack Colby was a degenerate human being, probably a drug addict, that he enjoyed fondling and abusing young women, and that he was a sadist. There were zoom shots in slow motion of organs in full blossom. The sound of sex was clear and unmistakable, as was Zack's repeated leering look of lust. As the lights came back up, Marcia waited as Shinogara talked with the group in rapid Japanese.

"You have done well, Miss Lee. When your Swiss bank opens for business on Monday morning, your account will be increased by two million dollars," said the pleased Shinogara.

Marcia was on the verge of telling Shinogara what she really thought about how Zack hung himself, but didn't.

What the fuck? she told herself. They don't care— you're the only one who's bothered. Forget it. It's just a job.

"Your limo and airplane are waiting, Miss Lee. Thank you very much," were Shinogara's last words as Marcia was escorted away from the celebrating Japanese businessmen.

It was a strange sight, but Marcia was glad to leave.

"Did you finish what you needed to in Dallas?" asked Shinogara.

"Yes, sir. We paid for six months on the house, in cash, so we have time to settle with them later. I didn't think you would want any suspicions raised."

Shinogara nodded approval.

"When do we go to Wyoming?" David asked.

"Tomorrow, if you are ready," Shinogara replied with enthusiasm.

"I am waiting on only one item, the dummied newspaper. I'm having several copies of tomorrow's *Dallas Morning News* expressed here. They should arrive tomorrow night."

"Do we need this paper?" asked Shinogara.

"Oh, yes. When the printer gets through with it, Colby will be convinced beyond a shadow of a doubt that he's a wanted criminal. The computer-generated graphics of his likeness are remarkable. The mark will be indelible in his brain. We need it to guarantee that he'll do what we want." David paused. "As for my team, we've been ready for weeks. We're very excited about this opportunity with VM and the 9350. What a stroke of luck!"

David was glowing with enthusiasm.

"Yes, yes," said Shinogara in a fatherly fashion.

"Will Marcia be there?" Kimura asked.

"No, her services are no longer required. She's done her job, now we must do ours," replied a stern Shinogara. "Are you concerned?"

"Yes, I am. It was she who controlled Zack Colby, manipulated him. He's never seen us, nor has he any idea of what will happen. I saw her give him drugs . . . I've never . . . but it's her sexual attraction that controls him. He can't resist her. I think we'll need her to help manage Colby the way we want. We don't want Colby to go off the deep end. I think she should be there, at least for a phaseout period—until we have him firmly under control," David said as diplomatically as he could.

"Nonsense," replied Shinogara. "We're perfectly capable of controlling this man. He doesn't want to go to jail. He won't want his family disgraced—he will have no choice."

Zack's weekend had been one of survival. The memories of Thursday night wouldn't go away. He couldn't get the image of the girl's naked twisting body out of his mind.

God, I'm sick.

His heart pumped with adrenaline-driven excitement generated by the thoughts of the week. He stopped thinking Why me? His only thoughts now were of the sexual gratification he'd gotten, the new horizons he'd reached. Going back to the humdrum of Cheyenne, of Cheryl and the children, was a step down. Just the thought of Marcia slowly bending over, arms locked on her calves, was enough to send him off to Fantasyland.

Zack hadn't wanted to go home. He'd known what was ahead. The joy, the children, the games, the presents he managed to remember at the airport in Dallas—along with the hugs and kisses from a loving wife, a woman who thought he could do no wrong—a woman who based her whole existence on him as their way out of Cheyenne—it would be too much. How could she compare to . . . the sex machine he'd been with in the last four days and nights? Even though she was only twenty-eight, Cheryl's body was reflecting the physical drag of two children. Her thighs were . . .

Stop it! Jesus H. Christ! Stop it!

No, he couldn't stop it. The sight of Cheyenne was doubly distressing. An indefinite haze hung over the valley. Zack's first thought was of steers being slaughtered, of beef being slung into boxcars.

Will you stop it? he chided himself. OK, OK. Why don't they have a god-damned rest area on this side of the highway?

Zack wasn't Mr. Mellow as he first went one exit east on I-80, then turned off onto College Road at the first exit, cut through east Cheyenne, and drove up the top of the bluff to his home, which was nicer than 99.9 percent of the homes in the city. He did his best to cover up, considering the nearly overwhelming flow of love from his anxious family. He begged off conversation with Cheryl, claiming flight delay, tiredness from the drive, et cetera, and went to bed.

The weekend was passable, but only barely. He felt bad on Sunday, and complained he thought he was getting the flu. But he felt like shit. The following day was Monday. It was the worst Monday morning in the history of Monday mornings. His head hurt, his arms and legs felt sore.

"You don't have a temperature, honey," Cheryl said, trying to convince Zack that it wasn't the flu bug.

Every motion Zack went through felt like it was one gear out of synch—he was in slow motion and the world was on fast forward. The children seemed like little gnats, buzzing and hovering and totally irritating. Cheryl's voice seemed more shrill, almost grating.

Get out there and sell those computers, Zack boy, he

told himself.

Zack's first day back on the job got worse.

He made it through his first call, a follow-up on an invoice at the state comptroller's office and delivery of some sales brochures. His ten o'clock call was out at Warren AFB, procurement. He'd scheduled a meeting with Captain Andrews and Major Jordan to try and convince them that under air force purchasing regulations, the purchase of two 9350s could be done sole-source and didn't require a formal RFP (Request for Proposals), which would bring in competition and delay the purchase by eight to twelve months.

Zack noticed that it was 9:45 as he pulled into the open parking lot across from the brick procurement building. He had to park in the back of the lot because air force folks were early risers — the lot was mostly filled by 7:15 every day. Zack got constant kidding from procurement for scheduling meetings so late in the morning — at the crack of ten, they'd laugh. With his briefcase opened on the passenger seat, Zack briefly looked up and saw the marketing rep from Digital Equipment Corporation (DEC) get out of her car. Tall, black hair, she struggled slightly with her skirt as she tried to be dignified while she got out of her little sports car. Zack's smile froze on his face as his arms and legs began to weaken, to tingle, and his heart began to beat rapidly. His head rolled back on the seat rest, but his mind's eyes never left the pretty young DEC rep's legs as she, seemingly in slow motion, got out of her car, her skirt rising above her knee.

No, he thought. It wasn't . . . Who? . . . It was Marcia! How can she bend over like that? Yes, yes . . . hit me Zack! Hit me! Harder, harder. Oh, God how can she hump like that? . . . It feels so good. No, no . . . it was Heather kneeling in front of him, her

87

sweet lips massaging him. . . . Oh please take it off . . . please oh please . . . Her sweater rose over her breasts. . . . She slowly dropped her short skirt. . . . Oh please bend over please bend over just let me get behind you. . . . Oh yes oh yes . . . God Marcia God God . . . Oh

Zack's eyes snapped open to a view of the ceiling. Both arms were extended as were his legs. His suit pants were warm with ejaculate, his shirt damp with perspiration. The clock read 9:56. He'd been out for eleven minutes.

"Jesus." Zack's body surged with adrenaline. "What's happening to me?"

The raised skirt and curved leg of the pretty competitor had triggered a delayed rush caused by Marcia's chemical cocktail. Zack wasn't at his best with Major Jordan and Captain Andrews. Fortunately, his dark blue suit hid the wet stain, but his moist underwear was a constant reminder of what had happened. His arguments weren't convincing. Twenty minutes later, as Zack walked back to the car, he knew he'd been weak and that the systems would go out for competitive bidding—even though the total hardware and software would be less than three hundred thousand dollars. The pretty DEC rep had been eating his lunch on the base.

Tuesday morning Zack felt moderately crummy, better than Monday, but not good. Still in his pajamas at nine-thirty, Zack stumbled down to his office and started a pot of coffee. The green light on his answering machine was blinking. He pressed the Play/Start and listened to the message.

"Mr. Colby, my name is David Kimura, and I represent a firm that's moving to the Cheyenne area within the month. We're supplying critical products and services for a"—Kimura paused, implying that he shouldn't disclose what would follow—"classified project at Warren Air Force Base. We'll need several computers for this company, in the 9350 class or above—we're not sure yet of the total computing required. We'd like to buy IGC equipment if we can. The president and chief officers of the company will be in the Cheyenne area today and would like to meet with you, if that's convenient. He'll be staying at Holding's Little America hotel at the Lincolnway exit on Interstate 80. Please call as soon as you can," said the voice, not without a touch of urgency.

Zack checked his appointment book only to find that he had two calls he'd promised to make downtown in less than an hour, and a demonstration this afternoon. Zack dialed the number for Holding's.

"Mr. Kimura, please," said Zack, now pert and alert.

"This is David Kimura," said the businesslike voice.

"Mr. Kimura, this is Zack Colby of IGC. I got your message. Unfortunately, I'm pretty well booked up today. Is there any way we could meet tomorrow morning?" replied Zack, hopeful.

"Very unfortunate," Kimura replied in a stern, disapproving voice. "My president will be here for only a day. Perhaps the Digital representative could make time for us."

The old Hated Competitor Trick. This normally sent salesmen off into the business equivalent of a feeding frenzy—juices stirred, appointments could suddenly be canceled or skipped, magically there was time where there had been no time before. This instance was no different.

"Yes, I think I can rearrange my schedule . . ."

"Would lunch be convenient?" asked Kimura, politely.

"Lunch? Certainly." Zack looked at his nearly empty wallet. He would have to plastic lunch.

"Excellent. I will meet you in the lobby of the Little America Inn at eleven-thirty. I assume you know where it is?" Kimura asked.

"Certainly. Little America at eleven-thirty. How will I recognize you?" asked Zack, not remembering David's name.

"I'm sure I'll be the only Japanese businessman dressed in a blue suit in the lobby," David said, laughing.

Zack laughed with him, then thanked him for the consideration and hung up.

He said systems—plural, Zack thought. Multiple. Damn! A bluebird! An honest-to-God bluebird.

If these people were serious, he might be able to get an order and time it so that it came after the last quota adjustment for the year, which was normally October. IGC manipulated the sales quota of its marketing representatives so that nobody would get rich. Even though the salesmen were on a sixty-five-thirty-five salary-commission plan, IGC management could manage a rep's income to the nearest dime by upping or lowering sales quotas based on a rep's backlog of orders to be installed and his forecast of revenue, which since 1989 was the primary yardstick for quotas. But nobody got blamed for not forecasting a true bluebird. When competing against the System, a rep always tried to save the Big Order for late November, and get the system installed by December 31, so that all bonuses would be paid, all income earned.

At 11:25 Zack walked into the lobby of Holding's

Little America.

"Hello, you must be David Kimura," he said, smiling at the slightly younger man.

Kimura was shorter than he, but appeared to be fairly muscular—bulky, might be a better description.

"Yes, I am. Thank you for coming, Mr. Colby," David replied. "Please follow me. I've taken the liberty of ordering lunch." Kimura smiled as the two men walked down the corridor toward a small suite of executive rooms in the rear of the sprawling motel.

Zack, as a representative of the premier corporation in America, exuded a professional confidence that was just shy of a swagger. He could walk into any corporate office and intelligently discuss computing solutions to computing problems—except when he had a wet dream in the customer's parking lot, now forgotten.

Kimura led Zack into the large suite, which appeared to be the size of approximately three large motel rooms. The living room area had two comfortable couches in an L-shaped configuration and several modern chairs, with appropriate tables. Along the center wall was a twenty-five-inch TV, a VCR, and a wet bar. A divider separated the living area with the small kitchen. A bedroom and two bathrooms were farther back. Zack had no idea such a layout existed in Cheyenne and mentally filed it away for potential business show purposes.

There were three men in the room; all appeared to be in their fifties, and to Zack they all looked the same—grim types.

"This is Mr. Colby of IGC," David introduced.

While Zack's handshake was taken by each of the men, names weren't exchanged. By the time Zack sat down he knew the name of only one man, David Kimura, who now stood near the door.

"Thank you for coming, Mr. Colby," said Shinogara.

Shinogara sat on the left end of one couch, Zack at the right end of the other. Between them was a bulky wooden end table with a heavy yellow lamp with a large shade. The shade made it difficult for Zack to see Shinogara's face without bending forward. Zack was slightly uncomfortable.

"David . . . Mr. Kimura has told me that your company is planning to build here in the Cheyenne area and that you're interested in buying computers. Is that correct?" asked Zack.

"Not precisely, Mr. Colby," Shinogara said slowly. "We do, however, have a business arrangement we would like to discuss with you."

"I don't understand," Zack said simply. He was puzzled.

"Perhaps our intentions will be more clear if we show you a short film . . . yes, I think so," Shinogara said, nodding to Sukawa, who depressed the Play button on the VCR.

The first sounds heard were the unmistakable slapping of flesh on flesh during active sex. Then there were grunts and groans as the screen slowly faded from black.

"Yes, hit me! Hit me, Zack!"

Then the screen was filled with Zack humping Marcia's high saddle.

Oh shit oh shit oh shitohshitohshit.

Zack's face imploded—his cheeks drew in, his mouth dried up as his saliva glands stopped to watch the show. Seeing himself on film was paralyzing—his chest tightened as his brain, overloaded with too many decisions and too much information, forgot to allow him to breathe. It was as if Zack's brain sent out an all-points bulletin that said "You're on your own" to all the other body parts.

Zack felt his neck, face, and chest turn red as embarrassment flushed through him, followed quickly by flash point anger.

"You have remarkable stamina, Mr. Colby," Shinogara smiled evilly, mocking him.

Zack's brain was smothered with anger, although he dimly could sense the scope of effort that went into the film. The quality of the film was crisp and clear, the sound disgustingly accurate.

"You son of a bitch!" Zack shot out his right hand toward Shinogara and grabbed the older man by his tie and yanked it forward. He was immediately set upon from behind by David, who in no-nonsense fashion wrapped Zack's arms behind his back.

"Sit down, Mr. Colby," instructed Shinogara, loosening his tie.

"How did you get this? Marcia was in on this? Why? Are you pornographers? Why me?" Zack angrily shouted.

"Sit down, Mr. Colby," repeated Shinogara as he sat down.

The other men backed off slightly.

"We could have made this much worse, you know. *Much* worse. This is a fine film. We could make money on it—but we aren't interested in the film itself, only the effect of the film. Not many men have an opportunity to live out their fantasies, Mr. Colby. We have a business proposition for you. That's why we've invited you in while you are dressed as a businessman—all wingtipped and white-shirted. We have you by the "short hairs," as I believe the phrase goes. One suggestion that was bantered around was to have Miss Lee bring you in naked, blindfolded and totally erect; then you would be forced to face the truth with all of us

93

present. There were other suggestions, but you can imagine what they were. Today, we offer you an opportunity to make the right decision as a businessman and to keep a portion of your dignity. You look like a sensible man, so we expect you to do what is needed," Shinogara said firmly.

Shinogara hadn't made his decision on how Zack's denouement would occur until they had reached the motel the night before. The choice had come down to the total destruction of Colby's spirit versus an appeal to logic. Regardless of which approach was used, the end result would be the same. Shinogara needed what was inside Zack's brain and access to his house in order to accomplish his goals. He needed Zack's cooperation.

Zack's bright flush had fallen to a sweaty glow.

"Do you want to see more? It's really quite remarkable," asked Shinogara, pretending to be civil.

"Why me? I don't understand. Why me?" demanded Zack.

Zack tried to see the answers from the other blocks of stone, but without success. He began to laugh nervously.

"You guys picked the wrong man to blackmail. I don't have any money. What do you want — my mortgage? My stock? Is that it? Is that why you went to all this trouble? I mean, I was in that house for four nights and had no clue I was being taped. No clue! What's it all for?" Zack was ready to beg, if required.

"We don't want your money, Mr. Colby," said Shinogara coldly.

The only sound in the room came from the hum of the air conditioner. Then the ice maker in the kitchen punctuated the silence by dropping a finished product with a *clunk* into a nearly empty bucket. Zack's brain

94

whirred through a new data base called If They Don't Want Money Then What the Fuck Do They Want? His brain kept coming back with No Record Found.

"I don't understand. What do you want?"

"We want your computers, Mr. Colby."

My computers? Zack thought. They're demo units.

"My demo units? I mean—why? They aren't mine. They're company property—IGC property. They aren't mine to give, for Christ's sake," replied Zack.

"No, you don't understand."

That was evident, Zack thought.

"We want the sign-on codes and access to the IGC computer system in Denver, the one that runs your version of the IBM PROFS software. There'll be other things that we'll need, but right now that's the essence of what we want."

Zack still didn't understand. You want to send electronic mail to IGCers? he thought. Why on earth would you want to do that?

Regardless, prickles of dread started to form on the back of his neck and down his sides and in the pit of his stomach. Shinogara could see some dim recognition in Zack's eyes, but they were still clouded by Zack's pure blue training and approach to business. He wasn't dishonest, so other people weren't, either.

"We'll enter your house and you'll open up both the personal computer and the 9350 for us to use. You'll provide us with any local log-on codes, manuals, and an explanation of programs that we may not be familiar with. You'll provide your sign-on codes for the PROFS system in Denver. You'll provide us with internal directories and telephone numbers upon request. You'll obtain telephone numbers and PROFS IDs for locations not in master directories, such as the PC disk in Yorktown, the trouble hotlines in Boca Raton, Austin, Endicott, and San Jose—and there will be others.

"We'll be represented by David Kimura, an experienced programmer. To your wife, who right now believes you're out earning a living, you'll say nothing. David will be your new systems engineer."

Zack was astonished. And terrified. And filled with righteous indignation.

These assholes are going to try and steal IGC secrets, he thought.

Zack was getting close, but he still didn't have it. Actually, it wasn't important that he understand. He understood what Shinogara wanted, and from Shinogara's standpoint that's all that was required.

"No way! No fucking way! Do you understand? Read my lips . . . you bunch of pipsqueak chink bastards. No . . . fucking . . . way am I going to let you do that. No way!" Zack shouted while he crossed his arms and shook his head vehemently.

Zack pointed his finger at Shinogara and shouted at him.

"You can show that to my wife—I'll take it. She'll forgive me. Once you're exposed, she'll understand—she'll forgive me. I might lose my job—no, hell no—they'll thank me for turning you in. No way! Just no way!" Zack repeated.

Shinogara sighed, reached for his briefcase and put it on his lap, then snapped the clasps open. He reached inside and pulled out a series of pictures. At the same time he nodded to Yamamoto, who started the VCR in a silent whir fast-forward.

"These are pictures of the Texas State Penitentiary. It's located on the outskirts of Austin. Unlike federal prisons, which do have a certain number of country club locations, the Texas penal system has no such luxuries. The Texas State Penitentiary is a miserable hellhole, Mr. Colby. We sit here on a comfortable October day, yet we have air-conditioning so that the room temperature may be controlled to seventy-two degrees. We certainly wouldn't want to get too warm. The temperature in Austin hovers around one hundred degrees from June through September. It feels like the surface of the sun."

Shinogara stood up just as the VCR came to a clicking stop.

"The Texas State Penitentiary contains a collection of nasty criminals in a state known for strange people. Here are some examples of the type of people you'll be associating with when you're convicted of your crimes."

Shinogara dropped five pictures in Zack's lap.

"I'm not the one who's guilty, Mr. Colby. It's you! It's you and your . . ."

Zack's attention was rudely slapped by the assorted photos of truly ugly beasts — mostly surly black and Hispanic men — vicious animals. Shinogara purposefully raised the specter of racism, which brought up the deepest of fears inside poor white Zack.

"These pictures are of hardened criminals who are serving life sentences. What do you think these . . . *men*"— Shinogara bit the word off as if it was a question mark — "will do to a child molester?" Shinogara asked quietly.

"I . . . I . . . I don't," stuttered Zack, who began to understand the pickle he had gotten into.

Still standing in front of Zack, with the cuffs of his white shirt still crisply peeking out from the sleeves of his coat, Shinogara handed another picture to Zack. It was a gross picture of a huge black man on top of a much smaller white man, just in the process of anal rape — the ultimate white male horror.

"Do you enjoy anal sex, Mr. Colby?" asked Shinogara, drilling Zack with mental bullets. "From your performance last week, I would guess not. It seems to me that you like the soft bottoms of young women," Shinogara continued. "Yes, soft bottoms," Shinogara said, as he walked casually around the room.

Shinogara sat down on a now-cleared section of the couch, perhaps six feet from Zack. The other men had quietly moved, knowing that Zack was completely trapped. Shinogara could have stopped but he drove the final nails into Zack's brain. He pressed the Play button on the VCR and watched as Zack and Baby struggled on the floor. The tape rolled through sounds of whipping and crying, of blood and rape.

"Her name is Julie Evans. She's fourteen years old and lived in the neighborhood. We abducted her for you. *You* raped her within an inch of her life. Your filth, your lust—is *disgusting! Here!*" Shinogara threw down clippings from the *Dallas Morning News*. The rape, abuse, and abduction of valedictorian Julie Evans was big news in Dallas.

HIGHLAND PARK TEEN KIDNAPPED, RAPED AND TORTURED

NAKED AND PHYSICALLY ABUSED, YOUNG JULIE EVANS WAS FOUND YESTERDAY AFTERNOON ON A SURTRANS TRAIN AT DFW BY FOUR MIAMI-BOUND TOURISTS. APPARENTLY DRUGGED, EVANS, 14, LAST YEAR'S VALEDICTORIAN AT HIGHLAND PARK MIDDLE SCHOOL, HAD BEEN KIDNAPPED THURSDAY AFTERNOON WHILE WALKING HOME FROM SCHOOL, AND HAD BEEN SUBJECTED TO A BIZARRE SERIES OF SEXUAL TORTURE FOR NEARLY TWELVE HOURS. EVANS, A PRETTY BLOND, WAS ABLE TO GIVE DALLAS POLICE A SKETCHY DESCRIPTION OF THE MAN—A

WHITE MALE IN HIS MID-THIRTIES, (SEE SKETCH, BOTTOM) BROWN HAIR, APPROXIMATELY SIX FEET TALL.

EVANS REPORTED THAT SHE WAS KIDNAPPED BY AN INDETERMINATE NUMBER OF MEN AND WOMEN WHO FORCED HER INTO A PARKED VAN AS SHE WALKED ALONG CEDAR LANE IN HIGHLAND PARK ON HER WAY HOME TO 1134 HILLTOP ROAD. HER KIDNAPPERS WRAPPED HER IN A BLANKET, THEN DROVE AROUND THE CITY FOR NEARLY AN HOUR, CHANGING VEHICLES AT LEAST ONCE BEFORE STOPPING.

EVANS WAS UNABLE TO PROVIDE A DESCRIPTION OF THE HOUSE SHE HAD BEEN TAKEN TO, REPORTING ONLY THAT THE ROOM HAD A TALL CEILING, MIRRORS ON THE WALLS, AND THAT THERE WAS A LARGE BATHROOM ATTACHED. UPON PROMPTING BY DALLAS POLICE, YOUNG EVANS RECOUNTED THE ENSUING EVENTS THAT INCLUDED MOLESTATION, SODOMY — ORAL AND ANAL — RAPE AND BONDAGE BY THE MAN DESCRIBED ABOVE. EVANS WAS APPARENTLY WHIPPED AFTER BEING TIED UP. THE PASSENGERS WHO FOUND HER, WHO REFUSED TO BE IDENTIFIED, VERIFIED THAT SHE HAD INDEED BEEN BEATEN WITH SOME KIND OF INSTRUMENT, POSSIBLY A WHIP.

Zack read the news clippings at the same time the image showed a close-up of a tender bottom being viciously beaten by the tip of a riding crop — the girl's cries for help were ignored, her legs twisted and twitched with each stroke.

Zack was devastated. The destruction was complete. Shinogara nodded to David, who approached the slumping Zack Colby. Shinogara turned the VCR off.

"I'm going to be your constant companion, Zack," David said, his arm around Zack's shoulder. "You've got to compose yourself. All this will pass."

Shinogara's expression changed from hard to fatherly.

"We realize that this . . . arrangement may be difficult for you. We know how dedicated IGC employees are, but we also know that we have you in a very difficult position."

Shinogara waited until Zack's red eyes met his.

"I want you to understand—more importantly, I want you to believe in your heart—that I'll think nothing of turning this evidence over to the authorities, to your company, and to the media, if you don't cooperate. Do you believe this?" Shinogara's eyes drilled holes through Zack's brain.

"Ye-yes," Zack croaked through a mouth drained of saliva.

"Good. We're not evil monsters, Mr. Colby. We're businessmen. I realize that you may have to make a new start someplace when this affair is completed."

Shinogara nodded to Yamamoto, who placed a tan briefcase onto the glass-topped coffee table in front of Zack's couch. The case was so new that the leather was unscratched and smelled fresh.

"Open it, please," Shinogara instructed Zack.

Zack clicked the dual locks and opened the briefcase. It was filled with cash, neat stacks of fifties and hundreds, each bundle wrapped with a crisp green official bank binding.

"Five hundred thousand dollars, cash. Untraceable United States currency, Mr. Colby. More money than you've ever seen."

Zack looked up at Shinogara in astonishment.

"With your brief tenure with IGC . . . what is it?

Four years?" Shinogara asked Zack.

"Yes."

"Then you must be making about forty thousand. With social security, federal and state taxes, you net perhaps twenty-four thousand of that. If you continue to sell computers and advance up the promotion scale, your gross earnings should approach eighty or ninety thousand dollars in another ten years. This briefcase represents the approximate net earnings for a twenty-year career that you, in all likelihood, will have to forfeit."

Dazed, Zack fingered a packet of hundreds.

"All in all, Mr. Colby, you should consider yourself fortunate to be involved with businessmen as generous as we are."

Shinogara rose and extended his hand to Zack, indicating that it was time for him to leave. Zack stood up and absentmindedly took the older man's hand in return. Shinogara stood close to Zack and made direct eye contact.

"It's important that you not do anything rash . . . that you follow the instructions of Mr. Kimura to the letter. Life can be simple or it can be very complicated. You have very little to go to the police with if you decide to abandon your good senses. We're faceless Oriental businessmen. I have a tape of you committing disgusting acts, which I'll not be reluctant to release to the authorities if you don't follow our instructions. On the other hand, if you do, this briefcase of cash will be yours. The choice is up to you. Good day, Mr. Colby." Shinogara nodded curtly.

David held out his hand and guided a stunned Zack Colby from the couch toward the door. Zack was ashen faced, and nearly stumbled as David walked him back to the lobby, then out into the parking lot to Zack's car.

David opened the door and Zack slid inside. Perspiration had gone right through his shirt and had dampened his suit coat.

"Are you going to be all right, Zack? Do you need some help getting home?" asked David.

With a mumble Zack shook his head.

"I'll see you tomorrow, Zack." David smiled.

"Tomorrow?" mumbled Zack.

"Yes, tomorrow. You may have the afternoon off."

After a long minute, Zack started the engine, then backed out of his parking spot. He was a man on remote control. Everything he saw was in his peripheral vision. He was devastated. His life was over.

Chapter Two
Marcia Gets Squeezed

Like the cat that jumps in the lap of the one person who hates it, or the cigarette smoke that always seems to drift up an asthmatic's nose, peace and quiet were not to be Zack's fate. On the one evening in his life when he was desperate to be alone, when he needed time to settle his nerves, to sort things out, he was bombarded with the reality of family. Cheryl wanted to talk. The children not only fought, they brought a new decibel level to their intensity.

"Can't you children play someplace else?" he shouted.

With only the briefest of interruptions, both children looked at their father as if he was not only retarded but that he'd also asked them to play on the planet Xenon. The answer was obviously *no*. They resumed by continuing their circle around his chair and by competing for sole possession of the exact same toy at the exact same moment in time.

And Cheryl wanted to talk. More than that, she wanted him to answer. This required actual brain participation on his part. Unfortunately, Zack's brain had disconnected. *Sorry, too much information. I can't take any more calls. Try again later.* Only he couldn't try later.

Jesus Christ, what the fuck am I going to do? he wondered.

"and I wanted to hit that D'angelo woman today, I

just did . . . Mom called and . . ."

Zack's mind was screaming *aahhhhiieeee!*

". . . so what do you think?"

"I'm sorry, what do I think about what?" Zack feebly replied.

"You haven't been listening to me? You're gone all day and I'm stuck with the children and you won't even listen to me when I want to talk with you?" Cheryl shouted angrily. "Children, be quiet!" she shouted into the living room with her best Voice of Doom. The effect was the same as muting an obnoxious used car commercial on TV. Instant quiet. Zack's mind was forced to pay attention. He wished the children were playing instead.

Jesus Christ, Cheryl, he wanted to say, can't you see I don't want to talk?

"Hon, I . . ." But the words wouldn't come out. His brain was strobing thoughts—bing, bing, bing.

What am I going to do? Kill him. Jail. Rape. Kill him. Marcia—oh, God, her legs.

Zack's heart pounded, sweat beaded on his forehead and upper lip. The back of his neck was prickly, the back of his shirt wet with perspiration.

"I'm sorry, I've had a lot on my mind. Business, I'm afraid. Sorry. It must be the kids. I just timed out," was his lame response.

Lame or not, any response was better than being ignored.

Bing, bing, bing. Zack's brain tried to focus on one idea but couldn't. All cohesive thought patterns were being overridden by the visual memory of the tape and Shinogara's parting words about anal sex with large, mean black men. He involuntarily squeezed his cheeks together in a butt tuck even Jane Fonda would be proud of.

Jesus, am I in trouble, he thought. What the fuck am I going to do?

The telephone rang, startling them both. For the children it seemed to be the signal to resume their noisy play — Round Two, Kids from Hell.

"Hello," said Cheryl, expecting the call to be from Mom. Nobody else called them at night. Even though they'd lived there for nearly four years, their social circle was very small. It wasn't as if they didn't try. While they invited a lot of Zack's business acquaintances over, they rarely got a return invitation. One of the trade-offs in getting the house on the bluff was that they were nearly out of the city, certainly out of anything that would be considered a neighborhood. The nearest house was a quarter mile down the street, also on the bluff. But they were an unfriendly couple that went to Arizona every November for the winter. While the children had plenty of open space to play, there was nobody Cheryl could talk over the back fence with. In fact, they didn't have a fence.

Cheryl listened for a second or two, then handed him the phone. "It's for you," she said with a frown on her face.

"Who is it?" he whispered.

"A David Kimura. I've never heard of him, but he says he knows you."

He's calling here? Zack thought. What am I going to do? Do I pretend to know him?

"Hello," he said tentatively.

Cheryl looked on with temporary curiosity, then headed for the living room to try and round up the children.

"Zack, this is David. Just a reminder about tomorrow. There is much to do. I'll be over at your house at eight-thirty in the morning."

"Here?" Zack said in a normal voice, then quickly whispered while he covered up the phone. "You're coming here? What the hell do you think you're doing? You can't come here!"

"Your wife sounds like a very nice person. I'm anxious to meet her," continued David Kimura.

"You can't come here!"

"Of course I can, Zack. That's the whole idea. You're going to tell your wife . . . what is her name?"

"Cheryl," Zack continued to whisper.

"Yes, Cheryl. You're going to tell Cheryl that your branch's management has decided that because of your territory's tremendous potential, that you deserve to have a full-time systems engineer assigned to it. And I'm the one. I'm going to help you sell and install all those wonderful new computers," Kimura said calmly.

David paused. He had to get Zack Colby in line.

"Now Zack, this is very important. You've got to stop whispering. I know you don't want your wife . . . Cheryl . . . to know what terrible things you've done. You certainly don't want her to see that disgusting film. I want you to calm down and talk normally. Pretend that you know me and say something she'll hear . . . something like 'hey that's great.' Go on! Say it," Kimura instructed.

The children had been quieted down again. Cheryl's attention was refocused on him.

"That's wonderful, David. That's great. Tomorrow morning, then? Eight-thirty?" Zack said, forcing a smile to crack his face while he glanced across the room at Cheryl and caught her eyes.

She doesn't have a clue, Zack thought. Smile, God damn it! Smile! Give them what they want to see. Chameleonic. That's it. Come on. Relax. Do it! Turn it on. You're good, God damn it! Do it!

And he did it. Zack smiled.

"Good, Zack. I'll see you tomorrow morning at eight-thirty. I know where you live. I'm looking forward to meeting your wife . . . and to seeing what you have in your basement," said Kimura.

"Yes, I'm sure," replied Zack, now seemingly under control.

"Good, good," encouraged David.

"See you tomorrow," said Zack as he hung up.

Zack slowly replaced the phone in the cradle. For a split second he thought of calling his brother-in-law.

Call Scotty. Do it!

But the thought disappeared.

"That was David Kimura. I've got an SE. They've finally recognized it . . . that this territory needs some technical support," said Zack, temporarily composed.

"Oh, that's wonderful Zack! You've been after them for so long. Why now? What took them so long?"

"I guess it must be the systems we've got on order for the base . . . that and what I've managed to get started downtown. Whatever the reason, I'll take whoever it is," replied Zack.

"David Kimura? I've never met him, have I?" asked Cheryl.

"No dear, you haven't. He's about our age — seems pretty competent from what I've seen of him," Zack lied smoothly. "He's coming up here tomorrow morning around eight-thirty. We might want to have the house . . ." Zack's sentence faded off into implication.

"Here? Tomorrow morning? The house is a disaster. I can't have him seeing the place like this!" Cheryl moaned, immediately shifting into housewife mode.

Since their marriage four years ago, Zack and Cheryl had divided household responsibilities along traditional lines. There was Man's Work — the cars, the

107

lawn, the outside of the house, Big Decisions, bread-winning—and there was Woman's Work, which consisted of everything else. However overburdened Cheryl was, Zack made no attempt to enter the domain of Woman's Work. The unfair division of labor wasn't all Zack's fault, however. Not once in the four years had Cheryl even approached him about sharing some of the house maintenance or cleaning chores. The process would have been simple. Here, you do it.

To Zack's great relief, the prospect of a stranger coming to her house in the morning turned Cheryl into Vacuum and Pickup Lady. Zack quietly left the room and went downstairs as Cheryl began to spruce up.

Just relax, Zack told himself. This will be OK . . . everything will be OK.

Of course, it wasn't OK. That night Zack had trouble going to sleep, not a surprise considering how hyped his body was. At two-thirty he woke up, terrified. His heart raced. The memory of the afternoon came back in a rush. The cries of the girl and the frantic look of lust and God-knows-what on his face came back with double vengeance. Cheryl softly snored as Zack faced the demons of the night. Ten hours ago he had walked into a meeting expecting the biggest blue-bird sale of his career. Fifteen minutes later he was lower than white whale shit.

Who are those guys? he wondered. It doesn't matter. They've got you wired for sound. Whatever they want, you'll do. What do they want? It doesn't matter.

He had access to information and to data bases that were confidential and for company internal use only. Whoever these Orientals were—Japanese, Korean,

Chinese—Zack couldn't tell the obvious differences in races and had never cared—they had him by the balls.

Stay alive, he thought. Do what they want. Stay cool.

But Zack couldn't stay cool. The thought of the young girl . . . the pictures of the smiling face in the *Dallas Morning News* and the evil pornographic picture of the huge inmate performing sodomy were set side by side in his mind's eye. He could see the two as clearly as if they were projected onto the darkened bedroom wall. He had been led over the edge.

Trapped!

He was doomed. He couldn't remember how he'd even gotten home that day. The whole afternoon was a haze. David had finally escorted him out to his car and had stood there for nearly ten minutes while Zack had stared straight ahead zombielike, not moving a muscle, keys in hand. Somehow he'd started the car and gone a block or two and had ended up in the parking lot next to the stockyards, where he'd sat for five hours—oblivious of the sounds and smells of the stock in the process of being loaded on their one-way trip to Denver. Always with a good sense of humor, Zack would have appreciated the stockyard irony and analogy to his situation. His head was on the chopping block and he had about as much power over his situation as did the ground sirloin on hooves mooing in front of him.

Zack lay on his side of the king-size bed and listened to the thrashing of his heart and felt the sweat drip down from his armpits. He was drenched. His arms felt like they were pinioned, like someone had tied weights to his fingertips. He could feel his skin crawl.

God! Oh, God, I can't move. Oh shit, I'm in trouble.

And it was so.

"Hi, my name's David Kimura," said the smiling young man at the door. "You must be Cheryl. Nice to meet you."

Cheryl was taken aback slightly by the friendly nature of Zack's new systems engineer.

Where do they get them? she wondered.

She and David had to be nearly the same age, yet he made her feel so much older. He was true blue from his yellow power tie with blue stripes right down to the polished double-laced Florsheim wingtips.

"Zack! It's David Kimura here to see you," Cheryl shouted upstairs.

David had intentionally arrived ten minutes early. IGCers were always intent on keeping exact appointment times, so much so that salesmen would walk around the block or sit in the car instead of being early for a meeting. As a result, David's early arrival caught Zack off guard, which was David's intent. David also wanted to ensure that he met Cheryl and got off on the right foot. It was easy for him to turn on the charm. Cheryl Colby would like him, which would make it tougher for Zack to stray off the path—which David was sure he would try at some later point in time.

"Hi, Zack—sorry I'm early. There was no traffic on I-25 today and I just moved right along. Wow, this is sure a nice house. How long have you lived here?" David said amicably, turning his glance back to Cheryl.

While Cheryl noticed the friendly twinkle in his eyes, she had the impression he had just given her the quick male head-to-toe scan. All men did it. The degree of the scan depended upon the age and shape of the woman-object. Cheryl was sure she'd just gotten the complete scan.

Men! she thought.

With the conversation turned to the home and not business, the need to go into immediate details on their professional relationship was obviated. Coffee was offered and declined, weather was discussed and put away, and movement was made from the foyer to the kitchen.

"Well, I sure was surprised when they told me I'd be supporting Wyoming. I'll be honest, I don't know much about your territory. For the last couple of years I've been assigned to government accounts, mainly in the federal center in Lakewood. I've got VM, PC, and midsystems experience," said Kimura, shifting his eyes directly to Zack, almost encouraging Zack to continue by the movement of his shoulders and head.

"That fits my territory to a T," Zack returned with a forced smile, a bit unsure, but enough to get by Cheryl.

"Great. Did you say this used to be a doctor's office?" asked David.

"That's right," replied Zack.

"Well, I've heard about your toy room. I'm anxious to see it," smiled David.

Zack was having trouble keeping up with the obvious.

"He means your office, Zack," inserted Cheryl, picking up David's meaning immediately.

"Oh, yes. Do you want to see it?" said Zack.

"See it?" David turned to Cheryl. "I'll be a regular visitor here, I'm afraid. We're going to sell equipment and make a lot of money — get rich and famous. I hope you don't mind," David said, laughing.

Cheryl was caught up in David's enthusiasm.

"Not at all, not at all."

David turned to Zack. "Let's see what you've got — and you can start telling me about your territory. I've got some catching up to do," he said as he put a hand on Zack's shoulder. David's grip was hard, almost pinching — a reminder. The downstairs was connected to the upper floor via the upper and lower kitchens, each with a privacy door. Zack threw the lights on and the two men walked down the steps. David made sure the door was closed behind him.

Zack stood still while David quickly scanned the rooms, covering the basement with his eyes and hands.

"Can she hear?" David asked softly.

"No . . . she's never said so," stuttered Zack.

"Very soon this equipment will need to be turned on twenty-four hours a day, seven days a week. We'll make arrangements for a separate billing. You'll tell her a story — something she'll believe. Do you have any big accounts?" he asked, still in a near whisper.

"Yes . . . yes. Warren Air Force Base. I've got several —"

"Good, good!" David cut him off. "You'll tell her that there's a large government procurement that's going out for competitive bid — for mainframe and personal computers. It could mean a whole year's quota — perhaps two. David will need to use the machines during the day and have access to them when he's in Denver. This means the machines will have to be left on all the time."

David was intense, his eyes were fierce. Zack was scared.

"Wha — what are you planning to do?" Zack whimpered.

"What do you think is going to happen, Zack?" David whipped him with the question.

Zack's whole body shook. He felt like he was getting

hypothermia right here in his basement. A cold dread had settled into his soul. He was going to sell his company down the drain. Part of him wanted to jump on the thick man and choke him to death, but it was only a small part of him. Zack's legs were cemented to the basement carpet. Fear was the ultimate Super Glue.

"You're going to tap into the internal IGC system, get installed base, customer lists . . . whatever is available." Zack felt like a Judas, but had missed the mark by a light year.

David didn't reply. If Zack Colby felt this bad about someone tapping into IGC's system to get customer lists, then he didn't need to know the real reason — not yet. Still in his intense whisper, David laid it out for Zack.

"Do you remember the group of men you met?"

"Yes." Zack's mind forced its way back nearly twenty-four hours.

"These are powerful businessmen. I work for them. So do the people who work for me." Zack looked up. "Yes, you look surprised. I have very intelligent men who work for me. We know how to use this equipment. You can't get out of this by thinking that if you kill me you're off the hook. There'll be another to replace me if that's the case. Your wife and children will be in danger if we reach such a point. Remember this, Zack." David stepped very close to Zack. Up close, David's appearance was slightly different. While he was shorter than Zack, his body motions exuded strength and bulk.

He'd be tough in a fight, Zack thought.

"The men I work for are very patient. They can afford to pull back and try again. Their resources are virtually infinite. You, however, have a very tenuous lease on life as you know it. If things get bad, we'll drop you like a hot rock. A telephone call is all it will take . . . a telephone call to the Dallas police. The video is already packaged and ready for express mail. We would do it with no qualms. In fact, it would make our next blackmail so much the better—whether you went to jail or committed suicide, the next Zack Colby would know we meant business. Have I made myself clear?" David drilled.

"Yes," Zack nodded, but his eyes concealed the resentment and buildup of anger that he felt.

"Excellent," David smiled. "Now, I think we can start to get down to our business."

"You can't come over here any time you God-damn feel like it, you know," blurted Zack, oblivious of what David had just said.

"Lower your voice," David ordered. "I have no intention of living in your basement. Once we're set up, I can do much of what we need to do from outside your house. But the machines must stay on twenty-four hours a day. Do you understand? Turn them on now, please."

Zack was on the verge of exploding.

"Now, Zack," David said firmly.

Zack's anger abated temporarily and one at a time he turned on each piece of equipment.

"Explain the connections, please," Kimura asked, pointing to the equipment. He knew what each of the machines did, but he wanted Zack Colby to be involved—and he wanted to be sure. It had been three years since David had left IGC to join Makato Shinogara's organization. In the interim he had been doing mostly PC programming, and since then IGC had come out with a complete overhaul of its midline and top-end computers.

I'll never be able to manage him and finish the programming we need to do, David thought.

Zack went to a blackboard and quickly drew a series of boxes and lines.

"This is a 9350 Model 60 with two 800 megabyte disks, a communications controller, an Ethernet controller, and tape drive. It's got VM, TCP/IP and a lot of IBM software—PROFS, ACF/VTAM, 3270 PC File Transfer, Advanced Print Function, and Application Systems software installed. Attached to the print controller is a dual sheet feed 3720 laser printer," Zack started his spiel, almost relieved to do so. "The system console is an IGC model 30 that is dedicated for use by the system and can't be used as a normal PC. Connected via the Ethernet controller is a model 70, a 25MHz 80386 PC that's the fastest in the marketplace," Zack continued. "In addition to having a baseband Ethernet adapter card installed, the PC has a 3270 adapter which is coax-attached to the communications controller. The controller is attached to this modem which in turn is connected to the telephone dataset. The modem is used to translate computer signals into telephone signals and vice versa. Thus, from this PC I can demonstrate local PC processing, local host computing on the 9350 via the Ethernet attachment, and remote computing by the communications dial-in to my office in Denver."

"Excellent. That's what I thought, but I wanted to make sure," replied David, nearly salivating at the prospects laid in front of him.

"Thank you. Before we get to work, let me explain the groundrules and what's going to happen. We obviously can't spend every moment of every day down here. I will ask you a question, and you will give me the answer. Do you understand?"

"Yes."

115

"I may ask you to get something for me from IGC. This may be a piece of equipment, a feature, or . . . an authorization. At this moment I don't know your level of authority in the system. If I ask you to get something, you'll get it. Do you understand?"

Zack's jaw began to tighten, his teeth clenched.

"Do you understand?"

"Yes," he spit the answer out. Zack's face was getting red.

"You will not tell your friends, your wife . . . or anyone what is happening. If you suspect that someone may be on to what is happening, you will tell me immediately. Do you understand?"

"Yes." Zack was angry, but Kimura didn't care. He had to drive the stakes right through Zack's heart.

"We'll meet every day, either here or at a designated point. I'll contact you. You will give me a key to the house — to this door. You and your family will be followed. If you don't do all of these things, your wife and children will be harmed and you will go to jail and be raped until you die. Do you understand?"

Zack's jaw slackened but his glare was just as intense.

"Yes."

"Very good. Now let's start with the personal computer. Show me what's on it," said David, moving a chair close to the PC.

"I spent two hours with Zack this morning. He seems . . ."

David paused, his eyes closed, his head resting on a pillow. He absent-mindedly twisted the cord of the telephone around his right index finger as he spoke. He saw the events of the day in his mind's eye.

116

"He seemed willing to answer most questions about the computers." David paused. "But he needed constant encouragement when I asked him about IGC data — why and how the applications were used internally."

"What about the 9350?" asked a patient Makato Shinogara, now back in his Palos Verdes estate.

"There was no time. I'll do it tomorrow. But . . ."

"What?"

"It's his eyes. I'm not sure how long he's going to stay stable. That's why I didn't want today's session to go too long. I'm a project leader, Mr. Shinogara. We have a virus to infect IGC and I'll see that it is done . . . and done correctly. But, I'm not . . . a psychologist . . . I manage *things* . . . *projects*. Give me a computer and I'll have it programmed correctly. Give me a task and I'll perform it, no matter how difficult or what risk is involved. But I'm not sure I have the skill or experience to manage Zack Colby. His psyche is fragile. I tell one of my people to do something, and they do it. There are no questions, no interpretations, no cajoling. Am I making myself clear?" David asked his mentor.

"Yes, I understand. It's not our way. You must call me every day," replied Shinogara.

Xiang Wu at first sensed her presence, then looked up from the stack of papers on his desk to see the serene face of his twelve-year-old consort, a beautiful girl who knew not to disturb him, nor speak unless spoken to. The only time she was allowed to speak without prompt was in bed, where she would come to him all freshly bathed and oiled, wearing only the fragrance of flowers, her long hair tied back in a braid. Under her

117

loose but formal silks Wu knew there were the smallest of budding breasts and skin so soft that just the thought of running his hand along the curve of her young bottom was enough to arouse him.

"Mr. Chimichanga, sir," she said softly to his nod.

"Send him in."

The sweet thoughts of the young consort were quickly replaced by the rough reality of Jimmy Chimichanga.

"Ah, James! What is the news?"

Jimmy Chimichanga came into the room like a warthog on alert. His eyes danced from side to side, a scowl of insecurity played across his mug. Wu's neatness and efficiency made him feel strangely uncomfortable.

"Here." Chimichanga placed a sealed envelope on Wu's desk, then sat down without being asked.

Xiang Wu opened the packet and began to sift through a series of eight-by-ten glossy black-and-white photographs.

"These are her people—I recognize them. Who is this man?" Wu held up a picture.

"The girl, of course—the guy's name is Zack Colby. He was registered at the Sheraton, but moved in with the girl on Tuesday. He stayed a total of four nights with her at this place she and"—Chimichanga reached over and pulled out a picture of David—"this Kimura fella rented. They pulled up stakes last Friday."

"Gone? Done?" questioned Wu.

"I guess so," Chimichanga replied as Wu continued to sift through photos. "By the end of the week this Colby guy looked like dead meat—there, you can see for yourself."

Chimichanga pointed to a photo of Zack that showed how drawn and used-up he looked by the end

118

of the week.

"Where does this Colby live?" asked Wu.

Jimmy C. grimaced, then shook his head.

"We started out with a plan to follow the Lee woman and this Kimura character. I didn't have the people set up—he took a flight to Denver. One of my men followed him there but lost him at the airport—the logistics were impossible."

"What of the woman?"

"She came back to San Francisco. She hasn't been out of her apartment since she got back. I've got a twenty-four-hour watch on the building."

Wu paused, then thought aloud. "Shinogara's started his operation—but what is it? The Lee woman spent a week in Los Angeles, then two weeks in Dallas. Now she's done. You've got to find out who Colby is and where he lives."

Jimmy Chimichanga smiled. Wu could read his thoughts.

"No, James—not *that* way. She may still be working for him. We need to know the details of Shinogara's operation. This calls for subtlety, James."

"Bullshit. I'll get what you want from her in five minutes," Chimichanga growled. "I'd enjoy it."

"Perhaps later you can have your amusement, James. But now I think we need to pay a call on Miss Lee—to give her the opportunity to cooperate."

"It's time you and I got down to work. Today, I want to see your PROFS system. Would you log on, please?" requested David.

Zack powered the PC, which quickly cranked through its self-test, called up the batch file to load 3270 communications, then started the communications session with Denver.

"I rarely demo this," Zack said.

Response time between screen changes depended on the speed of the modems used, how busy the remote computer was—how many users were on the system, or how many applications were running—and the quality of the telephone connection between the locations. Zack thought U.S. West used tin cans and string between Cheyenne and Denver.

After a short wait, the red, white, and blue logo of the Rocky Mountain Information Center popped up on the screen—the main log-on screen for all internal IGC applications.

WELCOME TO IGC DATA
COMMUNICATIONS SERVICES
THE USE OF THIS SYSTEM IS FOR IGC
MANAGEMENT APPROVED PURPOSES ONLY
THE FOLLOWING ARE VALID ENTRIES:
XXX USERID—LOGON TO YOUR AREA INFORMA-
TION CENTER/NSS SYSTEM
WHERE XXX IS YOUR AIC/NSS
MNEMONIC
NOTE: YOU CAN USE XXX782, XXX792, AND
XXX793 TO SPECIFY DEVICE TYPES 3278 MODEL
2, 3279 MOD 2 AND 3279 MOD 3, RESPECTIVELY
(OR EQUIVALENTS)
CCDN—CORPORATE CONSOLIDATED DATA NET-
WORK
CCD-YYYY—CCDN YYY IS YOUR DEVICE TYPE.
VALID ENTRIES ARE: CCDN782,
CCDN792, CCDN793, CCDNPC
—AN APPLICATION IDENTIFIER EG,
HON

PLEASE ENTER CHOICE

"That's for logging onto the system in Denver," Zack pointed to the first line that read XXX USERID. "Well, actually . . . we go to Denver regardless," he corrected himself. "The other choices branch off to other applications outside of PROFS.

"All I can show you is the list of applications — I'm only authorized to go into a few of them," Zack said, worried and irritated.

FOR IGC MANAGEMENT
APPROVED PURPOSES ONLY
CCDN Network
Centralized Applications

Application Status   13:19, Thu Oct 16

APPL	STATUS	
= ALT	ONLINE	11:27
= BAD	ONLINE	23:48
= BTS	ONLINE	19:29
= COM	ONLINE	00:57
= COR	OFFLINE	13:11
= CRT	ONLINE	04:05
= DNT	ONLINE	19:15
= EMS	ONLINE	11:28
= ES-	OFFLINE	01:15
= EWX	ONLINE	01:17
= FKR	ONLINE	00:14
= HLP	ONLINE	01:57
= HYU	ONLINE	10:48
= ISA	ONLINE	11:28
= TIN	ONLINE	00:45
= TMS	ONLINE	00:43

APPL	STATUS	
= TRN	ONLINE	20:55
= TRS	ONLINE	01:54
= TRW	ONLINE	06:47
= TSA	ONLINE	04:41
= TSB	ONLINE	03:54
= TSC	ONLINE	04:41
= TSO	ONLINE	00:14
= TS1	ONLINE	03:54
= TS2	ONLINE	03:55
= TS3	ONLINE	03:57
= TS4	ONLINE	03:55
= TS5	ONLINE	03:57
= TS6	ONLINE	03:54
= TS7	ONLINE	03:54
= TS8	ONLINE	03:49
= LXX	ONLINE	03:05
= MCD	ONLINE	12:08
= NC-	ONLINE	22:57
= NHH	ONLINE	23:03
= PT1	ONLINE	22:59
= RLA	ONLINE	07:41
= RPO	ONLINE	10:10
= RA1	ONLINE	09:23
= RA2	ONLINE	09:23
= RCT	OFFLIN	01:15
= ROL	ONLINE	19:17

NETWORK CONTROL 1-800-IGC-CCDN
CCDN COORDINATOR CLASS INFO
= APPL NAME TO SIGNON.
= LOFF/LOGOFF TO EXIT CCDN
= CIM FOR INFO
= = > _____
PF1 = HELP   PF3 = RETURN TO MENU

PF7 = SCROLL BACK
PF8 = SCROLL FORWARD

Each abbreviation represented a different internal application someplace in the huge network. From his days as a systems engineer, David recognized = HLP as being a series of technical data bases where the answers to almost all data processing questions could be found. If the answer wasn't there, there was a way to ask some really smart people what the answer was.

"What are these?" he asked, pointing to the = TSl to = TS8 lines. They were vaguely familiar.

"Administration uses those — you know . . . order entry, accounts receivable . . . stuff like that," Zack said matter-of-factly.

"The administrators use the same system now?" David asked, his mind off to the races again.

"Yes."

The TS1-8 applications represented the culmination of IGC's twenty-five year effort to properly administer itself. The applications resided on massive 8090 mainframes in the basement of the Rust Bucket in Bethesda, Maryland and in other locations.

What if IGC couldn't enter an order — couldn't order equipment to deliver to its customers? David wondered. Marketing chaos. What if IGC couldn't keep track of the money it was due — the thousands of invoices that were collectible each month? Economic chaos. What if . . .

David had found the key. The system didn't have to be poisoned — only the ability to get to the system.

"Thank you. May we go back, please?"

Zack returned to the first screen and typed logon colbyzac.

ENTER PASSWORD _____

The characters would not be displayed as he typed. "What's your password, Zack?" David asked politely.

Zack ignored him and touch-typed the password, then pressed Enter. The screen changed to the main PROFS display.

ROCKY MOUNTAIN REGIONAL
INFORMATION CENTER
IGC PROFESSIONAL OFFICE SYSTEM (PROFS)

Press one of the following PF Keys

PF1	Process Calendars	
PF2	Open the Mail	****
PF3	Note Processing	* Main *
PF4	Notes/Messages	* Menu *
PF5	Document Process	****
PF6	Go to HON	
PF7	Telephone Directory	
PF8	RMIC Update	
	News	
PF10	PC Options Menu	
PF11	Info Center Options	

HELP: HELPRMIC

Time: 1:19 PM

OCTOBER

S	M	T	W	T	F	S
			1	2	3	4
5	6	7	8	9	10	11
12	13	14	15	16	17	18
19	20	21	22	23	24	25
26	27	28	29	30	31	

Day of Year: 281

PF9 = HELP   PF12 = END

124

"This is the main PROFS menu . . . virtually out of the can from IBM. We haven't modified it much."

"I asked you, what's your log-on password?" David said with growing irritation.

"Where you can do . . ." Zack continued.

"Don't play games with me, Zack. I know what the fucking menus are. I can read. Give me your ID and password!" David raised his voice.

"I can't give you that. I'll walk you through anything you want, but I'm not going to give you free reign—"

"You'll give me anything I want," said David, clearly angry.

"No!" said Zack.

David was astonished. Zack's mind must be tricking itself. Clearly, Zack understood what was going to happen to him if he didn't do exactly what he was told.

"Didn't I make myself clear these past few days, Zack? Do you think Mr. Shinogara was playing games? *Do you?* I don't have time to waste with you over bullshit games. You'll give me what I want or I'll have my men get it out of you—or perhaps your wife and children," he threatened.

David was visibly angry. For a long moment the two men seemed to be on the verge of a tumble. Zack could see the intensity in David's eyes—there was no fear, no pity.

"No, I can't do that . . . I can't . . . I can't," Zack stuttered. His mind tried to shut off what Kimura could do with unlimited access to IGC data.

David was an excellent technocrat but had no patience or skill in dealing with this type of situation. Colby understood what would happen if he didn't comply—then why wasn't he doing it!

"Zack, you must. I know how to operate a computer—I know IGC mainframes. I know VM I

125

know PROFS—I've seen all this before," David said as calmly as he could, as friendly as he could. "Please—you're making this too difficult on yourself. You've got to work with me—not against me. We don't want to send you to jail. . . ." His voice trailed off.

"WBP8YR. My serial number is 209443," Zack said with reluctance.

"Thank you. That wasn't so bad, was it? Please continue," Kimura said with Oriental calmness.

The unusual password was required by IGC's internal use of IBM's Restricted Access Control Facility (RACF), pronounced Rack-F. No trivial passwords were allowed—this included familiar combinations of keys and numbers, social security numbers, street addresses, common names, et cetera. While there was great grumbling and much forgetting of passwords, the system appeared to work. Of course, this only denied someone from casually breaking into IGC's system from the outside. As in any system, once the password is known, system security is deader than a doornail.

David's heart raced with his act of bravado with Zack Colby. While it was true he knew the system, it had been over three years since he'd used it. PROFS had been significantly enhanced in the interim. Phone directories—including PROFS mailing IDs! There were over 1,400 mainframe computers within IGC, all connected via PROFS.

TELEPHONE DIRECTORY

LAST NAME: _____
AND/OR
FIRST NAME: _____
OR
PHONE NO: _____

OR
LOCATION/BUILDING NO: _____

ENTER DIRECTORY: ____RMIC____

ENTER OPTION: ____T____

   T — For Terminal Display
   I — For IGC TIELINE Directory
   E — For EDITING Your Directory
   C — To Change Your DEFAULT
   D — For DISPLAY of Avail Direct

== > MAKE DESIRED REQUEST AND DE-PRESS THE ENTER KEY

Worldwide electronic mail existed within the company. Every plant, lab, education center, and headquarters location, and every marketing office at all levels—branch, regional, and area—was connected by PROFS. When first announced by IBM, IGC had installed it in 1982 for internal use. PROFS's electronic mail quickly became addictive. Installed initially to handle mail within an office, it quickly was improved to handle multiple locations. Then, as more and more users came onto the network, additional applications were demanded—PC support, file transfer, ease-of-use, document creation. The productivity gains within the company were staggering—yet, as IGC's customers would understand, the application required a great deal of computing power—and that meant IGC mainframes, which was the whole idea anyway.

"Go into document processing, please," instructed David, his attention back on the target.

PROFS MEMO/DOCUMENT PROCESSING

Prepare a Document or Memo

		COMMAND
PF1	Create New Document/Process Author Profile	MEMO NEW
PF2	Resume Work on Document Postponed in Your Personal Storage	MEMO n

Mail a Document

PF3	Re-Mail a Previously Mailed Document	MAIL
PF4	Mail a Non-PROFS File Using PROFS Electronic Mail	MAILDOC
PF5	Mail a PROFS Document to a User on a Non-PROFS System	SENDMEMO
PF6	Check the Status of Out-Going Mail	MAILMAN

Process the Mail Log

PF7	Search for Documents	SEARCH
PF8	Retrieve a Document from the Database for Update	DOCOLD
PF9	Maintain the PROFS Mail Log	MAILLOG
PF10	Restrict or Unrestrict Access to a Document	RESTRICT
PF11	Store a Softcopy Document (CMS file) in PROFS	STORE

To invoke directly from any PROFS Main Menu, use the Command indicated. Press Corresponding PF Key

PF12 = Return

Mail a non-PROFS file using PROFS electronic mail! David thought. Mail a document to non-PROFS system! The transport mechanism was there! No modifications would be required. IGC's internal system presented David with the capability to mail a document to any person within the company—worldwide. With the explosion and functionality of personal computers, only a very few old-timers kept the 3278/79 display terminals that had been around since the late 1960s. Everyone had a PC on his desk—a PC/XT, PC/AT, 3270 PC, or an IBM PS/2. Everyone was connected to PROFS. Everyone started his morning by flipping up the Big Red Switch on his good old IGC personal computer.

"What about normal personal computer applications—word processing, spreadsheets?"

Zack pressed Alt and the space bar at the same time. The screen instantly changed. Hidden behind the communications screen was a "window," a whole smorgasbord of PC delights.

David's mind was eight steps ahead of Zack's. He paid virtually no attention to Zack's perusal of the other applications on the Denver machine—not until he reached a menu that he didn't recognize.

"Wait a minute—stop for a second. What's this?" David asked.

PF3 Logon to Yorktown Disk

David could see Zack's jaw clench again.

"You can get to Yorktown? From here?" David asked.

Easy PC   Last Updated 10/15
Key an Option Number

1 USER	—	All about Easy PC. Including User's Guide and Fastpath.
2 ADMINEASE	—	Administrative Support Applications
3 MARKETING	—	Marketing Support Applications
4 SERVICE	—	Service Support Applications
5 BPMENU	—	Business Processes
6 CUSTOMIZE	—	Install/delete software, configuration options, and personalized menus and fastpath names.
7 PRODUCTIVITY	—	PRODUCTS, EDITORS, TEXT, TOOLS, and ACCESS HOST
8 UPDATE	—	Update Easy PC with latest level enhance

Zack shifted in his chair and coughed nervously. In the back of his mind Zack knew that these people were after more than just customer lists.

"Yes, I did this one myself. PCs are a hobby with me, so—"

"Is this the same Yorktown disk that is the think tank bulletin board," asked David, excited.

"Yes. How do you know about it?" Zack asked.

"I just do," smiled David Kimura.

130

When Kimura was a systems engineer, IGCers in Yorktown Heights were in the thinking stage of how to open the disk up to more users internally. The "disk" was actually a partition of a mainframe computer and constantly used by the major tech weenies within IGC's research facilities, plants, and labs. In 1986 it was opened to selected branch personnel, then finally to virtually all of marketing in 1988. Like any PC bulletin board, data was "posted" in the form of messages and notes. PC programs could be sent, exchanged, and even debugged. Everybody who used it was on the honor system—but from an internal security standpoint the Yorktown disk was a ticking time bomb—a bomb ready to maim, destroy, or disrupt data residing on personal computers in the most important technical offices within the company. An "It Can't Happen Here" mentality blocked the vision of normally clear-thinking individuals. The geniuses who wore togas and sandals to work, the ones who were paid to think nothing but smart thoughts—and who wouldn't be caught dead using something as mundane as PROFS—they used the Yorktown disk.

I've got them by the short hairs, thought David with a smile.

Zack noticed that Kimura's eyes had temporarily glassed over. The Cheshire Cat smile was obvious.

"What are you planning, you son of a bitch?" Zack shouted, knocking his chair over as he stood up.

David's reaction was instantaneous. Although quite a bit shorter, his arms were much stronger. David grabbed at Zack just as Zack started a wild, frustrated punch that missed. Ducking down and inside, David managed to pin Zack's right arm up behind his back, while grabbing him in a tight waist hold from behind.

"So you want to go to jail, is that it?" David said

131

through angrily clenched teeth. "I ought to break your arm." Kimura twisted Zack's arm up to the very painful point, hard enough to cause Zack to cry out in pain.

"Enough?" asked David, roughly. "Do you want your pretty wife to have some of this? Eh?" He emphasized with another twist.

"Get your hands off me! Twist. "No . . . no! Enough! That hurts," said a much more subdued Zack Colby, disheartened and disappointed.

David released his iron grip on Zack's arm, which fell to his side. The muscles screamed from the unnatural position.

"I think we've had enough for today, Zack. Tomorrow I'll bring in two additional modems. I want you to find the customization manual for this." David pointed to the 3174 Communications Controller. "I also want you to go to Denver and pick up a PROFS manual, a VM manual, a *Using CMS* instruction book, and any other procedural manuals relating to the 9350 and PROFS. Do you understand?" asked David quietly.

"Yes . . . I understand," said Zack with a hangdog little-boy look.

"Very good," said David. Not very good was what he meant.

"He's fighting me — this afternoon we literally struggled. I'm spending more time than I expected just trying to keep him under control — certainly more than I want. There is much we have to do — the potential for control is greater than we expected, but our programs must be modified. We can choke IGC down to the point where they can do nothing but sit on their hands. And, I've had no time to even start on Phase

132

Two. If we're going to time its implementation, then we've got to get started this week," Kimura spoke earnestly.

Phase two would be the second deadly blow to the corporate giant. Most IGC offices had direct dial capability — so that customers could call their salesman or administrator at their desks without the need of going through a person at a switchboard. Secretaries in IGC only answered the phone of the managers they supported, not the reps, SEs, or administrative people reporting to the managers. Most locations had a rollover capability, so that after three or four rings the call would go to PhoneMail, where a message could be left. When the in-basket of PhoneMail was filled, the call would roll over to the switchboard, which in normal times only had to answer the stray calls from customers who didn't know the direct dial number of their rep.

David had all the information in front of him that he needed to implement Phase Two — the direct dial telephone number of every individual in IGC. This information, combined with Zack Colby's internal telephone book, could and would be loaded into banks of personal computers located at fifty sites across the country. The personal computers would be used to auto-dial a number. The "message" would consist of a five-second pause followed by a high-pitched irritating sound, fifteen seconds in duration. It would only take one or two calls for a reasonable person to let it roll over to PhoneMail, which would very shortly be filled. At some undetermined point, PhoneMail wouldn't be able to handle the flood of incoming calls, and neither would the switchboard, so the phones would ring at the individual desks — and ring, and ring, and ring — driving everyone Screaming Yellow Bonkers. While there was no practical way to disrupt every IGC office, a careful selection of fifty buildings could and would bring internal communications to a halt. With the computers locked and the phones tied up, there would be no way for IGC management to globally attack a solution to the computer virus.

"Yes, I agree. You want me to call Miss Lee—is that correct?" asked Shinogara.

"Yes, sir," said David gratefully. "Very much so."

"I'll get back to you tomorrow," replied Shinogara crisply.

David hung up the phone, relieved that Shinogara had seen the light. He needed Marcia here in the worst way. There was so much to do. The PC virus needed to be tested on IGC's systems. The host virus needed to be developed on the 9350. And while David wasn't in charge of Phase Two, clearly his input and participation were vital to the success of the operation. It was more than one twenty-eight year old should be responsible for.

Shinogara knew he had to channel the brilliant young man's energy on the target ahead.

The Americans would pay, he swore, and pay big.

There had never been a question who the enemy was, never a question who was going to pay for past sins, never a question who would gag on the cold bone of revenge. The hated corporate enemy was InterGalactic Computing Corporation of Armonk, New York. Bigotry and racism stirred just below the surface—IGC represented the whitest of white, the superiority of the Caucasian race. But just as bad, just as maddening, was the air of smugness—IGC was the Moral Majority of corporate America.

We play hard, but we play fair—we don't lie, we don't cheat, we don't tell tales—even against those other meanies who are trying to do us wrong.

From the Japanese perspective, the corporate "rightness" exhibited by IGC and worn so openly on the sleeves of company personnel was a slap in the face to the manner in which business was conducted in Japan, and indeed the rest of the world.

Now was the time for payback. IGC would not only be made to look foolish, but they would be severely hurt financially, and if all went according to plan, lose the technological edge they appeared to be gaining—lose it for this century, and perhaps forever.

Shinogara smiled as he watched the setting sun—setting for IGC, but rising for Japan.

The Tojo virus!

From the first day of his assignment—the crown jewel in a long and distinguished career—there had been no question what he would call the virus.

It will be Tojo's revenge.

Although Shinogara had been but a boy in a man's uniform he was old enough to still feel the hot flush and shame of defeat. Hideki Tojo—premier, and yes, dictator—had been the Japanese general who had authorized the attack on Pearl Harbor. Later, as prime minister, it had been Tojo who had resolutely demanded that the war be fought to the last beach, to the last man. And it had been Hideki Tojo who had been captured, convicted, and executed by the United States military.

It was with reverence that Makato Shinogara attached the name of the fallen general to a project that would be referred to in Pearl Harbor terms by its victims for years to come. The electronic sabotage would be Tojo's legacy.

Ransom? Yes, there will be a ransom.

Shinogara smiled. But not money. No, that would be messy—too easy to trace. Besides, what would they ask for? Five billion—ten billion—how much? Electronically transferred? To where? The digital fingerprints could be tracked, people would and could be held accountable. IGC could afford ten billion and stay afloat as a company. Shinogara's objective was on a higher plane, world domination of the computer marketplace.

I will have their technology! I will rob them of their souls!

Shinogara's plan would cripple, perhaps topple, the American computer giant. November 19—the day before the American Thanksgiving holiday—is V-I Day.

Shinogara smiled. He had been a frail boy of twelve, too young to serve, but not too young to understand the pain and humiliation of V-J Day. . . . This time it would be victory over IGC.

Revenge would be sweet.

Marcia absentmindedly twirled the ice in her gin and tonic with a slender silver stirrer. At street level, twenty floors below, it was hot, uncharacteristically so. But at penthouse level there was just enough breeze to keep her at the edge of perspiration. A pair of sunglasses was all she wore as she alternated her attention between a trashy romance novel, now strategically placed in her lap, the gin and tonic, and her view of Coit Tower, the Bay Bridge, and far-off Oakland. She took a long sip from her drink and leaned back in her soft lounge chair and closed her eyes. She was tired. The three weeks in Dallas had been emotionally and physically draining on everyone. Last week had been as tough as any they'd gone through since she started the business.

The equipment truck had arrived just that morning. Tony and Bill hadn't let any dust settle before they'd picked up their checks and split, Tony to Reno and Bill to a quiet spot down the coastline toward Big Sur. Where the girls went was their own business—just as long as they were back in town in two weeks to get started again.

"How about something down and dirty next time?" had been the general consensus—something simple, something short!

The hot sun felt good. Perspiration started to run off her slender body, taking with it the stress of the last week. She had a choice of several jobs. Think about it later, girl. Concentrate on those rays.

Her phone rang.

My private number, she noted.

Droplets of perspiration poised delicately on her nipples and waited for just the slightest of movements, seemingly anxious to fall onto her flat, tan stomach.

"Yes?" she answered with a who-is-this in her voice. The attached recorder was activated with the first voice.

"Miss Lee? This is Makato Shinogara. I assume you have verified our funds transfer."

Marcia sat up in her lounger, alert. Droplets of perspiration fell from her breasts onto her legs. She put down her drink. Why was Shinogara calling her?

"Yes, thank you. Everything went very smoothly," she replied cautiously.

"Well, I wanted to say again how much we appreciated your work in Dallas."

"Thank you."

Why are you calling? she wondered.

"Ah, I wish everything was going smoothly with our Mr. Colby. He's proven to be somewhat . . . difficult."

"I'm sorry to hear that," Marcia sympathized.

"Yes, it is. I wonder if you would be receptive to a second contract—to keep Mr. Colby in the mood to cooperate."

"I have no obligation to accept, Mr. Shinogara. You know that. I told you in Los Angeles that I didn't like what happened to Zack Colby."

"Yes, I am aware of your—concern. I'm sure that will make Mr. Colby feel that much better. Unfortunately, we're in such a position that Mr. Colby either cooperates or . . . we will have to look at—other—solutions," replied Shinogara, no longer the smiling businessman.

Marcia returned Shinogara's coolness.

"When we first met, you said you were businessmen—not thugs. What are you implying, Mr. Shinogara?"

"I will be blunt. If it comes to a point where we're faced with either completing our project or protecting Mr. Colby's safety, I'm afraid we'll be forced to choose the former. From what I've seen, Mr. Colby will do anything you tell him. Whether he knows it or not, it's in his best interest that he listen to you. Money has a way of soothing a conscience, Miss Lee. It will be worth your while."

"How much worth my while?" Marcia asked, immediately wanting to kick herself for turning on her principles.

"Two million dollars," Shinogara replied.

Shit. The amount was much more than she ever thought he'd say.

"We're planning a status meeting in Denver, tomorrow afternoon. We'd like you to attend."

"What if I don't like it?" Marcia asked. "Are you going to threaten me, too?" she said with undisguised sarcasm.

"There are no threats, Miss Lee. We each must do what we must do—to follow our own consciences. If you have some professional concern about Mr. Colby, then perhaps you should consider our offer. Two million dollars is a great deal of money. With regard to your question—we'll reach a point and ask if you want to continue. If you say yes, then you are part of our team, and you assume the risks and responsibilities that go along with it. If you say no, then you leave and all is forgotten."

Absentmindedly Marcia scratched the top of her right breast without replying.

"You know that you only have a certain number of years in your business until your . . . assets are depleted. Mr. Colby is vital to the success of our operation, but he already knows too much. He either sees this to the end or . . ."

"All right, all right—give me a fucking break. I accept."

"Yes, I hoped you would. A limo will be by to pick you up tomorrow morning at eight."

"There will be two of us. A Mr. Turner will accompany me."

"As you wish. Good day, Miss Lee," said a very proper Makato Shinogara.

Marcia picked up her novel and threw it across the patio in disgust.

"Well, shit."

"You know, David is a really nice guy—I like him," said Cheryl, busy putting the finishing touches on her

If It's Thursday It Must Be Meat Loaf. "You ought to have him over for dinner one night—have him stay overnight—we've got plenty of room."

I'll kill the little fucker first, Zack swore silently.

It had been a hard day for Zack—a hard three days. His psyche was being slowly shredded. The normal sights and sounds of everyday life began to grate on him. His senses were set on edge—everything became as irritating as the shriek of a knife being sharpened or a Styrofoam cup being torn into tiny pieces. It took all of his concentration to not snap at Cheryl, although he'd been sharp to the children once or twice for no reason.

And then there were the blackouts—or fuzz-outs as he thought of them, moments when his eyesight seemed to . . . *thicken* was the only word he could think of. Things were there one minute, then sort-of there the next. Time would jump in minutes. This morning before David came, there was a whole hour lost. He'd come out of it—whatever *it* was—and found himself holding on to the arm rest of his chair in a death grip, and he was drenched with sweat.

What the hell's happening to me? he wondered.

There was no logical explanation—just as there was no logical explanation for why he was in the fix he was in.

Why me? God, why me?

Twice in the past week Zack had thought of suicide. He'd heard a voice, whose he couldn't tell.

It's the only way, Jack. Just go—fuck them all. Just go.

God, he was scared.

An instant before the phone rang Marcia looked up from her packing to watch the sun's reflection on the tall downtown buildings. The various hues of shielded glass caused a jumble of reflections that made it difficult to tell what was real and what wasn't. Still, it was strikingly beautiful. But Marcia's musing was interrupted by the phone, which she answered with some irritation. The tone of the ring indicated that Benson was calling from the guard desk.

"Yes, Benson—what is it?"

"A caller, Miss Lee. *Callers,* actually. A Mr. Wu and a Mr. Chimichanga."

"A mister *what?*" said Marcia, almost laughing at the odd names.

"Mr. Wu said he apologized for the intrusion, and for the lack of an appointment, but that he and Mr. Chimichanga would like to see you on a matter of importance."

"I'm sorry, Benson. I can't see them now. I'm busy," Marcia dismissed the guard.

"Mr. Wu thought you might say that. He says he wants to talk to you about a Mr. Shinogara," said the guard in a monotone.

A puzzled look crossed Marcia's face. It was nearly the last thing she expected Benson to say. She stopped in midpack, the telephone in one hand, a handful of colorful underwear in the other. There was no sense in involving Benson in the conversation any further. She wanted to tell Benson to search them for weapons or tape recorders, but Benson didn't need to dwell on what kind of business the penthouse lady was into. The Executive House was wired with panic button capability. Like many of the other apartments, Marcia could set off alarms from nearly every room.

"Send them up," she told Benson, hanging up.

Marcia walked from her bedroom down a short hall to the carpeted sunken living-dining room area, up two

141

steps, then across the elegant black marbled foyer to the elevator, which was nearly invisible, its doors designed in the same ornate pattern as the surrounding wall. She stood near the door and could hear the mechanism whir as it brought her guests up the twenty floors, finally reaching its destination with a soft announcing *ding*. The door whooshed open and out stepped as unlikely a pair of men as Marcia could have imagined.

An old Chinaman and an ugly pit bull, she thought.

Marcia wore a white pants suit and three-inch heels, which made her seem taller than her five-foot-eight frame. As it was, she was taller than the Chinaman and equal in height to the pit bull, although the thick man outweighed her by at least a hundred pounds. The ugly brute was obviously a bodyguard. Marcia's senses constantly calculated the distance from and effort required to get to the nearest panic button.

"Miss Lee? My name is Xiang Wu. This is Mr. Chimichanga, my associate.

Marcia offered the pair neither her hand in greeting nor the softness of her comfortable living room to sit.

"Do I know you, Mr. Wu?" Marcia asked, business-like.

Wu casually looked around Marcia's beautifully appointed apartment without answering directly. Marcia's eyes went from Wu to Chimichanga, whose stare was fixed on Marcia's breasts, a feeling that made her slightly uncomfortable.

"Very nice," Wu commented. "You've done well."

Marcia's question floated unanswered in the open space of the foyer. She declined to follow Wu into idle chitchat and made no reply to the compliment; instead she waited for him to answer. Wu's eyes came back to her. The small twinkle of pleasantness had turned cooler.

142

"Oh, most likely not. I am a financier. If my contacts are correct, most of your money has been invested in overseas accounts—of the Swiss variety," Wu replied in a matter-of-fact fashion.

Marcia was taken aback, inadvertently dropping her mask of confidence, revealing concern.

Who is this joker?

"How do you know that?"

Chimichanga moved ever so slightly closer to Marcia and Wu. Marcia reacted by moving back one step closer to the living room.

"It is my job to know, Miss Lee. Please don't be alarmed. Mr. Chimichanga is a business associate, although like your Mr. Turner—who is . . . not here, I believe—he has at times in his career done extensive . . . physical activity."

The threat was obvious. Marcia's breath seemed to be stuck in her throat. Her heartbeat picked up. Her skin prickled.

"I'm going to have to ask you gentlemen to leave," Marcia said firmly, her hand reached out for the elevator call button.

"I'm here on business Miss Lee, nothing more. I represent certain offshore interests—investors who are very interested in the plans of Makato Shinogara. I have made a practice over the years of making my investors' interests my interests. Therefore, I am interested in what Makato Shinogara is doing—as is Mr. Chimichanga."

Marcia started to protest, but Wu held up his hand.

"Please, Miss Lee. My investors have asked me to keep track of the comings and goings of Mr. Shinogara and his people. I've done this for three years now. I'm well aware of his home in Los Angeles, his programming staff, and his interest in IGC. But, recently this has become difficult."

Wu's words froze Marcia. Her hand was halfway to the alarm button, but her feet were leaden. Wu reached inside his coat jacket and pulled out an envelope, then handed it to Marcia, who came out of her brief stupor. Inside the yellow envelope was a series of glossy prints. Marcia shuffled through the pictures as Wu continued.

"Needless to say, we were very surprised to see you arrive on the afternoon of September 26. Although you and I have never done business before, I am well aware of your special . . . *talents*. As you can see, Mr. Chimichanga's men followed you to the suburbs of Dallas, where most of these photos were taken. Those, as you can see, were taken in Los Angeles coming to and from Shinogara's estate in Palos Verdes—a very nice place, I might add. The Japanese government paid over six million dollars to put Shinogara up in style."

They were all there: Marcia entering the estate, Marcia shaking hands with Shinogara, Marcia at the airport, Marcia and Joe in San Francisco, David and Marcia in Dallas. Marcia stopped when she came to the pictures of her and Zack. One picture of Zack showed an expression on his face that was a cross between astonishment and puppy love.

"OK, you've done your homework well. But what do you want?" Marcia said, as she handed the photos back to Wu.

"A simple request. We want to know what Makato Shinogara is planning to do. When, where, and how," replied Wu quickly.

"I never discuss a client's business with anybody else," Marcia declined politely. "How do you know all this. Better yet, *why* do you know it?" she asked.

"We know a great deal about Mr. Shinogara. For ex-

144

ample, he employs approximately thirty people on the grounds of his estate. His backing comes from the Japanese government through a group of powerful Japanese industrialists, all with the same objective — the destruction of IGC as an international corporation. Funding for the project began shortly after several major Japanese companies were discovered stealing trade secrets from IGC. Shortly thereafter, IGC precipitated the U.S. government's action against the Japanese for flooding the American market with low cost computer memory chips, nearly putting several major American companies out of business."

"So?" Marcia shrugged her shoulders. "Who cares?"

"I'm sure the FBI would care — to name one. A group of *foreigners*" — Wu spit the word out with sarcasm — "plans to harm an important American corporation. I'm sure that IGC officials would be interested — as well as their competitors. Perhaps even some investors would be interested."

Marcia sensed that Wu had spoken more than he had intended to.

Investors would be interested, she thought. This slime is a money-bagger.

"You want me to be a double agent?" Marcia asked without surprise.

"That's perhaps a bit dramatic, but yes, I think it fits."

Marcia's hands slipped over the panic button and found the elevator call, which she pressed.

"The answer's no. Now, you'll have to leave."

Chimichanga put his hand on Marcia's arm; his touch repulsed her. She tried to draw back but the pug's grip was firm.

"Get your hands off me!" Marcia said with a cold voice.

Wu nodded and Chimichanga withdrew.

"Before the elevator returns I hope you'll reconsider, Miss Lee. You are, as you Americans might say, in the big leagues now," said Wu.

"Are you threatening me, Mr. Wu?"

"Yes, I am. You have access to information that I need. I *must* have it—I *will* have it . . . one way or the other—with your cooperation, or without it. This is why I'm so fortunate to have Mr. Chimichanga as an associate. His methods are . . . thorough."

The whir of the elevator came closer.

"On a more pleasant note, my investors are willing to be very generous for this information. After all, we would like your full cooperation," Wu smiled unctuously.

"How generous?" asked Marcia.

"Three million dollars. Half now, half with the information."

Three million dollars?

"You're joking?"

"I'm not a humorous man by nature, Miss Lee," Wu replied.

The elevator came to Marcia's apartment, softly dinged, and opened.

No wasn't the right answer.

Chimichanga's hands twitched. Marcia could still feel the impression of his thick fingers on her arm.

"One-six-four-eight-eight-two. My account at the Bank of Geneva. I'll call tomorrow to verify the deposit," Marcia said in a clear voice, one that didn't betray the fear in her gut.

"Very good, Miss Lee. You've made the right decision. I'd much rather pay you than . . ." Wu's voice trailed off as he stepped inside the elevator.

Wu and Chimichanga exchanged a look that said leave her alone—for now, a look that Marcia saw. Chimichanga seemed to be disappointed, but followed

Wu into the elevator.

"How do I contact you?" Marcia asked.

Wu handed her a plain business card with his address and two telephone numbers, one a FAX.

"You may reach me at these numbers. I assume you will be returning to Cheyenne soon. It appears that Mr. Colby is quite enamored of you—and who can blame him, Miss Lee," Wu said with a smile, and bowed slightly.

The elevator doors softly closed. Marcia saw the reflection of herself in the mirror.

What have I gotten myself into?

Chapter Three
Offshore Interests

Patterned after the Hyatt Regency architecture, the middle of the Embassy Suites Hotel was a massive ten-story atrium with hanging plants on all levels. Sunlight filtered through the large skylight and gave the entire hotel a warm, pleasant feeling. The chirping of happy birds added to the ambience, although the birds were on tape, to avoid health problems. Marcia looked down to the cobblestone-paved courtyard below. The complimentary evening happy hour was winding down.

"Miss Lee, so good to see you again," Shinogara said graciously. "Is everything to your satisfaction?"

"Yes, thank you. We *do* get around, don't we Mr. Shinogara?" Marcia replied, flashing her best smile.

"I have a private room set up for us, if you don't mind coming this way." Shinogara held out his arm, then glanced back to see that Joe followed her.

"I don't think your assistant will be required," Shinogara said.

"Oh?" Marcia replied.

"Yes. We've rearranged the order of things to accommodate you. Your piece of the meeting is relatively small—there are many details to be discussed. They would bore you. The flight . . . you must be tired," said Makato Shinogara, all-knowing.

Marcia grabbed Shinogara's arm with an iron grip. Joe stood alert behind her. She leaned into him and angrily whispered between clenched teeth.

"I won't be patronized."

Shinogara was genuinely astonished. The young woman was intense. Shinogara looked around to see if anybody was within listening distance.

"I don't care how much money you're paying me—I want to know what's going on, when it's going on, and why it's going on. If I don't understand something, I'll ask a fucking question. If it's boring and I don't need to know it, I'll leave. But, I'll make that decision—understand?"

Marcia gripped his arm so tightly that it hurt the older man.

"First you threaten me, then you treat me like a moron. How dare you! I won't stand for it, Shinogara. You can keep your money. I can pay for my own way home, thanks."

Marcia released her hold. Shinogara took two steps backward and bumped against a door in a natural reaction to her physical and verbal attack. He was astonished at her ferocity.

"Get the bags, Joe. We're going home."

Marcia headed down the hallway toward the center of the building. Joe looked at Shinogara, then pushed past the smaller man and walked toward the pile of luggage.

"Miss Lee . . . Miss Lee . . . please . . . *please!*" Shinogara shouted as softly as he could.

Marcia rounded the corner and headed for the elevator. She pressed the button and could hear the whine of the motors as the glass box glided up to the tenth floor, and arrived with a soft ding.

"Miss Lee . . . *please.*"

Like the actress she was, Marcia got into the elevator and froze Shinogara in his tracks with the look of death. Before the elevator doors began to close she stepped out. Joe had all the suitcases in his arms, but rather than ask what the hell was going on, simply stopped and dropped them in the middle of the corridor, without a word.

The elevator doors closed behind her.

"I . . . I seem to have underestimated you, Miss Lee. Given what you've done so far, I'm not sure why. Perhaps it is your femininity. I don't have women working in my organization — all my employees are men, and that's as it should be. However, this is a special case. Your type of work is . . . your type of work requires a woman's skill. Please, to the meeting — and Mr. Turner is welcome to attend," Shinogara said with a bow.

The meeting room was small but plush. When the door closed behind there was no sound of the hustle and bustle down in the lobby. At one end was a flip chart stand, behind it a fully stocked kitchen and bar. A clean whiteboard with markers had been placed on one wall. In addition to Shinogara and David, there were four other men at the meeting, who in unison had risen when Marcia entered the room.

"Please be seated, gentlemen," Marcia smiled.

"Seated next to David are Robert Fujikawa and Albert Nojiri, systems programmers who report to David. You remember Mr. Yamamoto and Mr. Sukawa," introduced Shinogara.

"Gentlemen," Marcia nodded.

"We'll begin the meeting by explaining why we've asked for your continuing assistance and exactly what it is we want you to do for us. At the end of that time I'll ask if you want to offer your assistance at the contract price we've negotiated. If your answer is no, then you'll be asked to leave. If your answer is yes, then I'll ask you the second question. In the hallway just now you strongly indicated your desire to be a member of the team, to understand the scope of the mission. Certain knowledge,

Miss Lee, comes at the price of risk."

All eyes were on Marcia.

"In business terms, Miss Lee, this is called a planning session, or a strategy session. We'll be discussing details of our operation that are . . . confidential. We're businessmen, Miss Lee. This operation involves fortunes. The future of our companies . . . no, the *existence* of them, depends on its success. Three weeks ago you asked me a question — what degree of risk are we willing to take to ensure the success. You may remember my response. Whatever it takes." Shinogara leaned over his end of the desk toward her.

Marcia nodded. Yes, she remembered.

Yes, this is hardball time, she thought. He's giving you an out, Marcia. But . . . he's also explaining the rules.

"If you say yes to my second question — that yes you would like to stay and be part of the team — then you also at that point assume the same risks of the operation. Those risks include jail, and under certain circumstances, physical harm — perhaps even death. We have worked on this project for seven years, Miss Lee. We can't afford to have it compromised at this point. We'll do whatever it takes to protect ourselves and the operation. Do you understand?"

Marcia didn't blink an eye.

"Yes."

"Good. David — " Shinogara turned the meeting over to David, who stood up at the front of the table.

"Three days after his return from Dallas we met with Zack at a motel on the outskirts of Cheyenne. By the end of the meeting he was in near shock, as you can imagine. At the time we thought he was convinced he had no choice but to do what we told him to do. But since then there have been other times when he seems to forget — and he only remembers when a physical threat is applied. I don't know if it's a personality conflict or if there's something inside his head that's blocking out reality—"

"Which is?" asked Marcia.

"We could drop him off the edge of the earth and down a black hole."

"Can you bail out?"

Shinogara answered for David.

"Technically . . . yes, we can. This is a long-term operation, Miss Lee. The stakes are quite high. We can afford to pull back. But, as I discussed with you, we'd be faced with several unpleasant alternatives, one of which is the disposal of Mr. Colby—perhaps his family."

Marcia's eyebrows raised.

"Yes, we may be businessmen, Miss Lee—but the stakes in this business are very high. We'll do whatever it takes to win. If Mr. Colby's death . . . or *anyone's* death is required as a last resort . . . then so be it. We don't want him to share his troubles with his wife. His thoughts must be his own."

"And you want me to keep his mind occupied?" asked Marcia.

"Yes. The more he becomes involved with you, the less likely it is that he'll confide in his wife—or in IGC. As it stands now we believe he's weighing the consequences. And that will be fatal—to our plans . . . and to him."

Marcia felt herself sinking into a bog. Every step took her further into the morass, away from safety. She couldn't go back. There was no back to go to.

It's too late to be a good girl, Marcia, she told herself, too late to say you're sorry—no thanks, I know I shouldn't have gotten into this business in the first place. Say no and Wu lets that Neanderthal loose. Say yes and you're in the middle of industrial espionage, blackmail, and maybe murder. Give yourself up and you're in jail for the rest of your life. Run and they'll find you.

Marcia hardly paid attention to what David was saying.

"By Thursday of last week, I realized that Zack needed a short leash. He needed to be followed, to be contacted every day — and I had to do it. I found that he wasn't responding to me. There were times when I felt I was on the verge of losing him, and I think it was more me than anything else. I think Zack has such a negative reaction to me that it's getting in the way of his good senses. More importantly, I've found that I'm spending too much time worrying and following up on him, and not enough on our mission. I am a project leader, a programmer . . . not a nursemaid. There is much to do, and just enough time to do it."

"How long?" Marcia asked.

David looked at Shinogara, who nodded.

"November 19. Less than a month," replied David.

"Is that the end of it?" asked Marcia.

"From your standpoint, yes," Shinogara replied. "Once the operation has gone past the nineteenth, we'll be past the point of no return."

"And you'll be gone," Marcia interrupted.

"Yes — and we'll be gone," Shinogara acknowledged.

"So I don't need to stay until the nineteenth? My piece of this will be over sometime before then?"

Shinogara considered the questions.

"Yes."

"What about Zack Colby?"

"We've offered him a cash settlement — a half million. We've shown him the money."

Marcia could hardly believe Shinogara could keep a straight face and say the words.

There's no way he's going to let Zack loose with a half million in cash, she thought. No way. He's going to kill Zack. And he'll do the same to you.

153

"This brings me to my first question, Miss Lee. Do you wish to offer your services at the price we've discussed?"

"Yes," said Marcia.

I have no other choice.

"Then we have an agreement. I'll make the financial arrangements this evening," Shinogara paused. "Now, Miss Lee . . . you've had time to think about the second question."

"Yes. Clearly, there is no financial benefit to me to be more deeply involved with your operation — unless you tell me something otherwise. I'm going to get paid to do a job. But I wasn't going to say yes to the first question without saying yes to the second. If this operation is as important — as potentially dangerous, then I need to have as much information as possible, so that I can anticipate what may happen. If there are enemies or roadblocks ahead of me, I can't see them unless I know what to expect. I may not be interested in all the details, Mr. Shinogara, but I feel I need to have the option to hear them. So I've said yes to your money. Now I'll say yes to the responsibilities — and the risks," Marcia replied.

"So be it," nodded Shinogara. "Then we should begin our meeting, don't you think, David?"

Kimura stood up, then slid a typed piece of paper down the table to Marcia. It was filled with computer terms and definitions. Marcia scanned the paper and set it in front of her. David walked to the whiteboard and began to draw.

"We know that within IGC, the large majority of PCs are connected to mainframe computers. There are over fourteen hundred mainframe computers in this network, worldwide. In the last three years, in an effort to reduce the number of conflicting and obsolete systems, IGC has consolidated its various networks into one massive network. Thus, nearly all of IGC's internal applications may be reached from a single computer terminal.

"Our objective is to cripple these systems, to make them unusable . . . to bring IGC to its knees. PC productivity programs such as word processing, spreadsheets, data bases, will all be locked out — as will be access to informational data bases used by salesmen and systems engineers. Any information that an IGCer has put into a personal computer or PROFS library will be inaccessible.

"The company will come to a grinding halt. IGC will have two choices — comply with our list of demands, or replace their entire internal computer network. In our opinion, they'll have no choice. They may go kicking and screaming, but they'll give in. They'll give in because their major customers will demand it. You see, as IGC improved its internal systems it linked up all of its major customers at the same time. Now, customer executives may send electronic mail directly to their IGC salesman. That same executive can browse IGC's remote computers for the latest in product announcements, the answers to technical questions, and even receive IGC's monthly billing in a PC file format."

"I don't understand," Marcia interrupted. "Are you going to all this effort just for revenge? Is that it? You talk about a ransom — why would anybody pay you *after* you've destroyed their systems? It doesn't make sense."

"Our virus doesn't destroy data — it captures them, makes them unusable. We're going to hold IGC's data hostage," David said in a soft, clear voice. "Destroyed data can't be ransomed. If we were out for mere vengeance, there would be no ransom. We would destroy IGC's systems and move on."

Marcia knew enough about business to know that IGC was a fifty billion-dollar-a-year company with enough clean-cut salesmen that it seemed like there was one on every street corner.

155

."How much are you playing for here, David? How much is your ransom? How can you expect to get away with it?" asked Marcia, concerned.

The group laughed, including Shinogara, who spoke.

"You don't walk up to a company like IGC and put a gun to their head and say give me all your money, Miss Lee. Not when they *own* the banks. All you'll end up with is — how do you call it — funny-money. Money leaves tracks in a computer, just like a robber in the night with muddy shoes. How would we possibly spend twenty billion dollars — or fifty billion dollars? How would we store it? *Where* would we store it? The world would know who we were. No, our ransom is IGC's *technology* — its *thoughts* — its *future*. Even more important than money in the long run. We don't need to go into details with you. Continue, David."

Billions of dollars? Marcia wondered. Thoughts? Future? Technology? If this is what Shinogara wants, what the hell does Xiang Wu want?

Marcia began to feel more than a little uncomfortable, like the small-time but well-paid hooker she was. David moved over to the whiteboard and began to sketch, using different colored markers.

"Think of this . . . our computer . . . Zack's computer . . . calls IGC central maintenance in Endicott and not only sends a message, but also manages to send a one-block burst of data that sticks on the concentrator taking the calls. The next sick 9350 to call in gets a return message that updates its profile, gets our message, and the next day dials (307) 876-1126, which is the telephone number for Zack Colby's demo 9350. Included in it are the file transfer of several PC and 9350 files, none of which encourages peace and prosperity," David elaborated, obviously having enormous fun. "We should be able to even transmit our encryption program."

David stopped and began to write a number on the

board, beginning on the far left side:

7,958,580,674,663,953,034,919,936

"In order to reactivate one of their computers, the user must know the key — the decryption code that will unlock the program. There are twenty-six alphabetic characters and ten numerics, for a total of thirty-six possibilities. Thirty-six to the power of sixteen is this number," David said.

Marcia was staggered at the number. Hundreds, thousands, millions, billions . . . what comes after billions? Trillions! Yes, trillions. What comes after trillions? I don't know. And what comes after that? And after that? And after that? I don't know.

"While this is indeed a number, to you and me it's no more than an abstraction — it has no meaning. While a bank of fast computers might eventually come up with the right combination, the practicalities of doing so on a personal computer would be fruitless.

"Five years ago we wouldn't have been able to attempt this — we couldn't — because IGC was still using fixed function displays, the old 3278/79 terminals. PROFS wasn't as sophisticated, neither were the communications to the mainframe. Now they have intelligent terminals — PCs — newer and smarter communications controllers, better host and PC software. Three years from now, it'll even be easier — for the *first* person to do it. Once we do this, the whole field of computer security will be changed. The next people to try such a scheme will have a much more difficult time.

"Do you know how many *successful* sky jackings there have been? Ever?" David asked, his eyes going from one man to the next, then resting on Marcia's. *"One.* D. B. Cooper was the only man to ever get away clean from a skyjacking — and he got away with it because he was the *first!"*

Marcia wasn't following everything, but she wasn't

157

lost.

"Our program is sitting on Zack Colby's disk file someplace in the basement of the IGC building in Denver. There are approximately 250,000 people in domestic IGC. When you throw out the manufacturing and service employees, you're down to roughly fifty thousand—half of whom work in branch offices, nearly all with terminals. The other half work in area, regional, and headquarters offices.

"In the last three days, while logged on to the system in Denver, we've accumulated nearly eight thousand names and PROFS mailing addresses. We estimate it will take us approximately ten days to capture all of the addresses in the system. We'll have the capability of sending a note to any address within IGC's system.

"At nine-thirty A.M. Central Standard Time, on November 19, all screens will blank and an ominous message will appear on the screen. The encryption program will execute, encrypting all files, all directories, all data, all applications. At the same moment on the local VM system, each user's A disk will execute our encryption application, which will prevent any use of the programs until the right key, or password, is issued. The program isn't illegal, nor is the action. The files haven't been illegally corrupted or accessed. They've simply become protected!

"To summarize, we're in very good condition. We have access to IGC systems and have started to abstract information. The encryption program we have selected for the mainframe computers can be delivered and executed, nearly without change. We have a chance to infiltrate IGC Endicott and the maintenance program on the 9350. Any IGC customer who has access to PROFS will at some point in time receive a coated pill, a pseudomessage from IGC that has with it one or both of our programs. Our PC program needs some testing, but we're well ahead of schedule."

Shinogara stood up.

"Thank you, David. At long last we can see the end of the journey," said Shinogara, clapping softly. Shinogara continued. "Now, we will hear from Mr. Yamamoto, who will discuss Phase Two."

Shinogara sat down and the stone-faced Yamamoto stood up.

"Thank you. Very good David," Yamamoto complimented. "You must feel very . . . satisfied after all these years."

"Thank you . . . I do," said David.

These people are seriously talking, Marcia thought, about the economic takeover, by blackmail, of the sixth largest company in the United States. A company whose net income is more than all but seven countries in the world.

Marcia might have been a high-priced slut, but that didn't mean she couldn't read. Copies of *Forbes*, *Fortune*, and *Business Week* weren't on her glass-covered coffee table for nothing. Nor was the *Wall Street Journal*.

Yamamoto started to describe Phase Two.

"At precisely nine-thirty A.M. Central Standard Time, the phones will begin to ring at IGC," he smiled. "Ring isn't exactly the correct description. Peal, inundate, annoy . . . these are better words. Thanks to David—actually to Mr. Colby—we have a current listing of IGC's internal telephone numbers. The internal telephone book lists not only the location of each office, but who the top managers are. For the marketing branch offices they are kind enough to include the major account these managers support. There are certain offices that bear more attention than others." Yamamoto held up the latest *IGC Internal Field Directory*. "IGC has centralized into one building in New York — a *single* telephone exchange to attack. In Bethesda, Maryland, there are nearly a thousand people on the 301-564-2000 exchange. The same applies all across the country. We've analyzed it and come to the conclusion that if we concentrate our efforts in thirty-five buildings, we'll bring the internal communications of IGC to a standstill."

Marcia listened in a state of near astonishment as Yamamoto described how the telephone system, something called PhoneMail, would be inundated with calls, each leaving an annoying high-pitched signal as its message.

"Of these locations, we think twelve are critical—the new IGC building in Manhattan; the National Federal Marketing operations in Bethesda, Maryland; One IGC Plaza in Chicago; 425 Market in San Francisco; 33 Westchester in White Plains, New York; Atlanta Central; 500 Broadway in St. Louis; 11100 Santa Monica Boulevard in Century City, Los Angeles; One Main Place in Dallas; 1200 Fifth Avenue in Seattle; Old Apple Orchard Drive in Armonk, New York; Boston Downtown; and the Southfield, Michigan office outside Detroit.

"We'll be in place by the middle of November, and ready to go by the nineteenth."

Yamamoto sat down to the thanks of Makato Shinogara.

"We have also been working on Phase Three," said Shinogara, nodding to Sukawa.

"It's been my pleasure to come up with other ways to convince IGC's management that we're serious—in case we aren't taken seriously with our first two attacks. The things we've come up with are as harmless as junk mail and as serious as letter bombs. With the names and internal addresses of all IGC employees, we could prepare a tape and send it to all the advertisers in the top twenty computer magazines—a ready list, preprepared for

160

mailing labels printing. If each IGC employee receives a thousand pieces of junk mail per year—multiplied by a thousand employees in a building—just *sorting* the mail would be difficult, much less delivering it. And it would all have to be processed. What if there was a real order from a real customer in all the junk?

"Since we've not only the mailing address but also the telephone numbers, a related annoyance would be the increase in unsolicited telephone calls from vendors."

Sukawa turned to Shinogara.

"In our discussions with IGC management, you may want to include the possibility of letter bombs. Buried in all the junk mail could very easily be a small package with an explosive powerful enough to kill someone, or severely injure them. It could come in any fashion—UPS, Federal Express, or U.S. mail.

"We haven't done anything down this line yet, and it would take a great deal of effort, but now that we have the names and location of employees, in smaller cities it would be possible to find out the home telephone numbers of many of them. Some sort of regular harassment could be started, perhaps even with automatic dialing.

"We have examples of IGC letterhead paper. Although a reputable printer wouldn't attempt to reproduce the corporate paper, we're not under such guidelines. We could begin to inundate the local business communities with orders of goods and services—everything from pizzas to printers.

"With most of our people working on Phase Two, these ideas haven't gone past the development stage. But they're all possible, and can be implemented if necessary—if we switch our resources."

Sukawa sat down to the thanks of a smiling Makato Shinogara.

"Very good. Very good! After eight years we can finally see our work pay off! V-I Day is soon at hand!

There is much work to be done—let nothing stand in your way. Do whatever it takes to get your jobs done! Whatever it takes!"

Maybe it's all over. Maybe they're gone.
Maybe it was a dream.

And maybe there's a tooth fairy.

In the darkness of his basement, Zack sat in one of his comfortable chairs, a chair that hadn't cushioned the butt of a customer in nearly a month.

Maybe they were gone. David hadn't been to the house in the last four days. He hadn't even checked in. He'd done what David had asked him to do. He'd gotten the latest programming manuals for the 9350 and had given David the internal phone directory last Friday. He'd left the machines on twenty-four hours a day, and had told Cheryl not, repeat, *not* to come downstairs for any reason. Today he'd sent a PROFS note to Endicott to register the demo unit and request the maintenance patch. "It's a great selling feature," he'd said in the note, nearly gagging.

Turn yourself in, he thought. Call Scotty!

Behind him, the 9350 hummed merrily in the background, its console lights blinking with communications.

"Zack?" Cheryl shouted downstairs. "Can we go out to dinner? I can get a sitter," she said, a trace of hope in her voice.

Why not? he thought.

Cheryl was pleased and immediately went to the phone, somehow getting one of the high school girls on her sitter list to come over on short notice. Going out with the kids wasn't *going out*. An hour later they were halfway through the first of two planned bottles of wine—each glad to be with the other, and glad to be out

162

of the house. Zack now hated the house, hated the neighborhood, hated Cheyenne — and certainly didn't feel too good about himself. *What to do* was a mental buzzard that hovered over his every thought. Still, he managed to put on a good face with Cheryl. They both enjoyed Torino's, especially the pasta dishes. The portions were huge and came smothered in a delicious rich garlic sauce. The wine made Zack's spirits artificially soar.

The restaurant was about two-thirds filled, which was crowded for a Wednesday night. At the second or third gay here's-to-you toast, with their food half-eaten, and the ambience high, Zack's eyes focused on the booth directly behind Cheryl.

It can't be!

Torino's was no different from other restaurants — cleanliness was covered in a mask of darkened atmosphere. Sitting in a booth, illuminated by a ray of overhead light, was Marcia. In her left hand she held a delicately fluted glass of wine. Her stare was locked on him, her gaze burned the air over Cheryl's right shoulder, and into his eyes. Zack's face registered every degree of panic imaginable.

Oh God she's going to come over here oh please don't let her oh please oh shit why is she here oh my God is she beautiful please don't come over don't say anything I didn't mean it.

Marcia wore a simple sweater and skirt, appropriate for a casual dinner in Cheyenne. Her raven black hair was worn full and to her shoulders. Although not flashy, her choice of lipstick made her lips seem moist even from Zack's perspective across the room. Their eyes locked, and Marcia tipped her glass to him in a salute while at the same time she softly rubbed her right index finger on the tip of her left breast. The motion was smooth and over in an instant, imperceptible to everyone but Zack.

Zack dropped his half-filled wine glass right into the middle of the table, where of course the worst that could happen, did. As noisily as possible, the glass smashed into the serving dish, broke, and scattered its red stain in all directions. Since their table was in the middle of the room, the distraction and embarrassment were maximized—nearly to the point of pain. Waiters seemed to come out of midair and hovered with napkins, patting and drying what they could. After a few moments of terrible confusion and profuse apologies, Zack looked up.

She's gone!

Marcia had left. The tall fluted glass was all that remained. Zack's heart thrashed, the color in his face changed from pale to red to pale to pink in less than five minutes. He saw and talked to Cheryl through a mental mask, not really seeing or hearing her.

"Are you OK?" she asked.

Zack could tell that she was worried. Without saying so, her eyes reflected "what's wrong?"

Dinner was ruined, and they left. The sitter was surprised to see them back so soon.

"Were they good?" asked Cheryl.

"They were fine. . . . Oh, yes . . . somebody came by, just after you left," said the young girl as she put on her jacket to leave.

Zack's heart, which had finally parked itself after a prolonged period in overdrive, began to pick up speed again. The nerve endings from his feet to his fingers began to prickle.

"Oh?" questioned Cheryl. "Did you know him?"

"Her. And I didn't know her. She asked for you, though," said the girl.

"Me?" said Zack.

"No . . . for Mrs. Colby. A pretty lady. She didn't

164

leave a name . . . said she'd be back. I gotta go now. Thanks," said the youthful neighbor pocketing her money, unconcerned that Mr. Colby's stomach had just belched acid up to his throat and that his soul had taken a large step down into a black pit.

"I wonder who it was?" Cheryl questioned, her attention quickly occupied by the children.

Zack just shook his head, speechless.

Zack dreamt of Marcia the whole night. He slept soundly for three hours, then tossed and turned as rapid images flashed in front of him, images that wouldn't slow down enough so he could concentrate on any single one, as much as he tried. By three o'clock, Zack's mental midnight demons intensified into full-scale uppercase Anxiety Monsters.

Zack waited until nine o'clock without hearing from David. It was the fifth day in a row. He was afraid to leave, afraid to go out and pretend to sell computers, afraid that Marcia would show up at his house.

"Are you staying home today?" asked Cheryl, curious. "If so, would you mind pushing the vacuum cleaner around for me?" she said with a note of sarcasm.

That drove him out. Zack was not acquainted with the vacuum cleaner. The possibility that Marcia might actually come to their home bumped up against the reality of the dreaded Hoover. It was time to go.

Zack drove down Capital Street and parked across from the Wyoming statehouse. There were several law firms who were nearly on the verge of springing for one of the new IGC-40s and going on-line with the state's IBM 4381 mainframe. Zack had found that Keeping Ahead of the Joneses was very big in lawyerland. Briefcase in hand, Zack walked a short half block down a well-manicured side street to Lawyer Alley, where he went inside one of the offices.

He reached down inside himself, groped around, and came up with a big smile for the receptionist, who today was doubling as assistant power typist. It was traditional in law firms to grind out productivity from the lowest-paid employees. Entry level secretaries, who perhaps earned fourteen thousand dollars ended up working impossible hours on massive projects that involved skill and stamina. In order to maintain their jobs, these mostly young women would become overqualified — to the point where they would be doing paralegal activities — but continued to be paid at their entry level salaries. After three or four years their salary would rise to the point where the firm couldn't afford to pay the overtime, so they would be fired, and replaced by a new crop of eager high school graduates. Zack had a great deal of sympathy for the secretaries he met. The feeling must have been mutual, because he rarely had difficulty getting appointments.

This morning was no different. One of the white-shirted partners came out and met him, and the two men began to discuss the possibilities of networking the firm's personal computers and perhaps upgrading to a more powerful central computer. From behind him Zack heard a voice that drilled him between the shoulder blades.

"Excuse me . . . I seem to be lost. Could you give me directions?" she asked the young girl.

The rest of the words were lost someplace between Marcia's lips and Zack's brain. In midconversation, Zack turned around just as Marcia looked up from her position, hand on well-molded hip, behind the receptionist's desk. She wore a pink knit suit with a skirt that was short for Cheyenne, but made up for it by clinging

166

to her figure. Her legs seemed to go from here to there and back again. Marcia smiled seductively.

"Well," said the lawyer, thinking the smile was for him. "I haven't seen *her* around before. I wonder what trouble *she's* in?" he laughed under his breath in a manly way.

Oh, God. Why is she doing this?

Zack's good-looking lawyer customer suspended business and resumed chitchat as he looked at the beautiful woman in the short tight skirt bending over his secretary's desk. Marcia thanked the receptionist, threw a meaningful look to the men, and walked out the door.

Zack was forced to resume talking bullshit business. His mind was totally on Marcia. The partner wasn't listening to what he was saying any more than he was. In two brief moments she'd carried him away to na-na land.

By the time Zack got outside, she was gone. Adrenaline surged through him. Nearly frantic, Zack wandered back and forth up the side streets, looking everywhere for signs of his siren, his seductress.

It was this bitch that got me into trouble, he thought. It's all her fault. Where is she? Where is she?

Zack ranted to himself. His eyes reflected the frantic state of his mind.

Get a grip, asshole! he thought.

"I can't!" he muttered to himself, loud enough that he drew attention to himself from a pair of legislators, along with a strange look.

Zack looked like the Mad Stork, a tall but gaunt version of the good-looking man he was. The two weeks of dissipation and worry had started to take a toll on his body. He'd lost ten pounds and looked to be just on the other side of lean. The weight loss and total disruption of his sleep pattern had reflected itself in his face, mainly his eyes — which now alternated between red and puffy, and sallow.

Where is she? he wondered. She's got to be around here someplace.

While Zack knew her torture was deliberate, Marcia's presence had given him an overwhelming urge to be close to her. She was a drug he couldn't resist. Zack walked into the beautiful Wyoming state legislature building and sat down on a marble bench. The click-clack of high heeled shoes mixed with indecipherable pieces of conversations caused by the poor acoustics of the open foyer. The double bank of elevators played a discordant melody of nearby dings and far-off dongs as the passing of each floor could be heard even down in the lobby.

Settle down, he told himself.

Feet attached to busy people shuffled past him in both directions. Then as he looked up he first saw the legs, *her* legs, legs that were standing not fifty feet away on the opposite side of the building. Sunlight from the eastern exposure shone from behind her, outlining her whole body underneath the soft knit suit. She stood, arms casually to her side, head cocked slightly to the left — enough that her hair fell below her shoulder — and just stared at him. People passed between them, temporarily blocking his view. The sunlight seemed to strobe as she passed into and out of his vision as unconcerned workers went to and fro.

Then she was gone.

Zack dropped his briefcase and ran across the lobby toward the opposite side, leaving a messy puddle of paper on the cold floor. He ran past the empty guard's kiosk, and around a polished corner, where he just managed to catch a glimpse of pink as it slid past the building directory and moved to the left down a well-used corridor.

"Marcia!" he shouted, unconcerned with propriety.

He had lost her.

168

Where did she go? She was here. . . . Zack stood in the middle of the first floor intersection of two corridors, first looking down one, then the other. No Marcia. His instincts said she had gone right. Slowly he walked down the corridor, its offices filled with busy people. Past the drinking fountain a small hallway went toward a door that led to the stairwell. Marcia stood at the door, one hand on the knob. Their eyes met. Hers smoldered.

"You!" he shouted as she quickly opened it and slipped behind, the door closing heavily behind her. Zack, more than five steps behind her, caught the door before it latched, and slammed his way through.

Zack's tie was askew, his shirttail out, and he was slightly out of breath. His eyes went up the stairs but saw nothing but gray. Then out of the corner of his right eye he saw pink, and turned quickly. Marcia, hands on the wall, was backed into the corner behind the door. She gave him a sultry, arrogant stare that said, "Don't touch me."

Of course, that was exactly what she didn't want him to do. Zack was in a rage. He felt anger, lust, hatred, love — all the emotions that stir up the juices. But he felt them all at once — a rage of emotions. In an instant he was on her, backing and pressing her against the cold painted cinder block wall. His hands were rough, at first pinning one arm behind her while pinching and twisting the other. She struggled and moved against him, letting loose a small throaty cry of protest. At first he had no idea what he intended to do other than punish her.

Somehow her lips found his as his hands went from pinning to molesting. His left knee went between her legs, then the right. Her tongue found his, darting and sucking. His hands roamed the soft knit, first above, then quickly underneath.

"No . . . no, not here . . . please, Zack . . . not here,"

169

she cried huskily, urging him on.

The soft fabric tore and caught against the prickle of the cinder blocks as he raised it, his hands hungrily and roughly fondled her thighs, then slipped all the way up and under her panties.

"Oh, God Zack . . . no . . . someone will come . . . not here, please, oh . . ."

Her hands were on his belt, then his zipper, freeing his erection. He twisted and tore at the thin material, which was nothing more than a thong held by a clasp on each hip. With a pop the clasp gave in to his pressure. Her legs scraped against the wall as he lifted her up. Her arms were locked around his neck, then her bare legs wrapped around him, first the left leg, then the right. They were coupled.

"You . . . you . . . *bitch* . . . you . . . *bitch* . . . you . . . *bitch!*" he grunted, rutting in unison.

"Don't . . . please," she protested, but wriggled to his urgency, driving him onward.

oh God she feels good oh God she . . .

Not five feet from them, on the other side of the door, was a corridor busy with people. Suddenly the door opened and swung around, momentarily protecting them from being seen. Someone came through and continued up the stairs. Zack held his breath and stopped in midstroke. Marcia, her pink skirt up to her waist, her legs wrapped around his, her tongue dancing on his, stopped breathing as well. The feet went through the second floor door. With a pair of animal grunts, they resumed their passion, which took another minute to conclude. Panting and out of breath, and with the stairwell reeking of urgent sex, they pulled back from each other, both wet with perspiration. Marcia's skirt fell back into place, although it was ruined with pulls in the rear. Zack was a mess. Wordlessly, Marcia produced a handkerchief and handed it to him, so that he could clean him-

170

self. "David will be at your house this afternoon at one-thirty. You should be there," she instructed.

Zack's eyes must have shown wild confusion. He had nine different things to say but none came out his mouth. Marcia put a soft hand on his shoulder as Zack zipped up his pants.

"Listen to me, Zack. These aren't nice people. I'm the only thing that's keeping your worst nightmare off your doorstep. Listen to me! Meet David at your house this afternoon and do whatever he wants. They're ready to throw you to the wolves, do you know that? Don't screw up."

Marcia reached inside her purse and came out with a vial filled with red-and-white pills, high-impact amphetamines.

"I know you're under a lot of stress right now. Stress can make you do strange things—it makes you feel zoned out, sometimes almost paralyzed. You can't be like that, Zack. You've got to put on a good face. You can't afford any mistakes, Zack. When you start to feel stressed, take two of these—you'll be all right."

Zack looked at the vial dumbly. Marcia gently folded his hand over it.

"You'll be all right—just hang in there. I'll be with you," Marcia said, then kissed him with warmth and some affection.

Poor Zack, she thought. Poor little Zack.

Marcia took a man-sized swallow of scotch and let her head rest against the sturdy, but uncomfortable, backboard of her motel bed. It was OK that it wasn't too comfortable. No sense in falling asleep too early.

At least they have cable TV, she thought. Joe would go nuts without his ESPN.

"I'm afraid we're going to have a lot of days like this,

171

Joe," Marcia said to her big man.

"I enjoyed it. I like it a lot more when we can move around. I didn't like Dallas much," Joe replied.

"That makes two of us. Boy, am I tired. You did a nice job today, considering you were by yourself most of the time," Marcia complimented. "The equipment seemed to work pretty well."

There was a soft knock on the door. Joe opened it a crack. It was David.

"Come on in," she motioned. "Where are Wing and Wang?" she smiled.

"Albert and Robert enjoy programming. They are in their room. What did you do to Colby?"

"What do you mean?"

"He's docile. Whatever it is, keep it up. We've got a great deal of work ahead of us. Are you planning to meet with him tomorrow?" David asked.

"No," Marcia shook her head. "I don't want to set a schedule quite yet. I want him to think I can show up in his life at any moment. I want him to be thinking of me—just me."

Zack Colby understood computers, and he understood plain English. He smoothly explained to Cheryl that the big bid for the base was starting to roll and that David would have to start coming over more often, sometimes nearly every day.

"I . . . I'm not sure I like that, Zack," Cheryl replied. "I'm not sure I want him around when you're not here. I just don't like the idea of another man in the house when you're not around."

"Oh, it'll be all right. David's got to work on the machines. That's why we've got him. This bid could be a whole year's quota," Zack tried to reassure.

It wasn't working. Cheryl would have no part of it.

"No. I don't want him here unless you're here. He . . ." Her voice trailed off.

What are you going to tell him? she thought. You don't like the way he looks at you? Are you a big girl, or what?

"All right, I'll try to be home," reassured Zack.

It was exactly what he wanted to do anyway. Zack had no intention of leaving Cheryl alone with David. But it had to be Cheryl who insisted on it. There would be no "why aren't you out selling" questions.

Downstairs, David was pleased to find that Zack was beginning to cooperate.

"I've got the manuals you asked for. We should be able to tie into Endicott by the end of next week."

"Do you have a demo ID, separate from your personal one?" asked David.

"Yes," replied Zack without question.

"Very good. Don't attempt to use it. We'll be using it from another location," replied David, who was now assured that he could gain some time in getting the required list of PROFS user addresses for the virus, and the internal telephone numbers of all employees for the Phase Two operation group.

"OK, Zack—let's do some work."

By reading the manuals, the pair set up additional profiles on the 9350, including one for remote maintenance. Because motel rooms designed furniture to be theft-proof, including telephones, David was unable to use an internal modem on his PC. Instead he was forced to use the old-style acoustic couplers, which cradled the telephone but didn't provide as good a connection. Still, it enabled Albert and Robert to connect with the 9350 and to develop and test their encryption programs without the requirement of being in Zack's office—which was good for all concerned.

Zack then showed David how to pass through to the

173

Yorktown disk. David laughed when he read what he saw. While COBOL was the most prevalent VM programming language, most internal IGC programming was done in a language called REXX—the same that Robert and Albert used. Available for free use by anyone connecting to the Yorktown disk was a powerful PC editor called E3, especially designed to work with the REXX programming language. Inside the editor was a set of tools called E3REXXKEY. The handy routines allowed a programmer to streamline the code for maximum efficiency.

From their motel room David's crew could write the program on their PC by using the E3 editor. Connecting to the 9350, the file would be uploaded, stored, and any "dirty" conversion codes repaired. At that point, the program could be executed against some test data. "Wing" and "Wang" never had to get out of their pajamas.

When Taipei businessmen needed someone to invest their profits, they came to Xiang Wu. By Taiwanese law, individuals were allowed to take no more than five million dollars per year out of the country without prior government approval. But the government had no way to enforce the law. In a country with seventy-five *billion* dollars in cash reserves, everyone was anxious to invest in the United States. And in San Francisco, Xiang Wu was the man to see. For a fee, Wu put U.S. startup companies in touch with Taiwanese venture capitalists, men who were anxious to invest in any new American technology.

When Wu had discovered Makato Shinogara's operation, he had begun to carefully develop the interest of a group of powerful Taiwanese businessmen, whetting their interest with the possibilities of making fortunes with their investment dollars, although leaving the exact details undercover. From the investors' standpoint, details only got in the way. If Wu said it was all right, then it was all right.

Over the past two months Xiang Wu and E. Dexter Albright had created nearly a thousand accounts in legitimate brokerage houses across the country, all seeded with relatively small amounts of venture capital money from the Taiwanese investment group. The dollar amounts in each account were slowly increased, as was their activity.

Wu put down his reading glasses, then the letter which had arrived by express mail that morning. It was good news.

28 October
Mr. Xiang Wu
820 Grant Street, #2
San Francisco, California 94111
Dear Mr. Wu:
The stakes here are very high. Shinogara is attempting to blackmail IGC by sending a computer virus through its internal systems, currently scheduled for the 19th of November.

Apparently, it will cripple IGC's internal systems completely. It uses a process called encryption, which I am not totally familiar with. They believe IGC's customers will also be infected.

My role is to make sure that Colby behaves during the period between now and then. He is a somewhat unstable man. David Kimura, Shinogara's chief programmer, feels that unless IGC caves in and gives them what they want, they won't be able to "decrypt" the information on their computers. I hope I am saying this right. There is something to do with a "key" that unlocks the code,

175

and from what I have seen it would be a long shot.

We are currently at a place called Holding's in Cheyenne.

I will update you as I get new information. If you want to contact me, I suggest that it be done in person, but please be careful.

Very truly yours,

Marcia Lee.

Wu smiled, then folded the letter in two. It contained an economic hydrogen bomb. Serious investment in today's stock market took courage, persistence, skill, and luck. Stock markets could rise or fall fifty points at the drop of an economic statistic or the depression of an analyst's Enter key. The strength of an economic modeling program was just as important as knowledge of P/E ratios, if not more important. Insider information, triple-witching days, computerized trading were by-products of the stock market's entry into its Future Shock. Wu fingered the folded letter. Even an attempt at blackmailing IGC would send ripples—no, *shudders* through the market. Fluctuations in IGC stock could make or break the New York Stock Exchange by itself. A major "short" investment would reap the dreams of kings. A short is a situation where stock is purchased on the assumption that it will go down, not up. Paper profits are calculated as the stock falls, not as it rises. Selling short means that instead of buying a stock, the investor is actually selling the stock now, with the hope that he will be able to "buy" it back at a much lower price in the future. The difference is his profit.

The simply written piece of paper in Wu's hands was the absolute essence of insider information. "They believe IGC's customers will also be infected." Who were IGC's top twenty commercial customers? Name a big company. Aetna, GM, Boeing, Rockwell, Ford . . . pick twenty . . . pick thirty. They're all big. And they will also be infected.

Wu was on the edge of the coup of a lifetime. But he'd have to be cautious. With news of this potential, a meeting of his investors was in order. Wu tapped a two-digit combination on his telephone, which in turn dialed the 011-886-02 international, country, and city access codes for Taipei, Taiwan. The connection was remarkably clear. The phone was the private number of a man called Do Sing. There was no reason for false chatter — it was not Wu's way, nor Sing's.

"This is Xiang Wu. You've asked me to obtain certain information for you. I've received sufficient details regarding your objective. I believe it warrants a meeting of your investors," Wu said indirectly.

There was always the worry of phone taps, on both ends of the line. There was no reason to identify Sing, nor Makato Shinogara. Anybody tapping the line would know it was Wu calling.

"In San Francisco?" asked Sing.

"That would be best," replied Wu.

"One moment, please." The call was put on hold for no more than twenty seconds. "Will Tuesday afternoon be satisfactory?"

"I'll have your plane met at the airport. Have a safe flight," said Wu as he hung up.

From his desk drawer, Wu pulled out a piece of crisp white bond paper and wrote a brief note, then called for an assistant.

"This must be personally delivered to the Lee woman. You know what she looks like. No one must see you make contact with her. No one must read this message but her. See that she reads it and acknowledges it to you, then destroy the message. There will be no reply. Go," ordered Wu.

The one thing Marcia knew about herself was that she had a hard time relaxing. It was very difficult for her to turn her duty light out. She was always on call. Even when she wasn't following Colby physically, she was doing it mentally. And when she did try to come down off the work mountain, she was a Type A personality. She needed to be doing something. Anything. TV wasn't a good outlet. Books were OK, but even then she got antsy.

How am I going to set him up next? she wondered.

The physical explosion in the Wyoming state legislature building had been a fantastic setup. She'd gotten Zack to act out another fantasy. She'd get him so riled up, strung so tight, that he'd do anything for her . . . *anything*.

"I'm going out for a run," she told Joe, then took off west on Lincolnway. East would have taken her into the center of town. Jogging wasn't exactly in vogue in Cheyenne — that sort of thing is only done in LA and back east. Trotting through downtown Cheyenne in her tight little running shorts and halter top would be like waving a red flag in a bull ring. She'd have a trail of yahoos following her like a bitch in heat. After a mile up to the I-80 on ramp, she stopped for a breather. On the way out, she noticed a man walk up to one of the bus stops along the route. Hardly huffing, she passed him at a pretty good clip, but couldn't help but notice that he was Oriental. Nearly up to I-80 a bus passed her headed toward town. But on the way back the man was still there.

Why is that man still there? she wondered.

Marcia thought about crossing the highway, but decided against it. The motel was only a half block away, and Lincolnway was well traveled. Marcia picked up the pace as she came closer, determined to sprint past the man. Just as she passed him, he turned and spoke just loud enough for only her to hear.

"Miss Lee, I have a message from Mr. Wu."

Marcia stopped dead in her tracks, perspiration rolling down between her perfect breasts.

"What did you say?" she asked, astonished.

"I have a message for you from Mr. Wu. Please . . . we are not watched. Could you read it now, please?" The man took a twice-folded piece of paper out from his coat jacket and handed it to her.

I RECEIVED YOUR PACKAGE THIS MORNING. IT HAS BEEN WELL RECEIVED. THANK YOU. THE INFORMATION IS VERY USEFUL. I NEED MORE DETAILS ON THE TYPE OF DEMANDS TO BE ISSUED. IS THE 19TH STILL THE EXPECTED DATE? ARE THERE ANY NEW DEVELOPMENTS? CAN YOU DESCRIBE THE "VIRUS" IN ANY FURTHER DETAIL? IT IS IMPORTANT TO RECEIVE YOUR ANSWER BY TUESDAY AFTERNOON OR FAX (415) 545-4068.
WU

"I am to return with the note, Miss Lee. Do you understand everything in it?"

The messenger was in his early forties, although Marcia had a difficult time determining the age of Oriental men. He was intense and all business.

Wu sent a private messenger from San Francisco to Cheyenne to hand carry a nine-line note, she thought. Just fax me.

"Yes. I understand. I have the number. Are you to take a message back?" she asked.

Wu's messenger shook his head no.

"Well, tell Mr. Wu I'll give him what I can."

The messenger repeated her exact words, then nodded slightly and walked across the street. Marcia watched as he walked to a parked car, got in, and drove off toward I-80.

Unbelievable, she thought. He's going back to the airport and hop a private jet back to San Francisco.

Cars whooshed past Marcia, reminding her that she should return. Fifteen minutes later she was standing under a moderately cool shower.

"Hi. I've come to bury any hatchets that need to be buried," she smiled, a bottle of scotch tucked in one arm and a partially filled plastic ice bucket in the other. "What do you say?"

David looked at her with appreciative eyes. Like Shinogara, he too had seen her naked in every copulation position imaginable, and some that weren't. She was a strong woman — *forceful* was probably a better description. She was used to getting her own way. An open admission from her that their working relationship might not be in sync, was unexpected. It was welcome, but not expected. She had a job. He had a job. She didn't know it, but he had the opportunity for significant wealth.

"Yes — please come in," David said, opening the door.

There were no apologies for an untidy room. They'd been living out of suitcases since August. David had been "home" to Palos Verdes for only three days — hardly long enough to recharge his mental batteries. He needed time off, but knew that between now and the end of November, perhaps even longer, all workdays were twenty-four hours long.

"I just wanted to tell you that I was sorry that I've been a bitch. We're all alone here, and we've got to work as a team. I apologize," she said with apparent sincerity, holding our her hand to shake amends and bygones.

"Apology accepted, noted, and filed. I appreciate it. We *do* have to work as a team. What do you have there?" he replied, seemingly anxious to talk to someone other than his programmers, who were busy in their room hacking away at a 9350 problem.

"Dewar's White Label. I like it — it doesn't have the bite that Johnnie Walker has . . . it's more mild. And you know, I'm such a mild person," she laughed, managing to get just the right degree of twinkle in her eyes.

He laughed. He enjoyed her company. He had enjoyed Dallas. Even though she was a pushy woman, it was fascinating to watch another professional do her job — and in such remarkable fashion. Ice tumbled into plastic room glasses, scotch was poured, then consumed and refilled. A knot in the center of David's shoulder blades started to unravel as the liquor, but more importantly the chatter, started to relax him.

"I'm curious, David — what do you get out of this? I know what I get. What do you get? It's got to be more than satisfaction. I'll be honest, I'm getting more for this job than anything I've ever done before — *way* more," Marcia asked.

"I get a percentage of the profits. Some of the money won't be realized for many years to come, but there is a formula. We're all on the Formula — all except Mr. Shinogara. I don't know what they'll get, but I've calculated what I'll get." Part of David was reluctant to tell, but most of him wasn't. "I can clear up to twenty million dollars. And I will have my own company. I don't know what company it will be . . . a subsidiary . . . I don't really care."

David sensed her confusion.

"Oh, the company is in Japan. We're assuming that when we issue the demands to IGC that we'll need to be one step ahead of the FBI, perhaps the CIA. I'd be dis-

181

appointed in you if you hadn't been thinking along the same lines," David continued, glad to see the nod of her head. "I hired Albert and Robert. Each of them is on a salary retainer and can make one million dollars — a staggering sum for twenty-five- and thirty-one-year old systems programmers. Properly invested, they could start their own companies — or never look at a computer display again." David finished his second drink and didn't refuse when Marcia refilled the glass.

"When I came on board the programming was in disarray. There was no discipline, no objective, no definite goal. Mr. Shinogara knew what he wanted done, but didn't have the programming skills to fine tune the objective. Once we decided on the virus, picked the operating systems, and began to work on the encryption programs, then Mr. Shinogara could focus on how to bring it off. He's been a *very* patient man," Kimura said with admiration.

"I understand *what* you're doing, but I've never really understood *why*. I don't know why you're doing . . . why *we're* doing what we're doing," she asked, concerned.

David leaned back in his chair and took another sip of his scotch.

"You know it's not money," David stated the question rhetorically. "It's technology. Future technology. I know he's told you that we're representatives of various companies — not exactly employees, but close. Our Ministry of Trade would be able to define the difference, but I don't think the Department of Justice would. On all fronts of the electronics and computer industry, we — our Japanese companies — are competing with the United States. In market after market we've destroyed our competition. We produce better products at a lower cost. We do it by grinding productivity from the workers — who in turn don't mind. Our standard . . . standards of living have gone up and continue to rise. We

182

have beaten the United States in all industries with the exception of computing. And of all the industries the world might *expect* us to win easily at, we haven't — and for one reason: a company called InterGalactic Computing. In all other industries our products are excellent — not necessarily the cutting edge of technology, but well made. In the computer industry, IGC produces very good products at an above average level of technology — well above average. Not leading edge. But very good. It's for this reason we haven't been able to dominate the marketplace as we have in others. They — IGC — even beat our own companies, *in Japan!* Even with our government support! In order for us to beat them, we must make the next level of technology as commercially available as IGC's products are today. We must leapfrog them in technology and then apply our mass production skills.

"Everything they are researching, we are researching. What we want is their research."

Traveling west to east halfway around the world was akin to sending one's senses through the Twilight Zone via Altered States, but the five businessmen were used to it. Drinking nothing but water, they fasted the day before and slept on the fifteen-hour flight as much as they could. Paying no attention to the setting sun, they were quickly escorted through customs to an awaiting stretch limo that drove them up the Bayshore, then through the Embarcadero to Chinatown. All were hungry, which is what their host had expected. He, too, had made many trips back and forth to Taipei — Singapore — Hong Kong — Jakarta — Malaya — Bangkok. It was a grueling flight that left one disoriented, but in these circumstances there was no time to waste in letting the body catch up with the time changes. It would be forty-eight

183

hours before the effects were complete, but by that time they all would be back in Taipei — or in Honolulu.

The limo took them directly to Kan's Chinese restaurant at 708 Grant Street, a block and a half from Wu's town house. The commercial sections of Kan's consisted of a huge second floor area that could seat hundreds, and a more secluded third floor for larger parties. Behind the small bar area, through the coatroom, was a sumptuously appointed elevator that went to the fourth floor, where three very private rooms shared a very private view of downtown San Francisco. Tonight, the fourth floor belonged to Mr. Wu and guests, including E. Dexter Albright and James "Jimmy C." Chimichanga. An armed thug guarded the elevator, another stood next to the concealed stairwell leading from the public dining room on the third floor.

The five men were Chinese businessmen of varying ancestry, all with direct ties to or memories of what life was like in Imperial China. Two of the men lived in Taipei, the other three in Hong Kong. All were presidents or behind-the-scene financiers of the electronics industry on Taiwan. Politically and economically, the five men had worked modern-day miracles in the last six years. They had developed Taiwan into a financial world power by taking cheap, substandard products and applying the Japanese theory of management and production. They were a force to be reckoned with.

Taiwan was home of the "clone" computer, a term used to describe an IGC personal computer look-alike. Built for one-fifth the cost, the products sold in the American marketplace for one-half to two-thirds the cost of an IGC product, and for the most part functioned as well. It was this last part that in 1987 caused IGC to take the punitive measures that it did. Because the offshore versions were so well reverse-engineered, closely copying the original design of the IGC product, the American computer giant through its army of Armonk-based attorneys began to enforce the five percent royalty fee on all Taiwanese clone computers. Five percent of all revenue for products sold in the United States would be paid directly to IGC. This practice was approved by the American legal system in 1987 and began to be enforced in 1988.

It was not well received.

Citing patent infringements on the computers' BIOS (Basic Input Output System), the very heart of the system, IGC had won a major series of court cases. It had won nearly every court fight worldwide since the mid-seventies, since the infamous dismissal of the U.S. government's suit against both IGC and AT&T for predatory and monopolistic practices. Insiders at Justice look back to the day as being the beginning of the end for the entire department. Both suits had been under discovery and near trial for nearly a decade. Roomfuls of information had already been presented. Three judges had heard the case against IGC—entire careers had been spent on the cases. Dismissed. In one day.

The five men took their seats at the round table, deferring to Do Sing, who at fifty-eight was the oldest and richest of the group. Wu was flanked by E. Dexter Albright and Jimmy Chimichanga. After warm greetings and introductions, there was no discussion of business as the men ate through an eight-course dinner like the locusts descending on the plains of the Great Salt Lake. An hour later, with the table cleared, it was time for business.

Earlier in the day, Xiang Wu had received a second Federal Express package:

30 October
Mr. Xiang Wu

185

820 Grant Street, #2
San Francisco, California 94111

Dear Mr. Wu:

I've been more successful in learning exactly what this operation is really about. I didn't tell you in my first letter that this attack on IGC on November 19 consists of two, perhaps three phases.

Phase One is the computer virus — actually now that I've talked with David Kimura — it is at least two, perhaps three viruses. Each virus is a program that will encrypt the disk(s) and files — I think those are the correct terms — of personal computers and larger computers. In addition, David has discovered an internal "bulletin board" — something called the Yorktown Disk, a place where IGC's plant and lab people trade programs. In addition, he believes he can put the mainframe virus into an automatic maintenance program that IGC has and spread it that way. I still don't understand the details of how it exactly works, just that it will go off at 11:30 EST on the 19th.

Phase Two consists of a simultaneous attack on IGC's phone system. He — they — have banks of telephones in many locations ready to disrupt IGC offices with automatic calling.

They also discussed possible use of letter bombs, very high-pitched telephone signals, and other things as Phrase Three.

I'm sorry for not telling you this in my first letter, but I am just now learning enough to understand the significance.

They do not want money. They want IGC's plans for future technology. In addition to existing computer technology in disk drives and micro-

186

chips, they want all development plans for artificial intelligence (?), fifth-generation computing, and the most significant to them — something called "superconductivity."

I hope this has been of some help. By the way, your courier did well. He scared the shit out of me.
Marcia Lee

Wu's mind churned with ideas, all financial. Stacks of hundred- and thousand-dollar bills tumbled in his mind like a giant cement mixer stirring up a vatful of goo. He would be curious to see if Do Sing's mind would react in the same fashion.

"Thank you for coming on such short notice. I know you've had a long day, but I wouldn't have called you unless I felt it was important. And I think time is of the essence." Wu paused. "Shinogara is ready to launch an attack against IGC."

The five Taiwanese businessmen nodded their heads in approval almost in unison, then listened as Xiang Wu explained the details.

"Will it work?" asked Do Sing.

"There will be chaos in the marketplace," replied Wu.

"And you gentlemen know, when there is chaos, there is opportunity," added E. Dexter Albright.

"Can this hurt us?" asked Do Sing.

There was a short pause by the group as they thought of the consequences.

"I don't see how Shinogara will be able to hide the fact that the demands have come from Japan, or a Japanese consortium. IGC has a tremendous influence on the American government. I think there would be trade reprisals — demands for reparations from Japan. There could very well be sentiment for the passage of a generally disadvantageous trade bill — a trade war could easily start. If so, we could see an import tax on our products," said one.

"Not *could,* but *would.* I don't think there is any question that the Americans would retaliate against Japan. And I agree, I think we would be lumped in with them — as would the Koreans."

"It would be about time — somebody has to stop the Koreans," said another, disgusted at the competitive inroads made by South Korean computer manufacturers.

The Taiwanese firms the men represented had been on the leading edge of competition — competition supported by the U.S. government and its Most Favored Nation trade policy. The Taiwanese companies had succeeded because of very low labor costs. But soon they were undercut by the Koreans, who had yet to develop and match the quality control techniques of the Chinese, but whose labor costs were significantly less. In time, the Koreans would be undercut by the microchip companies in Singapore. Each man knew that in a price-only competition, Taiwan's spot in the sun would be short. If the trend continued, the entire electronics industry would be based in Mali or Zaire, the poorest of the poor.

"How will he prevent discovery?"

"He will leave no trace. When the demands are issued, he will be gone. This unfortunate man will be killed."

"As will the Lee woman," said Do Sing.

"Yes," replied Xiang Wu. "Shinogara will clear out, backstepping and erasing any and all possible tracks. Anyone left behind will be eliminated."

"We would do no different," said Do Sing.

There was general agreement.

"How else could this hurt us? What about the technology?"

"We have no one working on this superconductivity. We copy, not develop. Disk drive advances would be useful, as would microchip technology. But we buy chips from Singapore and Malaysia—we don't develop new microchips."

Once again, there was agreement. The Japanese ransom would only indirectly hurt them.

"How would this benefit us?" asked Do Sing.

"If successful, IGC could be crippled. From our perspective, we could profit with a twenty- to thirty-percent increase in market share," said one man.

"IGC could be hurt *and* the Japanese punished," added another.

It was generally agreed that this scenario would be the best of all possible worlds.

"Our lobbyists would have to earn their pay," laughed one man.

"What should we do?" asked Do Sing, realizing that the men had laid out the most likely possible occurrences. "What are our choices?"

"Do nothing," said one.

Let the chips fall where they may, but keep the lobbyists on guard to protect Taiwanese interests if something goes astray.

"Inform IGC, now—no, not IGC . . . . tell the U.S. government now. Call the FBI, notify Congress," said another.

Get the Good Guy Award. Penalties against Japan would occur for sure—Shinogara would be captured, Japanese companies embarrassed. There would be little to be gained from that scenario.

In the best case, IGC needed to be hurt.

"Help them," said a third.

"No, no . . ." Do Sing shook his head. "We don't want anything to do with this."

For such bright men, they were temporarily struck with tunnel vision. Their thoughts had no lateral movement away from the obvious: How does this affect *my*

189

company, *my* group of companies?

"Gentlemen, what will happen to the American economy?" asked Xiang Wu, trying to lead the men down a wider path, one that would be easier to tread. "What will happen if Shinogara is successful, or even partially successful?"

"You mean, if IGC is shut down — and perhaps its customers are hurt?" asked Do Sing.

"Yes. What will happen?"

"Businesses will close . . ."

"*Large* businesses. Fortune 500 companies will be crippled — at least temporarily."

"People will be out of work."

"What about *money?*" asked Wu.

The staggering economic disaster began to dawn on the five men.

"What would happen if Chrysler could make cars and GM and Ford couldn't?"

"Or if the assembly lines at Boeing stopped, but those at McDonnell Douglas didn't."

"Or if Hartford could process insurance claims and Aetna couldn't."

Thoughts raced through their heads.

"And what if we knew this, and nobody else did?" asked Xiang Wu.

"The Congress of the United States has just given the Republic of China unlimited rights and privileges to invest in the New York, American, Pacific, Chicago, and NASDAQ exchanges," Wu reminded. "And, you've been doing so. Mr. Albright has established accounts all over the United States for you to place your investments. You gentlemen have brought new money into the American financial marketplace."

Wu stopped. All eyes were on him. No one felt the effects of the long flight.

"We've been shortsighted in thinking about the possibilities," Do Sing stated plainly.

"If you knew that IGC stock would drop fifty points between November 19 and December 1, what would *you* do?" asked Wu. "I know what *I* would do."

"It won't just be IGC that drops," said Do Sing, becoming enthused. "*All* stock markets would drop."

"Gold would rise. Silver would rise," said one of the other men.

"Yes. Precious metals would skyrocket. As would the stocks of mining companies. The money won't go into old socks, but will be transferred to other assets," said Wu.

"Black Monday would be *nothing* compared to the chaos this would cause," said Sing, shaking his head.

"You are right, Do Sing. A forty-percent shift of assets could be possible. A few people will make staggering gains, while hundreds of thousands of people will lose everything. The panic selling will be unlike anything ever seen," said Xiang Wu.

One of the men rapidly worked an abacus, his fingers flying back and forth over the beads.

"The significance of what Shinogara is doing is greater than any financial event in history—"

"And they don't see it," Sing interrupted.

"That's correct, Do Sing. They don't see it. However, *we* see it. And that is what's important," replied Wu.

"What do you recommend?" asked one of the men.

"I'll speak first of the financial aspects, since that's my expertise—it *is* what you pay me to do. I think the markets will go down faster and further than IGC will. Whatever damage IGC's customers feel will be less than the insecurity felt by investors worldwide. I'd recommend buying precious metals and selling short in the American stock markets. I'd also recommend the same positions on the London and Tokyo exchanges, where the volatility will be beyond our imagination. I'd sell yen and buy marks and even francs. Money will flow so fast that it will take years to properly reconstruct what has happened. In particular, I'd sell short those IGC customers who are cash poor, who could least afford a major downturn in the market. While I'd include IGC in this position, I wouldn't concentrate on them. Staying completely away from *any* IGC stock would be suspicious, however, but don't overload. You want to come out of this clean. I'd sell all computer and electronics companies short, as I would major bank stocks — firms that won't be able to stand the pressure of such a large percentage of their assets disappearing. Fourth, I would take a minor buy position on mining stocks."

The five Taiwanese businessmen were excited — rapid conversation filled the room with animation. Xiang Wu held up his hand.

"And . . . and there is one additional point. . . ."

Do Sing held up his hand to the others, to allow Wu to speak.

"Yes, there *is* one other item. Regardless of what happens, it is in your best interest to have IGC crippled by Shinogara's attack. You've assumed all along that the attack on IGC would be temporary, that they would give in and hand over the technology, or that Shinogara would be found out," Wu said, then pointed his finger at the group. "That assumes that Shinogara gives IGC the passwords, or that IGC finds them out."

Xiang Wu let the conversation pause for five seconds, then continued.

"But, what if the passwords are lost — or stolen . . . or destroyed? What happens if IGC has no way of recovering the data on their computers? The odds of even finding one of the passwords is astronomical. What would they do? They would have to replace all of their internal systems . . . all fourteen hundred computer systems, all fifty thousand terminals . . . and start over again. And the encrypted data would remain lost — as surely as if it were put inside a time capsule and shot off into outer space. What would happen to your market share, then?"

The five men looked at Xiang Wu with dare-to-dream eyes.

"Shinogara would be blamed, IGC would be crippled, and we would reap the greatest financial windfall of all times," concluded Do Sing.

It was the golden trifecta.

"How do you plan to accomplish this?" asked Do Sing.

"We've been giving this some thought. That's why I've invited Mr. Chimichanga to this session. Mr. Chimichanga provides a level of . . . security . . . for our partnership that goes beyond what is available to other clients. What I . . . *we* . . . need to know from you gentlemen, is that you're willing to commit your financial resources to this project, and . . . to doing what needs to be done to ensure its success."

Do Sing led a rapid conversation in Chinese, then as a group all turned to Wu.

"We are," replied Do Sing. "Proceed as you see best."

Chapter Four
Night of the Red Dragon

"I'm off to the store. Can you keep an eye on the children?" said Cheryl, knowing the answer would be yes.

Zack could hear Brian playing in his room. Anne was still asleep.

"Yes," he said, as he pulled the covers back up over his head.

I don't want to get up, he thought. I don't want to get out. I'm not sure if I want to live.

The repercussions of actually thinking about suicide terrified Zack.

She'll hate me, he thought. They'll hate me. There's no way this can go undetected.

Darkness magnified reality; and today, daytime was no better. There was no reduction in how big his problems were. From the seclusion of his bed he heard Cheryl start her car, activate the automatic garage door opener, back out, and slowly drive down the street away from the house. The house was silent except for the play noises that came from Brian's room. Zack drifted into the semiconscious Land of Doze, where his thoughts and perceptions were half here and half there. He heard the front door open, then close. Either Cheryl was back quicker than normal, or he'd gone to sleep.

Footsteps.

"Well, look what I found."

Jesus H. Christ! It was Marcia.

"What the hell are you doing here?" he whispered, barely able to control his voice. "How did you get in?"

"The door was open," she replied simply.

Zack sat up in bed, feeling and looking stupid in equal proportions. He wore pajama bottoms that barely covered a morning erection. Marcia wore a light-colored cotton skirt and a pretty blue blouse. She walked over to the edge of the bed.

"You can't come here! You've got to get out!" he urged, nearly overcome with anxiety.

Cheryl's going to come home Cheryl's going to come home oh shitshitshit oh shit.

"It's not nice to point, Zack," she laughed, playfully touching his arousal.

She stood close to the bed, so close that he could smell her freshness — nearly taste her. She rested her right knee on the edge of the bed, and he instinctively reached out and touched her.

"Want me to go, Zack?" she whispered throatily, placing her hand on his, guiding it up and down the inside of her thigh. Her dress made a soft rustle as the material slid up and down her stocking-free legs. "Do you, Zack?" she mocked him.

Zack was terrified.

"She . . . she'll be . . ." he stuttered.

"She'll be *what*, Zack? *Back?* Yes, she'll be back," Marcia taunted, now kneeling on the bed, straddling Zack's legs at his knees. "She's gone to the store. She always goes to the store on Tuesdays and Fridays. Right? She leaves you with the kids so she can have some peace and quiet alone. I can't blame her. By my calculations, she'll be back in less than fifteen minutes — maybe ten. If it's any less, she's going to get an eyeful." Marcia smiled as she unsnapped the clasp on his pajama bottoms. "Oh, my," she teased in mock surprise at his condition. "Tell me, Zack . . . do you want me to go?"

As she leaned into him, his hands hungrily slipped under her dress and found nothing but smooth skin.

"I want you, Zack—I want you bad," she whispered, as her tongue found his ear and her body slipped into position. "Hurry, Zack . . . hurry. She'll be back . . ."

With his hands under her dress, cradling her smooth buttocks, Marcia moved her hips with a practiced urgency. She knew he was nearly paralyzed with fear, but still engulfed with lust. All his senses were on overdrive.

Oh God oh God she'll be back oh God she feels so good so good so good.

The intensity of his orgasm was heightened by the fear of discovery—by Cheryl, by the children.

I saw Daddy playing with a lady while you were at the store.

When he was through but still inside her, Marcia leaned back and wriggled her hips in a slow circle, giving him one last ride.

"Nice house, Zack. Should I go in and talk to the kids?"

His hands were still under her dress, and stayed there until she got up. Using the tissues from the box on the night table, she carefully cleaned herself, then handed the wet residue to him.

"Make yourself useful," she mocked. "She's pretty, Zack," Marcia said, holding a picture of Cheryl and Zack together in some previous happy moment—a moment never to be relived.

Without saying a word, Marcia found Cheryl's side of the dresser and ran her hand along her underwear, then her lingerie.

"Go! Get out of here! She'll be back!" he said urgently, wanting to shout but not wanting to alert the children.

"I'll be back, Zack. I'll be back. Keep looking for me.

You need me — you have a *hunger* for me," she said in a low and earthy voice.

She walked out of the bedroom and down the hallway toward the front door. Zack closed his eyes and prayed that Brian wouldn't be at the window. Naked, Zack went to the door and urgently motioned to Marcia. He then tiptoed past the kid's rooms.

"Go out through the office," he whispered, showing her to the stairwell.

Through it all, Marcia had a bemused smile that constantly threatened to break out into laughter. Once downstairs, Zack rooted through a desk drawer and came up with a duplicate key.

"Use this door and that driveway," he pointed to the business entrance.

Marcia nodded, then still smiling, left Zack standing in his office naked as a jaybird.

Please.

Five minutes later he heard the sound of Cheryl's car pulling into the driveway. He was sure Cheryl would come back to the bedroom and smell the sex, but it wasn't until fifteen minutes later, after unloading all of the groceries, that she came back to see if he'd made any progress toward getting up. Hearing the shower running, she went back downstairs to begin another day.

Inside the shower, with hot water splashing down on all sides of his body, Zack Colby shivered uncontrollably and began to cry.

"Hello, David," said Cheryl, opening the front door.

"Good morning, Cheryl," he replied, smiling and familiar.

Cheryl had gotten over her initial concern with David's scanning eyes, but still made it plain to Zack that she wanted him there when David was at the house. David, on the other hand, had done nothing to make Cheryl the least bit suspicious. He was always polite and gracious — even Brian and Anne liked him.

But Zack was different. His shifts in moods hadn't stopped. If anything, they'd gotten deeper. Although he never came out and said so, Cheryl thought that there might be something wrong between the two men. She'd asked him, but had been reassured no, nothing was wrong.

"It's this bid — it's really important," he kept saying.

She even noticed it when she and Zack were out together, on weekends or in the evening. Zack seemed to be on edge, like he was looking for something. He was nervous, even twitchy sometimes. They'd known each other for eight years, nearly a third of her life, and she'd not seen him like this. What made his mood changes so noticeable were the times when he seemed to have more energy than she thought possible — especially during sex. And it was the sex they had that especially worried Cheryl. It was so . . . *different*.

I'm not a prude, she told herself.

But Zack was so active, so . . . *consuming* . . . more personal than ever before. While she enjoyed their new variety, she thought that Zack somehow . . . wasn't there. He made her wear new clothes, sexy clothes. Not that she minded them so much, they did make her feel good. It was that he seemed to be watching her, but *seeing* somebody else. It was a weird sensation. More than once she thought he was seeing somebody else. She didn't know when or how, but his new sexual appetites had come from experiences he'd gotten someplace. They didn't just come out of thin blue air. But she wasn't sure. And not once did Cheryl associate Zack's acquaintance with David Kimura with the changes in his

198

behavior. But in the back of her mind she blamed it on IGC, on *business*.

"Well, Zack, today we're through with our lab tests— today we test it out for real. I assume you want to watch," said David, smiling.

It was David's arrogance that irritated and set Zack off. David insisted on telling Zack how smart he and his men were. Overconfidence was David's one major flaw. For the most part, Zack simply stayed downstairs and pretended to read while David worked with the 9350 and the PCs. With remote hookup capability, there was no need for David to constantly be there, but when he was, Zack had to be there as well—for Cheryl's sake, if for nothing else.

David powered up the PC, modified the date/time definitions, then established a link to Denver. Once inside the system, David quickly typed a letter.

TO: COLBYZAC(DENVMIC1)
FROM: COLBYZAC
SUBJ: REQUEST FOR ASSISTANCE
I AM IN A COMPETITIVE BID SITUATION AGAINST DEC AT THE STRIKE HQ, WARREN AFB, CHEYENNE, WYOMING. I NEED AN APPLICATION REFERENCE USING AN IGC-40, AB-400, OR 9350 IN THE AREAS OF INTERACTIVE GRAPHICS, TECHNICAL SPECIFICATIONS DEVELOPMENT, FORMS DESIGN, AND OFFICE AUTOMATION SUPPORT. CUSTOMER REQUIREMENTS INCLUDE ETHERNET, 3270, AND ASYNCH COMMUNICATIONS, UNIX APPLICATION SUPPORT, DOS/OS-2 PC SUP-

PORT, DOCUMENT DISTRIBUTION, AND
HIGHLY INTERACTIVE GRAPHICS TER-
MINALS.

IF ANY REP, SE, ADMINISTRATOR HAS
A REFERENCE ACCOUNT INSIDE THE
GOVERNMENT OR NOT THAT INCLUDES
THESE CAPABILITIES, PLEASE SEND ME
DETAILS AND DEGREE OF REFERENCE-
ABILITY.
THANK YOU.

The message was typical business. No one would mistake it for a Trojan Horse. Tagged to the message was a
nasty trail of dirty deeds. David filed the document
away, then switched back to his PC screen and issued a
series of Send File commands which sent the two Execs,
the high-level application program interface, and the
PC encryption program up to the host. He was now
ready to send the note, and the related files, to anyone
on the network. The first test would be to send the documents to himself, which he did. Three seconds later a
message appeared on the screen.

DO YOU WISH TO RECEIVE A NON-PROFS
DOCUMENT, Y OR N?

David pressed N. The message went away, the screen
went blank for five or six seconds, then the previous
screen reappeared. The PC's disk-in-use barely flick-
ered—but the transfer had been done in "background"
nevertheless.

David sat back in his chair, looked at his watch, and
waited. Neither man said a word for five minutes. Zack
was fascinated, nearly mesmerized, as he watched the
PROFS screen tick off the minutes and seconds. Eleven

o'clock passed. Thirty more seconds passed. *What happened?* Zack wondered. He was just about to speak when the PC display went blank. A boldfaced message appeared, ringed with blinking lights.

WARNING DO NOT TURN YOUR MACHINE OFF OR ALL DATA ON YOUR FIXED DISK AND DISKETTE DRIVES WILL BE PERMANENTLY DESTROYED. THIS IS NOT A JOKE OR A PRANK. YOUR FILES ARE BEING ENCRYPTED FOR YOUR SAFETY. IF YOU TURN YOUR MACHINE OFF YOUR FILE ALLOCATION TABLE WILL BE UNRECOVERABLE, ALL DATA AND PROGRAMS WILL BE UNUSABLE.

THIS ENCRYPTION PROCESS WILL TAKE APPROXIMATELY SEVEN MINUTES. PLEASE BE PATIENT. IF YOU HAVE ANY QUESTIONS, PLEASE SEE YOUR MANAGER.

"Please see your manager." David giggled at the thought. "The reason it didn't go off at eleven was that the PC clock wasn't set exactly with the mainframe. It'll happen in real life, too," David explained to Zack, who was astonished.

The PC churned and chugged through seven minutes and fifteen seconds of encryption before returning control to the C: > prompt.

"Go ahead . . . try to run a program," David said to Zack.

Zack typed in 3270 PC and pressed Enter, to bring up the host session.

PLEASE ENTER PASSWORD

Zack typed in DW4 and pressed Enter, to bring up the DisplayWrite 4 word processing program.

PLEASE ENTER PASSWORD

Zack put the DOS 4.0 operating system in the diskette drive and pressed Alt/ Ctrl/Del, the three-fingered combination to restart the machine. The PC went through the reboot process without checking the diskette drive first. It had been logically disabled.

"Well, that's one problem solved," said David, pleased with himself.

He tapped in 3270 PC and pressed Enter.

PLEASE ENTER PASSWORD

He typed in the password, a full sixteen digits long. After a five-second delay, the program began to initialize. Soon David was back into the Denver PROFS system.

"It works. Of course it works!" he nearly shouted. "I've got you, you bastards!" David clenched his fist, pumping his arm like the back who scored the winning touchdown.

"Now, I've got to get the file size down," he mumbled to himself.

Zack was astonished at how well it worked.

"Jesus Christ — what the fuck do you people want?" he shouted, his face turning red.

It was the note itself that rattled Zack's cage. The note was from him! From Zack Colby, marketing rep, Cheyenne, Wyoming — good old COLBYZAC.

"We've got over two hundred forty mailing lists, Zack. Nearly fifty-five thousand people. The Tojo Virus,"

David laughed, but saw Zack's blank eyes. He had no clue who Tojo was. "That's all right. Years from now they'll call it the Colby Virus," he said cruelly.

"You god-damned son of a bitch!" Zack leapt at David, grabbing at his upper torso.

It was another mistake. David had tremendous upper body strength. Zack found himself on the floor with David on top. In wrestling the move was called a Pancake. Flop—slam! Zack landed as a whoosh of breath left his body.

"Is everything all right down there?" came Cheryl's shout from the top of the steps.

David looked at Zack with eyes that could kill, eyes that said, "Do you want me to hurt her, too?"

"Everything's fine, hon. We just nearly dropped a machine when we moved it. We're OK . . . thanks," said Zack from his position on the floor.

Perspiring slightly, David held Zack by the front of his shirt.

"You're in over your head, Zack. Don't screw up now. Remember the money. I can leave at any time. One call . . . just one call, that's all it takes, and I'm gone. And you're in jail for twenty years . . . or *life*. And there'll be no money, Zack. So, get your shit together, hotshot. Think of the money. Got it?"

David released his iron grip on Zack's shirt with a disgusted snap of his wrist.

Zack got up and went into the bathroom, closing the door behind him. His heart raced.

The Colby Virus!

Traitor!

In the medicine cabinet Zack found Marcia's vial and popped two red-and-white amphetamines, swallowing the pills without water. The inside of his head felt like gnats were flying in formation. Up until the breath had

203

gone out of his body, Zack had thought—had rationalized—that he wouldn't be caught. No matter what happened, he would be exonerated.

They made me do it, he told himself.

No, Zack. They didn't make you do it. You did it. You let them do it. You screwed up.

There was no way out!

Give up! Give it up!

Turn yourself in. Stop it!

Perspiration rolled down his sides. The back of his neck was damp, as was his upper lip. He closed the vanity mirror and looked at a man with hollowed eyes.

That can't be me!

At that moment Zack Colby knew his life spirit was ebbing. He was hanging on to the facsimile of life—Cheryl, the children, the house—but it was the *other him* that was doing it. The real him was down in the basement gobbling amphetamines while a thick Oriental sat at his computer and sabotaged his employer. When it was all over it would be the real him who would pay. There would be no drugs to take him away, only the harsh reality of a cold cell. He would be out of work. There would be no money. His wife and children would be gone.

Zack's heart raced as reality forced its way into his brain, fighting tooth and nail against the high that had started. There was only one option.

Suicide.

6 November

Mr. Xiang Wu
820 Grant Street, #2
San Francisco, California 94111

Dear Mr. Wu:

We have had no direct contact with Shinogara this week, although David talks with him every night.

As you requested, I have additional details to report. We have been having difficulty with Zack Colby. I have supplied him with additional drugs, but it doesn't appear that he's able to handle them. His mood swings have become greater; however, I have been able to keep him under control, enough for David to do his work.

David told me that Shinogara has offered Colby a half million in cash if he cooperates.

The PC virus has been tested and completed. David has inserted it into the IGC computer in Denver using Colby's identification. In the past week he has made fine-tuning adjustments to the program. He apparently has been concerned with the size of the actual program to be downloaded when the virus attacks. I'm not sure of all of the details, but he has made it as small as possible, to avoid detection.

A related problem he was having was with the accidental deletion of the program by a user. That apparently has been corrected. If the program is deleted, either by the user or the computer itself, a message is sent back to Colby's computer in Cheyenne. A duplicate is automatically returned, using a different message than before.

All of the mailing lists are now completed. There are over 55,000 internal addresses, worldwide. November 14 is the date I keep hearing from him regarding the actual sending of the virus.

The second program is one that will affect all of

the applications and data on mainframe computers. Its function is similar to the one being used on the personal computers.

The date of November 19 is still a good one, as far as I know. If you don't mind, I think I will be gone by then.

Marcia Lee

"You won't see the sun on the nineteenth of November, Miss Lee," smiled Xiang Wu, putting the letter down on his desk.

In the last two weeks Wu and E. Dexter Albright had funneled huge sums of Taiwanese investment money into the United States, carefully spreading it across many accounts. IGC itself received very little play; however, the other electronics companies, cash-poor firms, and mining stocks received heavy action. Significant investments had been made in gold and silver on the London market, and equally large short positions on the Japanese yen were taken. IGC had been sold short in both locations, as had all of its major customers.

For Marcia, her temporary life in Cheyenne started to fall into a manageable routine.

"I'm watching you every step you take, Zack," she'd said after another of her surprise encounters.

She knew she was good at what she did, but Marcia was constantly amazed at how addicted he was to her body. She teased him unmercifully by showing up in public places at the worst times for him, normally as he was trying to maintain a facsimile of his life as a marketing rep.

She'd come right back and visited him Friday morning while Cheryl was at the store. She wasn't surprised to see that the children were safely in their rooms. He'd *wanted* her to come to his house. He *liked* the danger of their meetings. He was addicted to her as much as he was to her supply of red-and-white pills. But Zack had begun to send out signals that he needed help. After the first coupling in his bedroom and the nearly daily surprise encounters in the outside world, Zack's drug use began to become constant. His appetite was gone and he was losing weight. He wasn't sleeping. Although his facade was constant, inside he was crumbling. The demons of the night never went away. They stayed in his conscious twenty-four hours a day. Thoughts, evil thoughts, strobed and darted constantly, never leaving him alone.

Just when he thought he should kill himself, *she* would enter his mind, or rub up against him, or touch him, or . . . a thousand and one other thoughts.

David Kimura knew he was getting a good deal with Marcia. Whatever she was being paid, it was worth it. Zack Colby was a nut case, but Marcia had the nut crusher. Without her, David knew that he wouldn't have been able to finish the job. They would have had to abandon Colby and the Cheyenne project. It would have been years before another attempt could be made on IGC. While Zack might have been convinced that David and Shinogara would have called the Texas State police, more than likely Colby and his wife, and children, would have had to be killed. The project had to go on.

And they were making fantastic progress.

David had also found that he now had a comfortable working relationship with Marcia, and secondarily with Joe, who was hardly out of her sight. Unlike Robert and

Albert, he could talk with them about things other than computers and programs and viruses. With an IQ of 162, David was surprised how easily he could get along with Joe, whose blind devotion to Marcia was complete, which David admired. *He* would never have that kind of respect from his men. When Miller Time came, he preferred to lighten up with Marcia and her crew.

The four of them were in Marcia's room, as usual. Her stuff was all over the place. Sometimes her stuff got him excited, but he refused to show it. Joe and Tony were watching a Red Man Tractor Pull from Charlotte on ESPN and were each rooting for their own favorite Monster Tractor. David took a healthy hit on a cold Coors. He had begun to drink more than he ever had.

It must be the Cheyenne influence, he thought.

"When this thing hits, how are you planning to get out?" asked Marcia.

"We've talked about it quite a bit. Should we notify them ahead of time, should we wait, how do we do it — all the questions that need to be asked. *I* want to know, too. It's important. The decision affects how long I . . . have to stay here." David took another swig, which tasted good.

"We had to come up with a way to guarantee that our demands would be received by the chairman of the board, John Holton. We'll send him packages by Federal Express, Airborne, UPS, and even the U.S. Postal System. But we have no way of knowing if any of them will actually *get* to him. We could call him, and we may if nothing else works — but Phase Two may prevent us from getting through. So . . . we decided to use PROFS — use the system that we've sabotaged. We'll leave all the PROFS IDs of the executive offices in Armonk off of our mailing lists, so that when the virus attacks, it will leave those machines alone. Then we send

208

him our message. It will pinpoint our location, but by then we'll be long gone. By that time, the only thing we have to leave on in Colby's house is the 9350. We can log on to Denver from anyplace, even a pay phone. We could do it from Denver or San Francisco . . . or even Hawaii . . . or Tokyo!" David laughed. "The only things we have to have are compatible modems, programs, and the password. We will, of course, leave Zack's address off from any mailing list. We don't need to shoot ourselves in the foot as we do this," he said, pleased with himself.

"So, you're going to throw Colby over the side?" asked Marcia.

The thought troubled David, but not for long.

"Yes. I'm afraid things will go badly for him," David replied.

"But David — Zack knows what you . . . what *we* look like," Marcia replied, curious and concerned.

" Marcia, when I'm in Japan, I'm no longer David Kimura. Nobody will care, nobody will know," David replied in a tone of voice that implied the obvious.

It also implied the converse.

Marcia Lee would be known, she realized. Marcia Lee might be clean in the FBI computers, but not for long. Marcia Lee was in real trouble. I'm dealing with two groups of financial terrorists and one of the largest multinational corporations in the world. Where am I going to hide?

The thought was sobering. David would melt into Japanese society, guaranteed by Shinogara to be born again as a young corporate leader of some high-tech firm.

What will I have? she wondered. A pot full of money and maybe no place to spend it.

She was being paid several million dollars to personally fuck the brains out of one man over a period of seven weeks. It was an outrageous sum of money, and it had been deposited into her account.

But these people had money to burn. Money was no object. There were billions of dollars at stake. Nobody was going to ensure that a thirty-two-year-old good-time girl got out OK. Nobody but herself.

Marcia could see that David had no clue of what could, and probably would happen.

He doesn't realize it, she thought, but he's in trouble as well. No, he doesn't see it—not yet.

But Marcia could see it. Everybody in Cheyenne was in trouble. The big guys never share diddley-shit with the little guys. And we're just the little guys—the grunts, the worker bees, the slugs. We get the job done—and in this case, get paid well for it.

But who cares, if you can't spend it? All I am is a hired hand to both of these people. You've got to keep your head clear, girl—and be ready to duck and run when the axes fall—and there will be more than one ax to fall.

It was a very uncomfortable position for Marcia. She had to leave when it was the right time to leave—when she could leave with no harm, no guilt from her employers. If she disappeared and told them she was disappearing, then did it—she might get out with hair in all places. If Wu and/or Shinogara was angry with her, was trying to get her, then no place on earth would be safe.

"Are you going to give him the money?" she asked, curious.

She could hardly believe herself, but she actually felt sorry for Zack Colby.

"That's Mr. Shinogara's decision. If it was up to me, I would say no."

"No last-minute pangs of conscience?" she asked.

The question made David wrinkle his brow in thought.

210

"No, I don't think so," he said as he finished his beer.

"Well — when do you think *I* can leave?" she asked.

"When controlling Zack Colby is no longer important."

10 November

Mr. Xiang Wu
820 Grant Street, #2
San Francisco, California 94111

Dear Mr. Wu:

Since I have not heard from you, I assume that the information I have sent is what you want.

I have good control over Zack Colby, although he remains a very unstable person. My people and David's are getting along well, and appear to be working as a team.

David has informed me that he has made tremendous strides this week. He has infiltrated a form of the virus into IGC's 9350 maintenance program, and has actually started it. It appears as if it is infecting 15-20 machines per day.

David says that he will use the system to notify IGC of Shinogara's demands, although he does not have to be in the basement of the Colby home to issue the instruction. This will be backed up with a series of express mail deliveries to IGC headquarters in Armonk, New York.

If you agree, I see my involvement in this ending sometime before the 19th. I will require verification of the deposit in my Geneva bank account by this Friday.

Marcia Lee

Dear Miss Lee:

Your information has indeed been timely and well received. We think that your services will be needed by your clients up until the time the virus is dispatched generally.

We want to know more about the status of the other viruses, and more importantly about the plans for backup of the computer data files.

Most importantly, we need to know *when* the virus will be activated.

WU

"David, what happens if Colby's house burned down?"

It was the worst thing she could think of.

"You mean, now?" he replied.

Marcia thought, then answered. "Yes."

"We'd be in big trouble."

Burning his house down was the answer to Zack's problems. David appeared very uncomfortable at the question.

"What made you say that?" he asked, amazed.

"I don't know. I just did. It's true, isn't it? If Zack sets his house on fire — burns it up — then he's pretty much in the clear. What does he have to do with the programs you've already put into the system?"

"He logs on from his computer in the office and deletes the programs. A message comes back from the deleted program telling our program to replace itself on at a given address — but the message has been sent to himself. The controlling PC is gone, burned. The directory of infected IDs is gone. The message goes off into vapor. If it happens before we start sending our messages out to all the distribution lists, then the PC virus is never activated — except in those systems we've infected through Endicott. If it happens *after* we've sent the virus . . ."

"Do you have a copy of your programs — a backup? In case something goes wrong?" she asked.

The question made David uncomfortable again. She could tell from the look on his face and his semidefensive tone that he hadn't, but that he knew he should have.

"I'm not completely finished yet. We've been making so many changes," David replied, uneasy.

"Then the answer's no?"

David was an experienced programmer. His hands could fly across a keyboard translating thoughts from his mind to coded instructions in a blur of confidence that was staggering. His confidence could have been called overconfidence. Like many in the computer industry, maintaining proper backup procedures was something that oftentimes remained in a procedures manual and was not done in everyday practice. David had not made backup copies as he had gone from one version of his programs to the next. Reluctantly, he nodded his head.

"Then he doesn't know it, but if he kills you and Albert and Robert and destroys the computers in the basement, then he's on his way to being free and clear — is that right?"

David was clearly uncomfortable.

"Yes, that's right."

"Jesus, David . . . doesn't that bother you? You've assumed all along that it was the tape that has been keeping him in line — which it has. But the tape doesn't have anything to do with keeping *you* alive. The tape

213

keeps *Shinogara* alive. Zack kills you, takes the programs and turns himself into IGC and jumps on his sword—what happens?"

David thought for a minute.

"Zack bargains," Maria continued. "IGC tells Zack that it won't go to the FBI. Zack buys it, and confesses. The 9350 in the basement has an audit record of the machines it has infected. IGC finds out the location of the machines, then sends out a technician to have it fixed—before November 19. IGC fixes the problem, then calls the FBI, and fires Zack at the same time. Zack plea-bargains for the names of Makato Shinogara, David Kimura, and Marcia Lee."

"But," David said, "if IGC *doesn't* go to the FBI, which you and I both believe it will . . . but if it doesn't, then it fixes the existing problem, discovers the encryption viruses, makes its machines more secure, and fires Zack Colby. He still has our names. We have the videotape. We bargain with him, maybe give him some money to get started again, and we all disappear."

"So, right now Zack Colby's best path is to lay down and confess," said Marcia.

Honesty *was* the best policy.

"That means *you* have to make sure he doesn't go off the deep end—that whatever you're doing now, you keep it up. Keep his mind off the right track," urged David Kimura.

Both David and Marcia felt considerably more isolated the further they continued the conversation.

"So, between now and the time your viruses are ready—and distributed, whenever that date is . . . if Zack looks like he's going to explode, go to IGC . . . or the FBI, what do we do?" asked Marcia.

The conclusion was inevitable.

"Kill him. You'll have to kill him," said David simply.

"Me?" questioned Marcia. "Why me?"

"That will have to be your job, Marcia. Do you think I'm going to send Albert or Robert out to kill Zack Colby? If something goes wrong, *you've* got to take immediate action. *You've* got to kill him. We need the machines, we need the access," said David.

"I'm not a murderer," said Marcia, her face turning red with anger. "I have *no* intention of killing Zack Colby," Marcia replied angrily. "In fact, if you want to know the truth — if it wasn't for Shinogara's threats to kill Zack, I wouldn't be here. I don't need the money. I don't need the hassle. The man hasn't done anything to anybody — he's just a poor, dumb schmo."

"Don't get upset with *me*. Those are the *facts,* Marcia. We will have other problems as well," added David.

"Like what?"

"Like what are we going to do with his wife and children? We'll have to kill them, too — or keep them out of the way until after the virus explodes," David logically moved forward.

"Jesus! This is getting worse by the second," she paused. "OK, that's if he goes off the deep end *before* you send your viruses. What happens afterward? Say between the time you send them, and the nineteenth — if that's still your date?" she asked, not seeing how anything would be different.

"Then we don't need the machines in the basement. We can dial in from anyplace. We assume that I have a complete set, or sets, of backup disks. The mainframe programs we've created have been created using the REXX PC editor, so everything can be simply backed onto PC diskettes. However, we *do* need Colby's PROFS sign-on capability, his ID number," said David, his mind working quickly.

"Why?" asked Marcia.

215

"To send the ransom demands to IGC in Armonk — by PROFS. And, we need it in case something goes wrong. We need to be in touch with IGC all the way up until the last moment."

"But we don't need Zack Colby," stated Marcia.

"Right. If he screws up, he's dead. One of us will have to kill him." A look of determination crossed David's face. "I've never killed anyone before — although I've *wanted* to kill Zack a few times in the last weeks. But I would be able to do it. I've worked too long on this project — and there's too much at stake for me to let one man get in the way."

"What about his family?" asked Marcia.

David shook his head.

"I don't know. I just don't know," he said honestly.

David and Marcia were mentally exhausted after the verbal bout with reality. David knew he had to develop a good set of backup diskettes. Shinogara needed a copy, he needed a copy. Somebody needed to know what the encryption codes were.

"So, when are you going to be ready?" she asked.

"Friday. Would that make you happy?" he asked.

Marcia returned a genuine smile of appreciation.

"I'll be *so* glad when this is done," she answered.

"So will I," David said, getting up to leave.

"Wait a minute," Marcia held up her hand. "What happens on Friday? What happens *after* Friday?"

"We should be done testing all the programs by Friday morning. When I leave Zack's home that afternoon, he won't know that we're done. And I don't want him to know. I want him to think it's just another day. Since all we need is Zack's ID and password, we can start the virus from anyplace. Mr. Shinogara wants to do it from his estate in Los Angeles. And I can't blame him. The men have worked long and hard for this day," said David with more than a degree of satisfaction.

"And afterward?" she asked.

"We just have to make sure that Zack stays on the straight and narrow. With me out of the way, it should be easier," David replied.

"Out of the way?" questioned Marcia.

"Well . . . so to speak. I'll be here, but only if you think he needs reinforcement. There will be no need for Robert and Albert to be there. In fact, they'll probably be in the first group to evacuate. I'll be one of the last."

This was the first time David had spoke of evacuation. It gave her a queasy feeling in the pit of her stomach.

"When will you . . . evacuate?" she asked.

" We'll send out the express packages to John Holton on the afternoon of the eighteenth. I can leave any time after that. Like I said, the PROFS message can be activated from anyplace. If I can dial into the system in Denver from Zack's home in Cheyenne, or from Shinogara's home in Los Angeles, then I can do the same thing from Honolulu or Tokyo, with a portable PC from any telephone. It doesn't matter." David smiled confidently.

Marcia's mind reeled.

And what's Wu planning? she wondered. What's in it for him? He could be out to steal the ransom. But he'd need to know where the meeting was. He knows IGC's going to take a hit. He could go to the FBI and turn Shinogara in. So, what happens to me? I'm in trouble. Wu's a hero, and I'm in jail. OK, so he doesn't do that. Instead . . .

Marcia's mind couldn't come up with trie scenarios, so it shut down.

"Oh, yes . . . I almost forgot," added David. "If I do finish on Friday, Mr. Shinogara would like you to attend the meeting in Los Angeles as well. Zack won't notice —

in fact, he'll probably be grateful for a reprieve from us," David laughed.

13 November

Mr. Xiang Wu
820 Grant Street, #2
San Francisco, California 94111

Dear Mr. Wu:

David's virus will be started Saturday the 15th from Shinogara's estate in Los Angeles. David says that he will be through on Friday and that we will be going to LA for a meeting, most likely on Saturday. It sounds like they're planning a celebration after it's all done.

I've been invited and will probably attend, although not for long. I have some things I need to get done in San Francisco and will go there for the weekend, before returning to Cheyenne on Monday.

With regard to backup, David admitted that he had none, although he will have by the time he leaves. He says that he will have a backup as will Mr. Shinogara. David doesn't know the details of the meeting in Hong Kong; and neither do I. Shinogara is handling all of the "evacuation" plans.

David says that he will be one of the last to evacuate, as late as the morning of the 19th. The way he describes it, the message to John Holton (CEO of IGC) could be delivered from a PC anyplace in the world. They plan to activate Colby's ID and send the message internally.

Unless I hear to the contrary, I will return to

218

Cheyenne until the evening of the 18th, at which time I will take care of myself.
Marcia Lee

Wu could feel Marcia's stress.

"She knows she's a liability to Shinogara," muttered Wu. "She could always blackmail *him*."

And, in theory, she could blackmail *me*, Wu thought.

Xiang Wu handed the letter to Jimmy Chimichanga, who scanned it quickly, his face set in a wrinkled frown.

"Can you be ready this weekend?" Wu asked, turning in his chair.

The view of San Francisco was spectacular. Evening light obliquely splayed across the tall downtown buildings, making the streets below darker than they should be, and the people scurrying to their destinations more vulnerable than they knew.

Jimmy C. felt the paper in his hands, twisting it to the point of crinkling.

"Yes, I can be ready. They'll never know what hit them. What about the girl?"

Xiang Wu turned to Chimichanga, the fading evening light darkening his face. His mind quickly translated investment into the present value of people.

"Kill her. Kill them all. Everybody. Nobody comes out alive. Obliterate them! We'll decide on Colby later."

David went through a final checklist. He logged on to Zack's ID in Denver, passed through to the Yorktown disk, perused the files there, and was wordlessly amazed at the lack of security and the lack of concern for security by the high-tech users. They were invincible. The bulletin board notes were filled with I'm-A-Bigger-Tech-Weenie-Than-You information.

As he did on most days, Zack sat nearby, his arms crossed, his face filled with dark clouds. But this day was different. David seemed more relaxed, less hostile. Zack paid attention to what David was doing. He wasn't programming. He was checking things.

He's done, Zack thought.

Zack's first reaction was right on the money. Today had been different than all the others. David hadn't done any programming magic today. All he'd done was check things. There were no file transfers, no HLLAPI tricks, no talking to himself. Instead, nothing but smiles and snide remarks.

In the space of a month Zack's basement had been filled to bursting with computer trash — the technolitter of modern society. Wastebaskets overflowed with fanfold printouts, cellophane shrink wrap, and balled-up pieces of yellow paper. Floppy diskettes were everywhere — some labeled, most not. Diskette jackets, which in real life disappear as fast as paper clips accumulate, lay unmatched and empty in every nook and cranny throughout the room. Software manuals were rarely matched with their corresponding hard cases.

"Would you help me clean up?" David asked.

To Zack it was a clear signal that David was indeed finished.

"Are you done? Is this it?" Zack asked anxiously as he helped match software boxes to the right programs.

"Not quite — but we're getting close," David lied.

Short of leaving everything where it was, there was no way to cover up the fact that the end was near. David couldn't afford to leave behind any evidence or clues that might help someone figure out what he'd done. David methodically checked the area for any notes or papers that were his, inspecting each diskette to see if it had anything to do with his programs. Those that did went into his ever-present tote, a medium-size canvas bag from L. L. Bean with a red strip around the top. Standard-size briefcases weren't designed for tech weenies.

"Help me, will you?" David said as he walked to the door carrying three trashcans.

" You're going to burn it?" Zack asked.

"Yes—it's safer for everybody. Get the door, please."

Zack opened the downstairs door, let David out, then followed him carrying an armload of fanfold paper. Except for the overflow smog from Denver, Cheyenne was like a lot of other small cities in that there was no ordinance against burning. While there was trash pickup, many people like Zack and Cheryl simply burned whatever they could. The Colbys' incinerator was in the back of the house on the downslope side of the office. While David fired the mess up, Zack walked back inside. His body was in a high state of agitation. The amphetamines were making him hyper, and he knew it. He was on the verge of exploding.

Not now! Zack warned himself.

David felt flushed with victory. His job was virtually over. Three years of programming. Three years of self-denial and seven-day work weeks were almost at an end.

Just a few more days! he thought.

David could see the consternation in Zack's face. He had a nearly overwhelming urge to rub Zack's face in the dirt. It was mean and unnecessary, but part of him wanted to make Zack feel lower than white whale shit at the bottom of the Mariana Trench. Instead, he let Zack hunker back inside while he stood near the incinerator and started the fire—a fire that would burn off any trace of his work.

Victory!

From the basement Zack could feel the vibration from David's car as it started up, then backed out of the driveway. Zack didn't move. He sat down in the nearest chair he could find. Under his left shoe was a sheet of silver sticky-coated write protection tabs used to protect diskettes from being accidentally overwritten. Then his leg started to shiver, as if the tabs were trying to eat through the bottom of his shoe. Then the shiver rippled through Zack's whole body.

What have I done?

He stared at the black metal drawer, not knowing what to do, half expecting it to speak and tell him. Inside was dynamite. Was it his redemption?

Call Scotty!

The two young men had been best of friends while Zack and Cheryl were courting, and later while Scotty was going to college. But Scotty was with the FBI, and the FBI meant confession, and Zack's mind couldn't come to grips with confession.

Is there a way out?

Zack gripped the sides of his head with both hands, his fingers digging into his scalp. Fragments of images strobed through his brain. Dallas. Marcia. The three of them. The little girl. Hanging by a chain. Head back, blond hair hanging down, naked but a torn shirt. Photos. The cries. The *Dallas Morning News.* Drugs. David. The old man. The Texas State Penitentiary. Large black men.

Zack could see himself in every image. But he couldn't concentrate. Cheryl. The children. Mom and Dad. Scotty. The Good Life. The people he knew. Zack repeated scenes where he could see the respect in people's eyes, respect they had for *him.* There was laughter.

Concentrate! Do something!

But he couldn't. The good and bad thoughts began to mix together, sinking his resolve into mental concrete. He saw himself telling Cheryl what happened. He could see the look of hurt and anger in her eyes, the revulsion.

No honey, please. I didn't mean it. I'm sorry. Please.

But her face mirrored more than disappointment. It was disgust.

What do you want, Zack?

I . . . I . . . want it all.

What Zack couldn't see was that he had to cut it off, give up something to get something. But what he couldn't do was identify his bottom line, the absolute minimum he was willing to settle for.

Was it the Texas State Penitentiary with sweaty ogres ready to rip his colon? he thought.

No, no . . . I don't want that. Please, no. Please.

You're helping these people sabotage your company, Zack! You're going to jail for that.

It was a white collar crime. They'd understand. I was forced to do it. Please.

Zack could see himself going to a minimum security lockup, just like on the news. The one where the rich guys, the white men, go to do their time. Behind the tall chain-link fence he could see Cheryl and the kids waiting for him.

But she still had the look in her eyes.

Zack didn't like that look.

He couldn't come to grip with the difference between hard time and *really* hard time. Not from a man whose hands were callused only on the tips of his fingers from keyboarding, whose worst injury was a paper cut. Losing any of his life was like losing it all — wife, children, friends, job, house, freedom, self-respect — they were all tied together.

At that very moment, 2:15 Mountain Standard Time Friday, November 14, Zack Colby had the means to save himself. The tiny voice of reason shouted up through his soul, but had no chance against the behemoths of fear and doubt. If he'd driven to IGC, or called Scotty, or had gone to the police, or had told Cheryl — if he had done any of these things, he could have been free.

Instead, he did nothing.

"You don't have to go, if you don't want," said David.

"Oh yes I do! This is payday, don't forget. I'm contracted to help you until the nineteenth, but I'm not waiting until then to get paid. You're going to be invisible people after the nineteenth and little Marcia is going to be quite busy covering her tracks. Won't we, Joe?" She smiled to her bodyguard.

"What does Shinogara have planned?" she asked.

David paused, considering his answer.

"He wants the whole group to see the virus started. In the big room — remember?"

"Yes, I remember. You can do that from there?"

"We can start it from anyplace — even the airplane if we had the right connection," David said, and smiled. "Then he has a celebration planned, I believe . . . a party."

"I'm *sure* I want to be around a bunch of horny, drunk programmers. You just made my mind up," Marcia laughed. "Joe and I will go home for the weekend — after we get our paychecks."

Shinogara's private twin-engine jet eschewed the lineup coming into the fog at LAX and requested a diversion to the airport in Long Beach instead. While there was no limo waiting, one was readily available and immediately chartered. The Long Beach airport was closer to the Palos Verdes peninsula and much easier to get to than the mess around LAX, even with its completed renovations.

David and his programmers were excited. For Albert and Robert, this was the end of their three-year assignment. They wouldn't go to Hong Kong with David and Mr. Shinogara for the ransom negotiations. With the help of several programmers at the mansion, the pair of young men would get choice entry-management positions in the electronics firms of their choice. In Japan there was already behind-the-scenes bidding for their services. Everyone on Makato Shinogara's staff was wanted. When the mission was completed, Shinogara himself would not have to work one additional day. When IGC paid its ransom, as it would be forced to do, Shinogara would hand the reins of the operation over to his counterpart, an equally talented man named Fujito, who was fully prepared to integrate IGC's technology into a wide variety of government-sponsored projects, both existing and on the drawing board.

Shinogara would then retire, receiving the grateful, but unpublicized, thanks of Japanese industry. His every need would be taken care of for the rest of his life.

It didn't surprise Marcia to see Shinogara greet them at the door. He'd done so every time they'd met. He still looked fresh and businesslike, this time dressed in a conservative gray suit which only went to highlight his mostly gray hair. But once the group stepped inside, the only similarity to her previous visits was that they were in the same house. Today Shinogara's house was at a near business frenzy. Actual people walked through the main house, even milled around in animated groups. Some even carried what appeared to be cocktails.

God, what will come of them? she thought.

The men were even *smiling*.

David and his programmers were welcomed with warm shouts. Even though she didn't understand a word of Japanese, Marcia could feel the genuine outpour of appreciation and thanks for David and his crew. David was in the Land Beyond, as were Robert and Albert.

"Will you stay the weekend, Miss Lee?" asked Makato Shinogara.

Marcia looked at the older Japanese businessman with different eyes. She sensed that this wasn't just a polite invitation. Yes would mean something different.

"No, I don't think so. David's told me you're planning a little celebration for your men. I think I'll pass, if you don't mind."

"So sorry. I think you would have enjoyed it," replied Shinogara, genuinely disappointed.

"David tells me that you're planning to start the virus from here," she stated.

"Yes—the men are very excited about it. You *will* stay for it, won't you?"

"Yes, certainly. But first, you and I have some business to discuss."

"I understand. This way please." Shinogara bowed and pointed her to his plush study, which was to the left of the entranceway and offered a clear southwestern exposure to the Pacific Ocean.

"I don't know what your plans are for David—and in fact, he's not quite sure—but, I'm very interested in you and I settling up before I leave, which will be shortly after this virus of yours is started. Frankly, I'm curious," started Marcia.

"I see," said Shinogara, hand on beard on chin.

"Yes. As far as I'm concerned, when David pushes that button, or whatever it is that he does, our basic

226

agreement is complete. Unless I don't understand something, it's my impression that once this thing is started, nothing short of the Second Coming is going to get it stopped. Am I correct?"

"Approximately," Shinogara admitted.

"You hired me to do a job, and I do what I'm paid to do. I'll stay with Zack until the evening of the eighteenth. By then you'll be long gone. Hong Kong—is that it?"

Shinogara had no comment.

"Whatever," Marcia continued. "I don't really care. My job is to see that Zack Colby goes nighty-night on the evening of Tuesday November 18. That thing of yours goes off at nine-thirty Mountain time Wednesday morning. I plan to be long gone by then, as will my people. In twelve hours I can be almost anyplace in the world, even from Cheyenne, Wyoming."

Shinogara nodded acknowledgment.

"So this is the last time you and I will meet. I'd like you to make a telephone call to the night manager at my bank in Geneva and authorize the transfer of the second half of my payment," said Marcia.

Her green eyes never left his steely grays.

"Very well," Shinogara said.

He picked up an odd-shaped modern phone, pressed a button, and waited for the automatic caller to be activated.

"English, please," Marcia added.

Shinogara nodded, then spoke.

"This is Makato Shinogara. . . ."

The Japanese security system used voice identification for verification of identity.

"Continue," the machine said in synthesized English.

"I authorize the transfer of one million dollars to the account of Miss Marcia Lee, account 164882, Bank of

227

Geneva. I authorize the transfer from the general fund."

Shinogara waited for fifteen seconds while the amount, Marcia's account, and the routing information were verified.

"Processing completed," was the reply.

Shinogara hung up.

"It is done," he said, smiling. "Shall we join the others?"

"Very well."

As he'd done two months earlier, Shinogara led Marcia out of the main house, now nearly empty, along the covered walkway to the computer building, and up the elevator to the second floor. This time the auditorium was packed with employees. An excited two-octave hum had begun to build as individual conversations bantered back and forth.

Like it was orchestrated by a master conductor, the sound of conversation dropped a decibal when Shinogara carefully led the tall and sensuous woman down the cascading steps to the bottom of the auditorium to a reserved seat in the front row. Marcia was the only woman in the room, her strikingly beautiful blue dress in stark contrast to the drabness of the men. She was a Technicolor woman in a sea of gray. Shinogara was to her right, David to her left.

Shinogara stood up.

The room instantly quieted.

"Fellow employees," came the stiff pronouncement, "our time is at hand."

The room exploded with thunderous applause.

"What we have worked for . . . what we have dedicated our lives for . . . has come to pass. We are about to deliver our blow to the enemy. A crippling blow! A staggering blow! A blow that he will never recover from. A blow that will make us . . . invincible!" Shinogara drew

228

the last word out.

Marcia was stunned at Shinogara's words. The old man spoke with the fervor of a battlefield commander. From up close she could see tears in his eyes. His words leaped out to the group, which as one returned them with a cheer of victory.

Suddenly, the room darkened and a map of the United States dropped from behind the podium. Lights littered the map, each illuminated dot indicating a separate IGC facility. Where there were multiple locations, the lights were larger. An overhead spotlight made Shinograra seem taller than he was.

"Gentlemen, I give you . . . David Kimura," said Shinogara, who bowed and gracefully took his seat next to Marcia.

The room went nuts.

Marcia could have been inside a North Carolina yahoo bar on a hot summer wet T-shirt night and the noise wouldn't have been greater. David didn't just walk to the stage, he was a *presence,* he floated — he was *fueled* by the outpouring of admiration.

"Thank you, thank you," he said, and smiled, then bowed. "I must credit Albert and Robert for their role in this — without them, it wouldn't have been possible," said David, generously sweeping his hands toward the pair, who rose briefly and bowed to applause nearly as warm.

For twenty minutes David went through the technical details of the virus, including the freebie 9350 from Endicott. Laughter cascaded at the description of how they'd fallen into the contamination of 350 plus 9350s and over 1,400 terminals.

"Yes . . . Yes . . . Yes!" came the voices.

While the conversation was mostly English, David did lapse into Japanese at particularly emotional times. Marcia didn't have to understand a word of what was

229

happening to understand what was *actually* happening.

These people were electronic kamikazes, she thought.

Marcia could see David was slowly bringing them up to an emotional climax. He was doing it better than she ever thought he could. At age twenty-eight, he had quite a presence. At some point, a large projection screen dropped on the right side of the front part of the room. It didn't obscure the large map of the U.S., which now had the targeted IGC offices with red lights.

David spoke rapid Japanese to Robert and Albert, who in turn tapped a series of commands into the PC on the stage. There was no hidden-rabbit trick here. They were going to give a cold demo to the group, so confident were they of their success. The large screen projected what was happening on the small PC screen. Everything was normal. David relayed what was happening — they were accessing the Denver, Colorado PROFS systems — live — on line — now! . . . David *was* a showman.

As Robert and Albert followed his instructions, David walked them through the files that currently resided on the Denver system. By an occasional "hot-key" to their PC session, David was able to explain, in excruciating detail, what the code actually was doing. He was often interrupted by applause from the knowledgeable group. The room grew silent as David reconstructed what would happen on the morning of November 19. He powered on — nothing — nothing — then, *blam!* On the screen was the do-or-die message of terminal encryption.

For a third time, the room went totally bonkers.

Shinogara came back into the room, arms in the air. For the next ten minutes he congratulated David and his men. He then introduced Yamamoto, who was in charge of Phase Two.

"Phase Two has been designed to choke IGC's communications system and to put additional pressure on them to quickly agree to our terms. We have chosen thirty IGC locations."

He pressed a button and thirty lights changed from white to red: Boston, Hartford, White Plains, Armonk, New York City, Philadelphia, Bethesda, Washington D.C., Raleigh-Research Triangle Park, Atlanta (two) Miami, Boca Raton, Dallas (two), Houston, Austin, Kansas City, St. Louis, Chicago, Cleveland, Detroit (two), Minneapolis, Denver, Seattle, San Francisco, San Jose, and Los Angeles (two).

"For each of these locations we have leased three separate facilities where we have installed forty computers each, all with an auto-dial modem. As you know, the computers need only an RJ11 connection from the PC's modem to the telephone outlet, which has been installed in all but two locations. These locations will be completed by Wednesday morning."

There was enthusiastic applause as he sat down and Shinogara returned to the podium. Shinogara then walked over to the keyboard of the PC, which had a 2,400-bits-per-second internal synchronous modem installed, hit a function key, and brought up the logo of the Rocky Mountain Information Center from the 3090 in the basement of the IGC building at 4700 Syracuse Street, Denver, Colorado.

Shinogara brought up Zack Colby's PROFS screen and went into

PF4 MAIL A NON-PROFS FILE USING PROFS ELECTRONIC MAIL

The screen prompted him for file name and type, which Shinogara typed in. The screen then came back and asked who he would like to send it to.

Shinogara skillfully identified the first of the two hundred lists, people who represented a cross-section of the IGC employee population — administrators, systems engineers, salesmen, staff people, managers.

SEND TO: ONE
FROM: DENVMIC1 (COLBYZAC)

The ONE represented a list of two hundred people, each with a PROFS node (DENVMIC1) and ID (COLBYZAC) like Zack's. The note had been carefully appended with .AT, which represented the coding in Zack's note required to suppress the displaying of the list of "carbon copies." It also prevented the sending machine from receiving a list of VM acknowledgments, a sometimes irritating feature of PROFS. In this particular case, it would have been very bad form for the other 199 people on the list to know that they too were being sent the same message. Also, since VM sent four display acknowledgments for each message-note sent back to the sender, without the .AT the Denver 3090 could be brought to its knees, since ONE was the first of over two hundred separate lists. And, each recipient thought that he or she was receiving an individual note from Zack Colby, poor beleaguered marketing representative from Cheyenne, Wyoming.

"The virus had been sent. Your years of work will be rewarded. Congratulations to all of you!" Shinogara beamed, then shot his right arm into the air, his hand in a balled fist.

"Tojo! Tojo! Tojo," he led the cheers.

It was all over but the shouting. The men were flushed with the pride of finishing a long and difficult project. As the meeting broke up, the men left the computer building in animated clumps. David and his programmers were the heroes of the day. Shinogara guided Marcia by the arm back toward the main house. Joe followed behind them. Most of the men were now milling around inside the huge living room area of the mansion, talking in rapid Japanese. It was a strange sight. Then she understood why. From out front she heard the wheeze of a bus as it came to a stop. From it came high-pitched voices of giggling young women.

Working girls, thought Marcia, nodding her head.

"You're welcome to stay, Miss Lee," said a beaming Makato Shinogara.

"No thanks. I don't want to get in the way of a girl making an honest living. This party's a little premature, don't you think?"

"Most of these men will never see each other again after this week. They all have, or will have, contacts in many different businesses throughout Japan. New identities have been guaranteed. It would be quite by accident that any of them should ever meet again. But if they do, this mission will be a secret they will carry with them for the rest of their lives. They've worked very hard for this moment, Miss Lee. They deserve much more than this little diversion," Shinogara replied, guiding Marcia to the front door. The foyer was filled with the electric sounds of pretty young women. Music competed with laughter. The party had begun.

"Let's go," Marcia nodded to Joe.

Shinogara escorted Marcia and Joe out to the curb.

"Very good, Miss Lee. Thank you for everything," bowed Shinogara.

"Good luck," she replied as she gracefully swung her legs from the pavement into the limo.

"Let's go home, Joe," Marcia said, and smiled as the driver slowly drove past the guard station and out onto Crest Road.

Propriety, etiquette, and other rules of behavior had been temporarily suspended at the estate of Makato Shinogara. The ladies knew how to party.

Inside the computer building David Kimura sat at the PC mounted on the stage. The link to Denver was still up. He would leave it on for the entire weekend, as long as he was out of touch with Zack Colby. Since the same ID and password couldn't be used twice in the system, David had no worry that Zack would sign on and try anything stupid. Zack couldn't erase the VM programs anyway because David had password-protected each of them before leaving. Outside, the heated pools and adjacent hot tub were filled with warm slippery bodies.

Makato Shinogara came into the nearly darkened room and down the steps to the stage, where his chief programmer was busy ensuring that the virus went to all of the mailing lists.

"How does it go?" he asked.

"Slow, but steady — we have nearly two hundred fifty lists in all. Even on a weekend it takes a while for the system to digest and process so many notes," replied a weary David Kimura. "I should be done within the hour."

"Good. When you're done I want you to enjoy yourself, David. Relax for a night. The women will be here until Monday."

David just nodded his head in a thanks-but-no-thanks manner.

"I still must get the ransom note typed and filed. I don't think I'll be much for partying afterward," David said, knowing that he would spend the night sleeping on a cot in his office, his ears filled with wax plugs to block out the noise.

David reached inside his tote bag and pulled out a manila folder and a box of diskettes with a red rubber band around it.

"I made a duplicate set of the program diskettes and decryption keys for you. Do you want them?"

Shinogara shook his head in a fatherly fashion.

"No, you keep them for me, please."

David handed Shinogara the folder. Inside was the ransom demand that would be sent to John Holton, president and chairman of the board of IGC.

"Is this what you want sent?" David asked. The emotion of the afternoon had left him drained.

Shinogara scanned through the letter, his attention riveted to the words that had been carefully crafted over the last two months.

"Yes, this looks very good," Shinogara approved.

"I'll time it to be sent five minutes before the virus strikes. Don't worry, I'll use some innocuous SUBJ—just something so that we can retrieve it quickly when we need it," David said, beginning to type the list of demands. "When we get ready to send it to Holton we'll make the heading as threatening as possible—something to get his attention—or his staff's."

David went back to work.

"I'll leave you alone," Shinogara said. "Don't be too long."

"Are you going to pay him?" David asked, curious.

Shinogara's slender body was outlined against the bright lights from the pool area.

"What makes you ask that?" Shinogara asked, equally curious.

"I just want to know, that's all."

"You don't think I should, do you?" asked Shinogara, reading the mind of his young protégé.

"No, I don't," David admitted.

"We are businessmen, David. And don't ever forget it. We've made a business transaction with Mr. Colby. The briefcase will be delivered to him on the night of the eighteenth, and you may tell him so when you return to Cheyenne next week."

David turned from the computer screen, a perplexed look on his face. He had hoped he would not have to return to Cheyenne.

"You understand why you must return, don't you?" asked Shinogara.

"Yes. I understand," said a very reluctant David Kimura.

"I have no one else with your combination of skills."

"You mean, if Colby gets out of line, I'm the only one who can threaten him physically?"

"That is correct," said Shinogara.

"And what if he *does* get out of line. What if Colby decides to give himself up?"

Shinogara paused. His face was black, in shadows, hidden from David's view.

"He *must* not. Do you remember a question that Miss Lee had for us when she first came here? She asked us how far we were willing to go? Do you remember my reply?" asked Shinogara, the teacher.

"Whatever it takes," replied David, slowly.

"Yes, *whatever* it takes. You are our critical link, David. And you know it. Zack Colby must not break down. IGC cannot find out about the virus before it strikes. You know this. If they have as much as an hour's lead time, all could be lost."

David's face was a mixture of uncertainty and pride.

"When will you be leaving?" David asked. "We've been concentrating on our programs for so long, I've not given much thought to what happens next. I'm not even sure where we are going. You've always been the one . . ." David's voice trailed off.

"Yes, I know." Shinogara stepped back to a position where the outside light obliquely crossed his profile. From his inside coat pocket Shinogara handed David a thick envelope. "The instructions are inside. Do you have your passport?"

David patted his back pocket.

"With me at all times," he replied.

"Inside are open-ended one-way tickets to Tokyo, Singapore, Honolulu, Jakarta, and Osaka. All flights leave from San Francisco, and connect to Hong Kong. Be assured, all is covered."

I'm a programmer, not a spy, David thought.

"Fog's coming in fast," the pilot said to the burly passenger.

Jimmy C. ignored the statement and responded by pointing upward with his index finger.

"Up. Now," he said gruffly.

The call to Wu had come in from the Lee woman's partner. The computer virus was irretrievably flowing through IGC's communications veins. It was time for Jimmy C. to carry out his part of the deal, which he was fully prepared to do.

By the end of the night they all would be dead.

The pilot had done his job and warned Jimmy about the weather, but he could see that his concerns were irrelevant to the situation. He was going to fly the helicopter, fog or no fog. As were the other five 'copters lined up behind him.

So up they went. Visibility was less than a half mile. To the north they could barely make out the headlights of the slowly moving traffic on the Santa Monica Freeway. To the east, the interchange of the Santa Monica and San Diego freeways was a mush of lights. Westwood and Wilshire Boulevard beyond were only imaginations. The earth seemed to end at the VA hospital in West LA. Closer, a few cars drove along Centinela Boulevard, mostly filled with Spanish-surnamed people. The Santa Monica airport was officially closed. Always a commuter airline terminal, the airport was filled with Pipers and Cherokees of all kinds. Tie-down service wasn't cheap, but the location couldn't be beat. And nobody wanted to try and land their twin-engine Beechcraft at LAX with a 767 ready to blow up its ass. The airport was comfortable, convenient, and relatively safe.

Tonight it was not safe. There was at least a three-hour delay in landing at LAX.

"Up," said Jimmy C.

The pilot went up—slowly, but up. It was eleven o'clock and Jimmy had to find out if the fog was going to be a friend or an enemy tonight. At five hundred feet they broke through the fog and began to parallel the Santa Monica Freeway toward downtown LA.

"This way," Jimmy pointed to the south.

"Can't do it," replied the pilot through the headsets. "Can't go through the LAX landing pattern. Big no-no. They'd get real upset if we bumped into a 747 or something. Got to go the long way around."

The long way around was really only ten, perhaps fifteen, minutes longer for the helicopter. They would have to parallel the Santa Monica Freeway, then turn south and to the same above the harbor. Even so, they'd have to cut their altitude down to a hundred feet, regardless.

As they crossed over Western Avenue they passed through the curtain into a crisp, clear night. Stars were out, the city bathed in lights. The pilot settled in at

238

seventy-five feet and accelerated. Neither man said a word. Ten minutes later they could see the oil refineries of Carson and Long Beach up ahead on the left. The pilot knew where Jimmy wanted him to go.

The fogbank appeared to envelop the whole Palos Verdes peninsula, from San Pedro to the south and east, all the way around to Redondo Beach on the north. From the junction of the Harbor and San Diego freeways, the pilot turned west, then south as he followed Hawthorne Boulevard. To their right were the huge think tank TRW buildings. Halfway up the peninsula the fog settled in like a nice old hat. The question was, did the hat have a hole in it? The pilot, now paying attention carefully, slowly entered the bank and proceeded south, raising his elevation as he did so.

"Listen, I've got to take it up. I don't know the hill that well. I don't want to run into the god-damned Safeway!"

Without acknowledgment, the pilot took it up to five hundred feet—pop—they were through! The entire Palos Verdes peninsula was indeed covered, all but the crest—and then, only part of it. Crest Road ran in and out of very dense patches.

"There!" pointed Jimmy.

It was the estate of Makato Shinogara. The red brick walls were illuminated all around the compound, which gave it a decidedly ethereal feeling—a wispy halo of artificial light. The main house was in dense fog, but the swimming pool, computer building, and two of the living quarters were in the clear.

Jimmy C. gave a thumbs-up.

"It's a go! The top of PV is clear, but you've got to hurry. I don't know how long it'll stay like this," said the pilot.

"Back off! I don't want them to suspect. Wait until the others get here!" shouted Jimmy.

239

* * *

One by one the five Rockwell helicopters lifted off from Santa Monica airport and moved in a similar pattern, first to the east, then to the south. Inside each helicopter were six fully armed members of Jimmy C.'s Southern California organization. When the helicopters arrived Jimmy's ground support would stage accidents on Hawthorne Boulevard, preventing any traffic from moving up the hill from either side.

At 11:10 David Kimura got up from his computer terminal. He was through. Finished. Done. Completed. Every last note had gone out. The ransom demand had been hidden in Zack Colby's note log, ready for retransmission on the nineteenth. He smiled as he looked out through the window at the hard-partying group. It was chilly outside and the fog was moving in and out. Yet, the happy programmers and their teenage nymphs played joyfully, mostly in the nude. Clothes weren't in fashion even in the main house, and certainly not in the Spartan living quarters, which were now beehives of foreplay—and end play.

What's that noise? David wondered.

Six helicopters came over the top of Palos Verdes and along Crest Road, then descended through the misty fog like vultures from hell.

"Unit one, take the main gate and security building. Units two and three, the dormitories near the north perimeter—watch for possible escapees over the wall. Unit four—strafe the main building. Unit five—take the computer center. Open fire at will," said Chimi-

240

changa, pleased.

The helicopters descended quickly and at the same time began to spread out, each to cover his assigned area. The swimming pool area became the killing fields of Rancho Palos Verdes.

"Did you see that?" exclaimed one "soldier," as Unit Two lowered above the swimming pool near Residence Hall One.

Naked people ran in every direction, a path of steam following their hot bodies to the edge of darkness.

"Fire!" said Jimmy.

And fire they did. The men were under orders to kill everyone and everything in sight. Not a living soul was to leave Shinogara's estate alive. Naked young prostitutes ran alongside naked middle-aged programmers. All received the same punishment as gunmen opened fire from the hovering helicopters. Screams of terror were mixed with screams of death as the soft spitting sounds from the automatic rifles were nearly drowned by the *thumpa-thumpa* of the craft.

David watched speechlessly as the first wave of gunfire opened, killing ten people instantly. Then he heard the shattering of glass and the ricocheting of bullets through the computer center as Unit Five started to land, spraying attacks on the windows as it did so.

Get out!

David's instinct told him that he had to run to the darkness of the perimeter to even have a chance. The helicopters would land inside the compound, do their damage, and be gone before any of their neighbors gave it a second thought. Shinogara flew in and out of the compound on a regular basis. It was his normal mode of transportation to and from the airport.

Wild gunfire ripped through the second-floor classroom, shattering glass. David dove for the floor, but realized that he had less than two minutes to save himself.

The lights. Get the lights.

David was familiar with the layout of the building, which was as typical a college building as one would find on any campus. Except that there was no basement. Because of the number of computers on the second floor, the electrical closet had been put there. David scrambled along the floor as Unit Five hovered ten feet, then five, then touched down in the large grassy area on the pool side.

David pushed through the door, then got to his feet and ran halfway down the fifty-foot hallway to the electrical closet; which was unlocked — once again because of the number of on-the-spot rewirings that had to be patched for this computer or the next. David pulled the master switch down and ran back toward the presentation room as the building, and more importantly, the grounds, were thrown into pitch darkness. Warrior cries of some type were heard all over. David knew they would be inside in seconds.

Get the diskettes. Get the diskettes and do whatever you have to, but get the hell out of here. Get the diskettes!

Without the diskettes there would be no way to barter technology.

Get the diskettes!

David stumbled back down the auditorium-style steps, stuffed Shinogara's box of diskettes and the thick envelope into the tote bag, involuntarily checked his rear pants pocket for his passport and wallet, then staggered toward the double set of doors that led to offices and storage areas behind the presentation room.

Run! Run!

And David ran like a drug-crazed banshee over blue-hot coals.

With his tote clutched to his chest, David shouldered the stairwell door, only to be stopped dead in his tracks by the sound of two men with lights strapped to their heads making their way into the foyer below him. Shots popped in the background, seemingly in all directions.

Damn!

Carried by instinct, David ran back through the supply room, stumbling over boxes, then into the relative light of the unlit classroom. Bullets traced through the night as men and women ran for their lives. The guard at the front gate was dead, his body dragged behind the wall.

David went to a window on the far wall, opened it, kicked the screen out, and jumped.

I hope this isn't the one over the loading dock, he thought.

In the distance Makato Shinogara heard the approaching sound of a helicopter but gave it no mind. Since he expected nobody, he assumed whoever was up there was confused by the fog. His attention was completely distracted by the pair of nineteen-year-old nymphs who at that moment were on top of him, servicing different pleasure points, and doing a very good job at it.

It wasn't until the night air was filled with a cacophany of helicopter noise that Shinogara pushed the young women away and scrambled out of bed. Naked, he ran to a window and saw a group of commandos kill the guard at the front gate. Two of the men went inside the blockhouse and seized control of the electronics. One man gave instructions to the rest. With beams of light shining forward from their helmets, the group advanced toward the front of the house.

It was then that Shinogara could hear the sounds of death in the rear courtyard. High-pitched screams for mercy mixed with the heavy sounds of beating helicopter blades and tinny sounds of lawn furniture being tossed around in the breeze.

In front, one of the attackers went to his knees and aimed what appeared to be a rocket launcher at the front of the house. In a rush of flames it spit a projectile. Instantly the house was shaken by a tremendous explosion. The two young girls, momentarily frozen in positions of love, screamed and tried to cover themselves up.

Downstairs, the heavy front doors had been blown open. The foyer and living room were filled with smoke and debris. There was a simultaneous explosion from the back of the house, this time with more devastating effect. Shards of glass flew everywhere. Screams of pain came from revelers in the living room.

Then there came death, through the front and rear doors, spraying bullets from semiautomatic weapons in an arc that created a cross fire in the living room. Some tried to run to the staircase leading up to the bedroom area, but were shot down. Naked young women ran in every direction, but were cut down with equal precision as the troops methodically spread out to every room.

"Upstairs!" shouted one man.

Shinogara had no weapon. He went to the window and tried to open it, but it was painted shut. His house was climate-controlled by a central heater-air conditioner. As a result, the windows had never been opened. Shinogara struggled to pick up a heavy chair and managed to lunge for the window, successfully breaking the lower half of it with two of the chair's legs. With the seat pillow he began to knock away the rest of the glass, just as three heavily armed men came into the room.

"It's Shinogara," said one burly, unattractive man, obviously the leader.

Shinogara turned to the men, instinctively putting the seat cushion in front of him for protection. With practiced ease, all three attackers let loose with a barrage of bullets that sprayed death in all directions. Hundreds of holes popped and ripped through silk sheets, soft pillows, young skin, and an old man. The carnage was complete.

"Find the programmer, David Kimura," instructed Jimmy C.

Fortunately, the window wasn't over the loading dock. David fell in a clumsy pile twenty feet below. The top of the box marked Kimura came off, its contents scattered on the damp ground. David quickly gathered them up like little lost sheep, then resumed his hot-coal sprint.

"There goes one of them!" came a shout, which was followed by several bursts of gunfire. Spits and tufts of ground splattered around him, but he wasn't hit. There were unmistakable sounds of rising helicopters, ships that David knew were coming after him. Searchlights glowed.

David ran into the fog. Its soft fingers grabbed and sucked him up, like the enticement of a sweet whore in a dark alley. And it was never so welcome. Something whispered in his ear to dodge the bullets that would surely come, and to change directions ASAP, which he did. Turning around as he ran, he could see the dim outlines of flashlights way, way far away, and hear voices shouting.

David was terrified, but was determined to put as much distance between him and—

With his head turned to look behind him, David ran

smack into the brick wall, then bounced back flat on his back. He was almost knocked out.

Voices. I hear voices. Hurry! Get up! Please oh please get up!

The part of his brain that hadn't quite gone dark finally was able to wake up the other senses and convince them that they were still indeed in a fire drill situation. The brick wall was ten feet tall. All of its lights were out. Fortunately for David, when the security building went, so did the systems. To the five-foot-nine David, the ten-foot-tall fence looked as tall as a basketball hoop — which it was — and David Kimura was no Michael Jordan.

You can't jump, he thought. You can't reach the top by jumping. Your arms are too short and you're too stocky. Forget it.

"Think!" he berated himself.

He had to put the obvious out of his mind. He needed a ladder, or a step, or something to help him get over.

Use your clothes.

David looked up at the wall. Every fifty feet was a dual-headed spotlight mounted in steel brackets on top of the wall. One light faced inward, the other outward. Still, it was ten feet tall. David shucked off his shoes, then his pants, and sat down on the damp cold ground. He took his belt off, which was the loop variety, and tied it back together again, this time in the last notch. He took his left pant leg and tied it like a rope to the looped belt, wrapping the pant leg around several times before knotting it. Then he did the same with the right pant leg. Now he had a pair of pants with a looped belt, a lasso of sorts. But if he had any chance of looping the belt around one of the ten-foot-high lights, he'd need some ballast. Thus the shoes. As best he could, he tied the shoes on opposite sides of the belt. It wasn't very good, but it gave him enough weight so that he could try to throw the shoes up and over the light, in hopes of hooking the belt. Finally, he took off his long-sleeved shirt and tied the sleeves to the waist of the pants. It was the weakest of the knots, but if he got it hooked, he probably wouldn't need the shirt anyway — except to get dressed with on the other side.

David was scared, but the scared kept him warm. On the third try the shoes sailed over the wall, the belt snagged the light, and the pants held.

David had never considered the fact that he might not be able to climb the thing once it was hooked.

And he never gave it a thought. He ducked down and looped the tote bag around his neck. All systems secured. It was by no means graceful, but driven by fear, David climbed the wall on the first attempt. His legs and arms had deep burns from scraping against the rough brick. David fell down on the other side in a thicket of scraggly manzanita bush. He could hear voices on the other side, but had to look out for himself — so as quick as he could, he untied his now too-good knots and got dressed. Then the voices were gone. The helicopters were in the air.

If they were in the air, then they must be on the ground, he thought. Get going!

David knew he was on the north side of the compound. He was in fog and bouncing down through grabby prickly bushes that seemed to know exactly where to poke the sharpest of needles. Thirty minutes later he ran through the backyard of a poshly located red-roofed California-style home, and dashed to the street. Dogs barked in unison as he ran away from Hawthorne Boulevard.

I have the diskettes, he thought. The project continues.

But there was no doubt in David's mind that he was the only survivor of the Palos Verdes Massacre.

247

* * *

As the helicopters rose, a medium-size white moving van with no lettering on its sides came through the front entrance, followed immediately by a paneled van with eight men inside. The gate was opened by Jimmy C. himself. Jimmy pointed to the pool area. Each of the men wore a mask and long rubber gloves. The disposal squad was here.

The area around the pool was a litter of dead nakedness. Young breasts were still warm to the touch. One by one the bodies were evacuated from the pool, the lounge chairs, the large grassy area between the buildings, the recreation center. Some had made it as far as the fence, but unlike David Kimura, they had neither clothes nor the comfort of the fog.

The cleanup took twenty minutes. There were sixty-two bodies piled inside the truck. It was 11:45 P.M. when Jimmy C. slammed Shinogara's iron gates closed and climbed into the front seat of the crowded van. The "accidents" along Hawthorne Boulevard were cleared.

From the San Diego Freeway, the caravan made its way to the Artesia Freeway, which eventually became the Riverside Freeway; then in two turns it found itself on I-10 heading for Palm Springs. Two hours later, the two vehicles exited onto a dirt road exit just north of the Chocolate Mountain Gunnery Range. They drove six miles up the dusty road to a point overlooking two hundred miles of desert to the east. There an eerie sight awaited them. Next to a flatbed truck was a large yellow Caterpillar. Beside them was a scooped-out path into the ground approximately sixty feet in length and twenty feet deep at its lowest point. The driver of the truck drove straight into the hole and turned the engine off. Both men squeezed out of the driver's side door and made their way back up the ramp to the surface, where the operator of the Cat had already fired up the hungry beast.

Jimmy C. and his men watched as the big Cat covered up the hole with the desert dirt and sand. The operation had been brutal but efficient. He had every reason to believe that the other half of the job had gone equally well.

At 11:30 P.M. a fashionably dressed young couple walked into the lobby of Marcia's apartment building, laughing loudly to unheard jokes. The girl was stunning, perhaps twenty years old. Both appeared to be drunk or high, or both. Before Benson could ask them who they were here to see, the girl caught her spiked heels and fell to the floor. Her raincoat opened and revealed a dress that was cut to her thighs on both sides, and down to her waist in front. Benson could see she wore no brassiere, in fact her young breasts were nearly out of her dress.

They were the last thing he saw.

Benson never saw the young man pull out a .25 handgun from his pocket, nor did he hear the five shots. The last thing he saw were the girl's legs.

The young man found the controls and opened the door to the penthouse elevator. The girl with the legs acted more like the street tough she was and pulled out a revolver of her own. The man reloaded. The elevator came to a stop and quietly opened up inside Marcia's darkened apartment. The girl went for the telephone, which she carefully took off the hook. The man waved, indicating that they should move directly to the back bedroom, which they did. With a flick of his hand he turned on the bedroom lights. This was instantaneously

249

followed by ten shots from two revolvers, all into Marcia's bed.

At twelve-thirty Sunday morning, Bill, Tony, and a handful of middle-aged men slowly filtered out onto a wet Market Street from the Roxy Theater after the X-rated twin bill was complete. Inside, the men had been well scattered throughout the dark theater. Nobody bothered anybody else. On the large screen the genital close-ups were more disgusting than titillating, but there were enough vignettes to satisfy most fantasies and there was enough privacy so that each man could masturbate at his own pace. If asked, they wouldn't be able to explain why they were there, not when there were so many real women and especially now that X-rated moves were so prevalent in video rental stores.

They walked south along Market, then turned left on Ninth. Neither was afraid of the sleazy neighborhood. Bill knew most of the punks and junks, they knew him and left him alone. He also knew that he didn't have to live there, a question Tony asked him over and over. Each man knew that he could tap into the "retirement" fund Marcia had set up—accounts in Geneva. But Bill enjoyed the life in lower San Francisco, the grimy coffee shops and corner delis and Oriental grocery stores.

The two men were lost in conversation. Neither saw the black Chevy, an old Impala, slowly creep up the street from behind, its headlights out. Walking in front of Wan's laundry, long since closed for the day, they never knew what hit them. Old Mr. Wan would find Bill and Tony crumpled in a pool of blood in front of his store but would be more upset that his plate glass windows had been shattered than he would be by finding dead bodies on the sidewalk.

250

* * *

For Jo Jo Joslin, the young and tempting Baby of the group, death came early in the evening. Alone in her second floor apartment, she'd gone to the door and looked through the fish eye to see who was knocking on her door at ten-thirty.

"Who is it? I can't see you," she said.

The reason she couldn't see was that on the other side of the door the eye was covered with the barrel of a Colt .45. In the hallway Jo Jo's shadow could be seen from under the door.

The two-shot explosion was enough to rip a gaping hole in the door and certainly loud enough for the other six residents of the building to hear. It was also loud enough to guarantee that nobody would stick his head out of the door to see what had happened. Jo Jo was blown back inside the room, her head nearly severed from the impact of the shots.

Of the crew, the only one who had a reasonable chance to survive the night was Heather Houston, who in her off time was a full-time hooker. If there was such a thing as sex addiction, Heather had it. If she'd been listening to the right radio station early Sunday morning she would have heard the names of Jo Jo Joslin and Bill Dworkin as having been killed in gangland-type slayings. As it was, she and the fourth gentleman friend of her evening were returning arm in arm to her upscale North Beach town house at four-thirty in the morning when three stocky men silently got out of a black Buick parked in front, opened their overcoats, and cut them both down with a barrage of semiautomatic gunfire.

"Is it done?" asked Wu, the telephone shaking slightly in his hand.

Only a few offices in the downtown area were lit at the early hour, but the dark skyline was still very visible against the pale of the morning sky. It was 5:30 A.M. on the morning of November 9 and the triumverate of Xiang Wu, E. Dexter Albright, and James "Jimmy C" Chimichanga nearly had a lock on the financial coup of the century, perhaps of all time.

Nearly.

Chapter Five
Diskette Inferno

"Where's the girl?" growled Jimmy Chimichanga, unhappy that the operation hadn't gone off perfectly as planned.

Buddy Gault shuffled his feet and started to hem and haw.

"I let you have the easy one — a *can't miss* — while I'm down digging graves in the fucking desert in the middle of the night. Where is she?" demanded Jimmy.

"I don't know" was all Buddy Gault could think of, but saying nothing at all was better than saying "I don't know," so that's what he wisely chose to do. Jimmy C. knew Buddy didn't know where the Lee woman was and didn't have a clue to her whereabouts.

"If the pilot hadn't been killed, he might have told us," Buddy whined, reaching for excuses. "Or the limo driver," he added as an afterthought.

But the pilot and the limo driver had been killed. Neither Buddy nor Jimmy had been directly involved, since each was busy on his own chores that night. Instead, the task had gone to another of Jimmy's men who had followed orders to a T. If there was to be any criticism after the initial outburst, it would rightly fall on Jimmy C.'s broad shoulders. Assumptions had been made.

"Ah, shit!" Jimmy waved Buddy off.

There was no need to grill him. Wu had distinctly told

Jimmy that Marcia had said she was returning home to San Francisco for the weekend. And she'd left for the airport in one of Shinogara's limos. The assumption had been made she was returning home.

"Why didn't you hit her at the airport? Why go to all the trouble at her apartment? All you did was make it complicated. Now we got the fucking police . . ." Jimmy C.'s voice trailed off as his thoughts were dark and confused.

As damaging was the possibility that David Kimura was at large. A man had been reported as having escaped along the west perimeter of the compound, disappearing into the fog. A random spray of rifle fire had yielded no body, although there had been no time to conduct a thorough search.

If Kimura has escaped and the Lee woman is at large, Jimmy C. thought, then they're better off together than separate.

At 4:15 Sunday morning David stood at the corner of the Pacific Coast Highway and Crenshaw Boulevard. He was drenched with perspiration, his clothes were torn, his face ragged with the exertion of running and scrambling eight miles downhill through scrub, backyards, and wandering neighborhood streets. He'd avoided dogs and streetlights as best he could, but was forever looking over his shoulder. Logic told him to avoid Hawthorne Boulevard if possible, at least until he was down off the hill. His descent down the northern side of the peninsula took him through the reverse stages of Dante's Inferno—the Seven Layers of Wealth, with Shinogara's estate on Crest Road being the highest layer, and the Pacific Coast Highway representing the lowest.

He stopped at a Denny's, which as advertised was

always open, and devoured a bacon cheeseburger and freshly cooked fries just out of the grease machine. They never tasted so good. A phone call got him a cab, but the driver took one look at him and made him pay in advance, which David did.

"The Marriott on Torrance, near Hawthorne," David said, sliding across the well-worn red vinyl back seat, exhausted.

The ride took twelve minutes.

"Good morning, sir," said the tall, black, red-uniformed doorman as he cheerfully opened the door for David, whose appearance closely matched that of a Cambodian boat refugee.

But Cambodian boat people don't carry platinum VISA and American Express cards, plastic backed by guarantees of a paper company set up to support Makato Shinogara and all his needs. In essence, the cards were backed by the entire wealth of the Japanese government.

"I want the best suite available," he'd said as he registered.

It was six o'clock and nobody was in the lobby. David looked past the registration clerk to the night manager.

"I need cash and clothes and a traveling bag, but more importantly, I need privacy. I'm not here."

The night manager understood and tapped out a short message into the hotel's computer system. David gave him shoe, pant, and shirt sizes, and told him to get two sets of everything. He palmed the large key and went to the bank of elevators, then to his three-room suite, where he mindlessly undressed, took a shower, and collapsed into the king-size bed, crawling naked under the crisp white sheets. He was instantly asleep.

Until the demons visited him.

* * *

"Aren't you glad we decided to come here instead of going home? I needed the break."

She knew Joe didn't mind that they'd gone to Reno instead of home. She also knew he'd be happy anywhere just as long as he was with her. Sometimes the relationship gave her a strange feeling. She'd never been that dedicated to anybody or anything in her life, and here was this big lunk that she knew would lay down his life for her — without thinking twice.

I doubt if I'd do the same, she thought.

It was unsettling.

But she had none of those thoughts as she flashed Joe her two hole cards, the nine and jack of diamonds. It was 5:45 Sunday morning and the poker room at Bally's was down to two tables. Up front near the chip cage were one- to three-dollar seven stud games, each with six old men trying to eke out a winning night with eight-dollar pots. In the back of the room at table eighteen was the fifty- to one hundred-dollar Texas Hold 'em game. A small crowd of off-duty dealers sat at a nearby empty table and watched the action, which had been hot and heavy all night.

Marcia was in seat ten at the south end of the twelve-person table, which was filled. She was the only woman. In front of her were nine stacks of one hundred-dollar chips, each stack neatly tapped out twenty chips high. The impressive black facade completely surrounded but completely protected a much smaller stack of royal purple chips, each valued at five hundred dollars. Six equally tall stacks of ten green twenty-five-dollar chips were piled up alongside, as were a smattering of red five-dollar chips and blue one-dollar chips, which were mostly used for dealer and waitress tips.

The hand had a feel to it. The cigar and cigarette smoke had just about reached Marcia's limit of toleration. She'd been there since the game had started at eight o'clock last night. On the way to the airport, Marcia had told the limo driver to take them to the Skywest terminal instead of the general aviation terminal, where Shinogara's private jet was located.

"Want to?" she'd asked.

Joe didn't mind. He'd just smiled and said sure.

Marcia knew half the players were professional gamblers, men who lived in Reno and went to the same table in the same casino day after day after day to withdraw cash from tourists.

The game was simple. Each player got two cards face down. The two players to the left of the dealer, who was marked by a rotating button, each had to ante a blind of fifty dollars. This was a forced bet and got the action going early. The actual dealer sat near the middle of the oval table, his pile of "checks" in an aluminum tray in front. It was as a limit game with four raises. After the first round of betting the dealer would discard the card on top and turn the next three cards face up on the table. These were common cards to all players. The objective of the game was the same as in seven-stud — to come out with the best five-card poker hand with seven cards. Except that in Texas Hold 'em, five of the seven cards would be common to all. After the flop, which in this case included the ace of clubs, the king of diamonds, and the ten of diamonds, there was another round of betting, this time more spirited.

Marcia had four to a flush and four to a straight flush. Two of the others folded in three-raise action, the pot rising to $1,900. The fourth, or "turn" card, was the ace of spades. Marcia could see the man in seat two nearly rise out of his chair.

He's got a full house or four sticks, she thought.

Seat four was dismayed and folded at the first bet. Seat eight foolishly stayed in through three rounds of betting, in which Marcia tested seat two with a raise.

257

The man was solid and came back with a raise, which Marcia just called.

Dumb bet, she told herself.

But she was up for the night and had played well—and besides, the game was just about over. If her hunch was right, there was only one card that would make her hand. The "river," or last card, had to be the queen of diamonds.

Which it was.

Because of the position of the button, it was Marcia's bet first. She did. Seat two craftily looked at his hole cards, pretended to think, then raised Marcia, with eight folding. Raise, reraise, re-reraise, call.

"Four aces," said seat two, proudly turning over his concealed pair of aces.

"Straight flush," replied Marcia, filling in the ten-queen-king of diamonds with the nine-jack in her hand.

The pot was over five thousand dollars, a beautiful mound of black and green.

It was the last hand of the night for the fifty-to-one hundred table. Soon the casino would start another day. By seven-thirty the demographics of the casino would change completely. Chased to bed would be the hard-charging heavy gamblers of the night. In their place would be the early-rising older folks, who would stop off for grapefruit and coffee before hitting the three-dollar blackjack tables and quarter slot machines.

The poker manager brought her five empty one hundred-chip trays, which Marcia filled with black one hundred-dollar chips, then helped her cash out.

In their adjoining rooms, Marcia and Joe slept until four in the afternoon. Marcia woke up in a semicoma, her body telling her that she didn't need to jump up and be pretty and alert. It was a great feeling to wake up, then roll over and pull the covers up. Nobody knew they were there. Not Tony. Not David. Not Shinogara. Not

Wu. Nobody. At four-thirty she lazily got up, took a shower, then called room service. A half hour later, at the beginning of the dinner hour, a huge platter of breakfast goodies was delivered. Casinos were on a twenty-four-hour schedule. There was a reason there were no clocks. And that included the room service menu. For the first time in what seemed like six months, Marcia devoured a full *Los Angeles Times* and a *San Francisco Chronicle*. It was wonderful. Tomorrow morning would come soon enough. They had tickets on a Skywest commuter that left Reno at 6:45 A.M. and would arrive in Cheyenne at 10:30. Then and only then would it be time to go back to work.

I think I'll order up a masseur, she decided.

As he slept through most of Sunday the demons quietly slipped into David's bed, crept under the covers, and began to torture his mind. David tossed and thrashed as he ran and ran and ran and ran for nearly seven hours. It was an exhausting dream, one where he couldn't stop running. *They* were after him. *They* were just behind him. *Stop! Let me stop! Please!* But they didn't let him. Bullets crashed around him. Dead friends fell on each side, only to rise and be dead again when the dream tape was replayed.

At three-thirty he awoke. As reality slowly entered his consciousness.

Who did this? he wondered. Shinogara must be dead. They all must be dead. Yamamoto. Sukawa. Albert and Robert. Who would be able to surprise Shinogara? Who was the enemy?

It wasn't the American government.

Marcia left after the presentation. She stayed only a short while. Did she . . . ? Was she . . . ?

David was ashamed of his thoughts.

Marcia wouldn't double-cross Shinogara.

But, she left early. She said she was going home. She got out before the attack.

How convenient.

David swung out of bed and reached for the phone. Nine plus one plus (307) 638-3301 got him to the operator at the Hitching Post Inn.

"Marcia Lee, please."

The operator put the call through, but there was no answer.

"Would you like to leave a message, sir?"

"Tell her David called. There's no return number. I'll call back," David added.

David was overcome with the need to return to Cheyenne. Sitting on the glass-topped table was his tote bag, now dirty and punctured in several places. But the two boxes of diskettes were safely tucked inside. He reached over and pulled out the one marked Master. He'd almost left them behind. Without the diskettes there would be no ransom.

How long would it take? he thought. A month? Two months?

The thought of having to rebuild the virus programs—and the decryption key codes—was terrifying. The last days had been typical of most programming he'd been a part of. Each of them had been responsible for a part of the code. In the end they'd put it all together and it had worked.

But reconstruction?

He'd need to be inside the heads of Robert and Albert, and the others at the estate. It wouldn't be impossible, but it would be unlikely.

But they were all on the diskettes, he thought.

David put the box back into the tote bag.

But more terrible thoughts confused his thinking.

I'm alone. Colby can identify me. But the virus exists,

260

it's real—it's going to go off. Colby can ruin it. And he would, too. Why not? If you were Colby and you knew that Shinogaro was dead—but he doesn't know! Of course! Why does he have to know. He doesn't. But what if Marcia tells him? She's got all her money. And she said that Colby had gotten a raw deal. But is she alive?

Did she do this to me? To us?

Did Marcia try to have us all killed?

Why would she do that?

David couldn't keep his mind on a single thread. Part of his logic said that Marcia couldn't be *that* good an actress. She couldn't be a double agent, working for somebody else. She'd have to realize that she too was in a lot of trouble, that she too could spend a lot of time in jail. Yet the opposite side of his reasoning could easily see Marcia in the role of double agent. She knew everything about the plan, the virus, the players, who and where people were. Everything. Everything somebody else now knew.

She's the reason all your friends are dead!

David shook his head in dismay.

Maybe Marcia's dead, too. Maybe they're all dead but you.

Given time the mind can come up with every imaginable combination, each worse than the last—because each new possibility was based on the previous worst possible.

He looked at the clock-radio, whose red digital figures said that it was 5:15. It was 1,155 miles to Cheyenne.

Don't be stupid, he thought. You're not driving.

David called the airlines. The remaining Continental and United flights were booked. The first flight out Monday morning was a 9:10 flight from LAX that got into Denver at 12:40 Mountain time Monday afternoon. David booked an available first-class seat.

He was going to Cheyenne.

"You're sure it was Kimura?" asked Xiang Wu, disturbed.

"No, but *somebody* got away. Short of digging them all back up and going through them one by one, I don't know. There wasn't time — we were busy. I know Shinogara's dead. I got him personally. But Kimura, no — I'm not positive."

"The fault is mine, James," replied Wu. "I made an assumption — rather, I let you make an assumption with my instructions. Either she was very lucky or she has a sixth sense. Perhaps it's just as well. It was a risky operation to begin with. She won't be able to return to her apartment — not with the police involved. They'll want her for questioning, which means her name will be in their computers. She has no home base to go to, which she'll soon realize. If she's smart — which I think she is — she'll leave the country immediately. And that's just as good for us. On the other hand, she might not have any knowledge of what happened. If that's the case, then she'll be returning to Cheyenne on Monday — presumably to see Colby."

Wu sat back in his chair and ran his fingers through his beard as he thought aloud.

"Yes — that's good. She'll return to Cheyenne," — Wu turned to Jimmy C — "and you'll be there waiting for her, James. Take care of her."

"What about Colby?" asked Jimmy C.

"Kill him," said Wu, his mind made up.

Jimmy C.'s head nodded in a consider-it-done fashion. "And his wife?"

"Kill her," said the old man grimly.

"And the children?" asked Chimichanga.

"Yes, them as well," Wu replied without batting a long eyelash. "Eradicate them, James. There is no reason for any of them to live. Find Marcia Lee. Kill her. Find

David Kimura. Kill him."

With the large sleeve of his garment Xiang Wu wiped a small dribble of spit that had secreted from his mouth while he poured venom from his heart.

"It's the only way," he added.

Jimmy Chimichanga nodded, then wordlessly stood up and showed himself to the door. He had work to do.

It was 49.2 miles door to door from the Colby home in Cheyenne to the Coldsmith family home in Laramie, where directions were given in relative distance from either the Cowboy Saloon or the Dairy Queen — the landmark on the north edge of town, the one with the sign that forever said Go 'Pokes in big red letters.

Dad Coldsmith was a retired professor from the University of Wyoming, and occasionally was asked to provide emergency assistance on a class or two, which he gratefully did. He missed teaching, but not the administration of teaching, the paperwork and bullshit, especially the bullshit. Mom Coldsmith was a professional mother, and like all grandmothers, she doted on her grandchildren and softly but unmistakably reminded her offspring that they should call and see their mother more often. More than once Cheryl wished that she was in New York, like Scotty, although she'd only been there once, hated it, and knew that she wouldn't ever go there again voluntarily.

This weekend having Mom and Dad close by was a blessing for Cheryl. Zack was troubled. Storm clouds hovered on his brow. He was moody and seemed like he wanted to tell her something, but just couldn't get the words out. As they did when they stayed overnight, Cheryl and Zack slept in Cheryl's old double bed and the kids slept in Scotty's room. Sleeping in her old bed always brought back memories of good times. It was the same bed that she and Zack had first made love in nearly seven years ago. It had been a passionate coupling, filled with mutual pleasure and the anxious anticipation of being caught in the act by one or both of her parents, who at the time were out of the house. Since then, every time they slept over, the memory of that first time was enough to bring more passion into their lovemaking. It was a good bed. A *productive* bed. Brian was conceived in this bed on an overnight stay. They'd been so noisy that Cheryl was sure that Mom would say something in the morning, but she didn't.

But there was no threat the bed would be used for love this Sunday night. Zack had gone off early. Cheryl sat out in the front room with Mom and let her troubles out.

"Something's bothering Zack, something terrible. And I don't know what it is. He's been so *different* these past weeks. I don't know if it's work, or what. He snaps at the kids, snaps at me — and for no reason. At least I don't think so. Maybe so . . ." Cheryl's voice dropped off.

"Would you like me to take the kids for a few days?" Mom asked, knowing that the answer was surely yes.

Cheryl looked at her mother with gratitude and nodded her head.

"I wasn't going to ask. Thank you. I think we really need a couple days alone," Cheryl said gratefully.

Cheryl leaned over and kissed her mother on the cheek, then softly walked back to her bedroom. Zack was in a restless sleep. Cheryl slipped under the covers and tried to come close to him, but Zack's psyche wanted no part of affection and rejected her, even though he was asleep.

We have to talk, she thought.

* * *

"Coldsmith?"

Not on Sunday. Gimme a break, Harper.

"Yes, sir—it's me," Scotty acknowledged with resignation, knowing that a nice Sunday afternoon was going down the tubes.

"Are you scheduled for court this week?"

"No—it's in recess until after Thanksgiving. I think the judge wanted to take the week off—which isn't a bad idea. I was planning to—"

"Good. I want you to meet Bevins and Griswold at the LAPD station in Rolling Hills in an hour. I told the captain that's all I could spare today. They'll fill you in there."

"—go home myself this Wednesday."

"There's been some kind of shooting. No bodies, but a lot of evidence. I knew I could count on you."

"Al—I'd planned to go back home on—"

Al Harper—Scotty's division chief while he was on the temporary assignment—hung up before Scotty could get his request finished. He was assumed to be on a twenty-four-hour schedule.

"Damn," Scotty muttered as he held a dial tone in his hand.

Even though he got from Inglewood to Rolling Hills in less than an hour, Scotty was the last one to arrive and got an evil look from the police captain—more for his casual appearance than his tardiness.

Jesus, it's Sunday, for crying out loud, Scotty thought.

"Nice that you could make it, kid," razzed Bevins, a twenty-year veteran. Since there was no way to win, Scotty just shut up and listened.

"To repeat"—the captain looked at Scotty—"we received two complaints last evening about a loud party

265

up on the hill—the first one was at 10:15, then three more a half hour later. Two of the neighbors said it sounded like the Fourth of July. But by the time a squad car got up the hill everything was pretty quiet. The lights were on and the gate was closed. The officers couldn't hear any noise, and since they couldn't see much with the fog, they figured the party had died down and that the complaint had pretty much taken care of itself. Well, this morning one of the neighbors was out walking his dog and saw blood on the driveway—then noticed a huge hole in the front of the house—like it had been blown out. It's on Crest Road—a pretty ritzy place, if you haven't been up there."

"What'd they find?" asked Bevins.

"Total destruction. Blood everywhere. But no bodies. It's a son of a bitch. You won't believe it."

And it *was* a son of a bitch.

Scotty was amazed. There were thousands of shell casings scattered at random over the mansion grounds, all 9mm semiautomatic. A bazooka had been used to blow open the front door.

"Unfuckingbelievable," had been Bevins's first reaction at the pool area.

Discarded clothing lay scattered across the grass. Partially consumed bottles of liquor were everywhere. The pool was a nasty tint of rust. Hardly a window in any of the buildings was intact.

"Who's the owner?" asked Scotty.

"Tax records in Sacramento list the property as being owned by a ProSun Corporation—not an individual. The taxes are paid out of an account at Security Pacific downtown. We'll have to follow up on that tomorrow. The police have interviewed most of the neighbors. Nobody on the street ever met any of them—but it sounds like they came and went in style—lots of limos," said Bevins.

The guard station had been riddled with bullets. By the bent grass on the lawn, and depressions in the ground, there was evidence that several helicopters had landed—which backed up the impression the shell casings gave that a full-scale assault had occurred. It also backed up the reports of the neighbors.

Inside the main house, which was easily accessed through a large hole, all was in shambles. Expensive furniture and appointments were shattered, scattered, and strewn. Near the front door was a small room where a sophisticated switchboard had been installed, which of course had been destroyed. Scotty looked at the multiple call directory, which seemed more in place in a large business than a private home, even a large private home.

The phones, he thought. Telephone records. There's always a track.

(213) 521-2010.

Scotty committed the number to memory and moved on through the house to the backyard, then to his left toward the dormitory. The rooms weren't what he expected. While Spartan, there was a personal computer and printer in every room. The bookshelves were lined with programming manuals. Scotty counted twenty-four smaller rooms and six larger rooms in the two-story building.

Thirty people lived here—all of them computer people, he concluded.

Other than the photographs, there was no evidence of any women. The door to each of the rooms had been opened or, in some cases, blown open by gunfire. Six of the rooms were devastated. Sheets were damp with blood. Blood splattered the walls and floor.

Massacre.

It was easy to come up with the names of the men. Underwear was tagged, as were shirttails.

Just like in college.

Bevins was less glib as he and Scotty went through the other building, which was obviously a work area.

"We're talking about some bucks, here," Bevins said as they walked into what had been the plush auditorium.

Glass and bullet casings littered the floor. Scotty walked down the steps, then up one step onto the raised floor of the stage, and stood in front of a personal computer, which patiently waited for somebody to instruct it to do something.

"It's still on," Scotty mused out loud. "Whatever happened here happened so suddenly that whoever was sitting here didn't turn the machine off.

The computer's screen displayed:

ROCKY MOUNTAIN REGIONAL
INFORMATION CENTER
IGC PROFESSIONAL OFFICE SYSTEM

Press one of the following PF Keys

PF1   Process Calendars

PF2   Open the Mail   ****

PF3   Note Processing   * Main *

PF4   Notes/Messages   * Menu *

PF5   Document Process   ****

PF6   Go to HLP

PF7   Telephone Directory

PF8   RMIC Update News

PF10   PC Options Menu

PF11   Info Center Options

HELP: HELPRMIC

NOVEMBER

S	M	T	W	T	F	S
						1
2	3	4	5	6	7	8
9	10	11	12	13	14	15
16	17	18	19	20	21	22
23	24	25	26	27	28	29

Day of Year: 320

PF9 = HELP   PF12 = END

The screen made no sense to Scotty, nor was his mind tuned to it.

What happened here? he asked himself.

While he normally had a good sixth sense, Scotty wasn't on the room's wavelength. He wasn't getting any good vibrations or cosmic messages.

It's probably Bevins's fault, he told himself.

Scotty looked back at the screen, which was vaguely familiar. But he couldn't put his mind's finger on it, and since his mind was already cluttered with the remnants of death, he turned and walked off the stage, leaving his brother-in-law still logged onto the IGC system in Denver.

The twin jet Lear began its descent to the Cheyenne airport as it passed south of Medicine Bow and just north of Laramie. Making a sharp bank north of Warren AFB, the pilot brought the sleek silver-and-black aircraft down over I-25 to a smooth landing at 10:35 Mountain time Sunday night. The air was crisp, the lights of the nearby capital city sparkled.

Seated in the nothing-but-first-class seats were

Jimmy C., Buddy Gault, and a thug named Jose, who was clearly not used to flying. The plane was Wu's private jet and cost over two million, not including the plush interior, which added nearly another half million to the total price.

"Get us something with four-wheel drive. I don't care what it is—Blazer, Bronco—something with bulk and plenty of room," Jimmy instructed Buddy, who took off on a run when the forward hatch was opened.

All three men were dressed in comfortable clothes, woodsmanstyle, as if they were hunters. Jimmy C. wore a plaid shirt, worn khakis, and a faded blue parka vest.

Twenty minutes later, after using one of his many false IDs, Buddy came back with a two-year-old red Blazer.

"Have the plane ready to go and plan to bunk down here until I get back," Chimichanga instructed the pilots, who knew Jimmy C.'s routine pretty well. "I don't want any delays taking off."

If Jimmy came back and one of the pilots wasn't there, the pilot would be returning to San Francisco on a commercial flight—then shortly thereafter be looking for another job. It took Buddy and Jose a few minutes to unload the boxes of "equipment" and supplies—three AK-47s, a flamethrower, a hand-held rocket launcher, and an assortment of Colt and Beretta handguns and related ammunition. With Gault driving and Jose in the backseat, Jimmy C. turned to Buddy Gault.

"OK, where the fuck are we?"

Finding the Hitching Post Inn hadn't taken brain surgery skills. From the airport they found Lincolnway and drove west through town, past the old Union Pacific station, then went under the railroad tracks before slowly passing the motel. Wordlessly, Jimmy motioned with his finger for Buddy to cruise the parking lot, which was only a third filled. Jimmy wasn't sure of what he was looking for—maybe the woman would be easy to spot. Circling the motel, Jimmy pointed to a nearby telephone booth next to an Esso station.

"Over there," he instructed.

Buddy did as he was told. Jimmy C. was out of the truck almost before Buddy came to a stop. He lumbered into the booth and his thick fingers ripped through the U.S. West Yellow Pages until they found Motels and the telephone number for the Hitching Post. Not finding a quarter in his pocket, Jimmy snapped his fingers and got one tossed to him, then called the motel.

"Do you have a woman named Marcia Lee staying at the hotel?"

It was one of those marginal questions that motel clerks sometimes answer, but shouldn't. Phrased differently, "Can you ring the room of Marcia Lee?" and there was never a problem. In this case the weekend clerk combined the two.

"Would you like me to ring her room?"

"Yeah," Jimmy smiled.

Won't she be surprised, he thought.

"I'm sorry, sir. Miss Lee seems to be out. May I take a message?"

"No. That's all right—I'll see her later," Jimmy said, almost laughing.

He hung up, got back into the truck, and ordered Buddy to pull into the motel's registration area.

"Get us two rooms," he ordered.

For an instant he had the idea of getting rooms as close to the woman as possible, but that would require a little parking lot persuasion with the registration clerk, who in turn might tip her off.

"Two? You mean I gotta sleep with him?" complained Buddy.

At eleven-thirty Sunday night Jimmy C. found himself inside the nicest of the two rooms, preparing for a night's sleep, while Jose and Buddy Gault found themselves alternating an all-night watch duty from inside the Blazer. Buddy wouldn't have to sleep with Jose.

"Fall asleep and I'll cut your balls off," Jimmy had said as he closed the door.

Skywest's seats just weren't designed for big guys. Marcia knew Joe was uncomfortable, both from his seat and from flying in the twin-engine prop. Everything seemed so close, including the ground. The flight to Salt Lake City took forty-five minutes longer than it would on a jet and Marcia was glad she hadn't gone for the second cup of coffee before taking off. There was no restroom on the plane. A curtain dangled in front of the passengers in seats 1A and 1B, separating the paying customers from the paid pilots, one of whom added to the atmosphere by wearing a long white scarf wrapped around his neck Eddie Rickenbacker-style. Everybody had an aisle and a window seat.

It was a quarter of eleven when Joe pulled their rental car, left at the airport over the weekend, into the parking lot of the the Hitching Post Inn. The red light was on Marcia's phone.

"This is Marcia Lee in Room 168. I have messages?"

"Oh, yes, Miss Lee. A Mr. David has been calling nearly every hour for you. Let's see" — she paused while she counted the pink message slips — "he's called ten, no — eleven times."

Eleven messages?

"When was the last time?" Marcia asked.

"About an hour ago," the clerk replied.

Marcia thanked the clerk and slowly replaced the receiver on the cradle. David's behavior didn't match his personality.

Something's wrong, she thought.

Leaving eleven messages was the act of someone who was in a panic. There was an emergency of some kind. Marcia sat down on the edge of her bed, fished through her worn leather purse, and came up with her little black book. Her fingers quickly sifted through and found Shinogara's number in Los Angeles, which she dialed.

"I'm sorry but the number you have dialed is temporarily out of service. Please try your call again later."

What? Out of order?

Marcia quickly redialed, a look of puzzled worry on her face. Adrenaline started to kick in and her heartbeat picked up. She got the same recording.

Shinogara had the latest of everything.

"What's wrong," Joe asked, easily sensing that Marcia was disturbed.

"I can't get through to Shinogara. The telephones are out of order. And David's been trying to reach us for the last twelve hours. I don't know what's happening. I don't like it, Joe."

Neither did Joe. Marcia was his rock, and his rock was wobbling. Without looking in her book, Marcia dialed another number.

"Come on, Tony—answer the damned phone!" Marcia muttered, not quite under her breath.

Joe was fascinated by Marcia's temporary loss of composure. Impatiently, Marcia depressed the disconnect button in the cradle of the phone to get a dial tone. The fingernail of her right index finger snapped off at the tip, leaving a jagged end.

"Damn!"

Marcia knew she was letting her emotions get uncharacteristically out of control.

Is this the kind of day it's going to be? she wondered.

Things had gone so well. The end was in sight. She

dialed another number.

"Executive House answering service."

"This is Marcia Lee. Do I have—"

"Oh, Miss Lee—thank God you're all right! We've all been so worried! Thank goodness!"

Marcia's neck muscles sagged and she felt the pinpoint prickle of a headache behind her left eye.

"What are you talking about?"

"The police have been here several times asking for you. They want you to call them right away!"

"What's wrong?"

"Poor Mr. Benson—"

"Benson? What are you talking about. You're not making sense," Marcia lowered her voice as she got hold of herself. "Please tell me what you're talking about."

"Mr. Benson was killed Saturday night. And your place was ransacked. Someone said there were gunshots! I'm so glad you're all right." Then the operator started to come down. "But the police want to talk to you. They've called twice. Please call them."

The operator gave Marcia the telephone number of a Detective Bryant of the SFPD, which Marcia didn't bother writing down. There was no way she'd be talking to a policeman about anything.

You can't go home again.

It was a strange feeling. The Executive House had been her haven—a comfort that she'd worked hard to get. The apartment had been her security blanket, her fort. And now it had been violated. While she knew she could replace the things she'd accumulated—it wasn't the same. Somebody had the power over her—the power to make her feel unclean, violated—the power to decide whether she lived or died—the power to control where she lived.

Marcia's hard shell of self-confidence had been meanly assaulted.

274

"Somebody's tried to kill us, Joe," Marcia said softly.

"Who?" said Joe, surprised.

"I think it's Wu. Would you try to get in touch with the others? We need to warn them," Marcia asked. "I need to think for a few minutes."

While Joe went to his room to call, Marcia tried to get her thoughts moving in a pattern. It was difficult.

Were the others . . . ? No—come on, nobody knows where they live. Shinogara doesn't, for sure—at least I don't think so. Wu? Wu knew where I lived. Yeah, but so did Shinogara. But his phones are out of order. And David's trying to reach you. He wouldn't—not eleven fucking messages! Wu. It's Wu. He had pictures! Remember? Wu had God-damned pictures of us! Tony and Bill and—shit. Heather and Baby. Not them.

Marcia jumped as the phone jolted her out of her bad thoughts, startling her.

"Hi," said the voice.

It was David!

"Where *are* you?" were Marcia's first words.

"Why'd you do it?" David said coldly.

"Do what?"

"Don't play games with me, Marcia. You know what I mean. You're trying to cut yourself in on this. I've got to hand it to you, I didn't think you were smart enough. You've got bigger balls than I thought." David was vicious.

Marcia's face flushed.

"I still don't know what you mean, David," she replied simply.

She could tell that David was taken somewhat aback and was shaken. There was doubt in his voice, perhaps even a quiver.

"You left early—it *had* to be you. Who else would it be?"

"What's happened, David? Tell me," Marcia said as

calmly as she could, over the pounding of her heart. She could feel the pulse in her neck throb.

"You really don't know, then?"

"No."

"Shinogara's dead. They're all dead. I was the only one to escape." David's words tumbled out. "It was a massacre — all my friends . . . Mr. Shinogara — I know he's dead. I just know it."

Marcia sensed that David was on the verge of tears.

Dead? All dead?

She wanted to shout at him, but didn't. But the news was enough to stun her system. Breathing was difficult as her chest constricted.

"Marcia?"

"Yes — I'm here. I don't know what to say," Marcia stalled.

You still need him, her mind shouted without telling her why. She spoke as calmly as possible, although she knew she was louder than normal.

"David — someone tried to kill me on Saturday night, at my apartment in San Francisco. The police are after me. I thought it was you. I still don't know —" Marcia let her thoughts trail off to allow David to fill in the blanks.

"No — I wouldn't — I didn't . . ." David stuttered, his venom gone and forgotten.

"It may be more than that. I haven't been able to reach any of my people — Tony, Bill . . . the girls."

Marcia could barely keep from throwing up. All she could see were images of the cheering crowd in the auditorium and the busload of pretty working girls.

All dead.

What about Zack?

"Where are you, David?"

David paused before answering.

"Los Angeles. Everything's been delayed this morning because of the fog. My flight's ready to leave in a few minutes. I've got to go."

"Why?" asked Marcia.

"Why what?" he replied, confused.

"Why are you coming back?"

"To keep Zack in line, of course," David said, pedantically.

"You can't be serious." Marcia was amazed. "You're not going ahead with this, are you?"

"Of course. The virus is already started. The operation is still on. We've got people in Hong Kong—" David stopped in midthought.

He hasn't told anybody yet, she sensed.

"—ready and waiting. This is my job, Marcia."

"David—think, for Christ's sake! Right at this moment we don't even know if Zack Colby is alive. If they know about me and they knew about you, then they sure as hell know about Zack."

Marcia was about ready to wet her pants she was so anxious to leave. Exit doors were slamming all around her. She just *knew* that Wu was watching her.

God damn—I mean, he knew—he knows—I've been staying here.

Marcia knew she was in big trouble.

"Look David—I've got to go. Don't come here, OK?"

"No—I've got my job to do."

"No—I mean, don't come *here*—to Cheyenne. Let me meet you someplace. I'll meet you at Stapleton. Just don't come here. Not yet. I'm getting out of here. It's too dangerous."

"What about Colby?" asked David.

"I don't know. If they tried to kill you, and they tried to kill me, then they'll try to kill Zack."

David thought for a moment.

"So let them," was his cold reply.

Shit, she thought. Let them. Just let them. Marcia's distaste for David and his plan was rising as fast as her

277

hatred for Wu.

They're all sons of bitches. Who's to say Shinogara wouldn't have tried the same thing with me once the job was done? After all, I'm just a loose end — nothing more.

"There's a bar where the moving escalators stop, halfway down the United terminal," she said, slowly.

"I know where it is. I've got to go — they're loading."

"I'll be there at" — Marcia looked at her watch, which now read noon — "four-thirty. Wait for me."

Marcia hung up before David could say another word.

A lot of her was scared.

I'm in way over my head, she thought. I've got to warn the Colbys.

Marcia threw her remaining clothes into a suitcase, sat on it to get it closed, looked around to see if she'd left anything, then closed the door behind her. She knocked on Joe's door.

"Let's go — we're in trouble!" she said urgently.

"I can't get any of them," Joe said as he checked his .38 for a full round. "What's wrong?"

"I'll tell you in the car — *hurry!*" Marcia urged.

Joe had never seen Marcia so excited. Her fear was contagious. Marcia's eyes darted from car to motel room to parking lot to another car to the street and back again. Joe revved the royal blue Taurus, popped the brake, out of the parking lot, and sped up Lincolnway toward town.

"Where're we going?" he asked.

"Zack's house."

"What's wrong?"

Marcia turned around to see if they were being followed. She couldn't see anything. But her gut told her that Wu's men were nearby.

"I hope we're not too late," she said, anxiously. "Damn! It's all my fault!" Marcia slammed her hand on the dashboard.

Joe turned to look at her, his peripheral vision trained on the road. Marcia looked him in the eye.

"They're all dead, Joe. Everybody. Shinogara. Tony. Bill — the girls — everybody. Wu's done it. And he's after us. We've got to warn Zack. They'll be after him, too — if they haven't gotten him already. He didn't deserve any of this. Then we've got to get the hell out of here. We warn Colby, then hightail it to Stapleton and get out of the country. OK? We first have got to save ourselves — then we'll think about getting even."

Marcia turned back again and scanned the cars behind them as they approached the turn onto College Drive, then turned left past the liquor store and headed north toward the bluff. Even from two miles away they could see the Colby home high and lonely at the edge of the small bluff.

"They've got all the cards. David's planning to go through with his plan — Jesus, how can he expect to do it by himself? Wu's going to nail him for sure. Damn, where are they?" Marcia said, turning around for a third time.

Marcia's jitters were indeed contagious.

"Nobody's back there, Marcia. We're all right. We're almost there."

Twice on the way home Cheryl had asked Zack what was wrong. The words were absorbed without reaction. He took Mom's offer to watch the children without a word of thanks, as if he weren't aware they were staying in Laramie. Although on the way home he appeared to be driving carefully, Zack was on remote control — sensing things on the road instead of actually seeing them. The nerve endings on his cheeks and neck tingled, as did the tips of his fingers and the tops of his hands. His chest was tight with emotion. It wasn't until he was parked in the driveway, with the garage door automatically rising, that Zack Colby came to grips with himself, with what needed to be done.

He began to shake uncontrollably.

"Zack, honey . . . what's wrong? Please tell me!" Cheryl reached over and put her hand on his quivering arm, herself nearly in tears.

"I . . . I . . . I've ddddone . . ." The words stuttered, then stopped. "I . . . I . . . I've done something wwwrong. Terribly wrong!" he blurted.

Cheryl's grip on his arm was hard.

"What *is* it?" she asked, afraid of the look on his face.

Zack looked like a prime candidate for a heart attack. His face was pale, his eyes glassy, his body shaking uncontrollably. Turning the ignition off, Cheryl got out of the passenger side, walked around, and then started to guide Zack toward the house through the opened garage. Tears welled in Zack's eyes, then began to gush.

"Oh, Cheryl, I'm so sorry. I'm so sorry! I've done terrible things."

Cheryl had to admit that, after murder, she thought of infidelity next. The two were right up there together. She also had a brief thought of her comfortable bed in the back room in Laramie where she could see herself tucked away, alone and safe.

From the garage they went through the laundry room, the kitchen, and finally to the living room, where Cheryl sat Zack down on the couch, then knelt down in front of him, her hands holding his.

"Tell me, Zack. Whatever it is, you've got to tell me."

And it was true. He did have to tell her. Either that or pop a gut or have his head explode.

"I think they're home," Joe said.

Marcia agreed with the assessment and motioned with her hand for Joe to use the downstairs parking lot. She didn't care if Zack or Cheryl overheard them come in, but silence would be preferred.

"Are you ready?" she asked.

Joe tapped the left side of his jacket and nodded yes. Marcia got out of the car, but didn't close the door. Joe pulled the keys out of the ignition just enough so that the irritating reminder buzzer wouldn't go off, and followed her toward the house. Using Zack's key, Marcia quietly unlocked the basement door and walked inside, Joe following. They heard voices upstairs. Even from here it sounded like Zack was crying.

Zack gasped for breath as a month's worth of tears came out in a gush. Cheryl could do nothing for him but be astonished. She'd never seen him cry before, not in their three years of courtship and four years of marriage. Not once. All he could do was blubber and say no and I'm sorry, but nothing coherent. She would just have to wait until the demons were flushed.

Zack blew his nose twice. His face was red with the exertion of crying. salty tears tracked streaks down his cheeks.

"I . . . I've done something bad, Cheryl." He finally completed a whole sentence.

While not in an ill temper, Cheryl was getting a bit impatient with her husband. From the look in his eyes, infidelity was almost a certainty, and it didn't please her at all.

"I gathered that, Zack. Now what is it?" she asked firmly.

Zack sucked in a deep breath.

"I'm being blackmailed. I should have given myself up, but I didn't. But I'm going to have to. I can't stand it anymore. I can't let them do it!"

"What are you talking about?" Cheryl screamed at him, her frustration level topped. "Tell me!"

Cheryl wanted to shake her jerk of a husband. From the corner of her eyes she saw a shadow in the kitchen. Then came the words.

"Go ahead . . . tell her, Zack," said Marcia.

Cheryl turned around, her face changing from anger to astonishment. Zack's jaw dropped.

Marcia stood in the doorway between the kitchen and the living room, left hand on her hip, right hand braced against the door frame. Joe stood quietly behind her in the kitchen.

"But make sure you tell her *everything*," Marcia said, her eyes boring into Zack's.

Cheryl screamed, then turned to Zack, saw the fixation in his eyes, then turned back to Marcia, now clearly identified as the other woman.

"What are you doing here?" shouted Zack to Marcia.

"Zack—who is this woman?" shouted a frightened Cheryl.

Marcia walked into the living room and stood in front of them.

"You both must leave," Marcia said. "Immediately. Your lives are in danger."

Zack's eyes were filled with an embarrassed dismay. Her words went right over his head.

"Who are you?" Cheryl demanded, getting up from her kneeling position in front of Zack.

Marcia ignored her question and gave Zack an if-you-don't-tell-her-then-I-will look. Cheryl saw that while the other woman wasn't more than five years her senior, she exuded a worldly experience that Cheryl would never have. Even though nothing was said, Marcia's simple body language made Cheryl feel like she was a girl standing next to a woman. Cheryl turned back to Zack, whose vocal cords were paralyzed.

Marcia turned to Cheryl, who was two inches taller than her.

"You deserve an explanation, Cheryl," Marcia started, their eyes locked. "I think things are going to happen quickly, and *you* most of all need to know everything. Your husband's a basket case. Any decisions the two of you make are up to you, but I suggest for your sake Zack"—Marcia turned to Zack, who was slumped in the couch—"that your wife makes the important ones. I'm going to have to be quick," Marcia started. "Your husband sold his soul for a piece of ass, *mine* mostly. But there were others, including a young woman that Zack thought was underage—*very* underage," Marcia started.

"You mean . . . ?" Zack sat up, astonished.

"Part of the setup, Zack. She was twenty-one years old. She worked for me. We just made her up that way."

"The newspapers! How . . . ?" Zack was confused.

And Cheryl was more so. She held her hand up in protest.

"Wait a minute!" shouted Cheryl, not believing what was happening to her. "What the hell are you two talking about?"

"Sorry." Marcia put one hand on Cheryl's arm. "Listen, you need to know this." Then she put both hands on Cheryl's shoulders and gripped the younger woman firmly. "I was hired by a group of Japanese businessmen to do a job—to find someone from IGC. The only criterion I was given was that the person had to have a computer and access to IGC's systems from home. That, and be willing to . . . play around. Zack fit the bill," Marcia told Cheryl straightforwardly, releasing her grip.

"I run a company that specializes in sexual blackmail. I set Zack up. It was my job to do so, and I was paid well. But other than being terminally horny, he's done noth-

283

ing wrong."

Cheryl's eyes teared but remained locked on Marcia's.

"You tricked me! You *slut,* you tricked me!" Zack shouted, and started to get up out of the chair.

Joe took a step forward, Zack sat back.

"David Kimura doesn't work for IGC. He works for the Japanese consortium. For the last month he's been using Zack's computers in the basement to program a computer virus, which is now in IGC's system," Marcia continued.

Cheryl turned to Zack with a devastating look of disappointment, the look he saw in his dreams.

"Oh, Zack—you didn't," Cheryl said, nearly heartbroken, her soul begging him for the denial that wouldn't come.

"I don't have time to go into it—but your lives are in danger, as are Joe's and mine. Some other people know about the plan. The Japanese have all been killed—my people have been killed." Marcia turned to Zack. "Yes, even that little girl—I know she's dead. You need to get out of here *now!* In the next few minutes. I'm sure they'll be here! I came here to try and make it up to you, Zack—but you need to hurry."

Cheryl's mind reeled. Zack was astonished.

"You're the weak link, Zack. You've always been the weak link. Now you're a loose end. Even though it's a risk—they'll come here—they've been cleaning up loose ends for the last three days."

"God damn you!" Zack shouted, getting up off the couch.

"Shut up, Zack!" returned Cheryl, angry.

"You've got to leave. Are your kids here?"

"The children?" asked Cheryl, concerned.

"Yes—the children, too. And your parents, too. And I'd do it now," said Marcia as honestly and as convincingly as she could.

Cheryl believed her, then turned to Zack.

"I'm going to call Scotty," she said.

"No! We're going to IGC," said Zack, a wild look in his eyes. "I've got his diskettes. I've got David's programs! He doesn't have anything! *I've* got them," Zack said, confidence building in his eyes. "I'll give them the diskettes, tell them what happened, and everything will be all right," he said, convinced of the impossible.

"What do you mean, you have David's diskettes?" asked Marcia, now curious.

"Downstairs—in my desk. I've got them! Son of a bitch!" he exalted.

"What are you talking about?" Cheryl shouted again, her tears welling back.

Joe was now in the living room, directly at Marcia's side.

"I've got you now, you bitch!" Zack pointed his finger at Marcia, his eyes crazed. "I've got the programs. I've got the decryption keys!"

Marcia was sorry she had come. It had been the wrong decision. What had started out as a mission of contrition had turned sour. She was going to have to do something with Zack, if he didn't see the light.

If Zack has David's diskettes, then what does David have?

Zack turned to Cheryl.

"Don't you see, hon? If all those sons of bitches are dead, then I'm the only one with the key—I'm the only one who can break the god-damn code! I'm free!" Zack shouted, mentally releasing himself from all his burdens. "Now, *you'd* better get out of here, Miss Marcia Lee," Zack said, a crazy look in his eyes.

Somehow he's switched the programs on David, Marcia thought. Her mind whirled. Let Zack tell IGC. You tell the FBI. Get Wu. No, No—that won't work. Wait a minute, wait a minute — IGC would pay dearly for the decryption diskettes. The virus is in their system. They'll need the diskettes in any case.

Marcia couldn't think.

"I'm calling Scotty," said Cheryl, reaching for the phone.

"You were right, boss," said Buddy Gault.

"Of course I was right," replied a scowling Jimmy Chimichanga.

Both Buddy and Jimmy peered through binoculars toward the Colby residence from a vantage point a half mile farther out of town, near the corner of College Drive and Dell Range Road, which was indeed the edge of town. To the north there was nothing but rolling prairie as far as the eye could see, without a tree in sight. In unison they moved their glasses as they followed Joe's slow approach to the Colby home.

"Are you ready?" Chimichanga turned in his seat and asked Jose, whose hands firmly gripped an army issue flamethrower.

"She's going inside, boss," Buddy updated. "So's the big guy."

"All right — *go!*"

Finished with his programming and satisfied with the program's effectiveness, David methodically backed up the hard disk onto a series of diskettes as Zack watched, fascinated. The process took a good ten minutes even though David used a fast backup program. While the next diskette was being dumped, David carefully labeled the previous one — Master, 1 of 9; 2 of 9; et cetera. He then took a second box of diskettes, ten to a box, formatted each one, then duplicated the master set onto the diskettes which would be labelled Backup, 1 of 9, et cetera. He put both boxes of diskettes

*into his L. L. Bean tote bag and returned his attention for the last
time to the PC, where he issued the fatal command:*

FORMAT C:

*which would wipe out the system's hard disk of all programs,
including the operating system, communication program, and of
course — the Tojo Virus.*

ARE YOU SURE (Y,N)

YES

"All right, let's clean up this mess," David had said.

Zack realized that David was indeed done. The virus was
ready. His heart pounded. Do something. What? As he helped
David clean up the messy room, a tiny thought blipped across his
mind: Those fucking diskettes can save your ass.

The diskettes had the programs and the decryption codes.
Everything could be redeemed if he had them.

And they might give you five hundred thousand dollars as well,
he thought, too.

Greed and redemption were tremendous motivators and were
enough for him to risk his life. Twenty minutes later, while David
stood by the incinerator and watched the flames slowly eat away at
the mounds of computer paper, Zack was back inside the office.

Zack's hands poised over the tote bag and lingered — should I?

Do it, for Christ's sake!

Zack reached inside his black metal filing cabinet, rooted under
the IGC Field Directory, and pulled out two boxes of diskettes. The cellophane made a soft crinkling noise as
Zack's hands quickly ripped the red pull tie on the new
box of diskettes and popped the lid. Through one of the
windows Zack could see David as he stood, back to the
house, near the incinerator.

Hurry!

One at a time, Zack peeled back the label on David's
diskettes. The adhesive on the labels was good enough to
stick but wasn't strong as cement glue. Diskettes in the
PC world were used and reused, labeled and relabeled.
Zack took each label, marked in David's handwriting,

and carefully transferred them to the new, unformatted diskettes out of his cabinet.

Zack was about to pee in his pants as he saw David poke around inside the incinerator with an old stick Zack kept by just for that purpose.

God, he's almost done!

And he was. Fortunately, so was Zack. In the last seconds, Zack remembered to switch boxes. David's diskette boxes were old, and dinged up from constant use. Zack took David's diskettes out and inserted his blank but labeled ones into each box, then put the two boxes back into the tote bag in the exact position they'd been in before.

Smiling, David came back into the office. Zack looked down at the floor in front of him. A sheet of shiny write-protect tabs had fallen out of his new box. It hadn't been there when David left. Zack quickly put his foot over the top of the tabs and returned David's smile as best he could.

Zack was drenched in sweat. Adrenaline pumped through his body.

What a stupid thing I've done!

There was great risk. What if David tried to use the diskettes before next Wednesday? He'd be killed for sure. Five minutes later, Zack collapsed into one of his soft customer-level chairs as outside, David started his car.

He'd robbed the robbers.

Since it was on level ground the Blazer responded with a leap forward and sped down College Drive toward the Colby home. Jose handed Jimmy C. an AK-47 and put Buddy's rocket launcher on the floorboard directly behind the driver's seat. When he stopped, Buddy would be able to slip it out quickly and without problem.

As usual, there was virtually no traffic on College. Buddy made the turn onto Bluff Court, ignored the driveway into the business entrance, and pulled into the residence driveway, stopping behind the Colby family car. Leaving the engine running, Buddy and Jimmy opened their doors in unison. Buddy grabbed for the grenade launcher while Jimmy slid the passenger seat back so Jose could jump out. The three men took ten steps to a position forty feet from the Colby front door, where Buddy knelt on the flagstoned sidewalk, one foot on the neatly trimmed front lawn — a patch of green in an otherwise sea of brown.

Click went the safety. The shell was already loaded.

"Obliterate them" had been Wu's words.

"Fire the fucker," said Jimmy with a cold voice.

Buddy's finger closed on the trigger and with a *woosh* the shell streaked toward the Colby front door, its path traced by smoke and fire.

Marcia sensed more than heard the sound of the rocket launcher and dove for Cheryl, who stood with the phone in her hand, halfway between Maria and the potential safety of the kitchen. At the same instant the room was filled with ten thousand bits of wood as the front door exploded back into the living room. The area was filled with a cloud of flying wood and vaporized Sheetrock. Shards of stained glass and pieces of metal finish turned to shrapnel. Living room furniture was upended, lamps were tossed , and glass-encased pictures shattered.

In the first three seconds of the aftermath, Marcia found herself on top of Cheryl, with Joe knocked completely down, half in the living room, half in the kitchen. Zack couldn't be seen through the choking dust and floating debris. They were all too scared even to shout.

Cheryl still clutched the receiver of the telephone, which was now in at least two pieces.

Marcia, her shirt on fire, grabbed Cheryl by her sweatshirt and on all fours dug and scrambled for the kitchen. Joe rolled over on his side and tried to pull back along with the girls, but his progress was immediately slowed by a sharp and twisted door hinge impaled in the meaty part of his right thigh.

"Down . . . stairs," Marcia grunted, pushing Cheryl into the kitchen.

The air in the living room was nearly unbreathable. Marcia could hear coughing. It had to be Zack, who had been knocked over the back of the couch and was lying on the floor between it and the wall.

"Zack!" shouted Cheryl, struggling to get onto her feet.

More coughing from Zack's general area.

Marcia slipped once on the slick kitchen floor, then got to a crouch, turned around, and saw Joe slowly pulling himself along the carpet, halfway into the kitchen.

"Joe!" she shouted, seeing that her friend was hurt.

Marcia scrambled back to Joe, just as she heard another noise out front.

"Cheryl! Where are you?" shouted Zack through the choking dust, as he slowly got up to his knees, then stood up.

The stoop was protected by an overhang which was held up by two fake pillars, each of which turned to sawdust in the explosion, collapsing the porch into a pile of rubble in front of what used to be the front door. The sound of the blast could have been heard down the hill only by someone who was particularly listening for such a noise. With the racket from jets taking off from the airport and nearby Warren AFB, and the fact that most

290

of the noise was sent to the north, where there was nothing but prairie, no one heard the blast.

Jimmy C. and Jose charged toward the house. Sounding like giant rats, they gnawed away at the front door rubble, knocking a hole for them to crawl through. Jose stood to Jimmy's left and slightly forward, his left hand covering his nose and mouth. Particulate filled the air.

The first thing Jimmy saw through the haze of the living room was the disheveled figure of Zack Colby as he got up from behind the couch. With a yell Jimmy let loose with a mean swath of fire from his AK-47, a path of death that cut through the room in an arc from left to right at hip level. To their right Jimmy heard but ignored a woman's scream.

Straight ahead of Jimmy, six four-inch bullets nearly cut Zack in half as the wall behind him popped with the onslaught. A large red lamp, miraculously unharmed and unmoved by the blast, exploded into a thousand pieces and flew in all directions. Jimmy thought he heard an *oh no,* but couldn't be sure.

At that very moment Xiang Wu was seconds from victory.

Jimmy smiled, quickly dropped the empty cartridge onto the floor, and slapped a new one into its place. If Jose had had an AK-47 in his hands and not a surplus U.S. Army flamethrower, he and Jimmy C. would have cut down their other three victims in a double sweep of death through the house. But Jose didn't have an AK-47.

Jimmy looked at Jose, whose finger was closing on the flamethrower — then to the room, whose air was filled with a billion pieces of tiny particulate.

"Nooooooo!" he shouted.

But it was too late. Jose pulled the trigger on the flamethrower. The fiery napalm shot through the middle of the living room, its fingers even reaching into the hallway leading toward the bedrooms. The weapon was absolutely the worst thing that Jose could have used. As the flames belched through the room, the particulate in the air was heated to combustion temperature.

The air in the room caught fire. The effect was a second explosion, this one much more powerful than the first, very much like a gas main being torched. The living room exploded, forcing red-hot air outward wherever it could find escape—through the front windows, down the hallway to the bedrooms, into the kitchen, back through the front door area.

Jimmy C. was knocked backward as if he had been pulled by a rope. Unfortunately, Jose's release of the trigger wasn't quick enough. Still belching, the flamethrower fell on Jose and torched him like kindling in a furnace, at the same time covering the living room drapes and the living room ceiling with hot death.

The living room had been turned into a five hundred-degree oven. Jose screamed as he was torched. Across the room, Zack Colby was doubly put out of his misery.

Across the room, the fact that Joe and Marcia were on the floor saved their lives. As it was, Marcia's hair was singed and her shirt was burned. When the second explosion ripped through the house, breathing became impossible. Farther back in the kitchen, Cheryl was knocked to the floor by the force, which also cleared her counters, smashed two sets of windows, and caught a pair of drapes on fire. Her skin was scorched.

"Come on, Joe. *Come on!*" Marcia urged, dragging the much heavier man across the kitchen floor.

Ignoring the pain in his leg and the fire in his lungs, Joe scrambled toward the stairwell leading downstairs. Marcia stumbled to Cheryl, who was knocked out. She would be dead in another sixty seconds if she stayed there, suffocated.

"Downstairs!" she shouted, grabbing Cheryl under her arms and dragging her across the floor.

The Colby home started to burn in earnest. In a few minutes smoke would be visible from all over town. Joe found the door and fell more than stumbled down the circular steps ahead of Marcia. At the bottom, he reached back up and took the limp form of Cheryl in one big arm, then helped Marcia, whose back hurt in a hundred places from the first blast.

Upstairs, Jimmy Chimichanga had been blown back through what had been the front door to the rubble-strewn front yard. Inside, Jose lay on the floor, dead and burning.

Downstairs, Joe hobbled down the hallway toward the far doorway to what he hoped would be freedom.

Following him, Marcia stopped halfway down the hallway, Zack's last words racing through her head.

I've got the programs. I've got the decryption keys! They're in my desk! Don't you see?

Marcia saw. She'd been in the house enough times to know the layout very well. Zack's office was the first office on the left, with a window that overlooked the city and the Rocky Mountains far away. As she ducked into Zack's office, ahead she could see that Joe had turned back.

"Marcia! We've got to hurry! It's clear! Hurry!" he shouted to her.

Marcia trashed Zack's neat stacks of IGC manuals and rummaged through his desk drawers.

"God damn it! Where the fuck did you hide the god-damn things?" she shouted.

Above her the house rattled and creaked and burned.

Next to his desk was a black two-drawer filing cabinet. Marcia fumbled with the handle, then yanked the top drawer completely off its casters, where it fell heavily onto the floor, tumbling out its contents. Her eyes fell on

293

two boxes of diskettes tucked in the back of a hanging-folder file cabinet; the boxes seemed to shout to her, "Me, me. Take me!"

Marcia scooped the box and popped the lid.

Master, 1 of 9 . . . 2 of 9 . . .

Marcia pocketed the boxes and ran for the door. The downstairs kitchen was on fire and the flames were advancing toward the open doorway at the end of the hall. She barreled through the screen door like a running back on drugs, then sprinted for the Taurus. Joe was ahead of her, carrying Cheryl like a sack of potatoes over his left shoulder. Joe reached the car, opened the door, and very gently placed Cheryl in the backseat, where she lay unconscious. Marcia ran for the car.

"Look!" shouted Joe, pointing up the hill, where the figures of Jimmy Chimichanga and Buddy Gault came sprinting around to the side of the house. Jimmy C., his shirttail out of his trousers, face blackened and burned, looked like the monster he was.

Marcia's anger was complete.

"Give me your gun!" she ordered.

Joe gave her his .38 Smith and Wesson, knowing that she'd never used a weapon before.

"You son of a bitch! You tell Wu that you failed — you miserable fucking son of a bitch! You tell Wu that I'm going to get him. Do you understand?" she shouted, then pointed the .38 toward them.

Jimmy C. dove for the ground as Marcia fired the gun three times, one shot by accident finding Buddy Gault's leg two inches from his left nut; he also fell to the ground, bleeding and in pain.

Black smoke had begun to rise out of the now-burning Colby residence. In the distance could be heard the sounds of a fire engine.

"Get the hell out of here, Joe," Marcia said, pulling the door closed at the same moment Joe gunned the car backward into a spinning K turn, then sped out of the driveway, across a wilted flower bed, and onto College Drive, headed north out of town.

The lone figure of Jimmy Chimichanga stood on the hill and watched as his targets fled, angry that he could do nothing but save himself. He had failed. Marcia Lee had turned out to be a formidable opponent.

"Son of a bitch."

Chapter Six
Scramble!

"You'd better call the police," said the yellow-slick-ered fireman, who turned from the cab of the fire truck and looked at the carnage from the Colby front lawn.

"It's out of control. Do what you can," the captain replied. "Damn, that thing went up quick," he muttered.

"Too quick," said the fireman.

Eight minutes later the first Cheyenne police squad car pulled up alongside the red fire truck.

"Holy shit," muttered the patrolman, reaching for the radio to call for additional units.

Fifteen minutes later Cheyenne detective Wyatt Steele, a tough westerner down to his genuine boots, climbed out of his Ford Bronco and approached the scene. Six squad cars, their blue and red lights strobing, blocked Bluff Court. Waiting for him to arrive was the county coroner, technicians, and two ambulances.

"Is this the way you found it?" Steele asked the fire chief, who nodded yes, which was verified by the patrolman.

"This was no ordinary fire, Wyatt," said the chief. "It was too hot. We should have been able to save part of the house. By the time we got here the whole house was burning at once. It shouldn't have."

Steele made a mental note and walked to the middle of the neatly manicured lawn. A body lay under a white piece of canvas.

"Pretty gross," said the Laramie County coroner. "You want a peek?"

Steele nodded and the coroner lifted the canvas.

The man's face looked like a tomato dropped on hot asphalt. He still clutched the beast that did him in, the army flamethrower. That explained why the fire was so hot and so consuming.

"Looks like the damn thing backfired on him," Steele mumbled. "You shouldn't be playing with fire, sonny," Steele stood up. "Who lives here?" he asked one of the patrolmen.

"The Colby family. Zack and Cheryl," he replied. "There was mail in the mailbox—I looked. He works for IGC." the patrolman pointed to the sign out at the street.

Steele walked back to the middle of the lawn, where a plastic bag fluttered in the afternoon breeze, weighted down by a large shell inside it. Steele looked around the area for footprints, but the Cheyenne fall had been long and dry. Even with constant watering, the Colby lawn was hard as a rock. He turned from the spot and looked at the rubble in front of the house.

A rocket launcher, he thought. A flamethrower and a rocket launcher. Just your everyday home-use items.

The dead meatball looked Mafia all the way.

"Is there anybody else inside?"

"We'll know in a few minutes—it's still too hot."

The Colby home made a series of groans as the weight of the structure crashed into the basement. After another twenty minutes the fire had reached the point where the first crew of firemen could enter the home. Only the overhead shell around the eastern exposure of the house had survived, that and most of what had been Zack's office. The rest was incinerated.

"Chief!" came the cry from the advance team.

Wyatt had been in enough situations to recognize the fireman's tone of voice. They'd found something unexpected, which in this case could only be a body — or bodies. A few minutes later a stretcher was hauled out with the charred remains of Zack Colby. Because he was on the floor his body wasn't completely charred, although his skin looked like a hot dog left too long on the grill. Wearing plastic gloves, the coroner searched the clothes and came up with a wallet from the back pocket, which he handed to one of the patrolmen, who in turn put the warm remains into a bag.

"How soon?" Wyatt asked the county coroner.

"This afternoon, Wyatt. I'll call you in the office."

Wyatt could hear the firemen tramping through the rest of the house.

"Nobody else, chief," was the all-clear signal.

The kitchen floor and back of the house no longer existed. In its place was a two-story pile of smoldering steel and wooden frames. Wyatt walked around the western side of the house and down the embankment to the business entrance. The sign read Zack Colby, IGC Corporation, Sales and Service, Please Call for an Appointment. The downstairs room looked like it had several computers, which now looked like they belonged in a house of mirrors. The keyboards were warped, the screens distorted. In one machine the gooey remains of a melted magnetic disk oozed out of its horizontal mouthlike slot like a computer version of Mr. Yuck.

What happened here? Wyatt wondered. Two people died violent deaths. The owner of the house was a salesman for IGC. Where is his family? Assault weapons were used. An intense fire started by a flamethrower.

Wyatt shook his head and walked back up the hill to the front of the house. This case was going to be one pain in the butt. It was major grist for the newspapers.

"Find out from the neighbors who these people are and if they've got any relatives in the area," he instructed the patrolman.

It was going to be a long night.

Why me?

For the second time in less than twenty-four hours Marcia's capacity to logically reason things out was failing her. She was bone tired and her back hurt. They'd driven like a bat out of hell for twenty minutes before getting off the highway at the first Colorado exit, taking a dirt road east toward a very small farming village named Carr. Halfway there Marcia ordered Joe to stop, which he willingly did. She'd almost thrown up when she had to help him pull the jagged piece of metal out of the meaty part of his thigh. The damned thing looked like a torn-off door hinge. While Joe held his hand over the bleeding wound, Marcia pulled two suitcases out from the trunk, ripped one of her blouses, and made a tourniquet. She then went to Cheryl, who lay sprawled across the back seat. The hair on the left side of Cheryl's head had caught fire when the living room had exploded. The skin on her left arm had first-degree burns, as did her neck. While her shirt had caught fire, the flames had been put out when Marcia covered her body, instinctively protecting her.

With no one coming in either direction, Marcia stripped to the waist, peeling back the remnants of her dress. Joe, his leg bandaged, inspected her back.

"Not so hot, Marcia," Joe said.

"Ouch," she'd said more than once as Joe used a pair of tweezers to remove tiny bits of shrapnel from her back. Once done, Joe covered the worst of the bleeding spots with the remaining Band-Aids from the first-aid kit. They would have to stop someplace soon to refill the supply and to get antiseptic ointment for Cheryl's burns. Aspirin was going to be the medicine of choice.

"I'll drive. You watch her," Marcia said as she switched seats with Joe, looking at the map.

Marcia drove through Carr, then turned right onto U.S. 85 and headed south toward Denver. It would take forty-five minutes longer than the interstate, but at least they would be off the main highway—in case the fleeing automobile had been recognized. Hertz wouldn't be pleased with the interior of the Taurus. Blood stains dotted and smeared the plush gray-blue interior.

"I've got to meet David at the airport, then we've got to get someplace and get patched up. She's going to be in some pain." Marcia nodded back to Cheryl, who was coming around.

By the time she'd gotten into the suburbs of Denver it was nearly five o'clock. In the backseat Cheryl was moaning. Pulling herself together, Marcia stopped at a Holiday Inn Crown Centre near the airport, registered the three of them into a large minisuite, then went to a nearby drugstore, where

300

she got a cache of commercially available feel-good products. Back in the room, she applied a cold solution of dissolved aspirin directly onto Cheryl's skin, then made her take some internally. She then cleaned Joe's wound as best she could and applied a real bandage to it.

"It's going to hurt, but I think you'll be OK. If it gets infected, we'll have to find a doctor. Keep ice on her burns and we'll just do the best we can," she instructed. "I'm going to the airport. I'll bring back something to eat."

Marcia looked at Cheryl, who lay hurting on the bed. She was coming out of it. She opened her eyes wide in fright; then they darted as she took in the room, now conscious. Then the thoughts flooded back. She was afraid and in great pain.

"He'll get you!" she shouted.

After he identified himself, Wyatt's call to IGC in Denver was put directly through to the branch manager, Al Benning. Wyatt knew the company was huge and made the logical assumption that somebody in the Denver office could give him some information on Colby's next of kin. When he was told that there were *three* IGC offices in the city, he was a little flabbergasted. Fortunately, the operator put him through to the landlord manager, Benning, whose territory included state and local governments and several remote territories outside of Denver, including Wyoming.

Wyatt quickly explained.

"There was a piece of ID in the wallet we found that was legible, indicating Zack Colby was its owner. We'll have tests done, but at this point I think it's safe to assume that Mr. Colby is the deceased. I need to know his next of kin, and I'm assuming you have that information someplace."

It took a few hurried minutes, but Benning's secretary managed to get to the personnel specialist before he went home for the day. Together the three of them went through Zack's blue personnel folder and came up with next of kin.

"What about Cheryl?" asked Benning, with Zack's jacket open on his desk.

"Would that be Mrs. Colby?" asked Steele.

"Yes," replied Benning.

"I don't know. She wasn't there."

"And the children?"

"No." Steele cringed. A wife and kids. Nothing's easy.

"Thank God. Well—Zack listed Cheryl's mother and father as next of kin not residing. They live in Laramie."

Benning gave Steele the telephone number and address.

"I'm not far ahead of the press, Mr. Benning. I'd appreciate it if you wouldn't give out that information to anyone. They'll get it quick enough, anyway," Wyatt requested as he hung up.

Mom and Dad, he thought. Not on the phone.

Wyatt got into his unmarked detective's car, put the bubble on the roof, and wailed through town to I-180, turned west on I-80, and covered the forty-eight miles between the cities in twenty-six minutes. It was five-thirty when he turned right at the Dairy Queen and pulled in front of the Goldsmith family residence on a tree-lined street. Two little faces leaned up against the inside of the door. Wyatt breathed a sigh of relief.

302

OK, no kids to worry about.

Steele knocked on the door, which was opened by a tall but thick woman in her early sixties, obviously Mom.

"Mrs. Coldsmith?"

"Yes?" she answered with a trusting smile.

"My name is Wyatt Steele—detective Wyatt Steele of the Cheyenne police department. May I come inside?"

At 6:15 Marcia slowly walked through the busy United terminal. She was sore and weary. The adrenaline that had flowed so strongly was gone. She was so tired that her thinking processes were numbed. She wanted to think, but just couldn't. Reaching the moving walkway, Marcia let it methodically move her down the terminal at five miles an hour. People passed her on the left, several bumped her legs with overstuffed carry-on bags. Marcia was in an alternate time zone, one of those slow-motion places where she was the only one moving at half speed.

Even as sophisticated and urbane as she was, as confident and skillful as she was, Marcia didn't yet fully understand the implications of what had happened in Cheyenne. She'd reacted on instinct.

Why are you here? she asked herself.

In a dream world she floated along with the bumpy rhythm of the escalator, oblivious of the holiday crowds bustling around her. Only five hours earlier her plans had been to come to Stapleton and take any flight she could out of the country. Now everything had changed. Everything.

This morning Wu had won.

He's probably gone, she thought.

Now, he hadn't. Now Wu was vulnerable.

Marcia's feet were rudely forced back to reality as the first section of the moving escalator reached the middle of the United terminal. Marcia was the only person standing still. She looked into the small walk-by bar. No David.

I'm so tired, she thought. I think I'll sit down here.

Which she did. It was a low, curved sofalike thing, like two love seats put back to back. Nobody else sat on it. Everybody was in such a hurry. After five minutes Marcia's eyes closed ever so briefly.

Damn, I could go to sleep.

"I didn't think you were coming," David said, sitting down behind her. "You look terrible," he added softly. "Is that blood?"

"Yes." Her eyes were still closed. "I didn't know if you'd come," she replied honestly.

"I almost didn't," said David.

David's eyes carefully scanned the terminal in all directions, seeing imaginary FBI agents everywhere.

"Zack's dead," she said softly, with resignation.

"What?" David exclaimed, nearly coming out of his chair. He dropped any pretense of being cool.

"Yes. Dead. They almost got me, too." Marcia shrugged off the near death experience. "The house . . . burned—it was terrible."

Her weariness covered her with a mantle of toughness that wasn't really there. Wu had nearly won. If Marcia was in a card game, she'd be drawing one to make an inside straight. David's skin tingled with fear. His mind could come up with nothing to say. But it was at that very moment—with thousands of travelers milling past their island of peace in both directions—that Marcia saw what she had to do.

There was only one path to safety and she had to risk it. The reward would be more than personal freedom. It would be redemption.

I will be avenged, she swore to herself.

Marcia's eyes brightened. She pushed back her weariness and concentrated on David. She put her hand on his arm, which instantly drew him to her.

"David," she said breathlessly, her eyes filled with an actress's tears. "Who are they? Why are they after us?"

The "us" didn't go unnoticed. Indeed, they were "us," and nothing more. Us versus the world. It was all she needed. David wanted to believe, and he did.

"I . . . I don't know."

"What are we going to do?" she said as she moved just an inch closer to him, the pressure of her hand increased in urgency.

After all, this is man's work, she implied.

There was obviously no need for them to stay in Denver.

"Are you all right?" David asked.

Marcia waved her injuries off.

"I'll be all right. The house was destroyed. They came with guns—the fire—it was terrible," she said, lowering her head as if to cry.

"We can't stay here—we've got to go—what about the—" David stuttered his thoughts.

"It's worse, I'm afraid," Marcia said, smiling inside.

Worse? David's face reflected.

"I had to bring Cheryl with me," she said simply.

"*Shiiiit!*" David said, too loudly.

"Shussh," Marcia replied.

"You're kidding?"

"No. I couldn't just leave her. She didn't do anything wrong, David. She's a woman—I couldn't."

305

Marcia pretended to cry. "It's dangerous for you to stay here," she said as she massaged his arm.

David's concentration was broken. He was confused. He was an excellent programmer—not a spy, not a blackmailer, not a murderer, and certainly not a sophisticate. Marcia's movements were too subtle. The atmosphere was electric around them—people and noise and pressure.

"I don't see how you can do this without some help, David," Marcia whispered. "Are you really planning to go ahead with this?" she asked, almost shyly.

"Yes," he said with determination, without a clue how.

Marcia looked around the terminal.

"Let me help. I don't think you can do this without some help."

He looked at her with skepticism.

"All right, I need a way out, too." David bought it. *Out* seemed a long way off. "The FBI's going to be all over this. I don't care what's happened—*somebody's* going to make the connection. Let me help."

"What about . . . her?"

"Cheryl?"

"Yes," David winced at the personalization.

"Her brother is an FBI agent," Marcia said simply. The sentence crushed David. His chest deflated and his shoulders drooped, as if some force had punctured his body and sucked out the air.

"That's right. Of all the people in the God-damned universe, we picked somebody whose fucking brother is an FBI agent."

One of the great things about living on the West

306

Coast—and perhaps the only good thing about living in LA—was Pacific Standard Time. Because the so-called civilized world ran on Eastern Standard Time, everything truly live came on the television at a decent time. "Monday Night Football" came on at six o'clock. A game could be bad but it was still better than the second hour of news, "Wheel of Fortune," and "Jeopardy." The Giants were leading the Eagles 10-6 midway through the second quarter when the phone rang. In his shorts, Scotty put down his beer and answered it.

"Scott Coldsmith?"

Long distance. "Yes."

"This is detective Wyatt Steele of the Cheyenne police department—"

Oh my God Cheryl's dead.

"I'm calling from the home of your parents in Laramie—"

Mom? Oh my God Dad's dead.

"Your brother-in-law Zack Colby has been killed—"

Zack? Zack?

"And we believe your sister is missing. The children are all right," said Wyatt, knowing the information would be devastating, which it was.

"Mom and Dad—"

"They're all right—as good as could be under the circumstances. They said you were with the FBI. You were on that spy case weren't you? I didn't know you were from this area."

Scotty sat down on a couch worn bare by years of beach rentals. A salty breeze blew in from the west and fluffed the thin curtains. In the last glow of the sunset Scotty could see a thick layer of dust on the table in front of him.

"I'm stunned—how . . . ?" Scotty started.

"It was a violent death, Mr. Coldsmith. It has all the appearance of a gangland slaying."

Gangland slaying! What the shit!

Steele's words weren't making sense.

This is Zack Colby we're talking about, he thought. The Zack Colby I palled around with in high school while he dated my sister in college. Zack Colby, a good bud. We went hiking together on weekends. He'd even leave Cheryl behind to go with me. He'd even go with me to the Cowboy on Friday nights for a hoot—treat me to a pitcher of beer and pour me in after the night was through. Zack and Cheryl—an All-American couple. Two great kids and a wonderful life. Gangland slaying?

"Have my parents given you a description of my sister?"

"Yes, they have," replied Wyatt. "We have an all-points out for her already." Wyatt paused. "I know everybody in town, Mr. Coldsmith. This is out-of-town action. The Colby home was burned to the ground. It was blown up. Somebody used a rocket launcher and a flamethrower on your brother-in-law. It sounds like somebody was very unhappy with him. It doesn't take too much to leap to the conclusion that he might have been involved in drug trafficking."

Scotty was stunned, overwhelmed.

"I haven't called the Bureau in Denver yet. There are some pieces of this that need FBI involvement—"

"I'll take care of it. I'll be there tonight," Scotty replied quickly, not knowing if it was a true statement or not. "How can I reach you?"

By the time Wyatt gave Scotty his home, business, and car phone numbers, he'd come back to life.

Zack dead?

"David, you need my help. You can't do this alone."

Those weren't exactly David's thoughts.

I've never killed anybody before. I can't kill her here.

For the first time David assessed Marcia as a potential adversary. He was obviously the stronger of the two, but she was tall and supple—and she had an inner strength that he'd already seen. She might be capable of considerable strength under pressure. In any case, David couldn't risk Marcia simply getting up and walking away. She was the last loose end.

She knows everything, he thought. *And Joe must know as much. And now Cheryl. Damn!*

"Yes, I could use some help. What do you want in return?" he asked, making the assumption that Marcia wouldn't do anything out of the goodness of her heart—she hadn't so far.

David's brown eyes couldn't conceal his thoughts. Marcia needed money like she needed a hole in the head. But he expected the obvious.

"Money, of course—and identification for Joe and me. Plane tickets would be a nice touch," she smiled. "I'm sure your rich go-betweens in Honolulu can come up with something nice—and quickly," she replied.

"Anything else?" David asked sarcastically.

"Yes, a briefcase of untraceable currency—two hundred fifty thousand dollars would be sufficient. Not outrageous considering what I've been paid to date, but barely enough considering what I've just gone through." Marcia gave him a hard smile. "In the end, Cheryl might be useful as a hostage. You've only got a couple more days left. *Somebody* has to be here to negotiate with those IGC people. You aren't going to be able to do it from Hong Kong."

David pretended that he didn't like what she said. In reality he was thinking, That's all? Marcia stood up and gave David an I'm leaving look. There was no response. She turned and walked toward the moving sidewalk, which was jammed with people.

"All right, I agree," she heard from behind her.

Marcia stopped, her back to him. They each were playing games. A confident smile crossed Marcia's face. She had him. She turned around and saw the anxiety in his eyes.

"Let's find a telephone. You've got some calling to do."

A canvas bag sat on the dusty table in front of the TV. The Giants were now leading the Eagles 24-9 and it was all over but the shouting. Al and Dan and the Giffer were trying to hype the Eagles' comeback but they all could hear the sound of the Nielsens falling in the background.

"Yeah?" was the reply on the other end of the long-distance call.

Typical Murphy.

"Hi—this is Scott . . ."

"Oh, shit—it's you," Monahan muttered.

"I'm calling to let you know I'm going back home, Murphy. There's been a problem. I want you to straighten it out with Harper in the morning. I'm on a case here, too."

"But . . ."

"I'm *going*, Murphy—"

Monahan listened as Scotty laid out the details,

realizing early in the conversation that he had no choice but to call the LA SAC in the morning and tell him what happened to his temporary agent.

"I want to be updated, Coldsmith—"

"Right, chief," smiled Scotty as he hung up.

Living in Playa del Rey, Scotty was fifteen minutes from the airport—less with the bubble. Even though the eight-thirty United flight to Denver was booked, his FBI badge would get him a seat. It would be after midnight before he got to Cheyenne.

In less than thirty seconds David was quietly speaking a mixture of English and Japanese to a wealthy rancher on the southeastern shores of the island of Kauai. A puzzled look came over his face. He turned to Marcia.

"He wants to know where to send them. Where are we going?"

"Where were you going if I didn't show up?" Marcia asked in return.

"San Francisco," David answered.

"OK. We can be there early Wednesday morning if we drive straight through. You can be there tonight if you want to," Marcia replied.

A question crossed David's face.

"I can't very well take Cheryl on a god-damned airplane!" she replied, acting exasperated.

"What about the Hyatt downtown?" he asked.

"No, something out by the airport. The Holiday Inn Airport. We've got outside access, it's spread out, and it's close to the airport. Tell him to FedEx it, care of your name. And the money. Don't forget the money," Marcia added, smiling to herself.

In another five minutes the conversation was concluded.

"It's done. The package will be there Wednesday morning," David said, a little proudly. "They are very anxious."

"I bet. Joe and I will be on the road tomorrow morning. There's no real reason for you to come with us, unless you want to. Just have a room reserved for us tomorrow night, late. If you're not registered or there's no note or I don't see you waiting for me — then we're gone and we let Cheryl loose. Do we understand each other?" Marcia asked, her hand on David's thick shoulder.

Although he tried to hide it, David's eyes flashed with resentment.

He wants to strangle me.

"Yes," was his simple reply.

He's in over his head.

Look who's talking.

"How are you?" Marcia asked as she sat down on the bed beside Cheryl.

"I'll be OK," replied Cheryl, unsure of the other woman. "What's going to happen to me?"

Marcia's face reflected "good question."

"I don't know. I didn't mean for any of this to happen. All I wanted to do was to warn you — and now I've got you — and I don't want you. Do you understand?"

"Sort of. But I don't understand — "

"Yes — I know. I wouldn't either if I was in your shoes. I'm not sure I understand myself. What I *do* want you to understand though, is that I mean you no harm."

"Oh, sure," Cheryl replied with deserved sarcasm.

Marcia's eyes rolled in dismay.

How can I blame her? she thought. I've fucked her husband, gotten him killed, kidnapped her, burned her house, and helped sabotage her husband's company. I'm a saint, right?

It didn't seem reasonable, even to Marcia.

Marcia sighed heavily and took her hand off Cheryl's leg.

"Yeah, I don't blame you. But I'm sure you *do* believe that I have to treat you as if you were a real hostage."

Cheryl's eyes agreed.

"Great. You don't know shit, but you know too much. I'd appreciate it if you didn't ask any questions, Cheryl. I can't answer them. I just want you to realize that when this is all over and done—I saved your life . . . and I meant to. If it wasn't for me, you'd be dead and burned—I know, I know . . ."

Cheryl started to say something, but the words were caught in her throat.

"Just remember it that way, please," Marcia said, then turned to Joe. "Listen, I've got to make a call." She got up and walked to the door. Joe handed her the key to his room.

"Hello," answered the soft voice of Wu's young consort.

"This is Marcia Lee. Let me talk to Wu," Marcia demanded.

"Very good. Please wait," came the polite response.

Marcia waited for nearly thirty seconds before Wu came to the phone.

"Miss Lee—this *is* a surprise."

"I bet," Marcia replied. "Your thugs left quite a

313

mess back there in Cheyenne."

"Regrettable," Wu replied conservatively.

"You *do* know that I have Cheryl Colby with me, don't you?"

Marcia could hear an audible intake of breath as Wu sucked it up.

"No—I . . . wasn't sure," Wu replied, hurriedly trying to gain composure. "Let me assure you, Miss Lee, none of this was personal. It was all business, nothing more."

"Well, it seemed pretty personal to me. And I'm sure it seemed *personal* to Shinogara and his men." Marcia spit out the words in anger. "Tell me, Wu. Did you have my people killed? *Did you?*"

"Yes."

"They were just girls, for Christ's sake!" Marcia said with vehemence.

"Yes, well—"

"Well, fucking nothing!" Marcia shouted.

There was dead air as Marcia tried to calm down and Wu tried to think of what to say to her next.

"I strongly suggest you consider your options, Miss Lee. We—that is, you and I—have no formal relationship. There's nothing but inference that ties us together. Who I am, or who I represent, is none of your business, as I see it. The Colby woman is a liability only to you—not to me. I think it's time that you begin to think about taking care of yourself," Wu said, in preparation to a disconnect.

"Are you aware that David Kimura is still alive?"

There was a pause.

"You have just confirmed it," Wu replied, leaving much unsaid.

"So you think you destroyed his programs?" Marcia asked in a near taunt. "Are you concerned about *that*

314

possibility, Mr. Wu?"

She could feel Wu tense up. There was no response.

"I'm sure you aren't aware of this fact"—Marcia said the words slowly, as if dragging a hot spear across a naked chest—"Colby switched diskettes on David. *He* had them this past weekend, not David."

"Oh?" replied Wu.

"And now *I* have them," Marcia said coldly. "A packet of nine diskettes—a complete set of Shinogara's virus programs. I have them—including the . . . decryption keys . . . as I believe David calls them. As I understand it, at this point these keys are more important than the programs. And I'm the only one who has them."

Marcia paused. The noise of I-70 was behind her, along with the roar from several jets landing at Stapleton. There was silence on the other end.

"Does this change anything?" she added, jabbing him.

"You could be bluffing, Miss Lee," Wu replied with a degree of disguised confidence that was easy to read, even over the phone.

"Until this very minute I haven't been able to put my finger on exactly what your game is—but now I think I've got it. You're a *money man*, aren't you?" Marcia asked, shrewdly grasping the tip of Wu's purpose.

She'd convinced herself that Wu was after the same thing Shinogara was—that the computers, the technology—the *things*, were the objectives.

So it was money all along, she thought.

"So that's why you were so interested in knowing exactly when the virus was activated. And I told you. If it wasn't for me all those people would still be alive," Marcia berated herself.

"It's just — *business*, Miss Lee," Wu replied in a fatherly tone.

"So who's in this with you?" Marcia asked. "Who are your partners?"

"I really can't disclose that information, Miss Lee."

"*I* have the decryption keys, Mr. Wu. I'm pretty sure IGC would be interested in them — don't you think? I'm also pretty sure that the FBI, the SEC, and a number of other federal agencies would all be interested."

"Perhaps. Are you proposing something?" Wu asked, his voice no longer confident.

"I think you have a new partner, Wu," Marcia replied coldly. "Of course, it's just — *business*. Nothing else, you understand. Just — *business*."

Wu accepted the heat without comment.

"What are you proposing?" he asked.

"I want to know who I'm dealing with. I want names. I want to meet these people. I want guaranteed compensation — ten million dollars deposited in my Geneva account. I want passports, new identity — and transportation out of the country for myself and my personal bodyguard, Mr. Turner," replied Marcia.

Wu didn't bat an eye. "In return . . . ?"

"I give you the box of diskettes. You can do what you want with them."

"I'm not sure . . ." Wu started to reply.

"Yes, you are. Call them. Make a decision. I'll talk to you tomorrow. Or should I call IGC? They'll be pretty anxious come Wednesday morning, I'm sure. I'll bet they'll be interested now, too."

"David Kimura doesn't have the programs?"

"David has nothing. *I* have them. I'll be talking to you, Wu."

Marcia hung up, smiling grimly. Her instincts were coming back.

Scotty managed to sleep for an hour on the flight to Denver, awaking minutes before the seat belt announcement as the plane encountered the usual turbulence crossing the Rocky Mountains. It was midnight by the time he'd rented a car and started north out of Denver on I-25.

The conversation with Mom and Dad had been frantic. There would be time to visit and comfort them, but his first objective was to see what he could do to help in the investigation—to see what the Bureau could do to help the Cheyenne police.

I'm not ready for Mom and Dad yet, he thought.

Scotty took the Lincolnway exit on I-25 and went toward town. The lights at the Stage Coach Inn and the Budget Motel were out except for the No Vacancy sign. Neither had a night clerk. Scotty pulled into the Hitching Post Inn, asked for and got a room, showing his badge to get the government rate of twenty-six dollars a night. The per diem in Cheyenne wasn't like LA or New York. He'd have to keep it under fifty bucks or he'd have to pay the excess himself, including the rental car, a subcompact Toyota that just wasn't built for a man of six foot four.

I'd hate to chase anybody in this, he thought. FBI agent nabs kidnapper in low-speed chase along I-25.

The thought made him smile—as did the room, which had a bed to fit his frame. Scotty tried Steele's number at the police station, but at 2:00 A.M. it was best that he got a night's sleep.

It might be a while before he'd get much rest.

* * *

"I'm Scott Coldsmith." Scotty held out his hand.

It was seven o'clock Tuesday morning and the station was nearly empty. Wyatt looked at the young man in front of him and mentally grimaced at having called him mister over the telephone.

This boy would never be a mister, he thought.

Scotty had seen the look before, a kind of oh, sure kid disdain that was easy to get in a first impression.

"I'm actually older than I look," Scotty said.

Steele, the epitome of craggy rugged western toughness, looked up from his desk and made eye contact. There's some substance there, was Steele's impression.

"What, nineteen?" Steele jabbed.

Scotty smiled politely. Without offering Scotty a seat, Wyatt rolled back into his squeaky old chair and put his boots up on his metal desk.

"I want protection for my parents—and for my niece and nephew. Can you arrange it?" asked Scotty, with a cold, businesslike tone in his voice, no longer the kid.

"It'll be done this morning," replied Steele.

"And a telephone tap. Can you get caller ID installed?"

Steele frowned. Caller ID had been test-marketed across the country for public use, but to this point was only used by police and emergency 911 systems.

"We don't have it here. But I'm going over to U.S. West this morning on a related matter. I'll ask."

"Related to what?" asked Scotty.

"Your brother-in-law had three separate telephone lines into his house—two into the basement, which apparently he used as an office. Do you know anything about what he did?" asked Steele.

318

"I haven't been back here since they moved into the house. Zack sold for IGC, that's all I know. What about the bodies? Is there anything in the system?"

"We're still waiting. As far as the rocket launcher goes, there was a match at the National Crime Information Center—the army reported it missing six years ago out of Ft. Bragg. But who knows?" Steele shrugged. "We got the autopsy report back last night. Zack Colby was shot six times in the chest and stomach by a semiautomatic rifle. I'll have somebody out digging through the living room this morning. Something must have gone wrong with the flamethrower—I can't figure out why this one thug died."

"Prints?"

"No. Maybe your lab boys can pull something out—ours couldn't. The flamethrower backfired—something went haywire. There wasn't much left of him."

"My sister . . . ?"

"I don't know. It's hard to reconstruct what might have happened. There are some tire tracks in a flower bed by the second driveway—the one he used for business. We could probably use some help on them. But the inside of the house was pretty well decimated. These were not subtle people, Mr. Coldsmith. They were there to kill people and to destroy whatever evidence there might be in the home. They did a pretty darn good job, too," Wyatt concluded. "Oh, yes—your sister. Your parents came up with a recent photo, which we'll use—the *Cheyenne Eagle* will have it in their afternoon edition. Until we're contacted, I can't chalk this up as a kidnapping. Right now she's a missing person, nothing more."

"Have you been in contact with IGC?"

"Yeah." Steele flipped a notebook back two pages.

319

"They gave me your parents' phone. I talked to a man named Al Benning. He's the branch manager — a sales manager. Mr. Colby reported to him."

"You can assume I'll be your contact on this case, Wyatt. Who's the SAC in Denver you deal with?"

"Alex Hastings. Good man."

"Have you called?"

"I figured I'd wait until you got here."

"Well — I've got to get things straight with Hastings, then I'll be at IGC. I'll call in."

"Most likely I'll be at U.S. West. I've got a good contact. His name's Pete Goodman — at this number." Wyatt wrote down a number on a memo slip and handed it to Scotty. "There's one other thing," Wyatt started.

Scotty had started for the door, but stopped in his tracks.

"He was using drugs. The autopsy found a high level of amphetamines in his system," Steele said, knowing what Scotty's reaction would be. "I'm sorry I had to tell you, but you had to know. Your brother-in-law was up to his neck in something. You and I both know that this stuff doesn't happen at random."

There was nothing Scotty could say. He appreciated the older man's gesture of sympathy.

Drugs? What the hell did Zack do?

"Mr. Benning's office," replied Mary, a gray-haired, soft-spoken woman of fifty-six who managed Al Benning's time like it was her own and made the space around the branch manager's office as difficult to get through as a German mine field. Mary listened to the conversation, jotted down a note, then walked into Al Benning's office and handed it to him. Al was

320

in the middle of listening to a loss review with the state of Colorado marketing team. What he heard between the lines was that the team hadn't done its homework, and in fact had even misinterpreted the bid specifications — offering a more powerful and more expensive computer than was needed. It was too late in the year to lose big orders — and Benning hated to lose. This loss would hurt the performance evaluations of all concerned.

With a scowl on his face Benning read the note: FBI Agent Scott Coldsmith in lobby — Urgent subject.

"OK, that's enough. Mistakes have been made. I've got somebody I have to see, but I'll want to finish this later — no matter how late it goes," he instructed the team, who were glad to have a reprieve, no matter how temporary.

Mary poked her head back inside Benning's large office, a third-floor corner with a panoramic view of the Rocky Mountains.

"I'll go down myself. Get Zack Colby's personnel jacket and find Ted Springs," he instructed, sending Mary off like a heat-seeking missile on a dual-function task.

IGC lobbies had become formidable since the infamous Rust Bucket massacre of 1983, when a fired employee drove his car through the glass doors of a two-story office building in suburban Bethesda, Maryland, and opened fire, killing six employees and holding another seven hundred people in terror for an afternoon. From a marketing perspective, the buildup in security didn't help IGC's image as being a cold and difficult company to do business with, but it did make sense given the times, and nobody much complained.

The lobby clock read ten-thirty when Benning stepped out of the elevator. At fifty-two, he was as high on the corporate ladder as he was going, but that suited him just fine. To go further would mean a move away from Denver, and most likely a divorce. Benning earned a $150,000 salary with the opportunity for an additional $75,000 in various quota, revenue, and expense bonuses. He had 26 first- and second-line managers reporting to him and a total branch population of 228 employees. His set of accounts brought in $180 million dollars in revenue each year. Al Benning was underpaid considering his duties and responsibilities. Nobody got to be a branch manager in IGC without an ability to ask the tough questions, and Al Benning was no different. Yet he was fair and generous at the same time. As a result, he'd earned a degree of loyalty that was typical within the company.

Scotty thought Benning sure looked the part—neatly trimmed graying hair, crisp white shirt, blue-and-red striped tie, a six hundred-dollar blue pin-striped suit, and a polished pair of black Florsheim wingtips.

"Mr. Coldsmith? I'm Al Benning, branch manager of this facility. May I see your identification, please?"

"Certainly," replied Scotty, holding his badge in front of him at shoulder level for Benning to read.

"Follow me, please," Benning said, turning toward the elevator bank.

Five minutes later Scotty was seated in a comfortable chair in front of Benning's large rosewood desk. As introductions were made, Scotty took notes.

"Ted Springs is—was—Zack Colby's direct line

manager. Ted is a marketing manager and reports to me. If you don't mind, I'd like my secretary Mary to sit in on this meeting and take notes."

"No problem," replied Scotty.

"Your badge identifies you as being from New York," Benning opened.

Scotty explained. But he didn't tell Benning that Denver SAC Alex Hastings was more than glad to have someone cover a case in Wyoming. Hastings spoke of the state as if everything above Ft. Collins was in the Yukon.

"I don't have anyone I can spare. I'm down three on my head count and everybody's pulling ten-hour days. I'll give you whatever logistical support I can, but unless this case of yours gets real bad, I'm afraid you're on your own."

Hastings had been brutally honest with him.

Al Benning and Ted Springs listened as Scotty went over the details.

"I've more or less assigned myself to this case, Mr. Benning. Zack Colby is . . . was . . . my brother-in-law. Cheryl Colby, my sister, is missing and presumed kidnapped. They came home together yesterday, their car is still in the garage, and only Zack's body was found in the house. And he was murdered," Scotty continued, shifting his attention from Springs to Benning and back.

As cool as the IGC managers were, neither man wanted to be involved in death — violent death. No amount of Dallas training prepared managers for completing the blocks in the death form, the piece of paper that finds its way to corporate personnel in White Plains, New York, and initiates the surgically clean separation of the former employee from the company. Like a butcher knife on a hard tabletop —

whack goes the American Express card, *whack* goes the Hertz card, *whack* goes the Blue Cross coverage, *whack* goes the separation statement and salary check, *whack* goes the life insurance check. *Whack, whack, whack, whack, whack!* All from one little form, Z120-0500. Also automatically generated from the form is an appropriate floral arrangement and personalized letter from the chairman of the board to the spouse of the deceased employee, suitable for framing.

"The autopsy showed that Zack had used drugs for some time before his death," Scotty continued.

Benning and Springs jointly sucked their breath.

"Gentlemen, I was born and raised in Laramie. I went to the University of Wyoming, as did my sister and brother-in-law. They're as square and honest as two people can be. But something happened to Zack, and I'm going to find out what. I'd like to know who he's seen — who's talked with him — did he have to fill out sales reports of any kind? I assume IGC salesmen must have some sort of weekly or monthly record keeping. Where's he been the last two months? Who's seen him?" asked Scotty.

Mary pulled out a stack of Zack's weekly time cards and flipped through them while Ted Springs went through the written weekly activity report submitted by salesmen to their manager each Monday.

"Other than a trip to Dallas in early October, it looks like—" Mary was interrupted by a gasp from Ted Springs.

"Oh, my God."

Ted's hands shook as he quickly sifted through the reports.

"We've been so busy . . . I didn't have time to read them all . . ." he stuttered, handing the handwritten reports to Al Benning, who looked at them sequentially, frowned, then handed them to Scotty.

Zack's neat handwriting and concise descriptions had degenerated in the last six weeks to the point where the words were illegible.

"Looks to me like Zack was crying out for some help," Scotty said.

Scotty looked at the reports, then at Zack's expense account while in Dallas. His time cards indicated he'd been in his territory every day since the class in October.

"I'm not a psychologist, but it certainly looks to me like something happened to him while he was in Dallas—wouldn't you say? I'd like your help in locating anybody who might have seen or talked to Zack during that week."

A semi-pained look briefly crossed Al Benning's face, which was not unnoticed by Scotty.

"This is a formal investigation, Mr. Benning. If need be, I can get our Dallas office to get a warrant for the records."

"There's no need to threaten us, Mr. Coldsmith. I understand your position, both personally and professionally. It's late in the afternoon, two days before a four-day holiday weekend. My concern is not *whether* I'll help you, but rather *how* I'll do it. I've got considerable red tape to cut through," Benning said, taking a deep breath as he spoke. "If you're willing to stay here, I'll do the best I can to get whatever you need."

"Thanks," said Scotty, smiling. "By the way, what have you told the reporters?"

"Absolutely no comment. Every reporter has been referred to our corporate external communications office in New York. At the local level we issue no statements of any kind to the press."

Without further ado, Al Benning pulled his *IGC*

Internal Field Directory from a bookshelf in his credenza.

"Ted, find out who's in charge now of marketing training in Dallas. I've got to call Bob and let him know that I might ruffle some feathers up the line," Benning smiled.

Scotty thought that Benning actually relished the task. When it came to a choice between tweaking procedure or conducting a loss review, Al Benning much preferred tweaking.

After only ten minutes and three transfers, Al got to the director of marketing training, Gabriel Sanchez. Al explained the bare bones of the situation, then put Scotty on the speakerphone to lay out what he knew.

"Hold the line. I'll find out who was class manager. What class was it?" asked Sanchez.

Benning looked at the branch copy of Zack's expense sheet, a white form still referred to as a "green sheet," a color from a previous incarnation.

"It was a workstation update, class number 66548, October six to ten," replied the branch manager.

"I'll be right back," said Sanchez.

In a few minutes they could hear sounds coming from Sanchez's office in Dallas.

"I've got Walt Goodfellow here. He was class manager."

Walt was introduced.

"I've got the attendance sheet for the class. It shows that Colby was there each day, but I'll be honest with you — I can't picture him. There were sixty people in the class, and while I was class manager for the workstation update, I was also teaching individual

326

subjects in two other classes during the week. Maybe if I had a picture I could place the face."

Scotty produced a head-and-shoulders shot of Zack and Cheryl.

"Can you fax it?" Scotty asked.

Yes, they could. Sanchez gave them the number of his fax machine, a bulky IGC Scanmaster, one of the thousands of unsold machines left over from the company's failed attempt to break into the facsimile marketplace. Mary took Scotty's picture of Zack and went off to the machine.

"You'll have it in a minute or so," said Benning.

"Did he have a roommate?" Scotty could hear Sanchez ask Goodfellow.

There was a pause and a shuffling of notes.

"Sorry—they stayed at the Sheraton, but the hotel took care of assigning rooms. They probably have it someplace—but it's been six weeks. If they're like most places, it'll take a couple of days to get somebody to do it," Goodfellow explained.

Both ends of the telephone paused to think. It was four o'clock Eastern time. Branch switchboards were closed. Central Headquarters was closed.

"What about PROFS?" asked Benning.

"And send them *what?*" asked Sanchez.

"Make it urgent, confidential, eyes-only. It sure beats trying to call sixty people and go through the story sixty times," replied Benning.

PROFS was to be used for business purposes only. Sending this kind of note would definitely be irregular. In his fifth-floor office overlooking Williams Square and the bronze mustang ponies, Gabriel Sanchez shifted uncomfortably in his chair. He was a director in the corporation, head of all marketing training for domestic operations, and three giant career steps above Al Benning on the corporate ladder. Yet, he didn't have the authorization to send this kind of request through the system.

"I know what you want to do, Al, but I'm going to have to contact someone in corporate communications—Fred Crowe's group. I'm sorry," said Sanchez.

Al Benning's eyes closed in frustration.

"Gabe, this is *very* important. Do you know Crowe?"

"Yeah, I know him," replied Sanchez.

"Can you call him for us?" asked Benning. "And give us a call back. We'll open a three-way conversation," said Benning.

There was more commotion on the Dallas side as the fax of Zack and Cheryl came through.

"That's Zack Colby?" exclaimed Walt Goodfellow.

Scotty looked at Al Benning and leaned closer to the speakerphone.

"Do you recognize him, Walt?" asked Scotty.

"Yeah, I remember him. Every once in a while we get somebody like this, a guy who comes to Dallas, parties every night, sleeps in class every day. This guy was comatose in class—a zombie—a member of the living dead. I almost sent him home, I remember that," Goodfellow said with conviction.

"Can you make the call, Gabe?" asked Benning.

"I'll do my best."

Cynthia Rosen was on the fast track. A former marketing manager in the Parsippany, New Jersey, branch office, she was now spending her two years on staff before getting her own branch office. It was a critical time in her life. When she'd accepted the job as Fred Crowe's administrative assistant, she'd made the decision that she wanted to go for the ring—go for as high a job inside the company as she could get. While it was a joint decision between her and her husband, neither really knew the family sacrifices that would have to be made. The children were third in life. Her husband was second—a distant second.

At age thirty-four, Cynthia had six 100% Clubs and a Golden Circle Award, and had been moved along as fast as she could accept responsibility. She'd been very careful about her selection of her staff job. She'd had several offers—two from marketing programs and another in the New York-New Jersey regional office. But it was headquarters experience she wanted. The profile was higher—the risks greater—but the potential reward was there. Nobody got to be a branch manager from a regional job—you had to go through Armonk or White Plains. Even so, there were too many former marketing managers who ended up as program managers in HQ, who after two years found they couldn't get their little marketing idea past the incipient stage. Instead of producing an idea and program that would really help the field marketing forces, all that was produced was a fancy foil presentation or perhaps a tray of colorful slides—all fluff and no stuff. The few people who made names for themselves were those who managed to take a good idea and translate it into reality—but it was a crap shoot. And Cynthia didn't like to gamble. But she was realistic enough to know that her career depended not only on her performance—which was basically a twenty-four-hour per day on-call job—but also on how well Fred Crowe did himself. If Fred screwed up there was no way any of the people Fred knew, touched, or had anything to do with, would succeed. It was that brutal and that simple.

And of course, one of the benefits of being an administrative assistant was that you got to mind the shop while the boss got to take the week off. But before leaving for upstate New York, Fred had agreed that she could take Wednesday off.

"If you've got all the reports ready, Rosen. I've got a presentation with Horton next week. Remember, I like backup charts for my backup charts. And lots of color—don't forget the color."

In her new job Cynthia had been forced to learn the PC all over again, down to a level of detail much deeper than she wanted to. Fred liked pie charts and bar charts and three-dimensional stacks. Three-quarters of the stuff she did never got out of his briefcase—it was just there "in case."

Why doesn't somebody pick up that phone? she wondered.

Then Cynthia looked at the clock.

It can't be four-thirty, she thought.

Nobody picked up the phone because nobody was in the office—just Cynthia Rosen, girl-wonder administrator, Queen of Graphs.

"Stop ringing!" she shouted.

But it didn't stop. In fact, the phone shrieked, "Pick me up, God damn it!"

Cynthia stumbled out of her office toward Betty's desk, where an angry light flashed in unison with each new ring. In the process she snagged her panty hose at the knee on a rough edge of her desk.

"Damn!"

She picked up the phone.

"Hello, this is Cynthia Rosen."

"Hello!" the voice sounded relieved. "This is Gabriel Sanchez. I'm director of marketing training in

Dallas. Is Fred Crowe still around?"

"I'm sorry, Fred's out of town for the rest of the week. He'll be back on Monday."

"Who's in charge while he's gone?" asked Sanchez.

"I'm Fred's AA. What can I do for you, Mr. Sanchez?"

Gabe Sanchez quickly explained what was needed.

"The branch manager in Denver, Al Benning, has this FBI agent with him. They'd like to have a three-way conversation if possible," said Sanchez.

"Go ahead," replied Cynthia.

The prospect of talking with an FBI agent wasn't something that thrilled Cynthia. What he would want from her—and from her boss—involved risk. Cynthia knew she would have to verify the agent's credentials and background before she would contact Fred Crowe. Fred had said that he could be reached, but it had better be important. The rightness or wrongness of sending the message itself was irrelevant. What was actually important was the decision, not the message. Would the decision to send the message be perceived to be correct—not just by Crowe, but by those in the chain of command in Armonk, all the way up to Mr. Holton's office, perhaps even by Mr. Holton himself. At age fifty-six, John Holton had four years left to run one of America's largest corporations, and arguably its most important corporation—four years before his mandatory retirement as chairman of the board at age sixty.

Whether it was right or wrong that careers—people's lives—depended upon the *perception* of decision making, was as irrelevant as the facts of the situation itself. It simply was. It existed. Cynthia Rosen could care less how many more years John Holton would guide IGC. What she cared about was that nobody of importance would criticize her or her boss for making a decision, whatever that decision turned out to be. At that moment, what frosted Cynthia's ass was that this decision had to be made at all. This wasn't one of the things covered in the Manager's Manual, the thick, black-bound, two-volume series given all managers. Inside were answers to everything that wasn't really important. But there wasn't a manager in the company, who, faced with lowering an employee's performance rating, wouldn't consult the manual for guidance to finding the Golden Rationale to get by the stressful event.

Cynthia Rosen certainly didn't get to where she was by making decisions by any rulebook, but even she would admit that it was nice to have a set of guidelines.

Page 841
What to do if the FBI Calls
(This Page Left Intentionally Blank)

Cynthia waited as Gabe Sanchez made the connection to Denver. Introductions were made.

"Miss Rosen, this is Scott Coldsmith. Has Mr. Sanchez explained what I need, and why?"

"Yes, but I'd like to hear it in your words, Mr. Coldsmith," came Cynthia's reply.

"One of your employees was brutally murdered yesterday afternoon—in the living room of his home, which was burned to the ground. He was killed by a semiautomatic assault rifle. An autopsy found amphetamines in Mr. Colby's system. Another man was inside Zack Colby's house—dead. And his wife is missing. We presume she has been kidnapped. Every minute we delay, the less chance we have of appre-

332

hending these people. This is a time-critical investigation, Miss Rosen," said Scotty in his best grown-up voice.

There was a pause on the other end as Cynthia finished her shorthand note taking.

"Why doesn't the FBI go through its normal channels, Mr. Coldsmith?" Cynthia asked.

There were restrained groans by the other IGCers.

"You're there, my people are there—but I'm here and so are the bad guys, Miss Rosen. There are lives at stake."

There was another pause.

"Mr. Sanchez," Cynthia started, "PROFS me the note, along with the distribution list. I'll get back to you tomorrow."

More groans, this time more audible.

"*Gentlemen,* this is *not* an approved way of using PROFS. I have to think about precedence. Is this a one-time shot, or am I committing the company to allowing the FBI to come in whenever it wants. What if the next time they want to see our employees' personnel jackets? And while I'm sure you're a legitimate representative of the FBI, Mr. Coldsmith—*somebody* has to verify it," Cynthia said, with a little steam in her voice.

Scotty was impressed by the woman.

"My office happens to be in New York City, Miss Rosen. I'm here because . . . your employee Mr. Colby is . . . was . . . my brother-in-law. It's my sister who is missing. My supervisor in Manhattan is Mr. Murphy Monahan." Scotty gave Cynthia the telephone number.

"I'll get back to you tonight, if I can," Cynthia said, just remembering that she'd planned to take Wednesday off.

"Miss Rosen, may I have your work and home telephone numbers please?"

Cynthia gave Scotty the numbers.

"And your position within IGC?" he asked.

"I'm the assistant to Mr. Fred Crowe, vice president of internal communications. We handle the worldwide PROFS communications network, internal publications, and a wide variety of other things."

One by one the lines were disconnected and Cynthia was left by herself.

Another pizza night for the crew, she thought.

Cynthia's first call was to her husband, Ted. They have to be late to the party.

"If I'm lucky, I'll be home by nine—knowing the Pattersons, the party will just be starting," she told Ted.

"I know, I'll get the pizza," he said.

What a good man.

Cynthia went back to her problem.

"Lives at stake" was definitely a benefit. Lives at stake is a tough one for anyone to criticize. Lives at stake is a free shot. No matter what happens, it's a gimme. The only "wrong" decision is one that jeopardizes those lives at stake. Anything else is irrelevant. Cynthia Rosen could see major benefits from making a no-brain decision.

Cynthia did indeed call Murphy Monahan, who at 7:15 in the evening was in the middle of his second shift of the day. Cynthia identified herself and asked about Scotty.

"Yes, he's mine. Why is he talking to you?" asked Monahan.

"I'm the red tape he's got to cut through," Cynthia

said after explaining.

"We don't normally send agents from New York out to Wyoming to investigate cases. We've got more than enough to keep us busy. But this one is kind of personal."

"So I understand," Cynthia replied, her conversation over.

Hanging up, she looked at her terminal. The Mail Waiting light at the bottom of her screen seemed to be on all the time. It never went out. There was always mail. The system was *too* good.

People spend so much time sending and answering mail that they never have time to do any work! she thought.

Another shrapnel wound from the information explosion.

Sometimes I just don't want any more damn data. Let me make my own decision, she thought.

Cynthia's next call was to the second-shift PROFS administrator in the basement of the huge Franklin Lakes facility, where she got the answers to her questions about the system. A recent change had restricted the "shareability" of PROFS notes marked Confidential. They couldn't be forwarded. Since nothing Classified, Restricted, or Restricted-Eyes-Only could be sent via PROFS, the central problem seemed to be with the classification of the message. Gabe Sanchez, director of marketing training, could indeed send a Confidential message.

But was it in IGC's best interests to do so? What was the gain? What was the loss? Were there legal issues involved? Could the FBI be setting a trap for an IGC employee? Could IGC be sued? What have we done with previous requests? What would we do with future requests?

What do you think, Cynthia?

Those would be Fred Crowe's first words after hearing a synopsis of the problem.

Well, Cynthia, what do you think?

Fred Crowe, dressed in warm and comfortable clothes, sat on a well-worn tree stump and watched the weather change. He loved it. It was going to snow.

Snow, you son of a bitch!

And it was so. Soft, tender flakes that delicately seemed to ask the ground if it was all right to settle down. Yes, it was OK. Fred watched from the front porch of his cabin on the southwestern side of Blue Mountain Lake. The eastern shore of the lake spread out in front of him. Everything was white, tipped with bits of evergreen. It was an incredible sight. Nobody was in the area but the Crowe family. The feeling of the 1700s and the early explorers of the New York Adirondack Mountains wasn't far from the seat of the pants.

What must it have been like? he wondered.

"It's for you," said his wife. "It's Cynthia."

Fred Crowe, designee to be the next chairman of the board of the world's most important company, could only grimace. Today, at that very moment, he didn't want to be anything but plain old Fred Crowe looking at the snow falling on Blue Mountain Lake.

"Yes?" was his stern answer.

There was no need to apologize. Fortunately, she'd gotten over that hump within the first sixty days.

She needed to learn.

But he couldn't tell her. Cynthia Rosen was chosen from a short list of very, very qualified candidates.

Young, aggressive, self-assured, talented . . . she had the potential to step into the upper echelons. Looks had nothing to do with it. Femaleness had something to do with it, but certainly not as much as it used to. Fred Crowe had many staff assistants, and approximately half were women. Those women that failed did so for the same reasons the men did. Fred could see no gender difference in performance, desire, or ultimate ability. The biggest weight they carried was mental.

Fred had chosen Cynthia carefully, but knew that he would drop her like a hot rock if she screwed up — certainly, if she screwed up. So far there was no reason for him to get a new AA.

"Fred, I've gotten a request from the FBI to send out a limited PROFS message regarding a case they're working on. An IGC marketing rep from Cheyenne was killed yesterday morning. Drugs were found at the scene. Apparently, the IGCer was being blackmailed. For what reason, they don't know. The FBI believes that there is a connection to a marketing class he attended in Dallas in mid-October and the agent wants to contact a limited number of IGCers who attended a class to see if they remember anything about the rep. The wife is missing and has been presumed to be kidnapped. So it's a time-dependent kind of thing," said a nearly breathless Cynthia Rosen.

Fred Crowe looked out of the cabin's front window at the soft snow falling on a cold gray-blue lake.

"And?" he continued.

"The FBI believes Colby, the dead marketing rep, started a drug habit sometime after a class in Dallas."

"What if an IGCer is involved?"

A slight pause.

337

"We didn't talk about that," replied Cynthia.

You never say "I don't know" to your manager. She continued quickly. She was now hooked into the situation. This was no longer a pain in the butt, but something real. There were real people who were in real danger. It made all the business forecasts, reports, and Big Decisions seem so small. And no matter how small a part it was, she was helping.

"What are our alternatives?"

"In order to meet the time dependency, we'd have to contact the branch manager in all sixty-two branch offices, get the home number of every employee on the class roster, and have the FBI contact them directly," replied Cynthia.

"No, we wouldn't let them have that degree of access," said Fred Crowe, thinking.

Crowe was familiar with the FBI's methods. The FBI thrived on information, sucked it up, stored it away. No piece of data was considered too small. He wasn't about to have the personal data on sixty-two employees end up in some NCIC dead file.

The real alternative was that Crowe would have to break off his vacation and come back to Armonk and talk with his counterparts in the marketing divisions. To prevent the FBI from having direct access to IGC employees, and yet give them the information they wanted, would entail a massive amount of work. The employee data was available in the master personnel file, including home telephone numbers. While each employee could have been contacted directly, without talking with branch management first, Crowe was not willing to dodge the missiles that would surely follow. A branch manager's employees were "his people." Even during business hours, contact between the management of one office and the employees of

338

another office was done after contacting the employee's line manager(s) first. For Crowe to call any of the people on the list directly would be a gross violation of internal protocol and etiquette. No matter how good the reason, Crowe would end up with shit on his lapel.

I can just hear them now, he thought. Sanctimonious crying over the dead body of Respect for the Individual . . . long may it live. No, I'm not going to touch that one.

"How are you planning to guarantee the employee's privacy?" asked Crowe.

The *you* wasn't lost on Cynthia. Decisions were like flypaper, make them and they stick with you—whether you want them to or not.

"I think Gabe Sanchez and Agent Coldsmith agreed on a workable scenario. The message would go out classified as Confidential," said Cynthia.

"How does the note read?" asked Crowe.

Cynthia's eyes went back to her terminal where Gabe Sanchez's note was on the screen:

"THE FBI HAS ASKED FOR ASSISTANCE IN A TIME-CRITICAL INVESTIGATION IN THE DEATH OF IGC EMPLOYEE ZACKARY COLBY OF CHEYENNE, WYOMING ON NOVEMBER 17. ALL ATTENDEES OF WORKSTATION UPDATE CLASS #66548 ARE BEING ASKED TO RESPOND TO THIS NOTE IMMEDIATELY. PLEASE CALL MR. GABRIEL SANCHEZ, DIRECTOR MARKETING TRAINING DIRECTLY AT (214) 668-7002 OR TIE-LINE 8-882-7002."

"Keep me informed on this, Cynthia."

"Will do."

Never let anything bite your manager in the ass. If something bad's going to happen, you'd better let him know first.

At 8:22 P.M. EST Cynthia sent the note out to sixty-two IGCers in sixty-two different offices across the country. She then called Gabe Sanchez.

"Fred wants to know what happens on this, Gabe," added Cynthia tactfully.

"I'll call you if . . . and when something happens," replied Sanchez. "I hope we aren't opening a can of worms, something we can't put back together again."

Cynthia could only silently nod her head in agreement as they each hung up. Precedence-setting was OK in certain situations—this wasn't one of them.

Oh, yes, she daydreamed. You remember Cynthia Rosen, don't you? She was the one who let the FBI have access to employee records and send notes on PROFS. Now they do it all the time . . .

The Rosen Initiative, a new Ludlum novel soon in a bookstore near you.

U.S. 50, proclaimed by Nevadans as the "Loneliest Highway in America," was all of that and more. After leaving I-15 in central Utah, the road topped nine mountain ranges and passed through only four towns in a distance of 460 miles. Halfway between the two ends of civilization was the tiny town of Eureka, a tough mining village of five hundred souls and county seat for a land mass the size of the state of Delaware. On Main Street, the only street, were two gambling saloons, a Chevron station, and an all-night café run by Pete and Lorraine, no last names. Eight police vehicles patrolled the five-block city, just waiting for something to happen. The newest building in town, in the whole county, was a brand new police station-courthouse-jail. Eureka wasn't a good place for pilgrims.

While Joe filled the van with gas, Marcia used the phone. This time Wu answered himself, picking the phone up on the first ring.

"Yes?" said Wu.

"Do we have a deal?" Marcia asked.

The day had been an excruciating one for Xiang Wu, and if possible, even worse for Jimmy Chimichanga.

Sweating, his heart racing with the exertion, Jimmy stood at the corner of the burning house and watched the woman get into the car. She turned and shouted some angry words up to him, words that he couldn't hear but understood. If he'd had one of the AK-47s instead of a nearly shot flamethrower, he could have dropped the bunch of them. But he didn't, so he didn't.

Jimmy briefly thought about chasing the Taurus, but with their head start he'd have to be lucky to catch them. Right then, he had to think about saving his own neck. The deal with Xiang Wu was getting out of hand. So Jimmy drove back down College, turned right at Pershing, then right again at Warren. Two blocks from the airport he pulled into a metered parking slot and stopped. He was still breathing hard. Sirens could be heard in the distance, as the first of four fire trucks clanged their way toward the Colby house.

Jimmy Chimichanga had a nagging suspicion that maybe Xiang Wu would think *he* was now a *loose end*. Jimmy carefully cleaned the flamethrower, the steering wheel, the driver's door, and the rear door, even though he didn't think he had touched it. He then locked the Blazer and walked the two blocks to the airport, through the small passenger terminal, and directly to his plane.

"Get out of here," he scowled at the pilots.

The pilot and copilot looked at each other with a where-are-the-other-guys expression, shrugged their shoulders, and followed their orders, lifting off from the Cheyenne airport at four o'clock. It would be a little after nine o'clock before Jimmy C. would be driven up in front of Xiang Wu's apartment on Grant Street.

Xiang Wu was not at all pleased. In fact, he was angry with Jimmy.

"You don't seem to realize the *importance* of this, James. Not only is the Lee woman alive, but she has the *programs* with her. You were *that* close. Why couldn't you finish it? We don't care who has the diskettes—just that they be destroyed. If three of you weren't enough to do the job properly, why didn't you take more. Why didn't you take ten, twenty—a *hundred* men?" Wu shouted at Jimmy Chimichanga.

Jimmy had no practical choice but to take the verbal pummeling. Xiang Wu's tirade soon shifted into Chinese, for which Jimmy was thankful. He didn't want to get angry with the old man; after all, Jimmy *had* screwed up. If he'd had his thinking cap on, or someone with him to make suggestions, he would have driven the Blazer out into the desert, dumped the guns, cleaned the vehicle up, and taken it back to the rental agency. Cars were always a pain in the butt. Instead, Jimmy stood in front of Xiang Wu's desk and took his abuse.

Xiang Wu went to the speakerphone, punched a

342

coded two-digit combination, and waited for the phone to dial.

"Yes, is everything all right?" asked a sleepy E. Dexter Albright.

"No, it is *not* all right. Mr. Chimichanga and his people have failed on their mission. Miss Lee is alive. Worse, she has the programs—the diskettes in her possession. And she wants to make a deal."

It was 11:10 Eastern time and past Albright's normal bedtime, but he was wide awake now.

"What kind of deal?" he asked.

Xiang Wu was distressed, no longer the gracious host, and was in severe jeopardy of losing his wily Oriental cool.

"Money . . . of course she wants money—ten million dollars. And she wants to meet with us—all of us. And passports, identity papers—that sort of thing." Wu waved his hand back and forth as if Albright could see him from three thousand miles away. "She wants to be our . . . *partner*, were her words," Wu added.

"Partner?" laughed E. Dexter Albright. "If she wanted to be our *partner*, she should have asked for a hundred times that. She's just made a lucky guess, Xiang Wu. She had no idea of what we're doing—the *scale* of what will happen."

"All this because James couldn't hold up his end of the bargain," Wu said without looking at Jimmy Chimichanga, who was now getting a little heated.

"Well, what's done is done. What else does she want?" asked Albright.

"A meeting on Thursday morning sometime, here in the San Francisco area—a meeting where money and identity would be exchanged for the box of computer programs," replied Wu.

343

There was a pause as Albright searched his mind for the obvious.

"How would you know if they were the right programs? How would *we* know?" asked E. Dexter Albright.

"Do Sing and his investors would know. They are computer people," replied Wu.

"That means Do Sing will have to be here . . . or there in San Francisco," said Albright.

"That is correct," stated Wu.

There was another pause as both men thought through their mental table of alternatives.

"Can we back out now?" asked Wu, knowing the answer.

"*Now?* You can't be serious, Xiang Wu. We've got a half billion dollars already invested, locked into short positions—dollar down, yen up, gold up, silver up, IGC down, Dow Jones down, AMEX down, computer and electronics stocks way down, the pound up. We're *committed,* Xiang Wu."

The two financiers had not only leveraged their clients' money, but their own fortunes as well.

"She's only one woman, Xiang Wu. *Make a deal!* Whatever she wants—just do it! Hell, we've got less than two days—and she's talking about meeting *after* the virus strikes. Make a deal. Pay her. Get the passports. Do you want me to fly out?"

Xiang Wu pondered.

"I don't think that will be necessary. She doesn't know about you. We need you in New York to manage the accounts. You'll be very busy for the next few weeks."

Wu hung up and turned back to Jimmy Chimichanga, his anger gone.

"When the Lee woman calls, we will agree on a

meeting place. You will see to it that she does not leave the meeting alive," Wu instructed. "Now, please leave me. I must call Do Sing in Taiwan. It's not a task I look forward to."

It was only four-thirty but it was already dusk in the desert. Neon signs advertised Bud and Coors and Rainier beer. If anything, the town seemed tougher at night.

"Do we have a deal?" Marcia asked.

"My associates and I agree to your demands, Miss Lee. I will have five million dollars transferred to your Geneva account this evening. The balance will be paid when you turn over the diskettes and we validate them."

"And the passports?" asked Marcia.

"Yes—I will have them with me," replied Wu. "Along with guaranteed transport to Taipei."

"Taipei? I'm not going to Taipei. You can forget that. Is that where your *investment* friends come from? *We* aren't going anyplace together. I want open-ended tickets on United, American, Delta, Northwest, and Quantas—for both of us," ordered Marcia.

There was a pause as Wu swallowed a retort.

"As you wish."

"I'll call you Thursday morning and tell you the time and place of our meeting. It'll be in the San Francisco area, someplace within an hour of downtown. I'm not going to give you time to set me up, Wu. I'll choose the place and the time. I've got the diskettes and I can give them to IGC at any time. I'll check with Geneva later tonight to verify your deposit. I'll call you Thursday morning."

Marcia hung up before Wu could say a word. She

knew he'd try to kill her again.

I would, if I was in his place.

No you wouldn't. You couldn't.

The thought seemed to regenerate her spirit. She dropped another quarter into the telephone and waited for the operator to answer. She gave the operator the overseas number she wanted dialed.

"Just a moment, please," the operator replied.

Placing a call from Eureka, Nevada to London, England wasn't something done every day of the week. Marcia smiled as she had a mental picture of a young girl sitting behind an old plug-style telephone bank, flipping through a manual to get the right routing codes.

"One moment please. Your call is going through," the operator replied crisply.

"This is Pete Goodman," answered a tired voice.

"Is Wyatt Steele there? This is Scott Coldsmith of the FBI."

Steele came to the phone.

"I hope you've having a better day than I have," Scotty started.

"I have. But I'm up to my eyeballs in paper. I've almost got too much information here. Everywhere I turn something new comes up," replied Wyatt. "Where are you?"

"Denver—but I'm coming back. The IGC people are doing their thing. Can I help?"

"You bet. Your brother-in-law had been making a *lot* of telephone calls. A lot."

"Have they called?"

"The kidnappers? No."

"I'll be there in an hour," replied Scotty.

346

"What have you come up with?" Scotty asked.

"There were three phones in the house—one upstairs, two down. Pete, here, got a printout of the detailed call record—incoming as well as outgoing—for the last eight weeks. This is what it looks like." Wyatt pointed to stacks of computer fanfold paper scattered across two desks. "The main telephone number for the residence has the usual number of calls. Most long-distance numbers were to the family in Laramie. But the numbers downstairs—there's a shitload of calls on those lines. I mean, a ton."

"What can I do?" asked Scotty.

Pete looked at Wyatt, then at his computer terminal.

"The only way to find out who these calls went to, and who they came from, is to use the computer. We used to be known as Mountain Bell. Now we, Pacific Northwest Bell, and Northwestern Bell are all U.S. West. So, if there's a number in the old Mountain Bell system, I've got access to it on this computer. Punch in a name or a number and I can come out with the billing addresses. Unfortunately, if I want to find a number outside my system, I've got to go to that particular company and have them help."

"How long will it take to go through all these?" asked Wyatt.

"Well, this is a lot of long distance calls, and most of them are out of the U.S. West system. I can get the calls collated differently—by area code instead of date and time. That'll speed things up. It would also speed things up if you two dug into the local calls. I'll let you use my terminal. Just type the telephone number."

347

Wyatt ran his finger down the long column of numbers as he and Scotty sat side by side. Since everything in town was on either the 632, 634, or 638 exchange, the numbers tended to look the same.

"Look at this," Wyatt said.

"Kinda pops up at you, doesn't it?" Scotty agreed.

The number 638-3301 repeated itself over and over.

"When does it hit the list?" asked Scotty.

"The first call was made on October seventeenth," Wyatt replied.

"Let's see," Scotty said, looking at the printouts. "There's nothing before then—look—the volume all starts after the seventeenth. After then it's almost every day. You got a calendar?"

Wyatt reached over behind Pete's desk and pulled his wall calendar down, then flipped the month back to October. The two men compared the dates.

"Every one of these calls was made on a weekday," Wyatt concluded. "Let's see what this number is," he said, punching in the seven digits.

"I'll be damned," Wyatt said.

"The Hitching Post Inn—Jesus, I'm staying there."

"So did somebody else."

"When was the last entry?" asked Scotty.

"It only goes through last week—through Thursday. There's at least one call every day," Wyatt replied.

"Either to or from the Hitching Post Inn . . ." Scotty thought out loud.

"From a telephone in the basement of Zack Colby's house," Wyatt finished the thought.

"Pete? Can you pull out the detail record of a particular record? It's a motel—the Hitching Post Inn," asked Scotty.

"I can't give you a room number, if that's what you need," Pete replied.

"It is," said Scotty. "Are you sure?"

"Well, I take that back. The detailed record shows the phone ID—that's what that two letter abbreviation means—A1, A2, B1, et cetera. That's the location ID of a particular set. All you'd need is access to the main box for the motel. The service technician keeps his papers there—it's easier that way. The ID matches a particular instrument with its physical location. Should be a piece of cake."

"Can you get the service rep who handles the motel over there in, say, ten minutes?" asked Wyatt.

"I'll see what I can do," replied Pete.

At 8:15 Wyatt and Scotty introduced themselves to the night manager of the Hitching Post Inn, who in turn called the day manager and owner. Everybody agreed that their conversation was better off kept private. At eight-thirty Jake Tibbits, senior repair technician, met them in the lobby and escorted the group to the wiring closet, which was accessed from the manager's office behind the registration desk. There were 211 rooms in the motel. Including the owner's cottage, the restaurant, bar, and pool area, there were 224 telephones in the motel.

"We're looking for ID number B9."

The technician paged through his records.

"Room 1204."

"Ah," said the day and night managers in unison; they both knew the room's occupants. "They came as a group—six rooms for six weeks."

By ten o'clock the maids had been interviewed, along with all the employees of the Hitching Post. A police artist would have composite sketches ready by daybreak — he'd personally promised Wyatt.

"If you look at the detail billing record — not all of the inbound calls to the Colby home came from B9. Some came from B8, the room next door," said Scotty.

"Three of the rooms were registered under the name of David Kimura," Wyatt said as he flipped through his notes. "The other two to a Marcia Lee, who paid for the rooms in cash. Kimura used a platinum American Express which was issued to a Pro-Sun Corporation —"

"What did you say?" exclaimed Scotty.

"ProSun." Wyatt gave Scotty a strange look.

"Jesus! Wyatt, I was on a —" Scotty's mind fragmented.

What the shit? he thought.

It was twelve-thirty by the time the two men dragged themselves back to Pete's office at U.S. West. By that time Scotty had been able to collect his thoughts and tell Wyatt about the massacre at Pro-Sun's estate in Palos Verdes.

"They were Japanese, Wyatt. I saw their pictures. Thirty men — all tech-weenie types. The maids said there were computers in B9. I'll bet you anything that in that stack of long-distance calls there'll be a bunch to that number in Los Angeles. I'd bet anything."

Scotty didn't need to bet. It was a sure thing.

"You bet — 213-521-2010 . . . every damn day," said Pete. "It's the only long-distance call that repeats. All

I could get was ProSun Corporation."

"I knew it!"

"But that's not all, my friends," Pete added, his fingers running down the long list of calls. "All these calls are from one computer to another computer — the one in Colby's basement."

Wyatt looked at Pete with doubt.

"Has to be, Wyatt. Look at them. Every last one of them is two minutes and forty-five seconds long. Every one of them. In the middle of the fucking night, most of them! The only thing that can do that is one computer talking to another." Pete smiled with satisfaction. "Some strange shit's happening here, Wyatt. You tell me what the hell a computer in a salesman's basement in Cheyenne, Wyoming is doing talking with another computer at Gulf Oil's headquarters in Pittsburgh? Or Rockwell's in El Segundo — or Coca-Cola in Atlanta — the fucking U.S. Postal Service in Washington — Aetna Insurance, Sears, Wells Fargo, Boeing — the list goes on forever."

Wyatt and Scotty were stunned.

"There are over three hundred different companies on this list. And every one of them's on the Fortune 500. What the fuck's going on?"

Chapter Seven
Revenge of the Tech Weenies

With Joe asleep in the passenger seat and Cheryl stretched out in back, Marcia guided the Taurus through its last forty miles by remote control. Her back hurt from the blast, her butt hurt from sitting eighteen hours in a row, her shoulders hurt from the driving, and her head hurt from looking at eight hours of oncoming headlights. It was twelve-thirty Pacific time when Marcia exited the Bayshore at the South San Francisco exit, turned left at the stop light, and pulled into the parking lot of the Holiday Inn-SFO Airport.

Waiting inside the lobby was David Kimura.

We're still in the ball game, she thought.

Marcia registered, got her keys and handed them to Joe, then walked with David through the lobby to the rear entrance, back out into the misty night air.

"I assume we have a deal," she said.

"Yes. I have everything," he replied.

"The cash?" she whispered.

"Yes, in my room."

Marcia followed David down a concrete walk to a pair of first-floor rooms near the back of the motel. David's was on the end, Marcia's next to it. They went inside David's room.

"This is for you," he said, placing two thick yellow envelopes on top of a briefcase; in the envelope, Marcia knew, was a half million in cash.

Joe came around with Cheryl on one arm and two bags in the other. They both stopped in the doorway of David's room.

"Hello, Cheryl," David tried to be polite.

"You son of a bitch!" Cheryl hissed unexpectedly, surprising herself as well.

Marcia scooped up the envelopes and briefcase, took the keys from Joe's hand, and unlocked the door to their room, hustling Cheryl inside. It wasn't the best of arrangements. They wouldn't be free to talk. Any of the cellophane-wrapped plastic glasses could be pressed against the wall to pick up conversation in the next room. Marcia went back to talk with David.

"Did you get the packages off?" Marcia asked.

"Yes—all of them," David replied. "Holton should have them tomorrow."

"Look, I've got to get some sleep. So do you," she said, closing the door behind her. "Relax. There's nothing you can do about anything now. Just wait until this morning—that's all. Just wait. Get some sleep," Marcia said, "you'll need it."

"Are you all right?" whispered Marcia.

Joe was softly snoring in the other queen-size bed.

"I'm scared," replied Cheryl, fear in her throat.

As they had done in Denver on Monday night, the two women shared the same bed. In the darkness, Marcia reached out and put her hand on the shoulder of the younger woman, whose body was turned away from her.

"I told you yesterday, and I'll tell you again," Marcia spoke softly. "I'm not going to let anything happen to you. I'm not proud of some of the things I've done. But these . . . *people* . . . who have done this—they're going to pay. And you'll be all right. Now go to sleep," Marcia said, squeezing Cheryl's shoulder lightly.

Scotty had a night filled with terrible dreams, what was left of it. Cheryl was with him part of the time, but most of the night was spent in nonsensical terror. Twice he woke up with a start, his heart beating fast, terrified. Once he was trying to breathe but he was underwater, waking up only when he could hold his breath no longer. Another time he was on a rope ladder on the face of Hoover Dam, scrambling up to a portal that never got closer, reliving moments in the past when he really thought he was going to die. With a rude buzz his restless sleep came to a merciful end at six-thirty. He rolled over and looked at the clock.

Mutant shit from hell, he thought ruefully.

Great. Just great. You'll look just fine at IGC this morning.

IGC? Damn. That's right. I've got to go to IGC. Get your butt in gear, boy!

A half hour later Scotty was in his car and on his way to Denver. He marveled at the number of people who made the daily drive in from Ft. Collins—even Cheyenne. The housing market was so different that it was worth an hour and a half drive twice a day.

Not me, he thought. No sir. Not me. I wouldn't drive an hour and a half. No, I'd rather live in a shit-for-nothing zero-bedroom hovel for a thousand a month.

Scotty could hardly believe himself. His mind had actually started to justify his existence in New York City. There was *no,* repeat *no* reason for him to be living in New York. He was a certified Hero of the Republic.

Heroes of the fucking Republic don't live in zero-bedroom one-thou roach-infested hovels. Not when they could be living in luxury in Cheyenne.

It didn't make sense. But it did occupy space and time. By eight-thirty Scotty found himself magically transported to the front of the IGC building in Denver.

"You've got bad news," said Benning, as he took off his suit coat and hung it up behind his office door.

"As a matter of fact, I think I do. How do you know?"

"I've been a manager for eighteen years. Before that, I was a salesman for ten. It's your eyes," Benning smiled.

Be direct, Scotty thought.

"Zack had several computers in the basement of his home—"

"Demo units," Benning inserted. "We'll have to get up there and inventory them when it's appropriate."

"Al, it was after two when I got to bed last night—this morning. Zack had three telephones installed—three separate lines. Two of them were in the basement and were apparently connected to the computers."

"For remote dial-in. We have internal applications that he could use—construct configurations, prepare proposals, ask technical questions—a library of information on line. And PROFS. There was no real reason for him to ever come into the office—he had the office right there at his fingertips." Al Benning's face changed as he said the words, his face reflecting the sudden realization of what Scotty would say next.

"We—the Cheyenne police and U.S. West employees—spent most of yesterday afternoon and evening going through the detailed call record of those telephones."

Al Benning closed his eyes and his chest sagged. Scotty could feel the man deflate like a beach ball. Al Benning knew what Scotty was going to say.

"One of the computers—right now I don't know which one—has received telephone calls from three hundred and twenty-eight other computers since November fourth. All the calls have been in the middle of the night. All of the calls were exactly two minutes and forty-five seconds long. The lateness of the calls, and the unusual timing, leads us to believe that the machines themselves initiated the telephoning. Why, or how, I don't have a clue. All of the calls were inbound to the machine in Zack's basement. They came from Gulf Oil, the Department of State, the Postal Service, Chevron, Boeing, Rockwell, the Hartford, the city of San Francisco, Bank of America — the list goes on and on."

With a dry tongue, Al Benning licked his chapped lips.

"Given Zack's unusual behavior — his drug usage, the reports we saw yesterday — I think Zack was being blackmailed and that somebody's been inside your systems. I'd like you to check it out for me. I can call in an alert at any time," Scotty finished.

With his phone on speaker, Benning punched out a two-digit code.

"Amy Engle," came the quick response.

"I need to see you in my office," said Benning in a tone of voice that Amy Engle recognized to mean right now.

"I'll be right there."

"Bring Ted with you," he instructed.

Thirty seconds later Amy Engle, a tall, well-dressed woman of forty-two, with short blond hair and legs up to here, appeared in the doorway. She was the branch market support manager, and the ranking manager under Benning. While the salesmen reported up through marketing managers, then to Al, the branch systems engineers reported up through SE managers to Amy, who in turn reported to Al. When Al was away, Amy was in charge.

Behind Amy, carrying a cup of coffee in a large Styrofoam cup, was the affable Ted Springs.

"No calls, Mary," Al said, closing his door. "We have a problem that for the time being has to stay in this room," Al started.

Al's eye contact was, mainly with Amy. If technical expertise was needed, she would be the one to get the right people. Ted Springs would get more coffee.

"We may have a breach in security, a bad one. The FBI and the Cheyenne police believe Zack Colby may have been blackmailed—for whatever reason—then killed, because of the demo equipment he had at home."

Scotty watched Amy's reaction. Within IGC the enthusiasm of the can-do marketing reps was always tempered by the maybe-it-can't-do reality of the systems engineers. With an eighteen-year background as a systems engineer, Amy's eyes flashed the fear of a worst-case scenario.

"Was Zack taken off PROFS?" she asked, turning to Ted.

"Ah . . . no, I was too . . ." stammered Ted Springs.

Benning gave his marketing manager a pair of dagger eyes. Taking a fired or deceased employee off of PROFS is normally done by either the manager or a senior person in the manager's group. Normally, it was done after someone went through and checked the person's electronic mail, the files on the system, and made sure everything was OK to deep-six.

"What kind of equipment did he have?" Benning asked.

"A PC—no, two PCs—a couple of printers . . ." Ted tried to remember.

"What about the 9350?" asked Amy.

Scotty could see Ted and Amy exchange meaningful looks. The topic of the 9350 had obviously come up before, and had been a sore point between the two.

"Oh, yeah—*that* 9350. He *needed* it. His people wouldn't come down to Denver to the customer center. I mean, you approved it Al," Ted said, looking around as if to say, "I had nothing to do with it."

"What about communications?" asked Benning.

"He had remote access to PROFS. Hell, I mean . . . we all do," Springs added, trying to justify something that he didn't need to.

"And the 9350?" asked Amy.

"They all have communications installed. *You* of all people should remember that," replied Ted, referring again to a previous conversation.

Amy walked over to Al's 3270 PC/AT.

"Log off for me?" Amy asked.

With a few keystrokes Benning logged off. Amy turned to Ted.

"Log on as Zack," she asked Ted.

"If I remember . . ." Ted logged on, then went to a managers-only application within PROFS. Each manager had the system authority to obtain the current password of any of his or her employees. Ted went through several menu screens, better than Amy thought he would, and finally obtained the correct code.

Al's phone buzzed. It was Mary. She would only disrupt him if it was an emergency.

"Yes, Mary?"

"There's a call for Mr. Coldsmith. Shall I put it through?"

"Yes," replied Benning, hanging up. "A call's coming through for you, Scott."

"Go back in and log on as Zack," said Amy, her anxious fingers twitching with the slowness of Ted Springs's typing.

The phone rang.

"This is Scott Coldsmith."

Scotty watched as the system six floors below them belched up an error message: ID ALREADY IN USE.

Scotty looked at Amy, who was looking at Al, who was looking at Ted.

"Zack Colby is logged on to the system," said Amy.

The three IGCers turned as one toward Scotty.

358

"That can't be," said Al anxiously. "If Zack's machines were burned in the fire, the line would have been dropped from Cheyenne. The system would automatically force him off."

Scotty concentrated on the flash of screens that went by in front of him.

"Stop!"

Amy turned around and looked quizzically at Scotty, pausing on the main PROFS screen.

"Damn! I've seen this before. I know —"

He knew. Scotty pictured himself in the large second-floor auditorium.

"Force him off!" said Al, his voice rising a bit.

Amy went to Al's phone and punched out a number.

"This is Amy Engle. I want you to force off COLBY-ZAC. Now!"

Amy stayed on the line as the PROFS administrator in the basement used her override capability and terminated COLBYZAC's PROFS session.

"He's off," she nearly shouted.

It was 9:22 Mountain time.

Amy's fingers rapidly tapped out COLBYZAC's log-on and password.

YOU HAVE 12,841 NOTES IN YOUR MAIL LOG.

"He's got nearly thirteen thousand unanswered notes in his mail log!" said the astonished Amy, pointing to the display.

"That's incredible," said Ted Springs. "Look, they're all the same subject," said Al Benning.

* * *

359

OPEN THE MAIL

Press the PF key for the document you want. Or, if you want to view all of these documents, type ALL here and press ENTER > > > >

FROM	TO	TYPE	DOCUMENT
PF1 RANDALLJ – BETVMIC1			
COLBYZAC – DENVMIC1		Note	11/19/89 07:38
	Subject: Competitive Reference Needed		
PF2 TOMGEORG – DALVMIC5			
COLBYZAC – DENVMIC1		Note	11/19/89 07:25
	Subject: Competitive Reference Needed		
PF3 YOUNGPAU – HOUVMIC3			
COLBYZAC – DENVMIC1		Note	11/18/89 18:35
	Subject: Competitive Reference Needed		
PF4 JACKSOND – SFOVMIC1			
COLBYZAC – DENVMIC1		Note	11/18/89 18:30
	Subject: Competitive Reference Needed		
PF5 UNGERPHI – NYCVMIC4			
COLBYZAC – DENVMIC1		Note	11/18/89 18:10
	Subject: Competitive Reference Needed		

There were eight notes per screen, 1,606 screens in total — all with unopened mail. It was an astonishing number.

"Oh, shit," said Amy Engle. "Excuse me," she added.

"Why the hell did he send out this kind of note to the world for?" asked Springs.

"You're his manager, Ted. I remember I got one from him," said Amy.

"So did I," said Al. "I thought it was a good way to use the system. I had no idea he was sending it out" — Al's voice dropped off — "to the fucking world! How many people *did* he send it to?"

"When did the original note go out?" asked Al.

"I don't know. It'll be in his Note Log," said Amy, pressing the PF12 key as fast as the system would accept it, to exit the program.

"God, his Note Log's got to be *huge!*" added Springs.

"Let's see his distribution lists," she said.

Amy's fingers jumped her through a few different screens.

"Jesus," she muttered.

"Shit!" Benning cursed.

DISTRIBUTION LISTS

1	21	41	61	81	101	121	141	161	181	201
2	22	42	62	82	102	122	142	162	182	202
3	23	43	63	83	103	123	143	163	183	203
4	24	44	64	84	104	124	144	164	184	204

The screen was filled with 220 numbers, and there were more numbers on the next screen. Each number represented a distribution list, an abbreviated way to send a group of people the same message without the requirement of typing in each name. Knowing what the next request was, Amy chose the distribution list labeled "1," and looked at who was on the list.

DISTRIBUTION LIST _____1_____
AABERGLE(DALVMIC1)
AAGAARD (ATLVMIC2)
AAHLSAM (BOSVMIC1)
AALBRIGH(BETVMIC1)
AAMESCHA(SFOVMIC2)
AAMONDT (DENVMIC1)

"Mother of God," exclaimed Amy Engle.

They paged through several other distribution lists. Each list contained the PROFS mailing address for approximately two hundred people. Each list was alphabetical. Occasionally one or the other would exclaim.

"Look at that." She pointed to an address on the

screen.

"FKFVMIC1 — Frankfurt, West Germany."

"GBR — London," muttered Springs.

"Zurich, Paris, Tel Aviv, Scotland . . . my God!"

"There are over fifty thousand addresses here," said Benning, stunned.

"Zack Colby couldn't have done this," said Ted Springs.

Amy typed the command FLIST at the prompt and pressed Enter. The command instantly listed the files on Zack's A disk, his filing space on the 3090 mainframe six floors below.

LVL0 —	A 191	900	BLKS 3380 R/W/		28 FILES 5 % — FILE 1 OF 1				
NOTE	OFSLOGF1	A0		F	80	100	3	11/11	16:08
OFSMAIL	OFSDATA	A1		V	51	33	1	11/11	10:15
OFSMAIL	OFSLOGF1	A0		F	80	100	3	11/10	9:28
LASTING	GLOBALV	A1		V	43	28	1	11/10	8:30
COLBYZAC	NOTE	A1		V	80	2158	43	11/09	14:22
PCDD	PRN	A1		V	1	2	1	11/09	14:22
HOSTDOC	PRN	A1		V	1	2	1	11/09	14:22
MISC	PRN	A1		V	105	4898	89	11/09	14:22
COLBYZAC	NETLOG	A0		F	106	163	5	11/08	11:30

1-HLP 2-BRW 3-END 4-XED 5-SPL 6-SB 7-SCB 8-SCF 9-SD 10-ST 12-CAN

"His note wasn't created in PROFS," Amy said as she pressed the PF4 key to XEDIT, to look at, the file called COLBYZAC NOTE A1. Inside she saw the original note. "There's got to be more to it than that," she muttered.

"Why would he send a non-PROFS note?" asked Ted. "Why go to the effort of using XEDIT when there's no formatting required?" he asked rhetorically to the group.

"There's got to be . . . what's that?" added Amy, pointing to the screen.

"I don't know," said Springs. "It's . . . it's . . . I don't know."

Amy paged through several blank pages at the end of the document, then ran into at least ten screens of gobbledygook, series of 1s and 0s. On the last page were several lines of what appeared to be file names.

"No wonder the God-damned file is so big!" said Al. "There's no way that note could be forty-three blocks big."

Each block of storage space was 512 bytes, or characters. Forty-three blocks would represent a file of approximately twenty-two thousand characters—plenty big enough for a tightly packed program.

"It's a program," stated Amy. "Shit," said the stunned branch market support manager. "There's a program of some sort at the tail end of the document. It's written in Assembly language, and very skillfully done," said Amy.

There was silence in the room as the global implications sank in. A man had been blackmailed and then murdered, his wife kidnapped. This was no prank, no practical joke.

"What does the program say?" asked Scotty.

"I don't have the slightest idea. We aren't programmers, Mr. Coldsmith. We help people understand how best to use their computers, help on applications—but we don't do any programming," she replied, sitting back in her chair. "I don't know what else to say—I think PROFS has been contaminated."

"Go to his Note Log," Al asked.

Scotty looked at his watch. It was 9:26.

Amy switched screens, jumping out of FLIST and XEDIT and going into Process Notes and Messages. PROFS stored a copy of all outgoing notes as a default.

"There's nothing there," Mary Beth said.

Indeed, there were only a few notes in the Note Log, which looked nearly identical in format to the Mail Log.

"I would have guessed that his Note Log would have been packed. He's changed his profile," added Ted. "He's turned the default off. We don't know how many people he's sent it to."

"Sure we do," said Amy. "His distribution lists are alphabetical. The responses sitting in his in basket were random. Whatever he sent, he sent globally—to all the distribution lists."

"To fifty-five thousand people?" asked Al.

"It appears so," replied Amy.

There was only a single page of items in Zack Colby's Note Log. The last item in Zack Colby's Note Log was:

PF8 COLBYZAK—DENVMIC1 HOLTONJO—
    CHQVMIC1 Note 11/19/89 09:25

Subject: Tojo Project—URGENT REPLY RE-QUIRED

It was 9:27 A.M. Mountain time.

"What the hell is that?" shouted Al. "What's happening here?"

"It appears that a dead salesman just sent a note to John Holton," said a stunned Amy.

"Oh, shit," Al cursed.

"It was a timed delivery. The note could have been in the system for who knows how long."

Amy pressed PF8.

SEND A NOTE
TO: HORTONJO
FROM: COLBYZAC
DATE: NOVEMBER 19
SUBJ: Tojo Project
      John Holton
      Chairman of the Board
      IGC Corporation

Old Apple Orchard Drive
Armonk, New York 10504

Dear Mr. Holton:

As of 11:30 A.M. EST this date, IGC Corporation should consider itself under siege. You no doubt realize that, as a corporation, you have a great deal of enemies within the United States and throughout the world. Your size and business practices preclude us, your attackers, from identifying ourselves. However, we assume that even you can hear the sounds of our attack as you read this note.

Be assured as you read our list of demands that we are aware that you will immediately call in the Federal Bureau of Investigation. We suggest that you go cautiously on this, since the FBI's objectives may not totally coincide with yours, and certainly not ours.

We will not be identified at any point in our discussions which we realistically expect must occur at some point in time — and very shortly.

We also caution you — be very careful in how you investigate this virus. There are several layers to it. Permanent damage can occur to your significant internal investment in hardware and software if you try to "solve the puzzle" we have set in motion.

We expect that you will quickly locate the source of this virus, but of course we will not be there, nor will there be any trace of us.

We selected an employee of yours named Zackary Colby, not entirely at random. To be fair to Mr. Colby's name, and his family — his wife Cheryl, his children Brian and Anne — we blackmailed Mr. Colby into allowing us to use his demonstration equipment for our nefarious purposes. Mr. Colby

365

did not know our objectives, which are outlined below — although he was aware of the consequences of his failure to follow our instructions. We have no comment on whether this mitigates any criminal penalties that may fall on Mr. Colby's head.

The essence of our virus is an encryption program. As you will painfully see, the data on your personal and mainframe computers have been completely secured. We have elected to use this methodology because of practicality. We felt you would be more susceptible to granting the five requests listed below, if there was a reasonable opportunity for you to obtain your data back in a usable format.

In order to decrypt your data, you will need to provide one of fifty randomly-selected 16-digit alpha/numeric combinations for each disk encrypted. I think you'll agree that finding the right keys to unlock your data is a fruitless task.

We have those keys, and we will be pleased to provide them to you — and recommend ways to use them to quickly reverse what has been done. However, we must receive satisfaction in five areas before we can give you those keys.

1. IGC will turn over all research material developed and discovered by the 1987 Nobel Prize winners in Physics, J. Steven Cravens and K. John Glaeser, research physicists at IGC's laboratory in Zurich, Switzerland, and their staffs, concerning the area of electrical superconductivity.

IGC is not the only source of research in this important new area. We will have scientists available who will determine the veracity of your response. While Bednorz and Mueller are your "big names," we want *all* of your available research, no matter what source.

2. You will provide the source code for all existing and developmental programs in the area of artificial intelligence—specifically, those programs under development at the IGC facilities in Yorktown Heights, Owego, the Watson Research Center, Raleigh, and San Jose.

Once again, we will have AI experts who are currently developing our programs at the meeting site to verify the contents of this response.

3. IGC will turn over all technical developments you have made in Fifth Generation Computing. Since IGC and the national computing companies of Japan are the only firms currently in this race, you will be helping develop an additional competitor.

4. From your San Jose, California, manufacturing facility, IGC will turn over all technical drawings and materials regarding existing and future plans for computer disk drive development.

5. From your Burlington, Vermont, manufacturing facility, IGC will provide all technical data regarding its memory chip manufacturing process, including the new 1MB, 8MB, and 16MB memory modules.

We admit that these demands are onerous, and will have the potential to disrupt IGC's income flow in the next decade, most certainly in the next century. However, we feel your choices are somewhat limited. By this time you will have no doubt heard from several of your major customers, who will have called you directly to voice their concern.

The legal issues involved could easily cost billions of short-term dollars in lawsuits. We believe we have a good understanding of your internal structure and operations. Without internal computers, it is our estimation that IGC will effectively be closed down until those systems are completely rebuilt. Replacing over 1,400 mainframe computers and 51,000 terminals will have a disastrous effect on your bottom line.

You may find that by acceding to our demands, that as a corporation you will be able to successfully move into the 21st century. If you decide to ignore our demands, or worse — to try and catch us . . . then it's entirely possible that one of America's largest corporations could be out of business within a relatively short period of time.

With regard to the meeting . . . it will be held in Hong Kong. We will provide detailed instructions on exactly where the meeting will be held within a day of your receipt of this note.

The group was stunned. Scotty looked at Amy Engle, who was ashen faced, drained.

"Can you print that?" Scotty broke the silence.

Amy quickly did five screen prints — one for each page of the document. The attached Quietwriter III printer quickly went into action. It would be the last document to be printed in Denver that day.

It was 9:30 A.M. Mountain time, 11:30 A.M. Eastern time.

In a single startling instant the screen went blank. The host session was replaced by a message:

WARNING
DO NOT TURN YOUR MACHINE OFF OR ALL DATA ON YOUR FIXED DISK AND DISKETTE DRIVES WILL BE PERMANENTLY DESTROYED. THIS IS NOT A JOKE OR A PRANK. YOUR FILES ARE BE-

ING ENCRYPTED FOR YOUR SAFETY. IF YOU TURN YOUR MACHINE OFF YOUR FILE ALLOCATION TABLE WILL BE UNRE-COVERABLE, ALL DATA AND PROGRAMS WILL BE UNUSABLE.

THIS ENCRYPTION PROCESS WILL TAKE APPROXIMATELY SEVEN MINUTES. PLEASE BE PATIENT.

IF YOU HAVE ANY QUESTIONS, PLEASE SEE YOUR MANAGER, OR CALL:
JOHN C. HOLTON
CHAIRMAN OF THE BOARD
IGC CORPORATION
OLD APPLE ORCHARD DRIVE
ARMONK, NEW YORK 10504
TELEPHONE: (914) 765-1900

Scotty's immediate impression of what happened next was that the IGC office was inside a German U-Boat and the whole Atlantic Fleet was above them. After a ten-second shock delay, the noise that erupted sounded like the business equivalent of blaring Klaxons—the horns that shrieked and reverberated as the captain shouted "Clear the deck! Dive, dive, dive!" into the intercom system. From Al Benning's office shouts could be heard—surprise and anger. Benning opened his office door. In the hallway IGCers scurried this way and that. Everybody was talking at once. Scotty mind's eye could see the water gushing through fractured stress points as the *click, click* of the plunging depth charges turned to the *boom! boom!* of nearby explosions. The look on the IGC faces quickly turned from shock and amusement to one literally of fear. Salesmen got up and moved away from their desks, as if the desk itself had beasts inside. Scotty's first reaction was to cling to the walls as the IGCers went into a state of electronic shock.

"What's that noise?" someone down the hall shouted.

It was the phones. Scotty watched as a marketing rep answered his phone, put it to his ear, then dropped the phone like it was a hot rock as a high-pitched tone pierced through the receiver.

Some voices were angry. Shouts were heard. Managers ran around in circles, then stopped. There was nothing to be done. Scotty reached for the cleanly printed collated pages in the printer's exit tray, then picked up the phone, which Amy had dropped.

"Your company is under attack, Cynthia. I have a copy of the ransom demands.

On the third floor of IGC's National Federal Marketing operations in Bethesda, Maryland, the U.S. Treasury marketing team was in a last-minute frenzy to complete its bid response to the never-ending Treasury Mini-computer Acquisition Contract (TMAC). Both of the branch's huge laser printers were miraculously working, regurgitating reams of proposal response pages. The fact that they were working on a lost cause had never entered their minds. They had five hours to go—to print the final response, make fifteen copies of approximately 1,800 pages, collate, stuff, box, and get the response down to the Treasury building by 4:00 P.M.

At exactly 11:37 the printers stopped their regurgitation because the host files stored on the FedRIC system had become encrypted. The bulk of the proposal's technical response now lay encrypted inside their secretary's PC/XT. Telephones, which seemed to be answered in a random pattern in the best of cases, now rang off the hook. After picking up the phone twice and receiving a high-pitched tone in each case, no one was willing to answer his phone. It was impossible to distinguish a real call from a phone bomb. The marketing team would be unable to submit its bid on time and no relief would be granted by the government.

Some of the phone calls that weren't picked up were from various federal departments and agencies who had tied themselves into IGC's internal systems to receive billing, product updates, answers to technical questions, and the capability to send PROFS messages directly to their marketing rep, SE, and/or administrator. Selected agencies included the White House, the CIA, the FBI, the DIA, the Department of the Navy, U.S. Customs, the NIH, the National Bureau of Standards, the Census Bureau, the Department of Energy (including the Forestall Building, Germantown, Oak Ridge, Los Alamos, Sandia Labs, Argonne Labs, and Lawrence Livermore Labs), the Department of Transportation, the FAA, and the Social Security Administration.

The viruses spread to each of the agencies, infecting some worse than others. Agencies whose mainframes were "pure-blue" and ran the VM operating system were highly infected, as were any personal computers that were logically linked via local area networks to the PCs with access to IGC's Federal Regional Information Center.

The telephone calls first went to the five branch managers within the National Federal Marketing complex. With the Bethesda facility effectively down and out, by 11:55 the calls were going directly to (914) 765-1900, the office of John Holton, chairman of the board.

The first viral infection within the Boeing Corporation was received at precisely 8:30 A.M. when the executive secretary to the chairman stood up and shrieked bloody murder as her brand new IBM PS/2 Model 70 went up in electronic smoke. Of the 55,000 terminals used throughout the company, over 23,000 were personal computers. Of the 23,000 machines, those belonging to corporate management and their staffs were affected, some 8,300 machines — all linked through a sophisticated series of local area networks, all infected by the company's 200 + PROFS IDs that linked various users to IGC's Northwest Regional Information Center in San Francisco and the branch office in downtown Seattle.

The address known as One IGC Plaza is an impressive forty-story ebony skyscraper that fits well into the downtown Chicago skyline and is located on the concrete banks of the Chicago River at the intersection of Wabash and Carroll avenues. The building was nearly entirely occupied by IGC employees and housed eight two hundred person marketing branch offices, two education centers, a regional office, an area office, an administrative services branch, two data centers, and two customer support centers. It was one of the few corporate-owned buildings of its size.

At 10:38 A.M. Central time, the elevators in One IGC Plaza came to stop in midfloor. In addition to locking three thousand personal computers and the data files stored on five 3090 mainframes, the Tojo Virus leaked out to the 4381 that controlled the administrative services of the building. In addition to heating, cooling, and lighting controls, the computer also controlled the elevator banks. While it was the proper use of computing, the VM operating system didn't make the distinction between the PROFS side of the computer and the Services data bases . . . it should have, but it didn't. When the Phase Two telephone assault began, the IGCers were trapped inside a modern mechanism of torture.

Thirteen blocks to the north, the virus began to ripple through the John Hancock Center. Eleven blocks to the south and west, the same virus began infecting computers throughout the Sears Tower. Both Sears and John Hancock were top IGC customers, and as a result each had several hundred electronic connections to IGC's systems at One IGC Plaza. In addition, major customers included Allstate, Blue Cross, Kemper, CNA, HFC, Wards, Walgreen, United Airlines, Amoco, and Motorola. Every one of these major customers was infected.

The corporate offices of Rockwell International's aerospace operations was located one block west of the intersection of Sepulveda Boulevard and Imperial Highway, one block due south of Los Angeles International Airport. As one of America's prime defense contractors, Rockwell's major investments include the B-1A Stealth bomber and America's space shuttle program. Its aerospace manufacturing and component plants were located in El Segundo, Downey, Anaheim, Canoga Park, and Palmdale.

The IGC branch office, located at 9045 Lincoln Boulevard, was one mile north of LAX and was a huge operation dedicated to the support of Rockwell, TRW, and Northrop corporations. Also in the same IGC building were the branch offices supporting the major airlines who use LAX. Scattered throughout LA were other large offices with direct communications with Hughes, ARCO, Lockheed, Farmers Insurance, Litton Industries, 1st Interstate, and Security Pacific National Bank.

At 8:37 A.M., with the screen of his 3270 PC totally locked and with over six thousand of his people in a similar situation, the president of Rockwell's aerospace operations bypassed what he knew was IGC's internal protocol, and dialed John Holton in Armonk directly.

He got a busy signal.

Located on a huge campus of interconnected buildings, Ford Motor Company's world headquarters depended upon IGC personal computers and mainframes not only for office functions, but more importantly, for the actual assembly of automobiles. Using a mixture of IGC Token Ring and Ethernet-based local area networks, Ford had used its investment in computers to temporarily vault past General Motors in the mid-eighties. Some of the PCs had been ruggedized to withstand the environmental conditions of a shop floor. They were all connected together via networking.

While the Tojo Virus didn't get down to the assembly level, it did wipe out communications between the manufacturing plants and various subassembly divisions throughout the country. Over twelve thousand computers had their files encrypted.

The chairman of the board was pissed.

At 18000 West Nine Mile Road in Southfield, a northwestern suburb of Detroit, the massive EDS/GM branch office went up in electronic smoke at the same time over twenty-eight thousand personal computers and networked 9350s began to have their hard disks encrypted. Even within IGC, the size of the EDS/GM operations was staggering. Located in three cities— Southfield and Bloomfield Hills, Michigan and Dallas, Texas—the three locations were comprised of five branch managers, twenty-six marketing managers, and twelve SE managers. Each manager had ten to twelve employees—all in the support of one customer.

At 11:38 the same instant the secretary to the chairman of the board for Boeing stood up and shrieked bloody murder, and the president of Rockwell International's aerospace group saw his 3270 PC do an electronic nosedive — the Hartford Insurance branch office was near the end of its November branch meeting. The Aetna and Travelers marketing teams had each crossed the magic quota barrier into the 100% Club and had been announced. Five SE Symposium nominations were given, as well as two IGC Means Service awards to selected branch administrators.

At 11:50, with fifteen minutes of the numbers review left to go, a very nervous receptionist stepped into the crowded meeting room, walked up to the first row, and handed a note to a marketing manager, who in turn read it, blanched, and handed it to the branch manager — actually interrupting his presentation, which was boring, anyway.

"Is this a joke?" asked the stern-faced executive.

"No, sir," she said, obviously scared.

There was a buzzing undercurrent in the room, filled to capacity with over 240 people.

"How many of our customers have connections to PROFS?" he asked the account execs and marketing managers, a number so large that they filled the first two rows. He ignored the rumble in the room.

Each of the managers nodded — Travelers, CIGNA, Aetna, Mass Mutual, and HIG. The branch manager's face got increasingly red, taking each yes as he would a slap in the face.

"We've got some real trouble here," he said, then turned to the assembled group. "While we've been in here, a computer virus has struck our company — through PROFS. Our phone system is under siege. But what's worse . . . our customers have been infected."

Groans went up from the marketing reps and SEs. The gigantic Hartford-based insurance companies were massive users of personal computing. Each company raced to implement new technology. Each had sophisticated local area networks, and ties to IGC through PROFS.

Once David's virus was received by a PC, it would be automatically replicated if the program found a DOS-based local area network program on the disk. Once on a network, the virus would latch itself on to the network file servers, then communicate itself to the other individual workstations on the network.

The insurance company group executives who began to besiege IGC during the November branch meeting didn't know themselves the full extent of the damage within their companies, and wouldn't for days to come. Over forty thousand personal computers were infected.

Scotty found himself standing in Al Benning's office alone, the list of demands in his hands. It was an amazing sight to listen to and watch. The phones were a cacophony of high-pitched tweets, an artificial plastic-sounding noise that was almost as irritating as the message being delivered. After five minutes, wonderment turned to annoyance, then to anger. It drove everybody nuts.

"Find Carlton," Al had instructed Amy as they left Scotty, each heading in a different direction, without explanation.

Hubie Carlton was the building services manager and had the key to the public address system for the building.

You've got to get this to Monahan, Scotty thought.

As Scotty started for the elevator, he was joined by many IGCers. Others went directly to the stairwell. Then came the announcement. It was Al Benning.

"MAY I HAVE YOUR ATTENTION PLEASE. MAY I HAVE YOUR ATTENTION PLEASE.

PLEASE CLEAN OFF AND LOCK YOUR DESKS. THE BUILDING IS BEING EVACUATED. THE BUSINESS DAY IS CONCLUDED.

DO NOT . . . REPEAT . . . DO NOT TURN YOUR COMPUTERS OFF. NO SECURITY VIOLATIONS WILL BE ISSUED. WE ARE AWARE OF WHAT IS HAPPENING AND WILL BE DOING OUR BEST TO SEE THAT IT IS FIXED. ALL DENVER BRANCH OFFICES WILL BE OFFICIALLY CLOSED ON FRIDAY NOVEMBER 21.

DO NOT MAKE ANY FURTHER OUTBOUND CALLS. THE SWITCHBOARD IS BEING DISCONNECTED WITHIN THE NEXT TEN MINUTES. THANK YOU AND HAPPY THANKSGIVING.

PLEASE LEAVE YOUR COMPUTERS ON! THANK YOU.

Without waiting for either Amy or Al, Scotty left the building and headed to the parking lot. The IGC building was in the heart of downtown Denver. The FBI's regional office was in the Denver Federal Center in suburban Lakewood, west of town — ten miles away and probably a half hour by car. On the opposite side of Sycamore Street was a small shopping center, including a Subway deli, a bank, a gas station, a Piggly Wiggly, and a dry cleaners. Scotty dashed across the street as hundreds of IGCers filed out of the building behind him. There was a pay phone at the gas station.

Scotty's first call was to Murphy Monahan.

"I'm sorry, Scotty — he's out to lunch," was his secretary's reply.

"Damn!" Scotty looked at his watch. It was 10:10 — which meant it was just after noon in New York.

Scotty reached into his jacket and came up with his notebook, then quickly fumbled for the last page of notes, which were on the descriptions of Kimura and the woman — then paged back. *There!* The telephone number of the IGC woman, Rosen.

She said she was going to take a leave day today, he remembered.

Scotty punched out the number, which was in area code 201, northern New Jersey.

"Mom! It's for you!"

Mom was in the middle of a pumpkin pie — several pumpkin pies, actually.

"Take a message, sweetheart," Cynthia returned the shout.

A half minute later Cynthia's oldest daughter came into the kitchen.

"He wouldn't leave a message. He says its impor- tant — really important."

This pumpkin pie is important, too, she thought.

"Who is it?" Cynthia asked; then she realized what the answer must surely be: that FBI agent.

"For crying out loud," Cynthia said, wiping her hands on a wet dishrag. "I told him I'd take care of it!" Cynthia marched to the phone, a tart retort burning her mouth.

"Hello," she answered.

"This is Scott Coldsmith," the long-distance voice con- firmed. "Something's happened to your company."

"I told you —"

What did he say?

Cynthia was stopped in mid-retort.

"I've just come out of Al Benning's office. They've

378

closed the building. The phones have gone haywire—
and there's a virus in your computers. It has to do with
the death of Zack Colby."

"What? What the hell are you talking about?" Cynthia couldn't comprehend what Scotty was saying.

"I've got the demands in front of me! Do you have a
fax machine?"

At 12:22 Eastern time, the main (914) 765-1900 ro-
tary switchboard at IGC's worldwide headquarters became overloaded. Combined with the knockout of IGC's
marketing, payroll, and administrative headquarters at
1133 Westchester Avenue in nearby White Plains, the
entire 765, 696, 694, and 686 telephone exchanges in
eastern New York State were put out of commission.

Up until the switchboard began to reject incoming
calls, John Holton's five administrative assistants, all
former branch managers, his two executive secretaries,
and all six of his available senior vice-presidents were up
to their bungholes in yellow message slips.

"What's happening?" was Holton's first question as
the phones in Armonk began to ring and the computers
stopped computing.

The third time he asked someone "What's happening"
and got an unable-to-cope blank stare in return, John
Holton became furious.

"Mr. Holton, the president of Coca-Cola is on your
line. And I've got executives from American Express,
Chase Manhattan, Metropolitan Life, Citibank, General Foods, Duke Power . . . they're all waiting! Why are
they calling?"

John Holton knew he was in big trouble when people
started asking *him* what the trouble was. The telephone
calls seemed to come in waves, rippling across America's
time zones: first the eastern companies, then midwest-

ern, then mountain, and finally a nearly bereaved secretary from Boeing who had come in early to finalize reports that were due that morning.

By 12:15 John Holton's office had become a war zone. Every telephone in the set of posh suites was occupied by a senior IGC executive, and each senior ear was being filled with the same information: virus, your fault, lawsuit, out-of-business, what are you going to do about it?

People began to flee the IGC corporate campus, some actually running to their cars, as if the virus would somehow strike them dead. Executives drained out of the building like blood from a dead body. No one wanted to be in the same building as Holton — somehow, *somebody* was going to get Major Blame.

At 12:22 P.M. Eastern time, telephone service in large portions of Westchester County, New York, came to a halt when the massive NYNEX switching unit in White Plains, an ultrasophisticated, specially designed computer, was no longer able to take incoming traffic from the various long-distance carriers. John Holton's telephone number had popped up on over four hundred thousand personal computers.

Holton let his telephone slide out of his hand, where it fell onto his executive desk with a clunk. An eerie silence fell through the blue corridors.

"Can somebody please tell me what happened?" asked Holton.

People milled around outside the IGC building, looking at it in awe as if the building was going to explode or jump or even talk. Scotty hung up and opened the phone booth's accordion door.

Where's a fax machine when you really need it? he wondered.

Scotty's eyes breezed the shopping center until they

landed on a Wells Fargo bank branch office at the far end of the center. He took off for the bank on a dead run, slipping and sliding through the packed parking lot like a halfback on a TD run. Nearly out of breath, Scotty slammed through the bank's doors, excitement flushed on his face.

"I need a fax!" he shouted.

Clearly this was the act of a lunatic. The bank's security guard reached for his weapon. A woman screamed in fright. Two children started to cry. Everyone seemed to talk at once.

"I'm with the FBI." Scotty flashed his badge to a well-dressed woman seated behind a nearly cleared desk in a glassed office behind New Accounts. "I need a fax machine—now!"

There was no time for soft-spoken conversation, pleases, or thank-yous. *I need a fucking fax, now.*

The manager came out of her office, looked at Scotty's badge, then his face.

"Follow me," she said. "It's over here."

All banking transactions—including the drive-up window—ceased at the Wells Fargo Sycamore Street branch office.

"Help this man," the manager instructed one of the tellers.

"Here's the phone number." Scotty handed the woman the 201 area code number of Cynthia Rosen's personal computer in the den of her four-bedroom home in Franklin Lakes, New Jersey. Attached to the PC was a thousand-dollar fax machine, a tax write-off made necessary by Cynthia's new twenty-four-hour workday. "I need a phone," Scotty instructed. "And some privacy—if you don't mind."

The manager looked around. The guard was still frozen in middraw. Three tellers all stopped in midcount. A full line of customers all turned toward them. The teller at the drive-in window had turned around, a pneumatic tube with cash and a deposit slip still in her hand. Even the driver of a pickup truck parked in the nearest lane could see what was happening inside the bank. The manager escorted Scotty to her office, where Scotty gobbled the phone.

"Dial nine?" he asked.

"Direct."

"Mr. Monahan! It's Scott Coldsmith! He says it's urgent!" shouted Murphy Monahan's secretary across the huge bullpen.

Cynthia stood transfixed as she read the five-page transmission from Scotty. Each demand was more onerous than the last. Ted came in and watched over her shoulder.

"You're *kidding*," he said, astonished.

One look at his wife's face said she wasn't.

"I've got to get this to Armonk," she said simply.

"You know it's started to rain," Ted said.

I have to go from Wyckoff to Armonk on the Wednesday before Thanksgiving, she thought, over the Tappan Zee bridge, and through Westchester County . . . and it's raining.

While it was theoretically possible to make such a trip, it was not possible on the Wednesday before Thanksgiving. This was the one day each year when sociologists scratch their heads in amazement over the apparent fact that everyone who lives in New York City has a grandma in Connecticut.

"I'll be back when I'm back," Cynthia said, looping her purse over her right shoulder.

If she'd had any foresight she would have told Ted to have a nice Thanksgiving.

* * *

"When are you going to call them?" Marcia asked.

She was quite comfortable and seemed relaxed. She sat in the middle of Joe's bed wearing a see-through summer nightgown and black bikini panties. The nightgown clung to her breasts as she casually paged through the morning *Chronicle,* appearing to read every other page. In the other bed, Cheryl leaned back against the headrest, her legs fully extended and crossed, fully dressed, with a glower on her face. David couldn't keep his eyes off of Marcia's breasts. The nightgown slipped and danced over her hardened nipples as she turned the pages of the newspaper. David's mind was confused, his heart beat faster than it should.

It was the effect Marcia wanted.

Seemingly absentmindedly, Marcia scratched an apparent itch on her left breast with the index finger of her right hand. The soft flesh jiggled underneath the flimsy gown.

"Well, things must be pretty hot at good old IGC this morning, don't you think?" she said, looking up at David. "When are you going to call them?" she repeated.

David was bone tired and desperately horny.

He looked at his watch and did the mental dance of the time zones.

"In a few hours. I want them to feel the full effect," he said, but without the normal David Kimura confidence.

David looked at Cheryl. Her brother is an FBI agent, he thought. His eyes went back to Marcia's nightgown, which now was draped over perfect breasts.

Think!

But he couldn't.

As he did every morning, Xiang Wu walked the three

blocks from his Grant Street apartment to his twenty-first-floor office in the Wells Fargo Building on Montgomery Street. However, this morning he smiled all the way.

The first rumors to hit the stock markets came at 12:10 P.M. Eastern time, 9:10 A.M. Pacific. The market, which had been up 8.27 at that point in moderate trading, started to wobble. Observers at the New York Stock Exchange would say later that they witnessed a financial feeding frenzy as the rumor of a disastrous computer virus within IGC became a reality. Huge blocks of IGC began trading. Insiders on the floor stopped in mid-trade, in midsentence, as the rumor spread. Like a cancer, the rumor of troubles at IGC immediately infected the stock of its healthy competitors. DEC, Wang, Intel, Microsoft, Iverson, and a host of other computer companies started to see more sell orders than buy.

Then came the flood of sell orders. By 1:30 P.M. the market was down 128.25 points and falling.

In his comfortable chair, Xiang Wu sat back and smiled.

At 1:50, Cynthia Rosen pulled into the nearly empty parking lot of IGC headquarters in Armonk. A brown UPS truck pulled past her as she used her badge to get inside. Stacked at the guard's desk were piles of undelivered express mail packages. The mailroom had canceled its afternoon pickup and delivery when the phones had started to go berserk. Like four other packages, the UPS delivery contained the same ransom note that Cynthia had in her briefcase.

Cynthia stood in the now-quiet chamber in her quickly thrown-together dress blues, neat suit, and crisp blouse. Her IGC badge was secured to the lapel in front. She walked past a huddle of secretaries and senior vice-presidents to an open door. Inside was John Holton, seated at the middle of a huge conference table. Holton was surrounded by white men, all still wearing their suit coats.

Unnoticed, Cynthia walked into the room.

"I have the ransom demands," she said.

In unison, all six of the men turned their heads up and looked at her.

"You're Crowe's AA, aren't you? Rosen, isn't it?" asked Holton.

How can he know everybody? she thought. I've never met him before.

"Yes, sir . . . I am. Fred . . . Mr. Crowe, is . . ."

"I know, in a cabin someplace upstate, on a lake — probably snowbound and drunker than a skunk," Holton added.

"Probably," she admitted. "I've been in touch with an FBI agent in Denver named Coldsmith. He printed the demands off of a dead marketing rep's PROFS Note Log," said Cynthia, leaving at least half of the story untold.

John Holton's mouth dropped in open astonishment and his five senior vice-presidents all said "What?" in unison. These were all men that Cynthia would want to work for someday. At that very moment she knew more about what was happening to IGC than all of them put together.

"Look at these," Holton said, holding up a fistful of yellow notes. "Cleveland — Standard Oil; Pittsburgh — Westinghouse, Alcoa, USX; Princeton — GE; Memphis — FedEx; Dallas — Mobil, LTV; Fort Worth — American Airlines; Houston — NASA, Exxon, Shell, Texaco; San Francisco — Wells Fargo, Bank of America . . . and there's more! So what the hell's happening?"

Cynthia Rosen took a deep breath.

"One of our marketing reps, a man named Zackary

385

Colby, while in a marketing class in Dallas, got himself into a situation where he was subjected to blackmail by these people." She held up the five filmy pages. "Colby had a remote territory out of the Denver commercial office, branch DP4, which covers most of Wyoming and parts of western Nebraska. What the blackmailers wanted was access to our internal systems — and they got it in spades. Colby had a 9350 demo unit as well as PCs and other equipment."

"*How* and *why* is the administrative assistant to the vice-president of communications dealing directly with the FBI?" Holton asked coldly.

I knew he was going to ask me that, she thought.

"Gabe Sanchez in Dallas received a request from Agent Coldsmith to send out a PROFS message requesting assistance in his investigation. Coldsmith wanted to find out if any of the other students may have heard or seen something. After talking with Fred and verifying Coldsmith's ID, I agreed that the request, while out the ordinary, could only reasonably be met by use of PROFS. I recommended it to Fred and approved Sanchez's request. Yesterday, through telephone records and hard work, the Cheyenne police came up with an astonishing list of telephone contacts made with the computers in the Colby basement. One of the machines Colby had was a demonstrator 9350. Just before the virus hit this morning, the Denver branch market support manager told me that she suspected a contamination of the Endicott customer support system.

"The team in Denver found that Colby, or someone, had created over 240 PROFS distribution lists . . . with nearly fifty-five thousand addresses, and had sent a VM-created document to every one of them. Buried in the document, in the back, was an Assembly program, which must be at the heart of the virus. The blackmailers allude to it in here," Cynthia stated, holding the faxed ransom demands.

"You've read it?" asked Holton.

"Yes, sir. I did."

Holton put out his hand and took the faxed pages from Cynthia and read the demands of the late Makato Shinogara. The IGC Chairman scanned the text quickly, then gave it to one of the VPs. He stood up and started for the door.

"We don't know the full extent of what's been done yet. I need to find a place where the god-damned telephones work. Rosen, you come with me," said Holton as he walked into his office.

Cynthia Rosen just about wet her pants.

The Holiday Inn on South Airport Boulevard, one exit north of the airport, was a hear-no-evil, see-no-evil, be-no-evil motel — one where businessmen poured through night after night and no one paid attention to anybody else. It was a perfect place to stay. Marcia would have preferred to return to her apartment, but the risks were too high — the San Francisco police still wanted to talk with her, Wu *had* still to be on the lookout for her — it was in his best interest to have her dead — and now the FBI, in the form of Cheryl's brother, had to be closing in.

Marcia knew that she either had to accept Wu's passport and diskette exchange or David's offer of new identity from his backers, or . . . her plan had to work. And her plan depended on tomorrow's meeting with Wu going off with exact timing. Everyone had a role — Wu, the FBI, David, Joe, and of course, IGC. All the pieces had to fit neatly together and be executed in the right sequence. The meeting would be at the Delta Crown Room at SFO. While she knew the place well, Marcia had used the previous hour to take the airport shuttle over to the Delta terminal and check it out one more

387

time. The airport was at near gridlock. So was the Crown Room. She waited until the attendant at the desk had a free moment, then made her reservation for a private meeting.

"The far room. It's very important," Marcia said, smiling.

The attendant wrote down her reservation in a daily log.

"No problem. This place will be empty tomorrow morning. I wish it was now."

Marcia quickly cased the room, making sure there were electrical outlets in case Wu needed one for his computer. There were several. One final check and she was done. Almost done. After taking the shuttle back to the motel, Marcia had one other thing to do before settling in with David on what would surely be a very long day. She drove into the city of South San Francisco and quickly found what she was looking for: a hardware store. In less than ten minutes she was on her way back to the motel, her purse two pounds heavier.

I'll never pass a metal detector, she thought.

Fortunately, she wouldn't have to.

What Marcia really wanted was everything. Money from Wu, money from David—and money from IGC, if possible. And why not? If David's virus is as bad as he says it is, she thought, then the starch should be out of their shorts by the end of the day. It would still be possible to bring off the Big Coup.

Now in David's room, Marcia watched as he dialed 545-2000, the main number for the IGC facility at 425 Market Street, near the Embarcadero business section of downtown San Francisco. David smiled, holding the phone up for Marcia to hear:

THANK YOU FOR CALLING IGC CORPO-
RATION. WE ARE CURRENTLY EXPERI-

ENCING DIFFICULTIES WITH OUR
PHONE SYSTEM. OUR OFFICES ARE
CLOSED FOR THE DAY AND WILL RE-
OPEN ON MONDAY MORNING, NOVEM-
BER 24. THANK YOU FOR CALLING AND
HAPPY THANKSGIVING.

"Something's working," Marcia smiled. "You've managed to knock out their phone system. You'd better start
trying to get hold of those people back east. They probably have a few questions," said Marcia smiling.

The smiles gradually turned to frowns as David repeatedly failed to make contact with Armonk.

DUE TO AN UNUSUALLY HEAVY NUMBER
OF CALLS INTO THE WESTCHESTER
COUNTY, NEW YORK, AREA, YOUR CALL
CANNOT BE PLACED AT THIS TIME. WE
EXPECT THIS DELAY TO BE TEMPORARY
AND SERVICE WILL BE RESTORED AS
SOON AS POSSIBLE. THANK YOU.

"I'd say that says your little virus has been successful,
wouldn't you? Maybe too much so. You had a phone
number on your message, didn't you?"

David looked stunned. Knowing that he would fail,
David tried the number again, with the same result.

"Call the police," Marcia said simply.

"What?" David said dumbly.

"I said, call the police," she repeated, picking up a discarded *Salt Lake Tribune* from the trashcan. "They're already involved. I'll bet anything her brother is in on the
case . . . what's his name?"

"Scotty," said Cheryl.

"Sounds like a brother's name. You can be sure that if
the FBI hasn't been involved in this before, they sure as

hell are now. This thing's probably done more damage than you thought. You've either got to make contact with them or we've got to get the hell out of here—false ID or no false ID, the FBI's going to be coming after us pretty hard."

David nodded his head in agreement.

This wasn't in the plans.

The Denver Federal Center is located just south of U.S. 6 at Kipling Street in Lakewood. All of America's favorite government agencies were represented in one collection: OSHA, IRS, BuMines, Interior, FAA, Justice, DOT, Agriculture, and others. The offices were a hodge-podge of tax dollars at work. Every hallway was painted a delightful shade of GSA green.

"Federal Bureau of Investigation," replied the male receptionist, a special agent named Thomas who drew the short straw and had to be duty-agent and sit out at the receptionist's desk.

"This is Wyatt Steele of the Cheyenne police. I'm looking for special agent Coldsmith—he's there on—"

"Yes, he's expecting your call. I'll transfer you," replied Thomas.

"He's made contact," were Wyatt's first words.

"What? Who?"

"David Kimura. He identified himself right off. He's skittish as hell, though. He hung up right away, worried about a tap. He says he wants to talk to IGC," said Wyatt.

"Did he say anything about—"

"Your sister? No," anticipated Wyatt.

"I've *got* to talk to him, Wyatt," Scotty replied.

"I thought you might. You'd be better prepared for a tap anyway. I told him to call back in a couple of minutes. I'll give him your number."

"Thanks," Scotty said, and hung up.

"Is there any way to get a tap on a line in here?" Scotty asked Alex Hastings.

"On the afternoon before Thanksgiving? We're lucky the damn phones work in here at all. Some days you're lucky if you can get a dial tone. When they built this place they took every last piece of thirty-year-old copper they could find and used it for the Federal Telephone System lines. It takes us ten tries to communicate something to the Hoover Building, just because the goddamned phone lines are so dirty. Get a trace? Good luck," said Hastings.

I guess that means no, Scotty thought.

The phone on Scotty's borrowed desk rang.

"Coldsmith," he answered.

"This is David Kimura," came the long-distance voice.

Shit!

Scotty looked at his watch, then noted the time on a legal pad in front of him. He wrote the words *long distance*.

"Where are you calling from, Mr. Kimura?" asked Scotty.

"I can't tell you that," said David, his voice sounding nervous. "I won't speak long—you'll be tapping the line."

Scotty swung his body around and leaned partially out of the door, as far as the telephone cord would allow him. Wordlessly, he waved down the hall to Hastings, who didn't see him. Frantically, Scotty snapped his fingers as loud as he could, finally drawing Alex's attention.

"It's him," Scotty mouthed in silence, then turned his attention back to Kimura. "No . . . no, this line isn't tapped. We just came here this afternoon. We wouldn't — "

"Has IGC received my demands?" asked Kimura.

"IGC? I don't know what you mean, David," replied Scotty.

"You're playing games with me! I'm wasting my time with you. I have the girl and — "

"You have my sister?"

"Yes, we do."

Scotty jotted *we* on the pad.

"Isn't there any way we can get a trace?" Scotty frantically whispered to Hastings.

"You'll have to get a court order, boy. I don't think we've ever had a trace set in this building before," Hastings mused.

"Don't hang up, David. . . . Is Cheryl all right? You haven't hurt her. . . ."

"She's all right, but I'm not. I'm angry! I want to talk to IGC!"

Oh Jesus and Mother Mary.

"I'll call back from another phone," David said, the long-distance line crackling with static.

"God damn it! God damn it!" swore Scotty. "He's going to call back. He's afraid of a trace. Can't we get one? He's giving us thirty seconds to a minute every time. He's jumpy as hell! They've got my sister and they haven't been able to get through to IGC," Scotty said, angry with himself because his emotions were going out with the tide.

"He can't get through to IGC?" said Hastings. "So he's going to use *us* as the go-between," he added, shaking his head in amazement.

The phone rang again.

"Coldsmith," he answered.

"I want to know if IGC has received our demands. I want to talk to them."

"Yes they have. You've disrupted them pretty badly,

392

but then you figured you would, didn't you?" Scotty praised Kimura's work.

"I want to talk with them. I've got to go now." Kimura hung up.

"Forty seconds," said Hastings, snapping off the stopwatch feature of his wristwatch.

Hastings gave Scotty an I'll-give-it-a-try look, walked back to his office, and called Wes Cooper, his counterpart at U.S. West in Denver.

"How would you like to tap a line for me this afternoon?" he opened.

"You want what?" was Cooper's reaction.

"Without a court order," added Hastings.

"Today? This afternoon?" Cooper's reaction continued.

"Here in my office. It's important. I wouldn't ask you otherwise, you know that."

Hastings smiled as his friend groaned. Cooper knew not to ask the details.

"I'll see what I can do," he replied, and hung up.

Hastings walked back to Scotty's borrowed office.

"He hasn't called back yet," said Scotty.

"Have you heard from your IGC contact?" Wyatt asked.

Scotty shook his head.

No turkeys would be eaten before their time — at least not in a small section of northern New Jersey. At 3:35 P.M. Eastern time a caravan of twelve automobiles rolled past the huge boulder in front of the glass entrance to the IGC facility at 400 Parson's Pond Drive. It was ironically appropriate that the building was the home of the National Service Division, IGC's repair and maintenance division. The division vice-president, considerably unnerved by the urgency of the visit and only provided with ten minutes notice, came out to meet the chairman. The cold November sky hinted snow but instead delivered a cold biting north wind that flapped the VP's suit coat as he stood waiting for the procession to arrive.

"Mr. Holton, so good to see you," he scraped, nearly bowing.

John Holton was not glad to see *anyone*. Inside Holton's limo with him were the corporate legal counsel, Mr. Kiley; the senior vice-president of the North-Central Marketing Division, Mr. Owens; the newly announced president of IGC World Trade, Mr. DeToqueville; and the administrative assistant to the vice-president of internal communications, Mrs. Rosen. Except for Cynthia, the men had the misfortune of being in the wrong place at the wrong time — inside the corporate HQ when the virus struck and the phones disintegrated. This was especially true for Mr. DeToqueville because he was only hours from returning to Paris, where IGC's overseas operations had its headquarters, and where he had his home.

The lead limo discharged its passengers, then car by car the others did the same. Each man used his badge to enter through the inch-thick lead glass doors that shielded the open foyer from the guard station inside. At 3:45 the main conference room was packed with forty-eight people. The RED corridor was shut off. A few remaining employees were asked to leave.

The conference room had two wooden flip chart stands, matching whiteboards six feet tall by twelve feet long at either short end, recessed counter space along the inboard length of the room, and floor-to-ceiling windows on the opposite side, opening to the New Jersey countryside. At one end was an audiovisual center, including two televisions normally used for sales presentations. John Holton got up.

"Do the phones work?"

Laughter wouldn't have been appropriate, and there was none.

"Yes," answered the VP of the National Service Division. "I want the switchboard open and manned twenty-four-hours a day with enough people to handle a flood of calls, if need be. I want the building cleared, except for the switchboard and the machine room. Is the operations manager here?"

This was Cynthia's turf. She found Harvey Cohen's eyes and nodded.

"Yes, sir." Cohen raised his hand.

"Good. Is someone from external communications here?"

"She's on her way," said someone. "She has to come out from the city."

Everybody understood the problem. External communications was responsible for IGC's face to the outside world, specifically the media. IGC was generally known as a very difficult company to get information from. Newspapers, trade magazines, television — all found the company to be cold and difficult to deal with. The situation was ripe for payback by the media.

"I'm hungry. Is the cafeteria open? We're going to be here until the situation is resolved."

The cafeteria was closed, but the NSD vice-president would personally see to it that the Marriott food service employees were brought back inside, and that food would be made available to the group.

"When we're done here, I want each of you to call home, tell your family there's been an emergency and where you can be reached — but say nothing of what has happened or what we are doing. Is that understood? Someone, or somebody, is attacking our company. It will be on the evening news all over the world, and in every newspaper. So, we aren't going to be able to hide it. Just tell your family that you'll be home, when you're home."

John Holton did not want his people to be worried about family. It was time to be worried about *company*. He went to the whiteboard behind him, uncapped a marker, and began to write.

DAMAGE ASSESSMENT
DAMAGE CONTROL
RANSOM DEMANDS
OPTIONS
LOGISTICS
OTHER CONSIDERATIONS

Cynthia's head was spinning. She had followed John Holton down the halls of IGC CHQ, jotting down his thoughts as fast as he could spit them out. Holton had walked down three corridors, nailing everyone from senior executives to flunky AAs like her. Holton's secretary was part of the group. Her name was Gracie. Gracie and Cynthia were the only women in the group of forty-eight.

"We are under attack as surely as if there were tanks and armed troops in the courtyard. We have the ransom demands. I want you to all know what they are. They could have asked for money — cash — but they didn't. Instead, they've asked for the heart and soul of the company — its research and development, the proprietary things that have and will make us great."

Gracie passed out a stapled copy of the five-page ransom demand. It had been a traumatic event over at CHQ finding a copier that could actually copy and collate fifty sets of the five pages quickly. The existing Series III copier line, which had been sold to Kodak in its entirety, was abused and maligned. If inanimate objects had feelings, then the Series III copiers felt pretty low.

Gracie had nearly kicked one machine when the collator simply refused to do its job.

"Gracie is also passing out your assignments. I want four groups: Damage Assessment/Damage Control, Ransom Demands, Options, and Other Considerations. Since Mr. Crowe is in a cabin in upstate New York, Mrs. Rosen will head up Damage Assessment and Control. Mr. Owens will chair the Options committee, Mr. DeToqueville will head Demands, and our corporate legal attorney Mr. Kiley will chair Other Considerations. It is now four o'clock. At five-thirty I want to meet back here and see if we can make any concrete decisions," Holton finished. "Rosen, I'd like to see you for a moment."

Cynthia gathered her papers and approached the front of the room.

"Yes, sir?"

"Have you touched base with your FBI contact?" he asked.

So when would I have time? she thought.

"No, sir."

"I don't want the FBI crawling all over us, yet. Not until we know what the hell has happened. At the same time, we've moved. If these people want to reach us, we're going to be pretty hard to find. If there's any talking to be done, we at least want a focal point. Make contact with him—in Denver, you say?"

"Yes, sir," replied Cynthia.

"Use this phone as the contact point." Holton pointed to the single telephone in the conference room.

Cynthia pulled out her black THINK pad where she'd written Scotty's number.

"Federal Bureau of Investigation," answered a male voice.

The connection seemed bad.

"I'm trying to reach Scott Coldsmith, he's—"

"I'll connect you," he replied quickly.

On the other end, Scotty jumped on the ringing phone, certain that it was David Kimura.

"I didn't know if you were going to call back or not," he said.

"Mr. Coldsmith?" questioned Cynthia.

The new voice threw Scotty off.

"Who is this?" he asked.

"Cynthia Rosen — of IGC," she replied.

"Oh, *yes* — I'm sorry, but we've been in contact with them," Scotty said.

"You have?"

"Yes. Apparently, they haven't been able to reach you back there in New York. So, they've been in contact with me."

"What do they want? Did they say anything?" asked Cynthia.

"They want to talk to your people. I'm reluctant to let them do it," said Scotty.

"Just a moment." Cynthia covered up the phone and quickly explained to John Holton what was happening; with a hand motion he told her to continue her conversation.

"Why is that?" Cynthia resumed.

Another pause.

"We're trying to set up a phone tap. Considering where we are, it's difficult."

Cynthia's gut feel was that for the time being it was better for the FBI to do its thing, and for IGC to do its — they needed to find out exactly what happened.

"The phones in Westchester County have been knocked out. We've moved our task force to a facility in New Jersey." Cynthia looked up at the expressionless John Holton. "I'm going to give you this telephone number, Scott — but it's between you and me. The press is going to be all over us . . . and we don't want them calling this number. OK?"

"Deal," returned Scotty.

"We're at (201) 848-1900. The conference room we're using is extension 1905, and you can direct-dial it without going through the switchboard. How long are you going to be at your number?" Cynthia asked.

"All day—and probably all night," Scotty returned.

"If you don't call us, we'll call you by"—Cynthia looked at her watch. It was ten after four—"by six o'clock—that's four o'clock your time."

"Agreed," said Scotty with enthusiasm, and they hung up.

Cynthia turned to Holton to see if there were any further instructions. His silence told her that everything she'd said was OK, and that she'd better hustle her buns to her Damage Assessment/Control meeting.

Does this mean I'm going to have to be a big girl now? she wondered.

"I can't authorize that, Mr. Hastings. This is a GSA building, not something *rented* by one of your branches. There are *rules* for situations like these."

The speaker was Augustus Raymond Johnson, regional director for the General Services Administration GSA and official landlord for the Denver Federal Center. Mr. Johnson had been regional director since 1975, surviving four changes in administrations and more than one or two scandals. Nobody was going to go poking around inside *his* telephone closets without his permission. Johnson didn't like the thought of the FBI putting a tap on a line in his building—no sir, not at all. Augustus leaned his portly frame back in his squeaky GSA chair and crossed his arms in the no position.

On the other side of the desk, Alex Hastings was angry enough to spit nickels. He gritted his teeth together, even though his dentist warned him that he'd have to have a retainer put in if he didn't stop.

"And . . . what . . . *are* . . . those . . . rules, Mr. Johnson?"

"Well, you've got to have a court order for one thing, which I don't see that you have. That'll do for starters," said Johnson.

"It's the afternoon before Thanksgiving—I'm not going to be able to get a court order signed this afternoon!"

Hastings responded nearly in a Kirk Douglas imitation. He was only missing the dimples. The barely restrained fury put Hastings at the top of a Type-A personality. He wasn't a man to take lightly.

This asshole isn't going to prevent me from doing my job.

Alex Hastings saw that it would be a futile effort to get GSA's help—and their approval was now only a formality. Hastings didn't give a rat's ass if the fat GSA director approved or not.

Cooper had come through—as Alex knew he would. Standing in the FBI waiting room was the Phone Man. Every building in the United States has a Phone Man, the wizard who can go into a ceiling conduit as easily as he can unscramble the jumble of wires in a phone closet. The Phone Man for the GSA Federal Center in Denver was Lew. Lew was not known to have a last name. Tall, lanky, and good-looking, Lew seldom ate alone. He *loved* servicing the Federal Center. With his heavy-duty belt slung around his hips, always laden down with tools and a portable telephone, secretaries hit on him like he was a returning GI. Lew never complained and gave good service.

Alex Hastings came back upstairs, shook Lew's hand, then asked him to step into his office. Lew ambled back through the bullpen area to the SAC's cluttered office.

"Lew, I need a tap on one of my lines. I've got a murder-kidnapper who's calling us every half hour and I don't have time to go try and get a judge to sign a god-damned court order. I can't tell you anything more. . . . I wish I could, but I can't."

"What line do you want tapped?" was Lew's instant response.

Alex smiled and headed down the hall to Scotty's borrowed office.

"This line," said the SAC.

Lew shook his head.

"This is going to take a while, Mr. Hastings."

"Can it be done?" asked Alex.

"It's *possible*. Anything's *possible*," he said, scratching his head with the edge of a pair of wire cutters. "You see, I know this building inside and out. Even though the building is less than twenty years old, the materials they used . . . well, they're old. The phone system is literally held together with chewing gum and paper clips," Lew said.

Lew walked over to Scotty's phone.

"The wire goes into the wall here, then down to the floor, where it crosses through a pipe to a relay out by the elevator—that's where all the phones on this floor are connected, not just the FBI's. From the third floor we go to the basement and outside—eventually it gets to the switchboard at my office. In order to get a tap on this phone, I've got to have that line secured all the way from my computer to this instrument. The problem is, this equipment is *crap*. What they need is a microwave on the roof and fiber optics in the building. If we had that, I could put Caller ID on in a couple of minutes."

"Can you do it?"

"I could get in real trouble for this." He shook his head. "No work order . . ."

By following procedure a tap on the line would have

been possible only after a court order and the proper work orders filed with U.S. West. Alex would have had to identify the need at least three weeks ahead of the occurrence. This would require clairvoyance beyond what was normally required to fill the position of special agent-in-charge.

"I'll get it done for you . . . but it'll probably be five before I can get it done. Is that OK?"

"Is that all right?" Alex asked Scotty. "There's no sense wasting his time if we won't need it by then."

"That will be great. I'll try to hold him until then," said Scotty with enthusiasm.

The two hours had gone by so fast that there wasn't a single member of the task force who felt like he'd managed to actually do anything of worth. But they had. As the group made its way back into the conference room, the second hour of the evening news had just come on WNBC, WABC, and WCBS in New York. One of the TV sets was turned on.

This morning at approximately eleven-thirty, a virulent computer virus of unknown origin swept through InterGalactic Computing Corporation, wreaking havoc on the computer giant's internal systems.

The virus is reported to be significantly different from the one that swept through the company on Christmas Eve 1987, leaving the firm with a twenty-four-hour case of the Blue Flu.

It's also different from the virus that was accidentally inserted into the APRANET communications network used by a brilliant graduate student in November 1988.

What makes this virus different is that this time

it appears to be real. Massive numbers of personal computers—initial reports are as high as one hundred thousand—have been infected.

What is terrifying is that the virus has spread to many of IGC's customers—all major users of IGC data processing—all important companies to the American economy.

Rumors are that the virus is part of an attempt to blackmail IGC. For an update on this, we switch to Franklin Lakes, New Jersey, where IGC officials as of this moment are gathering to sort out what has happened, and what can be done.

LIVE SATELLITE FEED

Hello, Kathy. I'm standing out in front of the IGC building in Franklin Lakes. Apparently the Westchester County phone disaster this afternoon was a direct result of the computer virus that hit IGC today. The switchboards at several IGC locations were bombarded with telephone calls from irate computer users—so much so that all Westchester exchanges were overloaded. For those of you in the Westchester area, your telephone service is expected to resume again this evening.

Inside, IGC officials are meeting to figure out exactly what happened and what they can do. So far, there have been no . . . wait a minute! Somebody's coming out of the building now. It appears as if we will have a statement after all.

[Camera shows gray-haired man of fifty-six being escorted by a woman approximately forty years old, and two security guards. There is a crowd of approximately fifty reporters outside, milling around.]

My name is Evelyn Bates, and I am the director of external communications for IGC. With me is the chairman of the board of IGC, Mr. John

Holton. I will read a short statement, which is all we will have for the moment, then Mr. Holton will make a short comment on the situation."

[Closeup shot of Evelyn Bates reading statement. Wind blows her brown hair across her face. The handwritten piece of paper shakes in her hand.]

At approximately eleven-thirty this morning, November 19, a computer virus was introduced to IGC's internal systems that has temporarily rendered them inoperative. The virus appears to have spread to some of our customers as well, with the same effect. We are working twenty-four-hours a day to provide a remedy, and hope that normal operations may be resumed on Monday morning. Mr. Holton?"

[Camera pans to distinguished chairman of the board, John Holton.]

I know each and every one of you wants to know every detail of what we're doing . . . of what's happening behind the scenes. That's your job. My job is to manage one of the largest companies in the world—and right now, that's a difficult one.

As you know, major corporations are rather secretive about how they operate internally. If you've been here before, you know we . . . IGC . . . are no different. Today's marketplaces are very competitive.

There is a computer virus within IGC. It has spread to more of our customers than we like. We are in the process of resolving the problem. And we will tell you when we have something definite to report. As of this moment, the virus has been "alive" for a little more than six hours.

"That's it?" [newsman]
[various shouting]

"What about blackmail? We've heard reports of blackmail! Are you going to cave in?"

"What about your customers? There are billions of dollars in corporate assets tied up with this virus. Whose fault is it? What is IGC's liability?"

"Do you have any evidence the Russians are involved?"

"I'm sorry, I have no comment."

[Camera shows John Holton, chairman of the board of IGC, retreating through glass doors.]

"Ladies and gentlemen of the press! You are on private property. Because of the sensitive nature of what is being conducted here, we must insist that you move back off of the facility grounds."

"Over there? By the road? We can't even see the god-damned building? Where are the toilets?"

John Holton walked back into a stunned meeting room. The dogs smelled fresh blood. Holton was fuming.

"I want a nationwide ISEN hookup for this evening. Ten o' clock. All branch offices. All regional offices. *Now!*" he ordered.

The assembled group had no idea who would have been responsible for such a task. The Interactive Satellite Education Network was IGC's innovative method for bringing classroom education to remote sites—to avoid the cost of transportation, rooms, meals. Classroom education, with interaction with the teacher, even if remote, had been brought to every large metropolitan area in the U.S. It was a tremendous cost savings, and nearly accomplished the same goal as live classroom education. Some was lost, but not much.

"Sir? Tonight?" came a question.

Apparently someone who had something to do with ISEN was in the room. Holton's look settled all questions. Two people scurried from the room.

"I hate that shit," Holton muttered, referring to the gaggle of reporters.

It was 6:20.

"All right, we're behind schedule. Let's hear what you've got," he said. "Assessment/Control?"

Why me? Cynthia thought. Why do I have to get up after the chairman of the board has gotten angry? Why me?

Cynthia stood up. Suit coats were draped everywhere, white sleeves were rolled up.

"The virus was initiated from the home of an IGC employee. The distribution method was PROFS. The employee was a salesman . . . marketing representative . . . from Cheyenne, Wyoming, who had access to IGC systems from home—from a remote territory. He put himself into a blackmail position, to the extent that his controller, or controllers, were able to send the virus through PROFS to every single address within our system—including our customers who have internal-use-only access," said Cynthia with a stone face.

She looked around the room. There were no smiles.

"The IGCer, Zackary Colby, is now dead," she added. "Shot. By whom, we don't know."

Blackmail. Virus. Death. These weren't subjects the average senior vice-president of a company thought of when he woke up and went to work in the morning.

"In the last forty-five minutes we've received good news and bad news. The good news is that Information Network was spared. The bad news is that our research and development plants have been contaminated via the Yorktown Disk."

There were moans of *damn* and *oh shit* mumbled through the room. Information Network was IGC's latest entry into computer time-sharing. If the virus had penetrated IN's systems, then it could have been pervasive across the country. IN provided relatively low-cost data processing services, even to the point of helping with application development. Its center was in Tampa, Florida. It wasn't infected.

The news about the Yorktown Disk was trouble. That meant that Yorktown Heights, the Watson Research Center, Owego, Burlington, Raleigh, San Jose, Santa Teresa, and even possibly the overseas sites in Scotland, France, Switzerland, and Japan were affected. But, the effect would be less because the virus would have attacked PCs only, and then only one at a time. Most users of the disk were "hackers" who wanted gossip and programs, or "teachers" who wanted to distribute their program or idea to a larger base of users.

"I'm afraid I have more bad news . . ." Cynthia trailed off. "We don't know the affect of the virus on our customer base. We know it is significant, but we don't know the extent. It's still out there. That's the problem. It could be sitting on a PC in Coca-Cola's HQ in Atlanta. The user was off for the weekend. He comes back, turns his system on, gets zapped . . . and because he's on a LAN, distributes the thing to other, currently uncontaminated, users."

"What *is* it?" asked someone, without raising his hand.

"We don't have it in our hands yet. From what the people in Denver said, it's an assembler program that was tagged to a non-PROFS note, then distributed. Like something you and I receive every day of the week. I haven't gotten it because I haven't been able to get enough of PROFS back up and working," said Cynthia.

Like the disparate pockets of people found after an atomic war, PROFS could find only a few users who hadn't been contaminated. The mainframe computers worked just fine. PROFS itself worked fine. Only there were no users available to listen. Everybody's ID had been sucked up by the virus. Everybody's terminal, his or her PC, had been wiped out. The only people left on IGC's worldwide system of 1,400 mainframe computers were a small handful of users who had refused to give up their 3279 terminals for personal computers. These people tended to be "old." In IGC, "old" was fifty. "Ancient" and "decrepit" were fifty-five. Anybody past that was "terminal."

On the afternoon of Wednesday, November 19, after scrounging the entire Franklin Lakes facility for three 3279 terminals, Cynthia Rosen sent out a broadcast message in the name of the chairman. It took two people to carry the clunky bastards, but each was installed, the 3174 recustomized, and the message sent.

TO: ALL PROFS USERS
FROM: JOHN C. HOLTON
Chairman of the Board
DATE: 19 NOVEMBER
SUBJ: BRANCH OFFICE STATUS
IT IS VITAL THAT WE RECEIVE A STATUS REPORT OF ALL THOSE SYSTEMS STILL IN OPERATION AS OF THIS DATE. A COMPUTER VIRUS OF UNKNOWN ORIGIN HAS ENTERED OUR SYSTEMS THIS MORNING. WE NEED TO KNOW HOW THIS HAS AFFECTED YOUR OFFICE. PLEASE ACKNOWLEDGE AS SOON AS POSSIBLE.

Cynthia had stood at her dirty, heavily smudged 3279 terminal and awaited the returns. The responders were from IGC's tertiary locations—the suboffices of major or nearly-major cities: Newport News, Virginia; Lincoln, Nebraska; LaGrange, Wisconsin; Lansing, Michigan; Richland, Washington; Bozeman, Montana; and

Eugene, Oregon. In all cases the reports were of actual cases of computer file encryption, or I-heard-someone-got-hit-someplace-else reports. Responses were more instantaneous from various PROFS nodes, locations where mainframes were installed. Each of those locations typically kept several 3279 terminals, which were strictly used for troubleshooting. The responses were typical: WHAT HAPPENED?????

What was depressing was that the devastation seemed to be across the board. The IGC Corporation was down and out. Cynthia continued.

"What's worse, the virus has spread to our customers. We don't know how many. We had nearly four thousand recorded messages on the Armonk switchboard before the Westchester phone system went down. We can assume there were at least ten times as many trying to get through. We don't know how many customers called their local branch office. We *do* know that any customer who tied into PROFS in the last two weeks was surely infected—regardless if their contact was merely to inquire about ivory letters." Cynthia was on a roll. "What makes it worse is that unlike the way our computers are connected in the branch office, that is by direct coax to the host, our large customers are all using local area networks of some kind—Novell, token ring, Ethernet, 3-COM, and others. Any customer using a DOS-based network operating system will have the virus spread throughout his network as well. I'm sure that's why we've gotten so many phone calls."

Cynthia put both hands down on the conference table and leaned forward.

"We did a quick test on one of the encrypted PCs. It's locked tight as a drum. You can't even do DOS commands without a password. You can't boot the machine from the diskette drive."

Cynthia walked over to a flip chart stand.

"We estimate that between ninety and ninety-five percent of our personal computers are locked — and the same percentage of all host files created by those users in VM. We don't know how many customer machines are affected. We don't know how many systems have been infected from the Yorktown disk.

"Furthermore, acting on the intuition of the Denver market support manager, we contacted the 9350 product support group in Endicott. A 9350 version of the virus was placed on the Endicott call-on disk. It appears from telephone records gathered by the Cheyenne police that the original program left there on November fourth. I gave that date to the manager in Endicott to use as a reference. He just about gagged. A quick check of his records indicated that over three hundred and forty systems could have been infected. And we have no idea how many terminals."

"That's a thumbnail sketch of damage assessment. On to damage control. The first thing we agreed on was to eliminate all remote access to PROFS — no customers, no remote IGCers." Cynthia gave the group a don't-shoot-the-messenger look. "I'm sorry, but until the virus is completely identified and the methodology outlined, our recommendation is that V-Net be shut down completely."

More groans. Cynthia was recommending that user access to and through all 1,400 processors be temporarily prohibited — no commission accounting, no payroll transactions, no order entry, no accounts receivable.

"Until we determine exactly what the virus is, we don't see that there is any other choice. Maybe we can have a handle on it by the end of the weekend — maybe not. The ransom note, the display message, and our brief testing all indicate that the files have indeed been encrypted. If that's the case, then without the key — the password — the files are locked."

Cynthia sat down, exhausted.

Charles DeToqueville stood up and walked to the front of the room and began to speak, his French accent a delight to listen to.

"We have been studying the ransom demands — not from the standpoint of how rational they are, but from the practical standpoint of how would we meet them. Although we each have our own opinion of who has done this, Mr. Owens has included an analysis of the possibilities in his section.

"With the telephone system out in Westchester County, we were unable to reach Mr. Hardy, head of the general technology division. So, we called the Burlington and San Jose plants directly. As you can imagine, neither plant manager was thrilled to talk about the possibilities of giving away the technology developed at both sites. My questions to each of them were the same: If we had to do it, could it be done? How much time would it take? What would the end product look like? And how would it be delivered? These are not trivial matters. Each one would take a task force to accomplish.

"In Burlington, we would have to disclose our manufacturing processes for the 4-megabit, 16-megabit, and 32-megabit memory chip. We have been delivering 1-megabit chips in our products for the last two years, and the 4-megabit chip will become generally available this year. The 16- and 32-megabit chips are still in development stages. In order to turn over the process, we would have to consider the actual microchip machinery itself, the skilled labor, as well as the development documentation. The documentation is less useful than one might imagine. What *would* be useful is one of the laboratories. It would take three to four weeks to properly disassemble one of the labs and move it to a new location. Even then, without the proper clean room environment,

411

quality control could not be guaranteed by any means. And of course, there is the issue of skilled labor to run the machines, perform quality assurance, et cetera.

"In San Jose, the development plans, prototypes, and manufacturing processes for the new 3395 disk drives could be delivered within two weeks—if the manufacturing process was required. The technology itself and prototypes could be delivered within days.

"We did not have enough time to contact the development labs in Owego, Raleigh, and Santa Teresa, where the bulk of our Fifth Generation Computing and Artificial Intelligence applications are being developed. We were able to reach appropriate management within Yorktown Heights. Most of the work in these areas could be reduced to 3380 disk packs and personal computer disks within a week, along with the appropriate documentation. The volume from each location would approximately fill half a medium-size moving van.

"Finally, I was able to reach Dr. Niles Heinrich, director of the Zurich Research Lab, at his home in Ruschlikon. He was extremely upset at the possibility of having to give up the research on superconductivity that his lab and other IGC locations have been doing for the last eight years. We are in a neck-and-neck race with the Japanese, but we are considered to be ahead. Both Dr. Cravens and Dr. Glaeser have made significant strides in the last year . . . we believe putting them well ahead of anyone else. Their latest findings on the new ceramics and higher temperatures have not been published. When Dr. Heinrich settled down, he explained that the research involved quite a bit more than just paper—a laboratory would have to be reconstructed, or torn down. It would take a month to accomplish and the research materials would fill several van loads," said DeToqueville.

"If we were to comply with the ransom demands, it

would take us approximately three weeks if we started now. Burlington's clean lab would most likely be shut down for a month. I don't have the statistics on the availability of 1-megabit chips, but I know every product we now ship uses the chips, so I would expect there to be delays in our product shipments."

"That assumes that we still have any customers," interjected John Holton.

There was nervous laughter throughout.

"I believe Mr. Kiley will cover that in the options section," DeToqueville said, then paused. "In summary, the demands, as we see them, are possible to comply with, but not in a short turnaround. Delivering this entire package in secrecy to an unknown destination within Hong Kong will be a logistical nightmare—if it can be done. Once again, I believe that falls into Mr. Kiley's arena."

Charles DeToqueville sat down, also with a discouraged look on his face. James Owens got up. After assignments as a branch manager, regional manager, and various staff positions, he was now the head of the North-Central Marketing Division—or the Nasty-Cold Division as it was referred to internally. NCMD comprised approximately half of the IGC branch offices, and about one-quarter of IGC's worldwide revenues. Mr. Owens was in a responsible position.

"We do have options—but, I haven't found one that I'm terribly thrilled with," Owens started.

"Option One is always the null option—do nothing. No response to the ransom demands. No response to our customers. Pretend it didn't happen, let the chips fall where they may. This one puts us out of business in the shortest amount of time. Since I enjoy my job and think I'm capable of taking on more responsibility, I'm going to recommend we reject this option.

"Option Two is the opposite—pay the buggers everything. As Charles has told us, the logistics of providing our enemies with our technology are *possible*. Right now we don't know who these people are. It seems unlikely that we would be able to construct a scenario that would provide them satisfaction *without* discovery of their identity. They would need technical people, a large facility, scientists to verify . . . and we know most of these people. Of course, it's possible that they really don't want *everything* we think they do. After all, it wouldn't be the first time we've sent *too much*. Perhaps they were only thinking of the documentation—the disks . . . I don't know. We need to talk to them. Option Two says that we pay them everything and we get everything in return— the keys to unlock our computers.

"Option Two also says that we will take care of the conversion of any of our customer's disks and pay for any actual expenses for what has happened. Mr. Kiley will have to get additional staff." Owens smiled at chief counsel Kiley. "Of course, we also have to fix our *own* problem as well—which we know we have to do in any case.

"My personal problem with Option Two is that I don't know what the long-term affects are for the company. I know that it gripes the hell out of me. The disk drive and microchip technology would only help somebody already in the business, and I have a gut feel that our marketing savvy could overcome the differences. As far as the Artificial Intelligence, superconductivity, and Fifth Generation Computing are concerned—I'm afraid I don't know. I don't have the experience or vision to project into the next century. The loss of AI applications would be a short-term loss, because our next generation of equipment will utilize these software programs. I simply can't calculate what the present value is of our research to date in relationship to when this technology becomes available. My guess is that it will make us something less than the best — and I don't like that, not at all.

"Option Three is a modified version of Option Two. Negotiate for a monetary settlement in lieu of the technology. Maybe this is the best. It certainly would be the easiest. Although I wouldn't like it any better than the other options. This option would be the easiest to get done within a reasonable time frame. I have no idea what the fair market value for our technology is — nor how to calculate it.

"Option Four — screw the bastards. Eat the machines, replace our entire V-Net, pay our customers for the damage, and replace their machines at no charge. Emotionally it's the solution I'd prefer, but we did some rough numbers and came up with ten billion dollars. That's a lot of money, even for IGC. And the number may be twice as high, given what the settlements would be with our customers — loss of good will, et cetera.

"So, we tried a ranking — and tried to look at it from different perspectives. I'm a marketing rep at heart — so my tendencies were obvious. If I have to pay, I want it done as quickly as possible. The longer this goes, the worse our market position will be. Option One was out. Between Options Two, Three, and Four — we get back into business quicker with Three. Negotiate and pay money. Two is the worst, I believe. It will take the longest to resolve. And the longer this goes on, the greater the possibility that these people may up the ante."

Owens sat down and legal counsel Kiley got up.

This wasn't a management development game where there was a right way to get through the maze, if everybody pitched in and worked as a team. Reality was a bitch.

"I've been in and out of your meetings for the last two hours. I've made some phone calls and jotted down some observations," said the rotund attorney.

"One—our stock started the day at 128.5. It closed this afternoon at 97.75. In the last hour of trading it went down eleven points. I've talked to the analysts on the floor of the New York exchange—we were saved by the bell. But, there's a stack of sell orders piling up that didn't get through. The market went down one hundred and forty-two points today, every last point of it after one o'clock. You listened to the newscast. You heard someone talk about blackmail. Word gets out—word *is* out. If we don't have a solution by Friday morning and announce it early, before the exchange opens—then Black Monday could look like Christmas in comparison. We simply don't know what the short-term effect could be. How many companies could be put out of business because of a drop in the value of their stock? How many people are in on margin? What is the programmed sell point for the mutual funds? There are a hundred other questions. But you get the point. We are the cause of it. What we do here—the decisions we make—will clearly affect the stock market. Not only the price of IGC stock, but the price of all stocks. The financial marketplaces will be in chaos," said Kiley.

There wasn't a soul in the room whose heart wasn't racing. The company was facing a financial Armageddon.

"Two—related to one, but different. The virus, through IGC's carelessness, has infected and damaged computer systems in other companies—our customers. I'm telling you now, no matter how hard my team will fight in court, the decision will not be in our favor. We will lose every case. Only an incompetent attorney could lose such a case. There is no argument! There is no defense. An IGC employee sabotaged PROFS, and in turn our customers' systems. No defense. None. The longer we go without solving the problem, the higher is our risk—our liability will truly compound daily."

People were hardly breathing. The weight of the responsibility was staggering.

"Three — who did this terrible thing? DEC, no. AT&T, no. Wang, no. Amdahl? No. CDC? No. I've narrowed my choices down to four: the Russians, the Japanese, the Chinese, the French. Yes, the French — as a government, not a computer company. We have virtually no idea what the government in Beijing has for computing. This type of demand could put them right in the ball game. The same applies for the Russians. Both the Chinese and Russians would use our technology to develop systems for internal use — for military purposes. The Japanese would use it for commercial purposes, as would the French. We've beaten both the Japanese and French national companies pretty badly in the last decade. I can't think of another competitor — can you? Is there someone else?" Kiley asked the group. There were no hands raised.

"OK, that brings up Four — national security. The technology demanded is clearly in the national interest of the United States. We could sell the technology to the Japanese and French, but not to the Soviets or the Chinese. We would fall under the guidelines of the National Espionage Act — nobody in this room wants to sell secrets to the god-damned Russians.

"Five — the FBI. From talking to Mrs. Rosen, I understand we are already dealing with the FBI in Denver, who have already been contacted by our mystery people. I can guarantee you, they will be here in force unless we can solve it ourselves. They'll be involved in any case, because federal laws have already been broken. We need to involve the FBI, and let them know what our decision is — but it's *our* decision to make. Our company is at stake. We can't let the FBI's need to capture criminals deter us from doing what is right for the company.

"So, what is our worst risk? Espionage—unwitting or not. Second, and more probable, the fallout from the infection of our customers—from a stock market value standpoint, as well as the actual damage to existing systems, and the loss of customer base that will surely follow."

Kiley sat down. As one, the audience started breathing again. John Holton got back up.

"I suppose in the long run, it's my decision to make. There is a great deal of work to be done—and we do need to talk to these people. Emotionally, I agree with Jim Owens—I'd just as soon bite the bullet and start over again, pay off our customers, and rebuild the system. Let the sons of bitches eat dirt for their ransom. It galls me to have a band of god-damned tech weenies hold us up to ransom—and to ridicule. Of the choices you've come up with, I think number three is the most practical—convert our technology to a dollar number. Pay the bastards." Holton shook his head in anger. "We've got to have the programs to unlock our systems—or we might as well put up a For Sale sign on that big rock outside . . . and in front of every other building we've got."

Scotty's phone rang again.

"It's me. Hang on, we'll find out soon enough," said Lew, who was buried inside the third-floor telephone closet, up to his eyeballs in multicolored copper wire.

An eternity went by in a minute. Scotty shifted his weight from foot to foot.

"Got it! Forty-eight seconds to get the exchange—another ninety-two, give or take a few, to get the line number," said Lew.

"What about the area code? These people are calling from out of state," Scotty asked.

"I don't know. This is a local call. It'll pick it up, but I don't know how long it will take. I guess we'll just have to wait and see."

"He's back!" shouted Agent Thomas, still sitting at the receptionist's desk. "Are we ready yet?"

"No!" came Lew's return shout. "No, wait a minute—yes! We have it!"

Scotty lifted the receiver.

"I want to talk to the IGC people. No more delays. I want to know their plans to meet our demands," said a determined Kimura.

"They . . . they aren't ready yet, David. You've hurt them pretty badly. Can you tell us where the meeting will be? Can you tell us that much?"

"No. I'll only talk with IGC," said David, who by now realized that he had opened Pandora's Box. "When will they be ready?" he asked.

"Any minute, now. What do—" The phone went dead. Kimura hung up. "Damn!" Scotty shouted, banging the receiver down.

Alex Hastings came back from his observer's outpost in the telephone closet.

"You couldn't keep him on the line any longer?" he asked anxiously.

Scotty shook his head. The phone rang again. It was Lew.

"Nothing. You were only on for twenty-five seconds. We simply need more time."

John Holton was furious.

There was no central maintenance in IGC's V-Net. Fixes, patches, updates—all had to be applied at the local host computer node. For such a huge system to be so compatible, so transparent from one location to another, was a credit to the PROFS software and the VM/SP operating system. But Cynthia and the folks in the Franklin Lakes machine room didn't have the ability to zap into the Denver system to tweak and twiddle. They had to rely on the systems administrators at each node to do apply system fixes as they were issued by CHQ.

Unfortunately, there was little to be done. Not without the decryption key. When the virus struck, it also encrypted all of Zack Colby's non-PROFS files — including the dummy memorandum, the encryption programs, the execs, and the HLLAPI download program.

"Can we break the program?" Holton asked.

"We have programmers in Yorktown and Endicott working on it. It's a very tight and economical program — well written. As of now, they haven't been able to penetrate the encryption program with an antibody solution."

"What about the FBI?" Holton asked.

"The agent I'm dealing with in Colorado, Agent Coldsmith, has been in contact with his counterparts in New York. They've gotten NYNEX to put a tap on the 1905 extension here in the conference room. They should be finished within the hour," replied Cynthia.

"Are they here now?" asked Holton.

Cynthia nodded.

"I'd like to meet them," requested Holton.

Cynthia went out to another empty office that had been commandeered for the FBI to use.

"Mr. Monahan? Mr. Holton would like to see you," Cynthia said.

Murphy Monahan had wreaked havoc with the Thanksgiving plans of several second-shift NYNEX managers. Twenty minutes after his call, even before his arrival at Franklin Lakes, the telephone crew was at the IGC facility. Cynthia introduced Monahan to Holton. Also present was chief counsel Kiley.

"Mr. Monahan, it's your job to catch the people who have done this . . . and it's my job to make sure that the IGC Corporation is hurt as little as possible. While these interests would appear to be the same, it's entirely possible that at some point they may not be," said John Holton.

"You're not going to *pay* these people, are you?" said Monahan, astonished. "We haven't even *started* yet. We know their names! We have their descriptions. By tomorrow we'll have their picture and description in every airport in the country. *Serious* crimes have been committed, Mr. Holton. Murder. Kidnapping. Sabotage. *To your people! To your company!*"

"Mr. Monahan, whether these people know it or not, they've got us by the balls. IGC is a sixty billion dollar a year company. In five years we'll be a hundred billion dollar company — if we get through this. This thing could literally put us out of business within five years. The economic repercussions for us — for the country — are staggering." Holton paused.

To Murphy Monahan, John Holton epitomized the image of the ruthless business executive.

"If you catch these people and we don't recover the computer programs we need, you may have done *your* job — but I will have failed. If you kill them, or scare them into abandoning their project, then this company will die from the lawsuits that will be generated. I can't allow that to happen. While I appreciate what your objectives are — it's my job to save this company. I appreciate the phone tap, but it's more important to me that I talk with these people rationally — as business people. In the end, I will make the decision that is best for my company," said Holton coldly.

"We'll be ready within the hour," said Monahan.

Murphy Monahan knew that he'd just met someone who wouldn't flinch at the implied power of the three letters F-B-I.

Cynthia had listened, and understood. While the FBI wasn't the adversary, they weren't necessarily on the same team.

Marcia could see that David wasn't getting anywhere. He didn't want to admit failure — he *wouldn't* admit failure. Yet it was just around the corner. Her plan would be destroyed. Kimura would sit around and get them all caught. He was letting the FBI dictate the pace. He was deathly afraid of a telephone tap — but he wasn't getting the right words in.

It was time to switch gears.

Marcia went back into her room and sat down on the bed next to Cheryl.

"We've been talking with your brother Scotty for the last couple of hours now," Marcia started.

"Scotty?"

"Yes. But David thinks the FBI is playing games with him, which they probably are. David needs to start talking with IGC. *We* need for David to start talking with IGC," Marcia said softly, the implication clear. "By this time tomorrow you'll be back home in Cheyenne with your two lovely children, and I've already told you that you won't have a money problem for the rest of your life. But Cheryl, you're going to have to lie to your brother for me. It will be very short, and you won't have enough time to say more than a few words — the words *I* want you to say. Your brother knows how to reach IGC and I need for David to have that number. Will you help me?" Marcia asked in an even but persuasive voice, touching Cheryl's arm with her hand as she spoke.

Please say yes please say yes.

She has to understand the consequences.

And the consequences were real. If she couldn't get

Cheryl to cooperate, she'd have to one way or the other. Fortunately, Cheryl realized the facts of the situation and nodded yes.

"Good. Thank you." Marcia was relieved. "We're going to go into the other room and call the FBI again. When your brother answers I'm going to talk with him. Then I'm going to hold the phone so you can talk with him. I want you to say, 'Scotty this is Cheryl, help, please help,' right into the phone. Understand?"

Cheryl nodded yes.

"If instead you say something like, "Scotty, I'm at the Holiday Inn-San Francisco Airport," I can't guarantee your safety. Do you understand?"

Again Cheryl nodded.

"Yes, David," started Scotty, but he was immediately interrupted by a muffled conversation on the other end.

"We have your sister."

A woman's voice. A cold voice. Again, muffled sounds — then a cry.

"Scotty! It's Cheryl. Help me, please. Help me!"

"That's your sister, asshole!" shouted Marcia. "By the time I finish with her tonight, she'll never want a man again! We're going to poke her so bad . . ."

Muffled cries.

Scotty nearly went berserk.

"Leave her alone! Leave her alone! You bastards — you sons of bitches!" Scotty was so angry that he was close to losing his capability of speaking, to that point where words were mutated someplace between the mind and the vocal cords.

"Give me the fucking phone number," Marcia demanded crudely.

"What number?"

Ground control to Major Tom! Ground control to Major Tom!

Scotty had become one hundred percent brother and zero percent FBI agent.

"The number for IGC! You give me their number now and we'll put her panties back on and she'll have a nice night's sleep. NOW, God damn it!" Marcia shouted; her words ripped through the connection, grabbed him by the throat, and shook him right down to his shoes.

"Area 201, 868-1905. Cynthia Rosen," said Scotty in a gut reaction. "Please don't hurt my sister. *Please.* You don't have to do that. She didn't do anything," Scotty begged.

"What was that name?" asked Marcia.

"Rosen. Cynthia Rosen. She's my contact. *Please . . .*"

The phone went dead. Scotty was drenched with sweat. His breath came in gasps, his heart raced.

Alex Hastings came running down the hallway.

"We've got the first two numbers of the area code — it's four-one, something. Congratulations. We *just* got it. Whatever you said, was *just* enough," said Alex, beaming.

Sniveling and begging had saved the day, Scotty thought. A snivel in time saves nine. Whatever it takes.

Hastings reached for a very well used phone book and fingered through the first few pages.

"Area codes. Write them down," he instructed to Scotty, whose hand trembled as he picked up a pencil. "412-Pittsburgh; 413—Springfield, Mass; 414—Milwaukee; 415—San Francisco; 416—Toronto; 417—Missouri; 418—Quebec, Canada; 419—Toledo, Ohio. Way to go, Scotty!" Wyatt congratulated. "Two seconds less and we wouldn't have gotten the second number—look at this! 401—Rhode Island; 402—Nebraska; 403—Alberta, Canada; 404—Atlanta; 405—Oklahoma City; 406—Montana; 407—east Florida; 408—San Jose, California; 409—east Texas."

"She's from San Francisco. That's where they are," Scotty said with determination.

"How do you know?"

"I just *know*," Scotty answered, his eyes glazed.

Scotty picked up the phone and called Franklin Lakes. The conference room line was busy. He then dialed the main 201-868-1900 switchboard number.

"This is Scott Coldsmith with the FBI, calling from Denver. I need to talk with one of the special agents there, please. The conference room number is busy. It's very important," said Scotty.

The switchboard at Franklin Lakes had been inundated with calls since the middle of the afternoon, many of them the crank variety from every conceivable source. Scotty was lucky that management had been sensitized to the possibility of a real call coming through the main line and not through direct dialing.

Scotty reached the FBI room.

"This is Scott Coldsmith, who's this?"

"Jesus, Scotty—this is Chad. Are you having a good vacation?" his peer said with sarcasm. "Remind me not to get your travel agent."

"Where's Monahan?" Scotty asked.

"He's in the conference room with the woman. Kimura's on the line now. He's nervous as hell. We've got him hooked up to a speakerphone," replied the fellow Manhattan-based special agent.

"Is the tap set?" asked Scotty.

"No—we're almost there," he replied.

"Delay him—do anything! It's a San Francisco number, I know it! The first two digits are four and one. Tell Monahan that I'm leaving. I'm going to San Francisco. I'll call you in a couple of hours. Can you call the regional office and tell them I'm coming?"

"Sure—no problem," Chad replied.

"I'm gone," said Scotty, disconnecting.

In every major city across the country, the ISEN (Interactive Satellite Education Network) classrooms were packed. A typical classroom had eight large tables arranged in two rows of four — sixteen students per room. For each pair of students there was a switch box with Talk-Question lights that allowed a student to query the main studio and to talk with the instructor. The major studio locations were in New York, Washington, Dallas, Atlanta, Chicago, and San Francisco.

This evening every education center across the country was packed with IGC managers. Along with Al Benning and Amy Engle, who represented the Denver Commercial Branch, the two other Denver branches, Salt Lake City, Montana, and Albuquerque also were in attendance. In Los Angeles, Dallas, Washington, and other major cities, there were so many offices in the surrounding area that each classroom was standing room only.

The scheduled nine o'clock ISEN session began promptly at nine-thirty. John Holton was grateful it was only a half hour late. Time was leapfrogging. John Holton's image appeared on the screen. He did not introduce himself.

"I will be brief this evening. There is much for all of us to do. I'm afraid our Thanksgiving will have to be postponed until this is resolved. This morning our company was attacked by an unknown enemy. What has happened is not a joke, not a prank. A well-programmed virulent virus has swept through our company, encrypting every file it has come in contact with. Many of our best customers have been infected as well. Our company is literally paralyzed. Because of their sensitive nature, I cannot at this time tell you the status or details of the ransom demands; however, I am personally involved in their resolution.

"The reasons I have called you together this evening are twofold. One: I want to know the status of your office. Two: I want to know which of your customers have been infected. Area one, your lines are open," said the CEO.

Area by area, region by region, branch by branch, each manager described what shape his or her office was in. It quickly became obvious that the telephone disaster was "limited" to the major cities across the country. Numerically, approximately sixty percent of the offices were still open. Every large office had done what Denver had done—close down. Even without chitchat, the roll call still took nearly forty-five minutes to complete. At one point Holton was interrupted by an aide who passed him a note. Holton read the note, scribbled a response, then continued talking into the camera.

When all the offices had been polled, a grim-faced John Holton resumed.

"We have done our best here to communicate with the thousands of individuals who represent hundreds of customers—your customers. It is vital for you . . . early Friday . . . or tonight if possible . . . even tomorrow on Thanksgiving . . . to call your customers directly. Call them and tell them not to overreact on Friday. We will have a solution—shortly.

"We have established a twenty-four-hour hot line here in our temporary headquarters in Franklin Lakes. The telephone numbers are (201) 868-1950 and 1951. You may be assured that whatever message you leave will be delivered directly to me. Good evening."

There was no wish of a happy Thanksgiving.

427

There would be no happiness in Franklin Lakes this evening.

Upstairs, Cynthia and a few of the other team members watched as John Holton talked to his top managers. The conference room phone rang.

"This is Cynthia Rosen," she answered, with more than a touch of tiredness in her voice.

"This is David Kimura. I want to talk to you about the details of our upcoming meeting and to see if you have questions regarding our demands. I was just given your name by Scott Coldsmith of the FBI in Denver. Each of our conversations will be short because I am fearful of a phone tap. I will call you back in fifteen minutes. If you have not done so, please have a list of your questions ready by then. When we are done with your questions, or when I feel we are done, I will give you the details of our meeting. Will you be the spokesperson?" Kimura asked.

"Ye-yes," Cynthia stuttered, surprised to be talking with the man who had devastated her company.

Kimura hung up.

Neither Cynthia nor any of the other managers was about to do anything without the approval of John Holton.

"Assemble the team leaders, please," she instructed one of her Assessment/Control members.

Cynthia quickly jotted a note and gave it to another man, who happened to be a director level—light years above her in position levels.

WE HAVE BEEN CONTACTED BY DAVID KIMURA. HE WILL CALL BACK IN 15 MINUTES. WE ARE TO HAVE OUR QUESTIONS READY TO DISCUSS. MAY WE CONTINUE

ON OPTION THREE WITHOUT YOUR PRESENCE? THE TEAMLEADERS WILL BE HERE. AS WILL THE FBI.
CYNTHIA ROSEN

Five minutes later, corporate counsel Kiley, senior VP James Owens, World Trade Corporation president Charles DeToqueville, and former marketing manager turned administrative assistant now primary contact with the Evil Force, Cynthia Rosen, all sat at the north end of the huge conference table. Also in the room was Murphy Monahan. Just as the meeting was to start, one of Monahan's agents entered the room and handed him a note. Monahan smiled and pocketed the note.

"This is from my agent, Scott Coldsmith. A trace on the line in Denver has been partially successful. We believe Kimura is calling from the San Francisco area. NYNEX isn't ready yet—they say they will be within the hour. It is *vital* that you keep him on the line long enough for us to get the tap secured."

"I believe we have sufficient questions to keep Mr. Kimura busy," replied Kiley.

"Do you still want me to be the contact?" asked Cynthia, now feeling the huge corporate structure she was representing.

"Absolutely, Mrs. Rosen," said DeToqueville, the ranking member of the group.

"I agree," said Kiley.

Owens had no comment. After it was all done, they would each go back to their respective jobs. More than likely, Cynthia would never see any of the men again, except in internal publications. There would be no tenth reunion of the Great Siege.

"I believe each of us has questions," said Kiley. "Cynthia, you need to get him to describe exactly what it is we're going to get for our ransom." He turned to Owens.

"Jim, Charles is going to describe the unwieldy logistics of several of the demands, and you'll need to get him to quantify those demands into dollars. I'll have to find a way to transfer the money to a place we both can consider safe."

"That's not going to be easy," said Monahan. "Just from what I've observed so far—this man is very nervous. *Inexperienced* is a better word. He sounds like this is way over his head, and I'm not sure why. Whoever these people are, they certainly know computers—enough to have half the Fortune 500 cranking up lawsuits against you. I'm not a computer whiz, but their demands seem to be sophisticated—"

"*Too* sophisticated," interrupted DeToqueville.

"Yes, I agree. Too sophisticated. Smart people, fancy demands for technology—why not money? Good old American greenbacks. IGC's got a stash of them in every drawer. From what I've read over the years, you must have a billion or so laying around in paper bags. Maybe a couple of billion. Why not ask for that?" posed Monahan.

It was a question they all had in their heads: Why not money? Why technology?

"The obvious answer is that they've got enough money," said Owens.

"They want our brains—our . . . *smartness* . . . our innovation," added DeToqueville.

There was silence in the room.

"I think your assessment of your enemy is correct. We're dealing with a *country*, not a *company*. Which goes back to my original question. Why is David Kimura—the supposed inventor of this virus—dealing with you? They must have professional negotiators. They've planned this for a long, long time. You don't just do something like this on the spur of the moment."

Monahan looked down the table at the group. The

phone would ring any minute.

"I've gotten away from the point I was trying to make. Kimura is inexperienced. I want his telephone number so I can catch the bastard and his friends. You want his programming to save your company. *He* will get upset. *You* can't. You've got to remain as calm as you can."

The phone rang, startling them all. It seemed so loud.

"This is Cynthia Rosen," she replied, inwardly nervous.

"What is your first question?" asked David Kimura.

"We have divided your demands into four groups, Mr. Kimura. I have three other people with me — Mr. DeToqueville, president of our World Trade Corporation; Mr. Owens, vice-president of one of our marketing divisions; and Mr. Kiley, our chief legal counsel. I represent the internal systems group," Cynthia explained.

Monahan was timing the conversation. The black box was not yet installed. When fully installed, it would not only trace the call backward, but would also record the conversation, as needed. The recording feature was controlled by a toggle switch on the top of the box. Kiley passed a note to Cynthia.

"We are prohibited by law from selling or giving technology to Communist countries or companies who do business with these nations. What assurances do we have that you do not represent such parties?"

"None. We have no affiliation with communist nations. Please have your questions in a list. Good-bye," said Kimura, hanging up.

"It's going to be a long night," said Kiley.

"Thirty-eight seconds. Not enough time," added Monahan.

The phone rang again. This time neither party identified itself.

"Next," said Kimura.

Cynthia began to read the questions as they were

431

handed to her from the others, along with those she had.

"What format will the decryption program use?

"How will we be able to verify it?

"Where will the meeting be held?

"In order to turn over our microchip technology, we would need to break down one of our clean room assembly labs. There is very large, very delicate machinery involved. This cannot be done overnight. We estimate it will take two van loads of materials to satisfy this demand, and up to three weeks to properly disassemble — and an equal amount of time to reassemble it, assuming the proper environment. How will delivery be accomplished and verified? Or, will documentation be sufficient to meet this demand?

"While less complicated a process, our San Jose plant estimates that the materials involved in the 3395 disk drive assembly will occupy approximately one-half van load of data. The same delivery logistics question applies."

"Good-bye," said Kimura, hanging up.

"We just got started!" said Cynthia, frustrated.

"Hang in there," encouraged Monahan.

The phone rang again. As Cynthia answered, the NYNEX service rep gave Monahan the thumbs-up. The green light went on the box.

"We're rolling," whispered Monahan.

"Because of the shortness of time, we have been unable to contact some of our plants regarding the artificial intelligence programs. Since many of these programs are customer-specific, and involve national defense — which we cannot disclose under any circumstances — is it possible for us to negotiate a dollar amount for these items?

"Internally, we don't use the term Fifth Generation Computing. Is it possible for you to clarify exactly what you want in this area?

"With regard to the superconductivity data — this is a very tricky area for us. Some of our —"

"Good-bye," said Kimura in midsentence.

"Shit!" said Monahan and Cynthia almost in a single voice.

For each of his first three calls, David Kimura had remained on the line for a maximum of thirty-eight seconds. Not enough to even register the first digit of the area code, which we know is 4-1, thought Monahan.

Cynthia looked up to see John Holton standing in the doorway. He'd come in unnoticed, but had observed the team he'd assembled, and seemed to be pleased.

The phone rang again.

David's room had two double beds. Because of the antitheft nature of the furniture position, he had to use the tiny table between the two beds as his working space. The phone cord had almost no flexibility for movement, so David was forced to sit on the edge of the bed. Marcia sat on the other bed and timed his calls, pointing to him and saying "time," never letting more than forty seconds pass. This was an important piece of the plan. David had to get through all of IGC's questions tonight.

Tomorrow was game day.

David furiously wrote down another long question from IGC, scribbling the words in a cipher only he could understand — a dribble mixture of Japanese and English characters. While he hadn't been forced to say much, Marcia could tell he was nervous — very nervous. He wasn't trained for this.

"Time," she pointed to him.

"Good-bye," he said, hanging up, a bit angry and more than a bit frustrated. "How can they have so many questions?" he asked.

"What kind of questions are they, David?" asked Marcia.

"Logical questions," he said with a big sigh. "I guess I'm going to have to make some decisions." He pondered for a moment before continuing. "I don't know what Mr. Shinogara was planning to do. Surely these questions would have come up in any case. I can't believe his . . . our . . . backers would be prepared to set up multiple laboratories," he muttered.

"Is that what they think you want?"

"They . . . they're not sure. It seems a lot. They say the only way they can properly deliver their microchip technology is to dismantle one of their clean room laboratories."

"Jesus Christ, David—that's fucking stupid!"

"And the same thing applies for both the superconductivity lab in Zurich and—"

"Get a grip, David! For Christ's sake, get a grip! You can't handle something like that. Neither can your backers. You know that. We've almost been killed a couple of times! You've been lucky to get this far. Jesus Christ!" Marcia muttered. "They'll end up bringing every fucking Tom, Dick, and Harry and a cast of a thousand other yo-yos. It'll be a zoo. Even if somehow they manage to get all that crap to fucking Hong Kong, what's going to happen on the other side? That's not exactly your home turf, you know. Unless things have changed a lot since I've been there."

Marcia might not be eloquent, but, as usual, she was right on the money. David could see what Marcia was seeing—truckloads of high-tech vans, hermetically sealed, lumbering through the narrow, twisting streets of teeming Hong Kong. Behind each truck are limos filled with white-shirted IGC systems engineers.

Where do you want it, boss?

Talk about tech weenies on parade.

But Marcia could also see David's consternation. The whole objective of the exercise had been to get IGC's technology. Hurt them in the head — not the wallet . . . at least not right now.

"Answer their questions, David. But be prepared to make decisions quickly. We've got the tickets. We can be on a flight out of here in any direction within twenty minutes. But we can't fiddledick around forever. These people are *smart*. They're going to catch up."

United's Flight 221, an uncomfortable stretch DC-8, made a slow, wide turn to the north, then turned west to cross the Rockies. Ten miles from the crest line of the mountains, the flight hit a brick wall of air and slid down five hundred feet in no more than a second. Fortunately, the Fasten Seat Belts light was still lit. Flight attendants knew never to get up too soon when leaving Stapleton. The effect was similar to a plunging out-of-control elevator in a fifty-story building. Although several people were on the verge, nobody threw up — once *that* process started, it quickly becomes a chain reaction in the plane. Everybody forgets to breathe through his or her mouth until it's too late. In a few minutes the captain returned the flight to its original altitude and the rest of the flight was OK — there were more drinks than meals served.

The flight landed on time at 8:45 Pacific time.

Scotty's drive into the city took thirty-five minutes, and another fifteen minutes after exiting the Bayshore to get to the Federal Center at 900 Golden Gate Avenue. Parking, even at night on the night before Thanksgiving, was a problem — as was Scotty's reintroduction to the one-way streets in San Francisco. Seventh to Market to Hyde to Turk to Polk to Golden Gate. It was a pain in the butt.

There was something about the smell of a GSA building, Scotty thought. They were all alike. Was it the guards?

More than likely it was the heating and air-conditioning filters that hadn't been changed in fifteen years. The same spores and fungus that prospered in the Denver system seemed to thrive in San Francisco as well.

The unfortunate special agent who had been stuck with third-shift duty for the Thanksgiving weekend looked up at Scotty from the receptionist's desk. His name was Rhodes. He had red hair.

"Don't tell me—*Dusty* Rhodes?" said Scotty smiling.

If he'd been back in New York City, Scotty just might have been pulling the same miserable duty.

The kid nodded, then inspected Scotty's badge.

"Are you alone?" Scotty asked.

"Until Friday morning, eight o'clock. I'm it."

Man, oh man.

"Well, Dusty—we've got a big case. And I have a hunch that you're going to be part of it."

Scotty spent the better part of a half hour explaining to the agent what was happening. He then called Franklin Lakes.

"We have an additional question regarding the safety—"

"Cynthia?" said Scotty.

"Scott? What are you doing on this line? Get off!" said an irritated Cynthia Rosen.

"Let me talk to Monahan please," requested Scotty.

"Call back on extension 1920," said Monahan, obviously grabbing the phone from Cynthia, then hanging up just as quickly. Scotty dialed (201) 868-1920.

"Monahan," the SAC answered on the first ring.

"Jesus, Murphy—you're quick," complimented Scotty.

"We've been busy while you've been flying through the night. Kimura has been getting a bit stronger. He

436

and the woman are working as a team. I can hear her telling him to stop — we just haven't been able to get any further than the first digit. They're about to drive the IGC people nuts," said Monahan, his adrenaline pumping.

I'm sure the feeling is mutual, Scotty said.

The phone rang for the twenty-second time.

"David, we just don't see how we're going to get Dr. Bednorz and Dr. Mueller to release their life's work. They're IGC employees, but they've got a special status in the world — they're research scientists. They've got so much of their work locked in their head. Without their cooperation, we're not sure whether the data you want is what you'd get. We haven't been able to reach either of the scientists yet. Isn't there any way we can negotiate on this issue?" asked Cynthia.

In the last two hours, with John Holton approving each step with a silent nod, they had negotiated a price of $500 million for dropping the Fifth Generation Computing demand. The artificial intelligence applications from Yorktown Heights and the Watson Research Lab had been agreed to, as well as those in the area of telecommunications under development in the Raleigh, North Carolina, plant. No price had been stipulated. IGC Lab managers in all three sites had been contacted. The materials could be produced. Holton had personally instructed the management team to begin gathering the appropriate materials and have them ready by Thursday afternoon.

The sticky issues had been the superconductivity and the microchip technology. David Kimura had been insistent on having both. He had agreed to schematic drawings for the internals of the unannounced 3395 magnetic disk units and the preliminary plans for the

3396 units. Prototypes of both were available and could be delivered easily.

"And David, you haven't yet told us how we are going to verify your program. It's very important to—"

"Good-bye," he said, hanging up.

"—us—you god damn son-of-a-bitch!" Cynthia slammed the phone down, surprising everyone in the room with the vehemence of her action. She needed to let off steam. She'd been word-playing with David Kimura for nearly five hours.

They were all in shirtsleeves. Empty coffee cups littered the room, along with plates of cold cuts brought up from Franklin Lakes' newest all-night deli located on the first floor of the IGC building. Holton reached across the table and put his hand on Cynthia's arm.

"You're doing a good job, Cynthia. It's frustrating, I know. I think anybody else in this room would have told Kimura to piss up a rope a couple of hours ago. You're doing just fine."

"Thank you. I just don't know . . ." Cynthia's voice trailed off as she put her head in her hands.

"What are you going to do about the remaining two demands?" she asked, hoping there was a way to resolve the issues. Time was beginning to become a factor. Unbeknownst to David, in less than ten hours Marcia was scheduled to meet with Xiang Wu and his backers, where diskettes would be exchanged for airline tickets, passport, and verification of deposit in her Geneva bank account.

"I don't know," he said, picking up the phone to call IGC for the twenty-third time.

David's back ached from being in the uncomfortable position for such a long time. Cynthia answered the

438

phone again.

"The superconductivity plans are at the heart of our demands," David started. "We would be willing to settle for schematics and layout drawings for the microchip technology demand. But we are unwilling to drop or to renegotiate superconductivity. I understand that you have logistic difficulties given that your Zurich laboratory is halfway around the world. But that's your problem. I'll give you an hour before I call back," David said forcefully, then hung up.

The call lasted only eighteen seconds.

"I'm going to get something to eat. Do you want me to bring you something?" Marcia asked.

David shook his head no, then yes. Then he lay back on the bed and was asleep within thirty seconds.

It was tough being a bad guy.

Chapter Eight
Thursday, 20 November
No Deals

It wasn't time yet!

The phone's ringing jarred them out of a semi-intensive discussion of Major Events. Even a very tired John Holton had been drawn into the philosophical discussion of superconductivity.

"We're not ready yet. Tell him that!" said Owens, a heavy undergrowth of beard beginning to show. They all needed a new round of deodorants. Murphy Monahan had gone downstairs to get something to eat, as had his single remaining agent and the third-shift service rep from NYNEX. *Free food!*

Cynthia went for the phone for the twenty-fourth time.

"We're not ready yet. You said you'd give us an hour," she said with a mild undertone of irritation.

There was a pause on the line.

"This isn't David. It's Marcia Lee. I'm calling from a pay phone. I know you have the FBI listening to this conversation, trying to get a tap on the line. You *have* to. It's late, but I have information that can solve all of our problems. I'm willing to make a deal with you—but only with me. Not with David Kimura," said Marcia. "Hello?" she added.

Cynthia fumbled for words. Everyone was alert. The adrenaline had kicked in for what seemed to be the tenth time in a single day—enough to make a person sleep for a week.

"This is Cynthia Rosen." Cynthia's hand hovered over the black box, its green light glowed, the little computer searching away for the far-off telephone number.

Cynthia's eyes asked the group, all of whom leaned over the table's edge in earnest interest. Her eyes found John Holton's.

Do I turn the tape recorder off? she wondered.

Cynthia found her speech.

"How do we know? Why should we make a deal with you, Miss Lee? You don't have the best of reputations," added Cynthia, with some sting in her voice.

Jim Owens's face contorted into a pained expression of *oh no, how could she say that.*

I'm tired of these people, thought Cynthia.

"I have the diskettes. He doesn't. He's bluffing you. Tell me to leave, and I'm gone!"

"No! Wait!" Cynthia shouted.

Murphy Monahan came back into the room, his hands filled with a plate of cold roast beef and cheese, pickles, cole slaw, and a mound of potato chips, all balanced on top of a giant Styrofoam cup of Coke.

For a brief second Monahan didn't realize that they were back in contact. John Holton nodded his head to Cynthia, who toggled the recorder to the Off position.

Marcia spoke to Cynthia alone. There was no speakerphone attached. No recording. NYNEX, however, was getting a fix on the location — and Cynthia knew it.

"I know who did this. I have names, places, people, times — and proof. I have the diskettes — the programs you need. We can make a deal. I'll call back in a few minutes. Screw around with me and I'll erase the fucking diskettes — or throw them into the . . ."

Marcia's voice trailed off. She'd almost given away her location.

"Don't go!" Cynthia shouted again.

Monahan nearly dropped his late-night snack all over the plush blue carpet.

The line went dead.

"You stopped the recording!" said Murphy.

"It was an accident! I got excited. I'm sorry," replied Cynthia.

Cynthia's eyes talked with John Holton's.

What am I supposed to do?

Monahan knew something was happening.

"What was that all about?" he asked.

Cynthia looked at John Holton again. The others sat immobile at the table, hardly breathing.

"Mr. Monahan, we have some information we would rather not disclose to you at this time. It's between them — and us. Only Mrs. Rosen has heard it. I asked her to turn the recorder off."

"These people are killers! Why?" Monahan nearly shouted.

John Holton stood up, put both hands down on the polished oak conference table, and leaned over toward the FBI chief.

"I told you there might come a time when our interests would diverge. You have your telephone information. We have information that we must consider to be proprietary — even to the FBI."

"I'll get a court order," threatened Monahan.

"And do what?" asked a cool John Holton.

There was nothing Monahan could do but follow up on what he had. John Holton walked around the table and stood nearly eyeball-to-eyeball with the SAC.

"Mr. Monahan, this doesn't mean we aren't going to cooperate. Far from it. We don't want to lose *any* of our assets. But we need time — *by ourselves*. We don't want you to leave. But we would like some time to discuss things — as corporate officers, perhaps not as citizens. We will cooperate in every way possible," said the smooth CEO as he escorted Murphy Monahan to the door. "Thank you. We'll call you in a few minutes."

At that moment the NYNEX service rep came and handed Monahan a note.

"They've got the first two digits of the exchange. Whatever you're going to do with these folks, you'd better do it quickly," Monahan said, walking back to his temporary office.

The conference room door closed behind him.

"We're getting closer!" shouted an ecstatic Scotty, on the phone with a very angry Murphy Monahan. "They're in the five-eight something exchange! Do you know where that is?" he asked Dusty Rhodes.

Rhodes pulled out the San Francisco Bay Area Yellow Pages. In less than a minute he had the page with the local exchanges.

"South San Francisco — San Bruno — Milbrea —

Burlingame. It's down by the airport area," said the red-haired young man. "What happened?"

"Marcia Lee called. Monahan says something's going on between Kimura and the IGC people. He thinks they're trying to work out a deal behind our backs. She called, but this time stayed on the phone too long. She's calling from someplace down by the airport. Who can we get?" he asked Rhodes.

"This time of night? I mean, morning. It's Thanksgiving."

The kid was right, even though the stakes warranted getting forces out of bed. There was so little time.

"If she's in South San Francisco, then she's at a motel—or a restaurant—or a phone booth. She's up and about. She's good looking and she's up and about. Someone's seen her! We need a car with a telephone—do you have one?" Scotty asked Rhodes.

"Yes," Rhodes said.

Scotty and Rhodes took off in a race against the morning.

"That's what she said. *She* had the diskettes—the programs we need. She wants to make a deal," said Cynthia.

"What kind of deal?" asked attorney Kiley.

"She didn't say. She said she would call right back. She says she knows who did this . . . names, places—everything."

John Holton looked at his group. We don't make deals with terrorists was ingrained into the American psyche.

The phone rang again.

"This is Marcia Lee. Is the line being tapped?"

"Yes," replied Cynthia, honestly.

"Is the FBI there with you?" asked Marcia.

"No. But they have a partial fix on your location," Cynthia blurted.

Somehow the truth seemed to be the best. Both Jim Owens and attorney Kiley started to object, but were held back by Holton.

"Let's see where this takes us," he whispered.

"I can hear voices, and I know I'm on a speakerphone. Who's there with you?" she demanded.

"I'm with our chairman of the board, Mr. Holton; our chief legal counsel, Mr. Kiley; the president of our World Trade Corporation, Mr. DeToqueville; and the head of one of our marketing divisions, Mr. Owens. Nobody else. But yes, the line is being tapped by the telephone company."

"I'll call right back." The phone disconnected.

Kiley started to give Cynthia a word of caution, then thought better of it. She was doing fine on her own. It was hard to say what the exact right path through the maze was—getting through was the important thing. The phone rang again.

"My name is Marcia Lee. I was hired to do a job by a foreign organization—David Kimura's employers. My specialty is sexual blackmail." Cynthia blushed, as did the men in the room. "Zack Colby was selected because he had computers at home and access to your systems. I gave him drugs and my body—and he gladly took both. So he was no choirboy. In the middle of October a second organization—also foreign—contacted me and subsequently hired me to be, in effect, a double agent. While

David Kimura and his people programmed your systems, I reported the activity to my second employer."

Marcia paused. The IGC conference room was still.

"All of David's employers and all but one of *my* people, *and* Zack Colby were murdered by the hired assassins of my second employer," Marcia stopped. "I'm going to go to another phone. When I call back in five minutes or so, I'm going to finish—then ask for your decision."

The line went dead.

Murder, blackmail, sabotage, Cynthia thought, perhaps even espionage. I'm not prepared for this—I don't know what to do.

But Cynthia wasn't alone.

The Big Carrot lay on the conference room table: a simple box of diskettes. She had them. The programs to make all of their systems usable. The programs to make all of their customers' systems usable. No lawsuits. No loss of productivity. No loss of ransomed technology.

A deal.

The phone rang.

"Have you made your mind up?" It was David Kimura.

Had an hour gone by already? It couldn't!

Cynthia snapped her mind back to the last time they'd talked with David. That was before they'd talked to Marcia Lee twice. And before they'd had a semi-falling-out with the FBI.

"We've reached one of the scientists, but not the other. Please, can't you wait a little longer? We're doing the best we can," Cynthia lied, with increasing sophistication and skill. "It's going to take us a while. We're tired. *You* must be tired."

"I will give you until seven o'clock to make all your contacts," David said, hanging up.

Not thirty seconds later the phone rang again.

"Was that David?" asked Marcia.

"Yes," replied Cynthia, holding her head with her right hand. She had a splitting headache.

"The meeting in Hong Kong is real. David believes he has two copies of his program—but he doesn't. I have the program. I have the decryption keys. Please listen to me closely. I have a meeting scheduled with my second employer. We have a deal. I give him the diskettes, he gives me a new passport, identification, and a nice deposit in my Swiss account." Marcia paused, knowing she was almost out of time.

"She hung up," said Cynthia, her head reeling.

Not a word was spoken as the four IGCers waited for Marcia's return call, which came exactly two minutes later.

"I could just as easily give you the diskettes. Zack Colby was blackmailed because David Kimura's employers wanted economic revenge on your company. The second group wants this encryption program to be permanent. They're in it for the gain to be made in the various stock markets throughout the world. They have invested staggering amounts of money already. I have their names . . . and I would be willing to testify against them. When this comes to trial, I want immunity. I want safe passage out of the country, and twenty million dollars deposited in my account. Today. What is your decision?"

"But today's Thanksgiving . . . it's a holiday . . . how can . . ." Cynthia stuttered anxiously.

447

"It's not Thanksgiving in Europe, for Christ's sake! Now what's your decision?"

"Yes," said John Holton, leaning across the table, interrupting Cynthia. "We agree."

"All arrangements must be in place by ten o'clock this morning—West Coast time. Remember, when you talk with him—David Kimura knows nothing of this."

"Yes, we agree," said John Holton.

"I'll call you back in fifteen minutes." Marcia hung up.

The chairman of the board of IGC had just agreed to making a deal with a blackmailing whore.

"Are you . . . we . . . *really* going to do this?" said James Owens in near shock.

"What do *you* think?" said Holton, smiling.

While Rhodes drove, Scotty made contact with Monahan, who was still steamed.

"They're making a deal with these people, Scott. You've got to find them."

It was the first time in Scotty's memory that Monahan had called him by his first name—and not the diminutive version everybody used.

"I only heard a piece of it before she . . . the Rosen woman . . . turned the speakerphone and recorder off. I *know* it wasn't an accident. They want to deal. The Lee woman has the diskettes—the programs they're looking for, not Kimura. They're around there someplace, Coldsmith—find them!"

The 582, 588, 587, and 589 exchanges were all in the airport district. There were nearly a hundred motels nearby, and who knows how many pay phones. Using the map and the motel section of San Francisco Yellow Pages they'd made the judgment to go south of the airport and come back north.

"There are more hotels to the south. The odds are better," said young Rhodes.

Better than what? thought Scotty.

The only people awake were party goers and night clerks. Scotty came out of the Sheraton shaking his head, in his hand a picture of Marcia, her face frozen in a moment of sexual energy.

"If we're going to get a visual tonight, we need some help. We're at the wrong time of the day. We need to get their descriptions to the day managers and the maids. Jesus!" Scotty hit the roof of the car with his fist in frustration.

Scotty was enough of a realist to know that getting the South San Francisco or Burlingame police to help an out-of-state FBI agent look for two criminals who *might* be in one of the motels or hotels along the airport strip—and that they had to be apprehended, not shot—and that there was a kidnapping involved . . .

You really don't want anybody else involved, do you?

No. Nobody else understands.

I'm going to get Marcia Lee. I swear that she'll never see the light of day again.

Marcia stood in the semidarkness of an outside phone booth at the edge of the Radisson Inn's parking lot, not two miles from the Sheraton Hotel. Outside the well-insulated rooms, the night air was filled with the sounds of airport and highway—the high-pitched whine of jet engines hurt the ears even from

449

this distance. Behind her, trucks lumbered along the Bayshore in both directions. The air smelled of exhaust fumes.

This would be the next-to-last call.

"Do we have a deal?" she asked. The very cool night breeze ruffled her hair and brought goosebumps to her neck.

"Mr. Holton has authorized me to say — yes — we have a deal. You were right . . . it isn't Thanksgiving in Europe," said Cynthia.

"Excellent. Here is what I want . . ."

Marcia rattled off items as if she was reading from a list.

Pay the bastards back in spades, she thought.

Marcia finished her requirements.

"Do you have everything?" she asked.

"Yes . . . yes, we have everything," replied Cynthia.

"It's now one-thirty in the morning. I meet with the people who want your diskettes at ten o'clock. I ask you one more time . . . do we have a deal?"

"This is John Holton. You have a deal. In return for twenty million dollars you will provide us with the programs to decrypt our computers and the names of the people who have done this. Is that agreeable?" asked Holton.

"Yes," returned Marcia.

"Good-bye, Miss Lee," said Holton hanging up.

"Mr. Monahan, could you please come back inside?" said James Owens.

Monahan walked back inside the large conference room. The IGCers were seated around the same end

450

of the table they'd been at for the last fourteen hours.

"Where's Mrs. Rosen?" he asked.

"She had to excuse herself. She was just too tired. The hours have been difficult," replied Holton, his hands folded across his chest.

Monahan could read eyes, too.

"Damn. You've made a deal with them, haven't you?" he said, amazed.

"Not *them*, Mr. Monahan—*her*, the one known as Marcia Lee," said John Holton. "IGC does not make deals with terrorists, Mr. Monahan. I thought I told you that. Please don't be offended by your exclusion this past hour and a half. We've had to make serious corporate decisions—the same kind of decisions a mother and father would be forced to make if their child were kidnapped. You are the police. But the first decision is ours to make. It's our decision to pay or not to pay. You were a part of the earlier meetings—but this last . . . is family. I hope you understand," said Holton.

Monahan's face was filled with anger and disappointment. He could barely contain himself.

"As I said, our enemy is split. We have just completed an additional call from David Kimura. We have verbally agreed to supply him with the superconductivity plans. He will call back one more time, this morning, with the details for the scheduled meeting in Hong Kong. We don't know when this will be, although we have urged him to be prompt. We believe, as a corporation, that we can forestall the dogs for a few days, but not much longer. We've asked him that the meeting be scheduled this weekend, if possible," rambled a tired John Holton.

"You said something about them being split?" asked Monahan, partially mollified, but not quite.

"We have no intention of bringing our superconductivity plans to Hong Kong. They will stay in our Zurich lab. We have no intention of disclosing our plans for microchip technology, which will remain in the vaults of Burlington. Likewise, we have no intention of handing over our secrets for future disk drive products, nor pay outrageous sums of money for our programming expertise," stated Holton firmly.

"I thought . . ." started a confused Murphy Monahan.

"Yes, so did we, Mr. Monahan. Marcia Lee has told us that David Kimura does not have the programs—that *she* has them. Something has happened to the enemy. There is disarray. There will be no meeting in Hong Kong. We have agreed to transfer twenty million dollars—a *piddling* amount considering what has happened, and what could happen—and have already done so. We consider it the cost of business. We'll add a few dollars to the price of our products or squeeze more productivity from our sales people—*something*—the money is not relevant." Holton waved his hand, trivializing the amount. "It doesn't matter because she won't be able to spend a dime of it! You'll catch her—the people that hired her—and a third group of people who have murdered at least fifty people in an attempt to see that IGC becomes permanently ruined!" Holton pounded the table angrily.

Monahan sat down in one of the comfortable chairs. It was a mistake. His legs started sending *oh no* signals to his brain. Thoughts weren't coming in a straight line. I want to sleep was mixed with Get off your ass.

"Mr. Monahan, I'm not anxious for the FBI to catch these people until we have our programs. You're familiar with personal computers?" Holton asked.

"Yes, we've finally reached the twentieth century within the Bureau—they aren't *yours*, but yes we have computers. Apparently IGC wasn't the low bidder. Internally, their official names are Intelligent Workstations. Given how they're used, I'm not sure that's the correct terminology," Monahan replied.

Holton walked up to the podium and returned with a PC diskette in one hand and a magnet in the other.

"This is a miniature magnetic disk, a floppy diskette. In principle, this does the same thing for personal computers as our 3380 disk units do for mainframe computers—they both store data. When I pass this magnet past this diskette, the data on the diskette becomes unusable. It's not just scrambled, or encrypted—it's *unusable*. Marcia Lee knows this. From our conversations with both David Kimura and Marcia Lee, we believe that Kimura is unknowingly running a bluff and that Miss Lee actually has the disks. We need those diskettes, Mr. Monahan," said Holton.

Monahan said nothing.

"In the last hour and a half we have talked with Marcia Lee three times. My gut impression is that she's a tough cookie. If she was trapped, I don't think she'd hesitate to wipe out a box of diskettes. All you have to do is pop the lid and run the magnet across the top. No more than five seconds. All gone," said Holton.

"What kind of deal do you have with her?" asked Monahan, now more curious than angry.

"She and Kimura have tickets on a flight to an unknown destination, leaving late tomorrow . . . *this* . . . morning, out of San Francisco International. Since our meeting with Kimura is scheduled to be in Hong Kong, we *could* assume that the flight would be westbound—but the earth is round, and you can get to Hong Kong from almost *any* direction. Kimura's employers were from Japan—essentially the Japanese government. We don't know their names, but she will provide them. We aren't surprised, but we need evidence to prosecute—*you* need evidence to prosecute. We need names, places—evidence.

"We have made the same comment you made earlier—why is David Kimura negotiating? The reason he is negotiating alone is that his group was assassinated this past Saturday by a group of Chinese who are attempting to manipulate the American stock markets by making sure this virus is not cured.

"You see, Mr. Monahan, Marcia Lee not only has the only copy of the decryption programs, but she also has the knowledge you and I need to prosecute these evil people for the things they've done. She says over fifty people in Kimura's organization have been murdered, along with four of her people," said Holton.

"And you've already paid her?" asked Monahan.

"Yes. She demanded verification before making the agreement, before telling us the information I've just related. Twenty million may be a lot to you and me, but it is insignificant compared to the billions of dollars worldwide that are at stake."

"So what does she want? What's the deal?"

"She claims to have a false passport, identification, and transportation—which may or may not be by air. Sometime this morning she will call us and tell us the names of the Japanese businessmen, the identification of the second group, *and* the location of David Kimura and Mrs. Colby. The meeting will be someplace within the airport—*anyplace*—apparently she's being a businesswoman to the bitter end. She's exacted a promise from them—money for the diskettes," said Holton.

"Why?" asked Monahan.

"I don't understand," questioned Holton.

"Why is she going to tell you all this?" asked Monahan.

"Some things in today's world *are* simple. Revenge. Nothing more. Sweet revenge. She wants to stick it to them because they murdered her people. She says that her meeting place will give her sufficient access for escape, yet there will be time for you to catch the criminals," said Holton.

"She doesn't think of herself as a criminal?" Monahan asked.

"I would guess she does, but not *that* kind of one," speculated Holton.

Monahan's brain seemed to be hitting on three cylinders. Something's missing—what is it? he thought.

"You *will* see that the airport puts on extra security, won't you? I'd hate to go to all this trouble, only to have all these people get away," asked Holton.

"Why has she done this, Mr. Holton?" Monahan asked. "I understand revenge and all . . . but she doesn't have to go to all this trouble . . . and neither

455

do you."

"Like I said before, Mr. Monahan. IGC does not make deals with terrorists—with criminals," said Holton seriously.

"But she *thinks* she's got a deal," added Monahan with a question in his eyes.

"That's right. After all . . . we're honorable people."

You son of a bitch, Monahan thought.

As Scotty began his hotel-to-hotel search, two miles to the north, Marcia returned to the lobby of the Holiday Inn, picked up two packages from the front desk, and handed the clerk a one hundred-dollar bill.

IGC had been receptive, but she was taking no chances. One of the packages the clerk handed her was filled with take-out food, which she first brought back to a very sleepy David Kimura.

He was sound asleep.

"What?" He rolled over toward her.

He'd been asleep for thirty-five minutes.

"How are you doing?" she asked.

"I've *got* to get some sleep," he said, seemingly drugged.

"What's the last word?" she asked.

"I'm going to call them tomorrow morning—what time do we leave?" His thought patterns were flipping.

"It's *today*. We leave *today*. In the next eight hours or so. What did you negotiate?" she asked, knowing full well that IGC knew David Kimura was full of shit.

"They agreed to everything! You missed it!" David's mind came back to reality. "They're going to meet us in Hong Kong! Next week!" he said excitedly, but nearly in a semi-drugged state.

David had been single-handedly negotiating with one of the world's largest corporations, under an FBI-dictated time-slice schedule, for nearly ten hours. It had been difficult beyond his imagination. IGC had redefined the meaning of methodical.

"I . . . I . . . must get some sleep," he said.

Marcia could see David's body shriveling into sleepytime.

"We should plan to leave here at eleven-thirty. I'm going to sleep as well. I'll have the front desk put a wake-up call for us at ten-thirty. Good night, David—I'll be right next door," she said with a smile.

You're history, asshole.

Even good guys get tired.

By four-thirty they had combed most of the lower motel group south of the airport. The hotels were larger than they looked. In a few, they actually got to talk to people who could look at billing records—nobody named Lee or Kimura, *many* people who paid cash, nobody good-looking with black hair who had been out in the night air for a walk, to a telephone.

The combination was improbable.

"Is anybody hungry?" said Scotty.

The answer was a universal yes. Of course, Denny's was Always Open. At six o'clock on a Thanksgiving morning, the tired pair walked out of the semi-fast food emporium to a radiophone.

457

Squawk-o-rama.

After an unintelligible repetition of the identifications, young Dusty determined that the call was for Scotty.

"Coldsmith! All hell is going to break loose there this morning. They're going to make a deal with her! *She's* got what they want—not Kimura! Sometime this morning she's going to make a break for it at the airport. IGC says that she's going to tell us where your sister is, where Kimura is, and who all these other people are!"

"Have they talked about Cheryl?" asked Scotty.

"They're going to release her—unharmed," replied Monahan. "I'm going to call the chief of airport security. I want you to break off what you're doing and go to the airport," instructed Monahan.

"But we're close! I know it!" protested Scotty.

"First things first, son," Monahan replied.

Damn.

"Airport," said Scotty, his face flushed with anger and embarrassment.

Monahan had been right—but it didn't take away the sting he felt inside . . . like a kid who'd been told to clean up his plate before he could go outside and play. Ten minutes later Dusty pulled up alongside the curb at the Delta terminal and asked one of the traffic cops where the security office was.

"Upper level—midway," replied the tall man, pointing across the airport to the United terminal.

Dusty drove down to the United terminal and pulled up to the curb. Scotty got out, flashed his FBI badge, and told the cop that the car was going to be parked there for a few hours.

God, I hate airports, Scotty thought.

458

Airports were just about the worst place in the world to try and capture any criminal, especially someone who hadn't been identified clearly. People all looked so *normal*. The last thing any law enforcement officer wanted to do was to have to draw a weapon in a crowded public place like an airport terminal. The *very last* thing anyone wanted to do was to have to *fire* the weapon.

Taking the escalator to the upper level, the three men sought the office of airport security.

Denton Holmes was not at all pleased to be awakened at seven-thirty on Thanksgiving morning, cheated out of a rare opportunity to sleep in late. His wife had been very reluctant to wake him, but the man had been so insistent.

"Dear . . . it's the FBI. Long distance. He says it's important. I'm sorry," she apologized.

Denton Holmes was the director of security for the San Francisco International airport, a job that was beyond bitch. SFO had four major horseshoe-shaped terminals, each with three usable levels—all in the open style of architecture common to many airports. Access for arriving passengers was a nightmare. A significant portion of his manpower was used in traffic control, not in airport security. The three lanes closest to the terminal were used for arriving passengers; however, the lanes were narrow and were on a gradual U-shaped turn. Outbound, on the other side of a concrete island, were three more lanes for the thousands of buses that made the various loop trips from hotels and rental car agencies. For deplaning passengers, the airport was as

459

unfriendly to use as could be conceived. Arriving on the middle level, passengers went down one level, picked up their luggage, then went back *up* one level, across the three lanes packed with departing passengers to the narrow island where everyone had to stand in the exact same space to catch rental cars or hotel buses. It tended to bottleneck. On Fridays it tended toward gridlock. On holidays it was worse.

Yesterday it had been worse.

Thanksgiving Day itself was a less-than-normal day—usually.

Denton struggled downstairs to the phone.

"Yes," he said, trying to impart a feeling of great inconvenience.

There was no pity on the other end.

"This is Murphy Monahan, special agent-in-charge of the Manhattan New York office of the FBI. Are you aware of the computer virus situation?"

Denton looked down at his copy of the *San Francisco Chronicle*.

COMPUTER VIRUS SWEEPS NATION
IGC, CUSTOMERS STRICKEN
STOCK MARKET TREMBLES WITH A CASE OF BIG BLUES

Denton picked up the paper, scanned it, then let it drop to the kitchen table.

"I see it," was his reply.

"The people who have done this are making a deal with IGC this morning—someplace inside your airport. Do you have a fax at your house?"

Installation of the fax machine in his office at

460

home had been an incredible convenience for Denton, but one that his wife hadn't cared for. It was bad enough that he'd get calls at all hours of the night and day—now *they* could send him *stuff* anytime as well.

"Yes," Denton gave Monahan the number.

"We're sending you a photo of a woman named Marcia Lee. She will be meeting with a group of men—either Japanese or Chinese—to exchange a box of computer diskettes. We are after both parties. The Lee woman believes that IGC will assist her and has agreed to provide the location of the group of men, sometime this morning. She believes that the timing will be close enough to let her escape, yet trap the group of men. She will tell us the identity of the men in the call. What I would like is added security at the street exits and security machines. I also need to know how I can contact you at any time over the next four to five hours."

"Anything else, Mr. Monahan?" said Denton Holmes with undisguised sarcasm.

"I think that's it," Monahan replied, the sarcasm unnoticed.

"Do you know what terminal—what airline?" Denton asked.

"No, we don't. It could be anything," replied Monahan.

"First of all . . . we're on a reduced morning shift and an even lower shift in the afternoon. I'll do the best I can, but on two hours' notice, I won't have a full complement. I can guarantee you that. You've been to my airport, I assume," asked Holmes.

"Yes," replied Monahan.

"Then you know that my terminals are physically

461

separated and are not terribly close together. It'll take a good ten minutes for my men to get from one to the other and get in position. Do you want to take a guess on where they might be, and load up—or do you want me to spread them out evenly?" asked Holmes.

This is one of those situations in life that is absolutely guaranteed to be a loser, Monahan thought. No matter which I pick, it would be wrong. The finger pointing would be pretty easy.

"No—spread your men," said Monahan reluctantly.

"I'll do my best," replied Holmes.

Monahan paused, long enough for Holmes's eyes to flash back to the *Chronicle's* headlines.

"I know you're going to think that this is typical FBI bullshit—but it's very important that my people be there. There's so much more involved. I don't want any of your people killed. And what is being exchanged between the girl and the men is vital to the country. Please don't take offense, but I'm having one of my best agents meet you at the airport. He's probably there by now."

It was hard for Holmes not to take offense, but he nevertheless understood. Most of his security force were paid little more than minimum wage. Airport security was generally a presence, not a force. His people were mostly black, mostly low paid, and mostly a front. There were exceptions, but most were not highly skilled police officers. The weapons they wore, they knew how to fire. It was a requirement. Knowing how to fire a weapon, and actually firing one in a combat situation, were two entirely different situations.

462

"How can I reach you?" asked Monahan.

Holmes gave him his pager phone, his car phone, his office phone, his fax phone, and the main security desk at the airport.

A man *can* have too many phones.

Marcia's internal alarm woke her after a nap of two hours and fifteen minutes. The room was chilly, but she had been sleeping close to Cheryl and had been warm and toasty. Still, she'd managed to wake up on time. It was an acquired skill. Marcia quietly rolled over to her side and slipped out of the comfortable bed, her feet softly padding on the worn carpet. She reached down and shook Joe, who was in a deep sleep. His internal alarm immediately went off. He rolled over, nodded acknowledgment to Marcia, then quickly began the process of waking up. Wearing only panties and a T-shirt, Marcia slipped on a pair of pants and a raincoat, then stepped into a pair of jogging shoes. As quietly as she could, she opened the door to the room, which had been left unlocked all night.

She stepped out into a thick, gray morning. The motel's interior courtyard was ringed with plants and bushy shrubs, all dripping with the morning mist. Marcia walked to the motel lobby, then directly to the first of two pay telephones, each of which was enclosed for privacy. Two businessmen stood in line as the clerk efficiently checked the men out. It was the same clerk who a few hours ago had received a crisp one hundred-dollar bill from Marcia for performing a simple task.

Marcia dropped a quarter into the telephone box

and dialed Xiang Wu's number.

"Good morning, Miss Lee," was his instant response.

"I trust you had a profitable day," she said, restraining her sarcasm.

"Indeed," was Wu's enthusiastic response.

Marcia looked at her watch, which read 7:40 A.M. She had a little more than two hours before the single most important moments in her life would occur. She ran a hand through her long black hair.

"Our meeting will be in the Delta Crown Room at the airport. Ten o'clock. Only three guests will be admitted. I have reserved a section of the room under the name of Lee."

"I assume the financial arrangements are satisfactory?" asked Xiang Wu, his voice not missing a beat even with the unexpected news.

"Yes. I assume you will have passports, identity, and airline tickets," Marcia asked.

There was a slight pause.

"Yes, I have them," Wu responded correctly.

"Good. I have the diskettes. I will see you at ten."

Marcia hung up, her heart racing. Small beads of sweat popped out above her eyebrows. Unconsciously, her mind had told her body that this was a Big Deal.

Marcia walked over to a table and poured a cup of coffee, then went outside and sat near the pool, unmindful to the wet dew that had accumulated on the rubber-thonged seats.

The nondescript black Buick pulled up in front of 820 Grant Street and casually blocked northbound traffic. Behind the Buick was an equally nondescript Chevy Caprice, which came to a stop not two feet behind. Inside were five men in need of a shave. Outside, no one made a fuss. To the residents of Chinatown, this Thursday morning was like any other. Thanksgiving was an *American* holiday. But in Chinatown, it was business as usual. The Buick's thick driver got out and positioned himself to open the back curbside door. Out stepped Jimmy Chimichanga. He wore the scars of recent battle. He nodded to the men in the Chevy, all of whom remained in the car.

Jimmy plodded up the steps to Wu's darkened stoop and knocked on the door. It was answered by a tiny china doll, who softly escorted him to Xiang Wu's office. Taiwanese businessman Do Sing was already seated. He did not get up to greet Jimmy.

"She wants to meet us at the Delta Crown Room at San Francisco International, in less than two hours. Only three people will be admitted to the room. With Do Sing and myself, I assume the third will be yourself. What will you do to insure the death of Miss Lee?"

Jimmy C.'s mind-tape went on fast forward. The Delta Crown Room was in the unsecured portion of the airport, in the U between two sections of gates. The unobtrusive entrance was surrounded by a series of highly profitable small gift shops—a newspaper and book stand, a T-shirt shop, a sports bar, a barbershop, and a candy shop. The room itself was approximately sixty feet long and ran behind several of the smaller shops, with floor-to-ceiling windows overlooking the apron of concrete on the inside of the U-shaped Delta terminal.

465

"She'll never get in," Jimmy C. said confidently.

"What if she is already there, Mr. Chimichanga?" asked Do Sing.

"Then, she'll never get out. There's only one entrance to the room. My men will be ready on all sides. She won't make it three feet past the door."

Xiang Wu nodded approval, then looked at his watch.

"We will time our arrival exactly for ten o'clock," he said.

"My men will be ready," said Jimmy C.

"Better than last time, I presume," Xiang Wu spoke harshly to the gangster.

Jimmy C. didn't respond.

Marcia's adrenaline had started to surge. It was game time. She was so nervous she felt like running, which she knew she might have to do in any case. She prepared for the morning by dressing in slacks, sweater, lightweight wind jacket, and jogging shoes. She called the front desk and canceled her wake-up call, then waited and listened for David's phone to ring and wake him up after four hours' sleep. The amount of time was just about perfect for her purposes — not enough for him to be rested and alert, but just enough for him to concentrate on one task. With her ear against the wall she could hear him sleepily acknowledge the call, then stumble into the bathroom.

"OK, fix her up," she instructed Joe. "Relax, Cheryl."

Marcia could see the fear quickly rising in Cheryl's eyes. Marcia sat on the edge of the bed as

Joe tightly wrapped her hands, then used two pairs of mail-order ankle cuffs used in bondage games to secure her feet to the bed rail. "Just stay still and nothing will happen to you. It's all going to be over soon. Remember—I saved your life," Marcia said, patting Cheryl fondly on the hip.

Marcia then bent down and kissed Cheryl on the cheek.

"I'll send you money within two months. Do something different with your life. You've got talent you haven't even touched," Marcia said, shouldering her purse.

She could hear the toilet flush in David's room. She walked to his door and softly knocked. After a moment David came to the door.

"We've got to leave by eleven-fifteen."

David nodded groggily.

"Can you make the call all right?" she asked.

Again David nodded. The call to IGC would be the last, and would include the directions to the meeting place in Hong Kong. But David would soon find out that dealing with IGC on anything, no matter how simple, wasn't as easy as it should be.

"I'm going to check out and clear the bill," said Marcia. "I'll be right back. I'll come and get you at a little after eleven."

She nodded to Joe, who was standing in the doorway of Marcia's room. When David's door closed, he handed her the briefcase, closed the door, and followed her. Inside Joe's pocket was the Smith and Wesson he'd not had a chance to use in Wyoming. Wearing nothing but the clothes on their backs, Joe and Marcia walked down the covered walkway to the motel lobby, went through the lobby and out the front set of double glass doors, quickly mingling with the other guests who were using the Holiday Inn's airport shuttle bus. In her right hand Marcia held a leather briefcase which contained $250,000 in cash, multiple open-ended airline tickets, two passports, various forms of identification, and a black-and-red box of 1.2MB IGC diskettes with David Kimura's computer virus programs and decryption keys. Her purse containing the back up disketes, dangled over her left shoulder.

The ride from the Holiday Inn to the airport terminal took less than ten minutes. After many years, the airport had finally widened the ingress and egress access lanes. The rental car area was still very clumsy to get to, but worse to get out of. At 9:45 Marcia and Joe got off the shuttle bus, crossed the three-lane drop-off area, and entered the Delta terminal.

In front of them were the ticketing counters, above them on the third floor were the business offices. Behind and on both sides of ticketing were the fifty-odd restaurants, gift shops, and assorted odds and ends that made the terminal a miniairport.

While Marcia's heart was racing, she felt in control. What was to follow would be the single most difficult thing she'd done in her life — and certainly the most dangerous. It would require nearly split-second timing, and a certain degree of athletic skill that she knew she possessed, but had never counted on to save her life.

The area behind ticketing contained the promenade of shops. At either end were the entrances to the gate areas, each protected by airport security metal scanners. In very busy times, up to four scanners could be activated. Unlike yesterday, today the traffic was light. Everybody was at Grandma's — the women gabbing and cooking in the hot kitchen, the men laughing and hollering in front of the TV while the Lions won and the Cowboys lost their respective football games.

Thanksgiving in America.

On the outboard side of the promenade, between the Italian restaurant and the sports bar, was the Delta Airlines Crown Room.

Marcia had membership in every airline's club room.

Opposite the tastefully sedate, but annoyingly restrictive, entrance was a bank of telephone kiosks, most set up for credit card-only calls. Only a few coin-operated phones had survived the onslaught of the Truly Long-Distance Service companies.

Marcia put her hand on Joe's shoulder, reaching up to do so.

"I'm going to wait for them over by the door. They will be obvious. When we go through the door, wait *exactly* five minutes. Then call IGC at this number. They're waiting for you. Read this message to them." She handed him a neatly written note.

She gave him a few seconds to digest it.

"Do you understand it?"

Joe nodded his head yes. He knew she was relying on him.

"Exactly five minutes," he repeated.

"That's right. The timing is *critical*. When you've made the call, come through the door. The attendant may ask who you are, but I will have told her to expect you. We'll be at the far right of the room," she said. "We're going to be OK, Joe." She smiled at

469

him, patting him on the arm.

Joe would have gone through the wall for her.

Marcia walked over and stood in front of the Crown Room door. It was 9:55.

Outside, in the bright November sunshine, arrived the limo of Xiang Wu. Wu gave the driver instructions to stay no matter what. In reality, they were fairly obvious. It was perhaps a fatal flaw, a chauvinistic mentality, that Xiang Wu had absolutely no idea that all hell was about to break loose. He would protect himself, but a woman was still a woman, and no harm could come from that.

And this woman was a whore.

Unnoticed, the black Buick and the old Chevy pulled up into the departing drop-off area and all but the driver quietly got out. Each man wore a sport coat that covered an automatic weapon of choice. The men entered the terminal, then quickly separated and melted into the small crowd of holiday travelers, gradually but surely making their way around the ticketing area to the promenade of shops behind. Xiang Wu and Do Sing entered the terminal, followed by an uncomfortable Jimmy C.

As was usual in airport terminals, nobody batted an eye, including the minimal force of airport security guards called up by Denton Holmes—a *very* unpopular man this Thanksgiving Day.

Jimmy's five men quietly cased the area and took unassuming positions with a clear shot of the Crown Room entrance, their rubber-soled shoes making quiet *squish-squish* sounds on the coated granite-tiled floors.

"Miss Lee, so good to see you again," said Xiang Wu to the tall black-haired beauty, who today could

470

look like a campus queen — her preppiness belying her preparedness.

It was 9:57 A.M. Pacific time.

"Mr. Wu . . . gentlemen . . . would you follow me, please," said Marcia, trying to temporarily submit her strength to the maleness present.

Marcia opened the door and walked inside. To her right was a cloak room for luggage and coats. Ahead was the receptionist desk. Behind and twenty feet below them was the tarmac area of the Delta gates.

"I'm Marcia Lee. I've reserved the meeting area. These gentlemen are my guests," said Marcia.

The general rule was that a member could bring in two guests. Today was light, exceptions were OK, and Marcia had cleared it ahead of time.

"Down there, gentlemen," said Marcia.

With the exception of Dallas and Atlanta, most Crown Rooms were similar — most of *any* of the frequent flyer rooms were the same. Each had a bar, some self-serve, well-used but very comfortable chairs and sofas, telephones scattered nearly on every table, three or four seating rooms, one or two rest rooms. Some had meeting rooms, or areas that could be used for meeting rooms. San Francisco was one of these.

At 9:59 A.M. Marcia ran into the first of her problems. Four businessmen sat watching the beginning of the Detroit-Tampa Bay football game in the secluded area Marcia had reserved. She looked back at the Delta attendant, who had immediately lost eye contact with her. I don't want to mess with those men, her eyes had said. Marcia retreated to the desk.

"I specifically reserved this area for this meeting.

471

Specifically! I want those men out of there. Now!"
Marcia demanded.

It was 10:00 A.M.

The Delta attendant looked at Marcia, then at the
three men she'd brought with her. It was the look in
the eyes of the men that gave her impetus to move
toward the back of the room to the group of now-
boisterous men. It was Thanksgiving . . . the men
were away from home . . . and the drinks were free.

"Gentlemen, I'm sorry—but you're going to have
to move. This area has been reserved for the next
hour. There's another television in the other room—
past the bar," said the Delta agent.

Xiang Wu was at the point of suggesting that they
meet in the far room, but Marcia pressed forward
with nonverbal communication with the attendant.
Her eyes and hands told of the urgency. It was *very*
important to Marcia. Xiang Wu was a bit mystified.

Grumbling, the men got up and moved. It was
unlike her, but she'd made a semiblunder. The god-
damned television! What would have happened if the
Detroit-Tampa Bay football game hadn't been available on another television could only be left to the
imagination. A horror show.

The time was 10:02 A.M.

Outside in the main terminal, the paging announcements for this person and that person to meet
this person and that person at this place or that
place went on and on and on. Recognizing thugs
when he saw them, Joe knew that Wu had brought
serious heat with him. While their eyes were on the
door, his eyes were on them. Then on his wrist-

472

watch. It was 10:02. He dialed the number in New Jersey, 1-201-868-1905.

It was busy.

Joe looked at the receiver.

It can't be busy.

Thirty seconds earlier the phone had rung at IGC's temporary World Headquarters in the cornfields north of Franklin Lakes, New Jersey. Outside, the huge boulder remained as stoic as the company's image. In the conference room were four white men, all between the age of forty-five and fifty-six, all representing the *corporateness* of the company. On Wednesday morning, thirty-six hours ago, they had each awakened to what promised to be a short-lived day of pretend corporate work. No real decisions were made on the day before Thanksgiving. All across America, IGC managers rejoiced at the holiday. It was their once-a-year respite from the rigors of attempting to fire marginal employees. From Thanksgiving to the Monday following New Year's Day, tradition was that employees, no matter how horrid their performance, were not to be fired. This was regardless of the massive amounts of documentation that the manager had accumulated against the employee. Every year there was a race to fire employees who deserved it — but before Thanksgiving.

Fire the turkeys before Turkey Day.

What had followed for the four men had been a corporate nightmare. Each of the men — Holton Kiley, DeToqueville, and Owens — was a corporate officer. They received stock options. Stock options were only good if the stock rose. The stock was about to take a header down a long chute. Nobody was pleased. Big bucks were involved.

"With regard to your last question, I'm not sure I understand. The exit is onto Pan Ni Street, and . . ."

It was David Kimura.

"Get that asshole off the god-damned phone," said John Holton under his breath to James Owens, the new speaker.

Owens disconnected by depressing the plastic knob on the receiver. The dial tone was back. They had diddle-daddled too long. *It was time.*

It was 1:03 Eastern time.

Do Sing set the portable PC up on the low-set coffee table in the sitting room area. The orange backlit display seemed to pop in the relative darkness of the room. Jimmy C.'s bulk blocked the doorway between the small room and the main lounge. The TV remained on, the Lions scoring on a pass interception. Cheers and groans echoed from the other TV room. Do Sing sat down in one of the comfortable chairs; Marcia and Xiang Wu remained standing behind him.

"You have documents for me?" she asked.

It was 10:05 A.M. Pacific time.

Joe's credit card call went through.

The phone rang!

"I am calling for Marcia Lee," said Joe.

"Yes, we are waiting!" replied Owens.

"Your line was busy," said Joe.

474

"Yes, yes—what is your message?" asked Owens.

Murphy Monahan stomped his feet impatiently.

"Are you taping this?" asked Joe.

"Yes, yes."

"Do you agree to abide by Miss Lee's terms?" asked Joe.

"Yes, Yes! Of course!" replied a sweating Owens.

"Good. Cheryl Colby is located in Room 118 of the Holiday Inn San Francisco International. It is located at 245 South Airport Boulevard in South San Francisco. David Kimura is in Room 120, next door. Kimura's employer was named Makato Shinogara. His company is a front for many Japanese electronics companies. They will all be represented at the meeting in Hong Kong. Miss Lee is meeting with Mr. Xiang Wu, San Francisco financier, and his backers . . . who she does not know. Wu authorized the assassination of at least fifty of Shinogara's personnel on November fifteenth in Palos Verdes, California. We do not know where the bodies have been buried.

"Miss Lee is currently negotiating with Xiang Wu and associates at the Delta Airlines Crown Room at San Francisco International Airport.

"Good-bye," said Joe, crumpling the note and hanging up.

He headed for the Crown Room door.

Using the phone in the conference room, Monahan quickly dialed 9-1-415-761-0800, the direct dial number to the airport security office at SFO. The large Rolm Corporation switch automatically determined which was the cheapest way to make the con-

475

nection, and did so transparently.

"Security," answered Denton Holmes.

"This is Murphy Monahan, let me talk to Coldsmith," he ordered.

Holmes handed Scotty the phone.

"Yes," replied Scotty.

"Marcia Lee is making a deal with a financier named Wu. They're in the Delta Crown Room. Get the sons-of-bitches!" shouted Monahan.

"They're at the Delta Crown Room," Scotty said, turning to Holmes.

"Follow me—we've got to run," said Holmes, who went to his portable walkie-talkie. "Close the Delta security gates! Notify the airline to hold all flights! Clear the area!" Holmes instructed.

Scotty, Denton, and Rhodes raced down the empty hallway, nearly sliding on the slick polished floor in front of the escalator.

"How far is it?" asked Scotty.

"About as far away as you can get!" said Holmes in a voice that told Scotty that he'd better conserve his energy for the dash.

The seeing-eye doors opened automatically for the three men. Denton turned to the left, and began to run.

"Over there!" He pointed to the Delta terminal, barely visible over the huge parking lot that filled the middle of the airport.

Run!

"I have the documents—if you have brought what we are seeking," replied Xiang Wu in his most unctuous tone of voice.

476

Marcia wanted to scratch his eyes out. The man made her skin crawl. The thick man blocking the doorway was the same man who had torched Zack's house. The bunch of them were filthy slime. Marcia placed her briefcase on the table next to Do Sing and his portable PC. She unsnapped the clasps and opened the case. Inside were stacks of fifty- and one hundred-dollar bills, a thick folder with David's passports and tickets, and a single black-and-red box with nine 1.2MB diskettes inside. A thick rubber band wrapped lengthwise kept the lid to the box secured.

"Traveling light, Miss Lee?" smiled Wu.

"Just the essentials, Mr. Wu," she replied in kind. "These are what you want. Now, let me see the documents, please." From his seated position Do Sing reached for the box of diskettes in Marcia's right hand. He was denied, as Marcia pulled back.

"Just a moment. You'll get your precious diskettes," she replied, a bit bravely considering that she was outnumbered three to one by men she knew would have no remorse in killing a woman.

Tough, confident talk was the best approach. From his inside coat pocket, Wu withdrew a thick packet and handed it to Marcia. Marcia scanned the passports for her and Joe, who just that moment walked through the Crown Room door and was given direction by the attendant. His presence made her feel good, but she knew she was behind schedule. The timing was critical—razor thin. Her legs were tingly, her stomach turning.

There were two passports, one each under the name of Smith and Ling—her new name. The airline tickets matched.

477

"Rebecca?" she questioned.

"It seemed to fit," Wu replied, smiling.

His fingers twitched in anticipation. Joe lumbered up beside Marcia.

It was 10:08 A.M. Pacific time.

"My associate, Joe Turner. These appear to be in order," Marcia said, as she put the new passports into the briefcase and closed it with a crisp double snap. She handed the case to Joe, who held it in his left hand. His right hand was free, ready to quickly slip under his sport coat to his holstered weapon. "Now, Mr. Wu, if you'll please make the telephone call," she said.

Wu's face crinkled with distaste, but he had no choice. The woman would be dead in a matter of minutes, but the money was irrelevant as pocket change.

"The diskettes," said Wu, more forcefully.

"Make the call, please. Make the connection, identify the account, authorize the transaction, and keep them on the line until your client has verified the contents of the diskettes. When he does so, then give the word to your agent," said Marcia, knowing that government agents and police had to be running toward the Crown Room.

She was playing it too close. She wouldn't make it. Would greed be her undoing?

Do Sing's hands twitched as Marcia dangled the box of diskettes out in her right hand. Using one of the automatic credit card telephones, Xiang Wu dialed the 41-22 country and city codes for Geneva, Switzerland and the local number of Xiang Wu's bank. There was no surprise on the other end. Xiang Wu had prepared the bank for the transfer of

478

the additional three million. There were no explanations required. Marcia's bank number and account were given. Xiang Wu turned back to Marcia.

"The diskettes, please, Miss Lee," he said firmly.

Marcia handed Do Sing the box of diskettes. Jimmy Chimichanga turned and watched. The portable PC hummed politely; its memory chips stood ready to process something.

Do Sing unwrapped the rubber band and took out the diskette labeled #1 and inserted it into the diskette drive. Marcia wanted to wet her pants.

Scotty had never run so hard in his life. His shoes seemed to be anchors. There was a three hundred-yard open space between each of the SFO terminals, which themselves were over a quarter mile in length. And, they had to take the long way around. Only crows could fly the straight route, which would bisect the fourth floor of the underground parking lot.

Scotty caught up with, then passed Denton Holmes, who would much rather have been home in his pajamas watching the football games. Unfortunately, Denton had been smoking for too long. The ten-yard sprint to the refrigerator had replaced the thousand-yard sprint to catch the bad guys. But he would later blame it on the age difference, which was partly true. Scotty had *age* and he had *reason* and he had *passion,* none of which Denton Holmes had in this case.

At 10:09 Scotty smoked into the Delta terminal, doing a near wheelie as he rolled through the now-cleared ticketing area. Holmes's message had been relayed to all security guards in adjoining terminals,

479

who descended on Delta like there was a pay raise waiting at the gate. The security checkpoints to the two gate areas were instantly closed. A line of complaining passengers, half of whom did not speak English or understand a whit of what was happening, noisily deluged the agents, who had simply turned off the machines and had mentally prepared themselves for the worst.

Oh please don't let them come this way.

"Where's the Crown Room?" Scotty shouted to a handful of surprised Delta ticketing agents.

"Around the corner, toward Gate B—on the other side," returned one woman.

Scotty and three of Denton's men who had picked up on what was happening, raced for the entrance door.

Delta Crown Room—Members Only

Marcia watched as Do Sing inserted the first diskette into the portable PC. He made no comment as he ripped through a DIR A:/P—whacking the Enter key with each new screenload of file names.

"Ah, ha," he exclaimed, finding a file called READ.ME created by David Kimura.

Do Sing's finger followed his speed-reading brain down the nearly illegible image on the backlit display. His fingers tapped out commands, searching for this file and that.

"Very good," he said twice.

"Are you satisfied, Xiang Wu?" asked Marcia, very antsy.

"Not yet. Not until—" Xiang Wu stopped in mid-sentence, his eyes locked on Do Sing's, who communicated a non-verbal yes to the financial specialist.

Xiang Wu smiled, then nodded to the beautiful woman in front of him. Jimmy C. calculated what would be required to dispose of Joe.

"Process the transaction," Wu said into the telephone.

It's time to go, Marcia thought.

Do Sing tapped a few keys. The portable had a fixed disk mounted onto one of its three available adapter cards.

```
C>_____
FORMAT A:
Insert new diskette for Drive A:
and strike ENTER when ready.
```

The PC began to reformat David Kimura's diskette #1. The portable 80386-based PC was quick about it.

"What are you doing?" asked Marcia.

"There's no need for *us* to use the program. It will just take a few moments, and everything will be erased. Then there will be no doubt. The virus will be permanent. No matter what happens," Do Sing laughed in a high-pitched voice. "I only need to erase one or two of these program disks before they all become impossible to reconstruct. Why wait?"

"Well, you'll be on your way then, Miss Lee?" said Xiang Wu, also smiling to the soft grinding sound of David Kimura's program diskette being wiped out. "I think we will stay here a—"

Wu's plan for Marcia to die in a hail of gunfire had backfired.

"What's that?" said Jimmy C., now alert.

481

It was gunfire.

The shopping promenade behind the Delta ticketing counters had become a killing zone. Jimmy C.'s five thugs opened fire on the first guards to run to the Crown Room door. Scotty, Denton, and Dusty Rhodes were in the second wave of authorities, along with five or six other security guards who had run with them from the United terminal.

"Stop, Freeze!"

But there had been no stopping, no freezing.

Two security guards were cut down in a cross fire. Shots popped from the barbershop, the sports bar, and the candy shop. Two elderly couples slowly made their way toward ramp B down the middle of the promenade when the firing started. One of the men was hit, all four fell to the floor, scattering packages and luggage across the slick surface. A woman with two children, one in each hand, screamed as the first two guards were shot and killed.

There was chaos in the Delta terminal as shouts of warning mixed with screams of pain and fear. Gunfire crisscrossed the promenade. Glass shattered in the bar. A carefully built pyramid of books was knocked down in the newspaper stand. A sourdough bread rack fell over and a bystander was shot in the leg. Luggage was dropped as people dove for cover.

"Over there!"

"Watch out!"

"Behind you!"

Scotty's momentum around the corner had propelled him smack into the middle of the chaos. Instinctively, he went to the ground, rolled toward the far wall, and came up firing. Two shots took out the thug in the bar, along with a row of glasses that hung down above the bartender's head.

When three of Jimmy's thugs were dead, the other two raised their hands.

"I give up!"

"Don't shoot!"

"Drop your weapon! Now!"

Guns clattered to the floor.

"Down on the ground!"

The men fell.

Scotty, followed by Dusty and two security guards, opened the door to the Crown Room. The Delta attendant screamed.

"What's that?" said Jimmy C.

There was a commotion coming from outside. Then through the door burst a young man and several uniformed officers, all with their revolvers drawn. The Delta attendant screamed. Marcia, Joe, Xiang Wu, and Do Sing were frozen in their tracks. Do Sing had both hands on the PC. Diskette #1 was history. Diskette #2 was in the machine and he'd just pressed Enter.

```
Format complete.
1213952 bytes total disk space
1213952 bytes available on disk
Format another (Y/N)?
Y
```

"Over there!" the attendant pointed.

The Crown Room foyer consisted of the attendant's desk, two corner couches, and a well-presented table with soft drinks, ice, mixers, and dry little finger fishes that tasted like cardboard bits. Carafes of tomato, orange, and grapefruit juice were iced. Tiny cans of Bloody Mary mix were lined up along with equally small cans of Tropicana orange juice for screwdriver mixers. To the left of the receptionist was the TV room, where the four football fans were stopped in midsentence. To the right were two rooms separated by low partitions.

"Coldsmith!" exclaimed Marcia, knowing she was in real trouble. She knew she was behind schedule.

Scotty pointed his revolver at the group.

"Marcia Lee, Xiang Wu — you're under arrest for the murder of Zack Colby, kidnapping, and other crimes," Scotty said, calmer than he thought he'd be.

Efram Zimbalist couldn't have said it better.

At that moment the Delta Crown Room began to explode. Of all the occupants, the attendant did the one smart thing — she ducked behind her desk. The men in the TV room for an instant seemed to be paralyzed, as if what was happening wasn't real.

"He's got a gun!" said one of the uniformed security guards.

Indeed, Jimmy C had a gun. And he began to use it. The first shots were wild and to the right, and devastated the neat table of morning drinks. All three of the large carafes of juice exploded as one bullet smashed through the thick portion of the glass container. Another bullet destroyed the large glass bowl which contained several gallons of chopped ice and the carafes. Everything on the table seemed to jump in the air, crash, and spill at the same time.

484

Scotty ducked and fired a shot which struck the wooden door frame next to Xiang Wu's head. Wu and Do Sing fell to the floor as Jimmy C. began to return fire.

"Now, Joe!" Marcia shouted.

Marcia went for the emergency door. Joe had a firm grip on the briefcase.

Do Not Use
For Emergency Use Only
Door Is Alarmed

Marcia pushed the flat red handle to the heavy emergency exit door down and out, which broke the security circuit, which set off the fire alarm, a whooping, nearly painful noise, which now competed with the popping of gunfire.

"She's getting away!" shouted Do Sing.

Jimmy C. turned and saw Marcia step through the doorway, Joe following. He fired a shot. It missed, dinging off the heavy door and ricocheting outside. Jimmy turned back to the advancing agents, then saw that Wu and Do Sing had started toward the door behind the fleeing Marcia and Joe.

Joe's big body got through the door and Marcia slammed it behind him. The grated landing was no larger than four feet square. Joe fell to the deck and put his back against the bottom of the door, his feet jammed against the metal guardrail on the opposite side. Joe was a human doorstop.

Inside there was chaos. Do Sing and Xiang Wu pounded on the door, shouting to be let out. Shots could be heard. Outside, Marcia pulled from her purse the length of heavy chain link Joe had purchased, reached up and snapped one of the J-hooks to the elbow of the sturdy door hinge at the top of the door. Quickly reaching over Joe, she attached the hook on the other end of the chain around one of the steel grates that made up the platform they were standing on. The chain then stretched across the width of the door and top to bottom, an excellent deterrent.

Click, snap, click, snap.

"Let's get the hell out of here!" she shouted at Joe, who scrambled behind her, down the twenty-five-foot-tall series of grated steps to the black tarmac below.

"Throw down your weapons!" shouted Scotty, unable to see around the corner of the far room, but able to see that bodies had fallen and the enemy was in disarray.

"Freeze, you son of a bitch!" Scotty shouted.

Scotty, the security guards, and the late-arriving Denton Holmes all advanced on the trapped group. Jimmy C. started to move toward the emergency door.

"Drop it! Freeze!"

Then he saw the door close. Xiang Wu pounded on the door. Do Sing shouted in rapid Chinese. Wu turned around and looked Jimmy C. in the eyes.

Jimmy decided it wasn't worth it.

"Drop your weapons! Down on the floor!" Scotty shouted, as the officers converged into the far room.

Format complete.
1213952 bytes total disk space

1213952 bytes available on disk
Format another (Y/N)?

Diskette #2 had been reformatted.

"Watch them," Scotty instructed as he ran to the emergency door and tried to bash through it.

He failed. But the door opened a crack, enough for Scotty to see to the bottom of the stairway. *She's down here!* he thought. *Get her! I can see them!* Scotty could just get a glimpse of two people at the bottom of the stairway.

"Shit! Shitshitshitshitshit!" Scotty screamed as he rattled the door in a fury.

He backed up and ran at the door, crashing into it with his left shoulder and the full force of his six-foot-four frame.

Shoot it!

Mindless of the possibilities of ricocheting bullets, or the possibility of injuring someone below, Scotty cracked the door as far as it could and shot at the chain attached to the grate. His first shot missed, but his second didn't. The chain broke in two and the door sprang open, crashing against the steel platform. In a flash, Scotty scrambled down the stairway, taking the steps four at a time.

He reached the tarmac. Running in constant motion underneath the terminal was the automated luggage-handling system, now mostly empty. Two planes were nearby, but they were outboard. Scotty could see a quarter mile in all directions.

Gone. She was gone!

She couldn't have run that fast.

Scotty did a madman circle, running aimlessly in one direction toward Gate A, then back to Gate B, then toward the luggage area. Marcia Lee was nowhere to be found.

"Arrrggh," he cried, slamming his fist into the ladder. The high-pitched whine of a nearby 767 hurt Scotty's ears. The smell of exhaust was enough to make him gag.

After all this—he'd lost her.

Scotty slowly climbed back up the steps to the emergency exit of the Crown Room. He looked around. There were no extra eyes who might have seen her escape down to the tarmac.

She didn't just disappear. God-damn it!

Scotty's self-flagellation was interrupted by a call on Denton's beeper.

"Message for Agent Coldsmith," the dispatcher blurted.

"Go ahead," said Denton.

"This message is from Murphy Monahan. David Kimura is in Room 120 of the Airport Holiday Inn. Cheryl Colby is in Room 118. Apprehend."

"I know where it is," Dusty Rhodes said.

Without a word, the two young men ran back through the Crown Room, past the collared crowd of criminals and out into the airport promenade, where they dashed for the exit doors. Rhodes's car was still there. In the next instant it was cutting through three lanes of traffic at forty miles an hour.

Holton, DeToqueville, Owens, attorney Kiley, and Murphy Monahan all waited in silence. Events were now out of their control. Holton gave Kiley a look that DeToqueville saw but Murphy didn't. John Holton's fingers were crossed.

Extension 1905 rang again. Holton briefly thought of having the phone bronzed for the duty it had gone through, but answered it instead.

"Hello," Holton said.

"The directions to the meeting are as follows . . ."

John Holton's whole face turned into a cold smile.

"There's going to be no meeting, David. There's going to be no exchange. The only thing that's going to happen is that you're going to go to jail for a long time. A *very* long time. I have at my disposal world-class corporate attorneys. You will never see the outside of your prison cell for the rest of your life. I'll see to it."

"Bu-but, you . . . I . . . you can't. Not now . . . the diskettes . . . I have," David babbled.

"You have *nothing*, David. *We* have them. We have your name, your backers' names. We have the murderers and criminals who tried to loot the American financial system. *We have you all.* You have *nothing.*"

Although he wasn't a vengeful man, John Holton would remember his final conversation with David Kimura as one of the most satisfying moments in his life.

David dropped the phone like a hot rock, tore open the door, then tried to turn the knob on Room 118, Marcia's room. It was locked.

"Open it!" he shouted, then pounded on the door. *"Open it!"*

Inside was a bound and gagged Cheryl Colby, terrified. The curtains were drawn so David couldn't see inside, which for Cheryl's sake was fortunate.

His stomach began to feel as if an evil mutated

growth had just hatched inside. It grabbed his inte:
tines and made him gulp back bile at the same tim(

He went back inside his room and turned on th
computer with a flip of the big red switch. H
opened the box of diskettes marked Kimura and ir
serted the one marked Backup 1 of 9. On the pro
gram was a copy of the operating system and th
initial panels of the encryption program. The 80386
based PC quickly went through its power-on sel:
test. Satisfied, it then searched the diskette drive fo
a copy of the operating system. The red disk-in-us
light flashed briefly. Finding none, it beeped twic
and flashed an error message.

NON-SYSTEM DISK OR DISK ERROR
Replace and strike any key when ready

David's heart jumped, his stomach turned.
You've put the wrong diskette in! Look at the label. H
fumbled with the diskette, flipping it out of the disk
ette drive. It was marked Backup 1 of 9. Davi(
began to pray to all forms of deities. He put i
another diskette and rebooted the machine.

DISKETTE READ FAILURE
STRIKE F1 TO RETRY BOOT

This was the message inserted into the system'
internal smarts by the manufacturer to tell the use:
that yes, indeed, he had put in the wrong diskette
and to please insert one that had the operating sys
tem on it.

David was sweating as he quickly inserted diskett(
after diskette. None had DOS on it. *One should hav(*

it.

OK, OK . . . you've just done something wrong. Go get a DOS diskette and start from scratch.

But David wasn't cool. His hands shook. He reached for his copy of DOS 4.0, then inserted the operating system diskette. The machine booted up just fine. The operating system was in memory. He took the DOS diskette out and inserted Backup 1 of 9 back into the diskette drive. He typed DIR A:

GENERAL FAILURE READING DRIVE A
Abort, Retry, Fail

"No!"
He tried another diskette.

GENERAL FAILURE READING DRIVE A
Abort, Retry, Fail

The dreaded Abort, Retry, Fail. *Fail* was the applicable word.

No, no . . . this can't be. It can't be. This is a blank diskette . . . I just can't . . .

The box marked Kimura fell to the floor, scattering the remaining diskettes. David fumbled with the second box of diskettes, still with its protective rubber band wrapped lengthwise around the top and bottom. The band snapped and fell to the floor as he released it.

"No!" David shouted, a dribble of spit at the corner of his mouth.

He was frantic. His hands and arms felt numb. His chest was tight. He put diskette #1 into the machine, closed the door, and pressed Enter.

GENERAL FAILURE READING DRIVE A
Abort, Retry, Fail

The grand·plan of Makato Shinogara was down the tubes.

The straightaway leading out of the airport had six lanes dropping down to four, which then split into two northbound and two southbound exits. Rental cars leaving the airport came in from the right and regularly caused spectacular accidents as rentals headed south had to cross over the two exiting northbound lanes.

"Wow! That was close!" said Dusty, unaware that he'd had a near-death experience and that his lifetime quota of near-misses had been reduced by one.

Mercifully, they only had to go one exit on the Bayshore Freeway, which in the South San Francisco area had been laid over unstable ground, causing the roadway to buckle and sway.

"You know where you're going?" Scotty asked.

Dusty answered him by peeling off the Bayshore at the Airport Road exit and wheeling through the traffic signal against the light. The kid's driving like he's just gotten permission from Dad to break all the rules, Scotty thought. The Holiday Inn was on the right, the northernmost motel in the airport group. With a hand motion, Scotty told Dusty to slow down, then pointed for him to pull into the lobby parking area. Scotty jumped out and was inside the lobby before Dusty had turned the ignition off.

"I'm with the FBI." Scotty showed the clerk his

badge. "There's a man in Room 120 that we're going to arrest, and there's a prisoner they've kept in Room 118. I want the keys to both rooms," said Scotty, holding out his hand.

Young Rhodes came into the lobby.

"I'm sorry . . . but I can't . . ." the clerk protested.

"Out of my way." Scotty swung his lanky body over the counter in a move that even he would consider to be graceful.

His fingers ran along the little cubbyholes until they found Rooms 118 and 120, and plucked out a duplicate key for each.

"You can't do . . . I can't . . ." the clerk stuttered.

"Show me where the rooms are," Scotty ordered.

The clerk finally realized that this was the point where a guest's right to privacy terminated.

"You go through the double door, and they're straight back—all the way to the end. They're the last two rooms on the right, pool side," said the scared clerk.

"That's fine. Now I want you to do me a favor and call the police—and an ambulance," said Scotty, thinking of Cheryl.

The clerk nodded.

Scotty pushed his way through the double glass door and found himself at one end of a large open courtyard. To his left was a large, well-manicured, grassy area leading to a semiprotected swimming pool, now drained. Straight ahead were Rooms 102 through 120, running in a row away from him, with 120 toward the back of the motel.

"See that area over there?"

Scotty pointed to a sunning area that had been partially shielded behind an elm tree and a large

493

clump of flowering bushes. Dusty nodded yes.

"Cover me from there. I'm going straight. If Ki mura comes out with a gun—shoot him. You'll hav a better angle," the detective instructed.

Scotty drew out his revolver, freed the safety, an quietly walked toward the rear of the motel, walkin on the grass instead of the concrete walkway to re duce the noise of his approach. Dusty made a quic dash to his left across the grass to the sunning area approximately even with Room 114. In front c Room 116 Scotty pressed himself against the motel' wall, then stooped down low to scurry under th window to Room 118. Back against the door h tried in vain to hear anything inside Cheryl's room There was nothing. Nearly on his hands and knees he crawled past the window to Room 120 an cupped his ear to the door.

A voice!

It sounded like he was shouting. In Japanese?

Scotty gently tested the door but its firm refusal t turn told him it was locked. He ducked around th corner, where there was a soda machine and an ic maker.

If you use the key, the door could be locked and latched He could have a gun. He could very easily kill you.

Next to the soda machine was a standard-size waste can—a little over three feet tall, green, with rounded top, and a push-through slot for the trash Safety back on, Scotty holstered and secured hi gun, then picked the trash can up with both hands Half-filled with garbage, the can weighed nearly fift pounds.

Scotty was a tall man and in good shape. Round ing the corner, he positioned himself and got a good

494

rip on his projectile, then in a single swoop lunged
oward the motel room, pitching the trash can side-
ays through the four-foot-square pane of glass at
he last moment. Rather than throwing the can,
cotty held onto it, driving it straight into the motel
oom.

The window shattered into nine million shards,
ome of which landed on Scotty, but most of which
howered back into David Kimura's room. A micro-
econd after impact, Scotty released the can, letting
: crash into the room, where it knocked over a
orty-watt lamp that sat on a small table next to the
eater-air-conditioning unit and was theoretically
sed for reading.

Ignoring the broken glass, Scotty climbed through
he window, where an astonished David Kimura had
nly begun to react. Instead of going for the door,
vhich wasn't locked on the inside anyway, David
hrew himself toward the tall special agent. David's
hick body hit Scotty in the midsection, much like a
ootball lineman practices on a dummy sled. Scotty
vas indeed surprised with David's compact bulk, and
hat his breath had been knocked out with the colli-
ion. The two men could do nothing but close-com-
at wrestling, something that Scotty soon realized
vouldn't be in his own favor if it lasted too long.

Where in hell is Rhodes?

David's tackling strategy soon changed to one of
attempted immobilization, which Scotty knew would
ie followed with the strangulation and/or termina-
ion phases of the short-lived combat.

This guy's a rock!

The two men thrashed back and forth over the
oroken glass, bumping into the trash can, rolling

495

over its smelly spilled contents.

Stop thinking and start hitting!

Faced with the prospect of fighting like an anim[ ]
Scotty let his adrenaline go right to the surface.

*This is the guy who set Zack up. The man who k[ ]
napped Cheryl. Jesus Christ! Beat the shit out of him!*

Scotty found himself on the bottom. Shards [ ]
glass cut into his back, straight through his jacke[ ]
each shard inflicting a sliver of pain into his shou[ ]
der and arms, occasionally the back of his thigh[ ]
His left hand found David's face and began [ ]
squeeze the oval bulk, trying to focus the energy [ ]
his entire body into the tips of five fingers. Dav[ ]
grunted and yelled, applying a choking hold [ ]
Scotty's neck, while trying to dislodge the agen[ ]
death grip on his face with his other hand.

A primal grunt came out of Scotty's being as [ ]
hit David's head with his right hand. *Whack!* Grun[ ]
Whack! Grunt! David's grip on his throat was tighte[ ]
Blackness formed around the edges of Scotty's ey[ ]
sight. Scotty's right hand pounded back behind hi[ ]
and was sliced by a piece of glass. His finge[ ]
twitched and reached. His left hand squeez[ ]
harder—*grip—die you motherfucker!* Scotty could sm[ ]
his enemy's sweat and the staleness of his tir[ ]
breath. He couldn't breathe. *How can he stand t[ ]
pain—I must have his eyes!* Scotty's fingers found t[ ]
long shard, which immediately sliced his fingertip[ ]
but grabbed the piece and drove it into Davi[ ]
shoulder blade with every last bit of energy.

David's cry of pain was immediate, as was th[ ]
release of his grip on Scotty's throat. Scotty push[ ]
backward with his left hand, twisting as he did s[ ]
driving David off Scotty's chest and onto the flo[ ]

next to him. The shard was stuck in his back. David cried out in pain, all his thoughts focused on getting the sharp pick out.

Scotty's attack didn't stop. He hit David across the face with a very bloodied right hand, yelling as he did so. Then he found himself on top of the bulky but beaten programmer.

"You . . . son . . . of . . . a . . . bitch!"

Pound! went David's head back against the floor, the sharp piece of glass embedding itself further into David's back.

"You god-damned son of a bitch!"

Pound! Pound! Pound!

Scotty was a madman. He slapped David across the face repeatedly with the full fleshy part of his fist — *hard — hard — hard!*

"Mr. Coldsmith! Scott!" came the shout from behind him. "Stop . . . please stop! He's out!"

Scotty turned to young Dusty Rhodes with the temporary look of a crazed animal feeding on the carcass of a just-killed prey.

Then he *saw* Rhodes. Scotty looked down at his enemy and cared not if he was dead or alive. His chest pounded with the exertion, perspiration poured from him, drenching his clothes right through the jacket. Blood was everywhere, and it was hard to tell whose was whose.

Oh, God I hurt!

The back of Scotty's jacket looked like it had the measles. It was filled with tiny punctures that went right into his skin, drilling pinpricks of blood in most instances, gushers in others. Etched — burned — on Scotty's throat were the impressions of David's fingers.

But his enemy was in much worse condition. Temporarily out cold from the beating, David's face was a series of black and blue mixed with nearly artistic streaks of blood, as if an abstract artist had swished and dipped here and there across his broad face. The shard of glass in his back wasn't fatal, but it was painful and very, very messy. But it was the impression left by Scotty's left hand that would be permanently reflected in David's physical appearance. As Scotty had nearly conceded death, his fingers had dug into David's throat, both cheeks, and the corner of his right eye.

The sound of police and ambulance sirens filled the air.

Cheryl!

As Scotty stood up, tiny pieces of glass tinkled to the floor.

"I guess I should have come through the door," he said in a low, gruff voice.

Scotty opened David's door from the inside just as the area seemed to be filled with South San Francisco police, guns drawn.

"My name is Scott Coldsmith, FBI," he said, reaching slowly for his badge. A few pieces of glass fell to the floor as he did so. "I am here to arrest a fugitive from justice named David Kimura, and to return him to New York. This is that man."

The Millbrae Medical Unit arrived just as Scotty fished through his coat pocket and found the key to Room 118, which he fumbled with in his anxiety, then opened.

Oh my God.

Scotty's heart was touched. It was all worth it. Cheryl was tied, trussed, and gagged; tears streamed down her reddened face. The look in her eyes said everything.

Please help me oh please help me oh thank you.

His conversations completed, Murphy Monahan paused, then carefully replaced the telephone receiver back in its white cradle.

"Well, you'll be pleased to know that we got them all. All but the girl. We got the Chinese financier, his Taiwanese client, the Japanese programmer—and they're all talking. They can't stop talking. But we didn't get the girl. Somehow, she managed to escape. We can't find even a *trace* of her. We got your diskettes . . ."

John Holton interrupted.

"My people have had a chance to look at the damage. The first two diskettes were erased. The damage is considerable. But, we have a story to tell the public. The evil people have been captured, and *they will pay!*" Holton smiled. "I don't know if we can reconstruct the lost programming, but we've got smart people—and our *customers* have smart people. *They* won't put up with the Japanese trying this kind of sabotage either. If we can't solve the problem, we'll get help. It's the *attitude* that counts. Without a known criminal, we—the stock markets, our customers—American industry—would have been in for very disturbing times," said Holton.

Monahan gave the IGC chairman a look out of the side of his eyes.

"I appreciate all that you and your men have done, Mr. Monahan. I hope I will have the opportunity to convey my appreciation to your young Mr.

Coldsmith. It sounds like he's done a terrific job. *I* could use some people like him. Maybe I'll try to hire him away from you," Holton laughed.

Murphy Monahan knew he was being sold a bill of goods. John Holton was the top dog of a company known for its marketing expertise.

"You made a deal with her, didn't you?" he asked.

A tired John Holton shrugged his shoulders and shook his head.

"A deal? I don't know what you mean, Mr. Monahan."

Postscript

Cynthia Rosen depressed the seat-back button and the comfortable leather seat reclined six inches.

God, it feels so good.

The Longest Day was nearly over.

"Would you like a drink, Miss Lee . . . Marcia?" she asked.

Across the aisle sat an equally weary Marcia Lee. Beside her was Joe, his shoulder in a makeshift sling from an errant shot fired from Jimmy C.'s gun.

Besides the pilot and copilot, the three of them were the only occupants of the modified 727—a corporate jet owned and operated by IGC Corporation. Painted big blue, the jet had been used for nearly twenty years for carting preferred customers to and from customized sales briefings in various parts of the country.

The afternoon was quickly turning to evening as the jet recrossed time zones and headed for its destination—Montego Bay, Jamaica.

"I think I will have something, thank you," replied Marcia, getting up and walking back to the galley. "Would you like something?" she asked.

Cynthia looked at her watch, which read four o'clock. Was this still considered working hours?

"It's got to be five o'clock someplace — pour me a couple of scotches, if you don't mind," said Cynthia, smiling.

Where have I been? Cynthia thought. What day is it?

These were both legitimate questions. The day had truly seemed endless to Cynthia. Starting at nine o'clock in her bedroom with a message on the recorder from Scott Coldsmith — *was that really today? No, it was yesterday.*

They'd worked through the night with options, finally settling on Pay the Bastards. Then the call from Marcia. *What caused me to hold back from the FBI?*

It was Marcia's voice. Whatever instinct it was, it had been correct. At two o'clock Monahan had been asked to leave. Marcia made her pitch. At three o'clock, by a three-to-one margin, the temporary executive board of IGC had made the decision to deal — no tricks, no subterfuge.

A deal was a deal. IGC employees didn't have the background to do otherwise. What they did was execute, and execute very well. If there was a problem — no matter how big or small — IGC could bring enough resources to solve it. The job always got done.

It had been John Holton who had known where the corporate jet was located at 3:00 A.M. Thursday morning—at the Westchester County airport. By 4:00 A.M. the jet, which had been refueled after a round-trip to Boca Raton with a handful of Chemical Bank executives, was ready for takeoff. A flight plan to San Francisco was filed. At ten minutes after four, with Cynthia Rosen as its only passenger, it took off for the West Coast.

At ten o'clock Pacific time, the jet landed at SFO and was immediately refueled. For Cynthia, landing meant that the very tricky part of the deal was just beginning. But her worry had turned out not to be a problem after all. The pilot and copilot knew what to do.

"Five minutes after ten? I can be there," said an American baggage handler, accepting the folded hundred-dollar bill.

To ensure his timeliness, Cynthia went along for the ride. She was terrified. The American baggage cart stopped at the bottom of the stairway ramp in front of Big Blue. Cynthia got in the front seat along with the dirty baggage handler, who then took her through the maze underneath the airport, finally stopping outside the Delta Crown Room at five minutes before the hour. Cynthia was so nervous that she nearly jumped out of her seat when the alarm went off at 10:09 A.M.

She hadn't known what to expect, but somehow the description and feeling she'd gotten from talking to Marcia, actually fit the person who took the steps nearly in a single leap.

"Get the hell out of here!" Marcia had shouted.

The baggage handler now started to show some nerves. Cynthia had never bribed anyone, but she took five twenties out of her purse and stuffed them into the surprised man's hand.

"Go!" she said, urging him on.

And go he went. It took less than five minutes for the baggage truck to completely cross SFO, dropping the trio off at a gate reserved for charter flights in the international terminal. With all the commotion up top, and the exits packed with extra security details, not a soul saw them. Ten minutes later Big Blue was taxiing out to the runway, ready to make its trip to Montego Bay. While its original flight plan was for Dallas, it would be changed while en route.

Marcia came back with two double scotches. They each took a sip.

"Do you trust me enough yet to give me the diskettes?" asked Cynthia.

"I've gone through life not trusting a soul—" Marcia stopped in midsentence. "No that's not right . . . I trusted my people," she said softly. "No one in this has lived up to his side of anything. But, I guess there's a first for everything."

Marcia reached inside her purse and pulled out the backup set of diskettes, then handed them to Cynthia. She looked out into the darkness over the Gulf of Mexico.

"I guess I didn't expect you to live up to your end of the bargain. I'm not exactly a nun," said Marcia in gross understatement.

"A deal's a deal, Marcia. We don't know any other way. It may be stupid, but that's the way it is.

I think we all agreed that we would have preferred to have you captured and locked away, but once we stepped over the line . . . well, it was like being a little bit pregnant . . . you know what I mean?" replied Cynthia.

"You always had an out, though. You did it because you were being ransomed," replied Marcia.

"Yes, but the *people* were just as important to us as the diskettes. Capturing Makato Shinogara's lead programmer, the head of a Taiwanese consortium, and a leading worldwide money peddler—*and* getting the diskettes. That was what we wanted. We couldn't have gotten it all without you. We would have been forced to go to Hong Kong. We're just no good at this sort of thing. We would have gone there and gotten slickered, I just know it. No, this was the best way. We closed our eyes to you and your past, and concentrated on business . . . our business. Our customers will be saved. We will be saved. The stock markets will rise and fall, but will balance out all right. Our competitors will get what they deserve. What we did today was unprecedented, at least in the modern company. I don't know how it was in the old days," Cynthia mused, the liquor starting to take effect.

"What will happen to the companies making up the consortiums?" asked Marcia, curious.

"They will take a tremendous beating. Their names will be found out. They will be barred from doing business in the United States—most likely other Free World countries will do the same. There will be trade sanctions. There will be significant pressure on Japan and Taiwan to press criminal charges on all involved. I wouldn't be surprised to see both Japan and Taiwan have their American stock market trading privileges suspended. There will be terrible turmoil in the world markets."

Marcia smiled.

"I sure hope so. I'm pretty well leveraged out. When I decided to go all the way on this, I called my London broker, cashed in my Swiss accounts, and sold the Japanese yen and the Taiwanese new dollar short—*way short!* I told them that whatever money came into my account was immediately to be transferred and processed in the same way. I had hoped something like this would happen. The sons of bitches deserved it," she smiled.

All they had to do was treat me right.

Cynthia dozed off for an hour or so, while Marcia stared out into the blackness. When the plane landed she and Joe would be on their own again, with only the clothes on their back. But she wouldn't be in jail, and with a new passport and ID, they could get to her money.

At 10:20 in the evening, the IGC corporate jet made the parallel run along the north shore of the island, then a long slow turn to the left, finally landing back to the east. The plane pulled up to a vacant jetway, one normally used by Jamaica Air. The copilot came out and released the front cabin door from the inside. An attendant opened the door. Joe got out ahead of her.

"I'm not going to wish you good luck, Marcia Lee. You don't need it," said Cynthia Rosen. "Remember . . ."

"I know . . . a deal's a deal. Pretty catchy concept," said Marcia, as she stepped off the plane and into the unknown.

"Let's go home," said Cynthia to the copilot.

Author's Note

I'll have to admit that *The Tojo Virus* was a more difficult book to write than I'd thought, even considering my background. I spent nearly twenty years with IBM in a variety of administrative, systems engineering, marketing, and management positions. I spent another year as senior vice-president of International Technology Corporation in McLean, Virginia, before striking out to write novels for a living.

Some thank yous are in order. First and foremost, I'd like to thank my wife Linda for not only giving me constant love and support, but also for providing the much-needed series of reality tests that any novelist needs.

There are several people within "IGC" who helped me with technical background details and who spent hours wading through the original manuscript, offering very constructive criticism. They've asked not to be identified, but I thank you anyway.

I'd also like to thank Craig Fiebig, a former cellmate of mine at IBM. Craig's now an account manager for Microsoft Corporation.

OK, you've gone this far . . . now you're concerned about computer viruses. What can be done? It's not an easy question to answer. But I do have recommendations.

Personal computers have proliferated because they provide instant gratification to computing needs—instant gratification when measured against the same kind of application response from mainframe computers.

After twenty years in the computer industry, it's been my experience that less than one percent of employees actually had to use PROFS or other mainframe mail packages for transferring PC programs. The development of "smart" terminals was something that had to happen. It only made sense for a PC to do local applications for someone and have the ability to talk to a mainframe application. But a corresponding development of smart communications software was not required. And it is this advanced communications capability that has, and will, aid computer viruses.

Current mainframe security is sophisticated enough to keep up with developments in hacker capability. What the PC world has developed is a "loose lips sinks ships" technology that has allowed the less secure machine, the PC, to communicate with and use the facilities of the mainframe as an equal.

PC viruses will continue until a "mainframe" communications mentality is implemented. I have the following suggestions.

1. If I was the MIS manager of a company with mainframes using mail packages such as PROFS, MAILWAY, or other programs like them, I would sharply curtail the use of intelligent micro-to-mainframe programs. I would provide users with host terminal emulation only, so that the mainframe pro-

grams could be used but not contaminated by file transfer.

2. In late 1988 IBM augmented PROFS with a SAFESTOR function that temporarily files non-PROFS documents by reversing the file name. Thus EXEC becomes CEXE. The user then may look at the document before either permanently storing it or executing it. This is a good approach, but I'd take it an additional step. I'd have the file name randomly scrambled. Somehow, I believe a clever programmer, knowing that "IGC" was going to reverse the file name, could figure a work-around. To avoid file names such as "1" or "IMI" or any other reversible name—if you're going to the effort to scramble—I suggest that these file names be changed to something totally random.

3. The local area network problem is much more difficult, but a mainframe solution that works will have to be implemented on these naturally open and unsecure systems. Once again, the mail programs are the culprits. In order to implement the scrambling technique outlined in number 2 above on a local area network, the server will need to have significant memory and much faster processing speed. The Intel 80486 is available now and the 80586/etc. are just around the corner. LAN operating systems and mail programs will have to be enhanced significantly so that incoming files will be a) scrambled, b) put in a secure hole, and c) available so that it is transparent to the user. Until that time, any LAN is susceptible to sabotage.

510

4. Daily backup of mainframe computers is standard procedure. It is, however, not standard on LANs, nor on individual machines who may have a micro-mainframe connection. In *Tojo* David Kimura inserted his virus a week before implementation. So in theory IGC could have used backup copies from *before* November 14 and they would have only lost a week of data. In real life, "IGC" only keeps its PROFS backup for three to four weeks. In writing the novel I elected not to mention or include this, since it wasn't really necessary and would have disturbed the plot. However, with the advances in disk technology, if I was that MIS manager again, I might be keeping system copies a bit longer.

In any case, PC users must take the time and *invest the money* for proper backup equipment, including external tape and disk units and removable disks. System backup should be the first thing done in the morning, the last thing done at night, or done as you walk out the door for lunch.

Anyway, that's my two cents.